MARGO'S GOT
MONEY TROUBLES

ALSO BY RUFI THORPE

The Knockout Queen
Dear Fang, With Love
The Girls from Corona Del Mar

MARGO'S GOT MONEY TROUBLES

A Novel

RUFI THORPE

WM

WILLIAM MORROW
An Imprint of HarperCollinsPublishers

MARGO'S GOT MONEY TROUBLES. Copyright © 2024 by Rufi Thorpe. All rights reserved. Printed in the United States of America. No part of this book may be used or reproduced in any manner whatsoever without written permission except in the case of brief quotations embodied in critical articles and reviews. For information, address HarperCollins Publishers, 195 Broadway, New York, NY 10007.

HarperCollins books may be purchased for educational, business, or sales promotional use. For information, please email the Special Markets Department at SPsales@harpercollins.com.

FIRST EDITION

Designed by Bonni Leon-Berman

Library of Congress Cataloging-in-Publication Data has been applied for.

ISBN 978-0-06-335658-0

24 25 26 27 28 LBC 7 6 5 4 3

For you

CHAPTER ONE

You are about to begin reading a new book, and to be honest, you are a little tense. The beginning of a novel is like a first date. You hope that from the first lines an urgent magic will take hold, and you will sink into the story like a hot bath, giving yourself over entirely. But this hope is tempered by the expectation that, in reality, you are about to have to learn a bunch of people's names and follow along politely like you are attending the baby shower of a woman you hardly know. And that's fine, goodness knows you've fallen in love with books that didn't grab you in the first paragraph. But that doesn't stop you from wishing they would, from wishing they would come right up to you in the dark of your mind and kiss you on the throat.

MARGO'S BABY SHOWER was hosted by the owner of the restaurant where she worked, Tessa, who thought it would be funny if the cake was shaped like a big dick, maybe because Margo wasn't married, was nineteen, and couldn't even drink, or because it was her professor who'd knocked her up. Tessa was an accomplished baker. She made all the restaurant's desserts herself and went all out on the penis cake: a hand-carved 3D phallus, twelve layers of sponge swirled in matte pink icing. She installed a hand pump, and after they sang *For she's gonna have a huge baby* to the tune of "For He's a Jolly Good Fellow," after Margo blew out the candles—why? it wasn't her birthday—Tessa gave the pump a sharp squeeze, and white pudding spurted out of the top and dribbled down the sides. Tessa whooped with glee. Margo pretended to laugh and later cried in the bathroom.

Margo knew Tessa had made the cake because she loved her. Tessa was both a mean and loving person. Once when Tessa found out the salad boy had no sense of taste or smell because he'd almost been beaten to death in his teens, she served him a plate of shaving cream and potting soil, telling him it was a new dessert. He ate two big bites before she stopped him.

Margo knew Tessa was trying to make light of a situation that was not happy. Turning tragedy into carnival was kind of her thing. But it seemed unfair that the only love available to Margo was so inadequate and painful.

Margo's mom, Shyanne, had told Margo that she should have an abortion. Her professor had been hysterical for Margo to have an abortion. In fact, she wasn't sure she wanted the baby so much as she wanted to prove to them both that they could not bend her conveniently to their will. It had never occurred to her that if she took this position, they might simply interact with her less. Or, in the case of the professor, stop interacting with her altogether.

While Shyanne eventually accepted Margo's decision and even attempted to be supportive, the support itself wasn't always helpful. When Margo went into labor, her mom showed up to the hospital four hours late because she'd been driving all around town looking for a good teddy bear. "You are not going to believe this, Margo, but I wound up going back to Bloomingdale's because it had the best one!"

Shyanne worked at Bloomingdale's and had for almost fifteen years. The way her legs looked in sheer black pantyhose was one of Margo's earliest memories. Shyanne held out the bear, which was white with a slightly constipated face. She did a high, squeaky voice: "Push that li'l baby out, I wanna meet my friend!"

Shyanne was wearing so much perfume Margo was almost glad when she went to sit in the corner and started playing competitive poker games on her phone. PokerStars. That was her jam. She chewed gum and played poker all night long, stomping those jokers. That was what Shyanne always called them, the other players: "jokers."

There was a nurse who was rude and made fun of Margo's name choice. Margo named the baby Bodhi, like *bodhisattva*, which even her mom thought was stupid, but Shyanne slapped that nurse right across the jaw, and it caused a whole kerfuffle. It was also the time Margo felt most loved by her mother, and for many years to come she would replay the memory of that slap and the perfect look of surprise on the nurse's face.

But that was after the epidural and the whole night of being rabid-dog thirsty, begging for ice chips and being given a yellow sponge to suck on, sponges being well-known for their ability to quench thirst. "What the fuck," Margo said around the sponge in her mouth, which tasted of lemons. It was after all the pushing and pooping on the table, and her OB looking so disgusted as he wiped it away, and Margo shouting, "Come on, you've seen it all before!" And him laughing: "You're right, you're right, I have, Mama, now let's have one more big push." And then the magic of Bodhi's slippery purple body when they put him on her chest, pressing the towels around him, his eyes pinched shut. She was instantly worried about the scrawniness of him. His legs, in particular, seemed underdeveloped in a tadpole kind of way. He was only six pounds, despite the song they had sung to her at work. And she loved him. She loved him so much it made her ears ring.

It was only when they released her from the hospital that Margo began to panic. Shyanne had already missed one shift to be there for the birth, there was no way she could take another day to help Margo home from the hospital. Besides, Shyanne was technically banned from entering the hospital after slapping that nurse. Margo told her mom that of course she would be fine. But driving out of that parking lot, her baby squalling in the hard plastic cage of his car seat, Margo felt like she was robbing a bank. His cries were so mucus-y and frail they made her heart race, and she was shaking the whole forty-five-minute drive to her place.

She parked on the street because their apartment came with only one designated spot, but when she went to take Bodhi out from the back, she found she couldn't understand how the lever that released the car seat from the base worked. She was pressing the button; was there a second button she was supposed to push simultaneously? She began jiggling the car seat, careful not to shake it too hard. If there was one thing everyone had been clear about it was never to shake the baby. Bodhi was crying frantically now, and she kept thinking, You do not have the calories to expend this much energy, you are going to die before I even get you upstairs!

After five minutes of straight panicking, she finally remembered she could just unfasten him, and after fumbling with the freakishly gigantic plastic clasp that went over his chest and pressing the stupid red button of the crotch buckle with the requisite superhuman strength (seriously, she pictured a family of rock climbers, used to hanging by their fingertips off cliffsides, who then decided to design baby stuff), she freed him, but then she had no idea how she was supposed to carry this tiny, fragile thing and also all her bags. Already the stitches in her downstairs hurt like crazy, and she regretted deeply the vanity that had made her pack jeans to wear home from the hospital, though let the record show that they did fit.

"Okay," she said seriously to Bodhi's tiny body, his face red purple, his eyes shut tight, "now don't move." She set him down on the front passenger seat, so she could slip the straps of the diaper bag and her overnight bag over her shoulders, crossed over her tits like bandoliers. Then she snatched up the tiny baby and waddled up the street to the slumped brown buildings of Park Place. They weren't exactly bad apartments, tucked away behind the excitingly named Fuel Up! gas station, but compared to the cheerful, whimsically bright 1940s homes that lined the rest of the street, Park Place looked like an uninvited guest.

As she climbed the outside stairs to the second level, she was terrified she would spontaneously drop the baby, his little form, like a Cornish game hen, spiraling downward toward the leaf-choked communal swimming pool. Margo went inside, said hi to her roommate on the couch—the nicest one, Suzie, who loved LARPing and sometimes dressed as an elf even on a random weekday. By the time she made it to her room, closed the door, shucked off her bags, and sat down on her bed to nurse Bodhi, Margo felt like she'd been to war.

I do not mean to insult people who've actually been to war; I only mean that this level of stress and physical hardship was entirely outside

Margo's previous experience. She kept thinking, as she nursed him, I am so fucked, I am so fucked, I am so fucked. Because all around her she could feel the echoey space of no one caring about her or worrying about her or helping her. She might as well have been nursing this baby on an abandoned space station.

She held the perfect purse of his warm body and looked into his pinched little face, the tiny coves of his nostrils mysteriously beautiful and fluted. She'd read that babies' eyes could focus on things only about eighteen inches away, which was exactly how far away their mothers' faces were when they nursed, and he was looking at her now. What did he see? She felt bad if he was seeing her cry. When he fell asleep, she did not put him in the crib like she was supposed to; she lay down next to him in her bed, aware that the battery of her consciousness was running out. She was afraid to fall asleep when she was the lone sole guardian of this tiny being, but her body was not giving her a choice.

I'D LEARNED ABOUT the terms *first person*, *third person*, and *second person* in high school, and I'd thought that was all there was to point of view until I met Bodhi's father in the fall of 2017. The course Mark taught was about impossible or unlikely points of view. I remember one day, a kid in class named Derek kept trying to Psych 101 diagnose the protagonist of this novella, and Mark kept saying, "The main character is not a real person."

"But in the book, he's a real person," Derek had said.

"Yes, insofar as he is not presented as a cat or a robot," Mark said.

"So, I am just saying, in the book, I think he has borderline personality disorder."

"This is not an interesting way to read the book."

"Maybe to you," Derek said, "but I find it interesting." He was wearing a black beanie, and you could tell his hair was dirty underneath, lank and soft, the fur of a sick cat. He was the kind of boy who was never romantically interested in me and whom I therefore spent little time thinking about. He probably watched a lot of foreign films.

"But the character would not be interesting if he were a real person," Mark said. "You would never want to know someone like this, you would never become their friend. They are only interesting because they aren't real. The fakeness is where the interest lies. In fact, I would go so far as to say that all things that are genuinely interesting aren't quite real."

"Real things are boring, and unreal things are interesting, got it," Derek said. I could see only the back of his head, but he sounded like he was rolling his eyes, which was brazen even for him.

"The point is," Mark said, "the narrator doesn't do x or y because he has borderline personality disorder. He does x or y because the author is *making* him. You aren't trying to have a relationship with the character. You are trying to have a relationship with the author *through* the character."

"Okay," Derek said, "now that sounds less stupid."

"All right," Mark said, "I will settle for less stupid."

And then everyone laughed like now we were all good friends. I did not say a word in that class. I did not speak in any of my classes. It honestly never even occurred to me that I should. Teachers always claimed part of your grade was participation. I'd learned long ago this was a bluff. I had no idea why anyone would choose to speak in class, but there would always be one or two who jabbered the whole time like the professor was a late-night host and they were some well-loved celebrity come to promote the movie of their own intelligence.

But the day he handed back our first papers, Mark asked me to stay after class.

"What are you doing here?" he asked.

"Oh, I'm enrolled," I said.

"No," he said, "this paper."

I saw now he was holding my essay in his hands. I could see it had an A written on it in red pen, but I pretended to be worried. I'm not sure why. "Was the paper not good?"

"No, the paper was excellent. I am asking why are you at Fullerton junior college. You could go anywhere."

"What," I said, laughing, "like Harvard?"

"Yes, like Harvard."

"I don't think they let you into Harvard for writing a good English paper."

"That is exactly why they let you into Harvard."

"Oh," I said.

"Would you like to get coffee sometime?" he asked. "We can talk more about this."

"Yes," I said. I had no idea yet that he was interested in me. It didn't occur to me at all. He was married, he wore a ring, he was in his late thirties, old enough that I didn't think of him in that way. But even if I'd known his intentions, I still would have wanted to go for that coffee.

He was my professor, and for some reason this mysterious title made him slightly nonhuman. In the beginning it was hard to imagine that I might hurt his feelings or affect him in any way. I did not make moral judgments about him either. I accepted him as he was, as though he had earned the right to be dorky and odd and adulterous by being better and smarter than other people, better and smarter than me. Mark seemed as whimsical and mysteriously useless as the city of Fullerton itself.

Fullerton wasn't really any richer than where I'd grown up in Downey, though it had a completely different vibe because of the colleges: Cal State Fullerton and its little sister, Fullerton College. In Downey, you could eat overpriced seafood in a dark restaurant pulsing with techno or wait in line for an hour to eat Instagram-worthy sweet rolls from Porto's. Fullerton, by contrast, was like an entire town run by maiden aunts. It had so many dentists and tax advisers you'd think people did little else. Even the frat houses seemed quaint and harmless, shaded by mature elms. Fullerton's money didn't come from industry. It came from its connection to learning, the colleges reason enough to keep the rents high and dollars flowing. Mark was a part of all that. He was a wind chime in human form, dangling dorkily from the glorious tree of higher education.

In the beginning, this made me feel like the power dynamic was in my favor. His professor-ness didn't blind me to his foibles: I registered fully the ridiculousness of his pants (green! corduroy!), his shoes (Birkenstocks!), the thumbed-through copy of *Beowulf* peeking out of his messenger bag (messenger bag!).

But it was almost like I was a character in a book to him. He couldn't get over it, the Kermit tattooed on my hip.

"Why Kermit?" he asked, the first time we slept together, rubbing Kermit's little green body with his fingertip.

I shrugged. "I wanted to get a tattoo. Everything else was, like, knives or snakes or serious things, and I'm just not a serious person."

"What kind of person are you?"

I thought about it. "A cheesy person."

"Cheesy!" he barked.

"Yes, cheesy," I said. "What, like, I believed in Santa until I was twelve. I don't know, I'm cheesy!"

"You are the most singular person I have ever met," he said wonderingly.

It was part of why I avoided ever telling him about my father. There are people who venerate professional wrestling and people who look down on professional wrestling, and I worried Mark would be the kind to venerate the thing he looked down upon. I knew my carny-ass bloodline would be an instant fetish for him.

The faker things seem the more intrigued we are by them—that was what Mark loved about point of view: the ways it was obviously fake or tried so hard to be real, which was, weirdly, another way of showing how fake it was. "The way you look at something changes what you see," he said.

It's TRUE THAT writing in third person helps me. It is so much easier to have sympathy for the Margo who existed back then rather than try to explain how and why I did all the things that I did.

THE THING ABOUT Bodhi's dad that was so confusing was that of course I only slept with him because he had the power, of course it was the fact that he was my English professor, my favorite class. And yet so much of what compelled me was the way he kept insisting that I had the power. Which one of us actually had it, though? I used to spend a lot of time thinking about this.

Aside from impregnating me and kind of ruining my life, Mark helped me a great deal with my writing. He went over every sentence of my papers with me, touching on each one and how it could be better. He would give me A's, then demand I rewrite the papers anyway. "What you are," he said, "is too important not to polish." He would point out a sentence I had written, demanding, "What were you trying to say here?" And I would tell him, stuttering, what I had intended, and he would say, "Just say that. Don't pussyfoot around."

It was only after he'd been helping me this way for several weeks that the affair started. One day, I was supposed to go to his office. When I got there, he said he couldn't focus and could we meet another day, and I said sure. But then we wound up leaving the building at the same time and that turned into going on a walk together, and he vented about everything, all his frustrations about the department and his wife and kids and how trapped he felt by his life. "And I don't even deserve my shitty life," he said. "I'm a horrible person."

"You are not," I said. "You're an amazing teacher! You've spent all this time with me, helping me."

"Every second of which I was desperately wanting to kiss you."

I did not know what to say to that. I mean, in a way I had a schoolgirlish crush on him, but I'd never thought about kissing him. I just felt glow-y and good whenever he praised me.

It was raining, and we had been walking in circles around campus. We didn't have umbrellas, but we were both wearing jackets with hoods. We'd stopped underneath a huge eucalyptus tree.

"Can I kiss you?" he asked.

I nodded. I mean, I literally could not have imagined saying no. I would have done anything he asked. He was short, maybe five foot five, my height, and I had never kissed a boy that short before, and it was kind of nice, with both of our hoods up in the rain. But even I was like, *We are kissing openly on campus? This seems like a very bad idea.*

The thing was, by the time everything was over between us, he had behaved so childishly, and I'd had to assume so much of the responsibility for what we'd done, that I didn't feel taken advantage of. I felt . . . pissed off. If he had actually been a grown-up, the whole thing never would have happened in the first place.

THE FIRST TIME Mark came to Margo's apartment, he wore a baseball cap and sunglasses, like he was trying to dodge the paparazzi. Margo had not attempted to clean or pick up for this visit, did not feel embarrassed about Mark seeing the stained pink velvet sofa, the mess of cords hanging from the TV. Her own frameless bed, a mattress and box spring on the floor. None of this troubled her. He was here to fuck a nineteen-year-old—what could he possibly expect?

"You have roommates" was what he said.

"I told you I had roommates," she said.

"I didn't think they would be home."

"Is that beer?" Suzie asked.

Mark was indeed clutching a six-pack of beer in oddly medicinal-looking bottles. Red Stripe. It was a kind of beer Margo had never seen in her life. Certainly, they didn't stock it at her work. He was still wearing his sunglasses indoors.

"Take those off," Margo said, and tried to pluck them off his face.

He swatted her away. "They're prescription."

"Pay the troll," Suzie said, and held up her hand to receive a beer.

"What?"

"Give her a beer," Margo said, laughing at him. He was holding the bottles to his chest like a child who didn't want to share.

"How old are you?" he asked Suzie. "Jesus, Margo, I didn't mean to—"

"Old enough to tell the dean, *now pay the troll*," Suzie growled.

"This was such a mistake," Mark said.

"Here," Margo said, and slipped a beer out of the six-pack and into Suzie's waiting hand.

"The troll is very pleased," Suzie said.

"Let's go to my room," Margo said.

Mark followed her down the hall, past her other roommates Kat the Larger's and Kat the Smaller's rooms, to her door.

"Welcome," she said, holding the door open for him, "to the place where the magic happens."

EVEN THOUGH SHE was not really attracted to Mark, the sex was surprisingly pleasant. She'd had sex with two other boys before: One her high school boyfriend, Sebastian, who had absolutely the best dog, a shepherd mix named Remmy, whose head smelled vaguely of peanuts and whom she definitely loved more than Sebastian. And the other, a boy she'd met at orientation the first week of college who never spoke to her again. Mark was different in bed from either of them. He was uncircumcised, a situation that made her curious, and she never did get to explore the elasticity of his penis skin to her satisfaction. But he was also capital *P* Passionate. That first time they had sex was standing up with her pressed against a wall. It seemed impractical and uncomfortable, but Margo assumed it was part of some fantasy he had. She could not see a reason for having sex against a wall besides a fantasy really.

When it was over, he sat down in her desk chair and spun around. She went to the bathroom to pee and thus ensure she didn't get a bladder infection, and when she returned he was going through her desk drawers.

"What are you doing?" she asked.

"You wander around like that in your underwear?" he said, looking up.

"They're girls," she said. "Why are you going through my desk?"

"Just curious."

She would have been upset if there were anything interesting in her drawers. If he wanted to examine her graphing calculator with the cracked screen, he could go ahead. He would never find her secrets. She didn't really have any. Or she did, but they were internal somehow, secret even from herself. For instance, she did not like him, not really, and the secret of her disdain was like a folded promise waiting in a drawer within her.

"Does your wife know you do this?" she asked.

"Uh, no," he said, and gave himself a little spin in her desk chair.

"But you've done this before?"

"With a student? No."

"With other women?"

He stopped spinning and appeared to be considering his answer. He opened one of the weird beers he had brought. He used the edge of her desk to pry off the bottle cap, and she was astonished by the rudeness of this.

"I've never told anyone," he said.

"What?" she asked, lying down on her bed, aware that even now she was trying to look cute in her underwear, her hip cocked a bit as she lay back on the pillows. From the hallway, she could hear one of her roommates throwing up. Probably Kat the Smaller, who was very much a puker. Things entered and exited her with a whimsy Margo could not imagine.

"I slept with my wife's sister on our wedding night."

Margo gasped. "Oh my gosh, you are a bad person!"

He nodded, brow furrowed. "I really am."

"But then you stopped sleeping with her sister."

"Yeah. I mean, there were a few more times after we got home from our honeymoon, but after that we stopped, yeah."

"Did you feel guilty?" she asked. It was hard to tell what men felt, she realized. She'd always wondered how her father could be so totally immune to her need for him, how he could pack a bag and be gone when she woke in the morning without saying goodbye. When she was a child, she assumed he was different with his real children, but as she'd gotten older and come to know him better, she understood he was that way with his wife and kids too. It was the wrestling life. Always getting on a plane. That was where he wanted to be: crammed in a rental car with two men who were both almost three hundred pounds, psychotically violent, and addicted to painkillers. The regular world had perhaps never been entirely real to him.

"This is going to sound so fucked up, but not really," he said. "I would just pretend I never did it. And since she didn't know I'd done it, it was like I hadn't."

HE WROTE HER poetry, ultimately almost a dozen poems, but she liked this one the most:

THE HUNGRY GHOST

In the dark, we turn to each other
Like deformed doves,
Confused that we have bodies.

I feel nothing,
Keep touching me,
I feel nothing.
I'm a hungry ghost.

We try to eat each other
But it is like trying to run in a dream,
The dark frozen ice of reality splintering around us.

CHAPTER TWO

Mark had two kids, a four-year-old named Hailey and a seven-year-old named Max, but he hardly ever spoke of them. He certainly didn't talk about his wife. All he wanted to talk about was poetry and writing and books. He would take me to Barnes & Noble: "Have you ever read Jack Gilbert? No? Okay, you must, it's a must," adding more and more books to the stack. Then he would take me out to dinner. It did not occur to me at the time to wonder how he was affording all of this on a junior college professor's salary.

He loved seafood. He was always ordering us things that filled me with mild dread, charred octopus or mussels that looked for all the world like the clitoris of a corpse stuffed inside a shell, and I would choke these things down with the same worried expression as a dog who's been given a carrot. Then he would tell me about a weird dream he had where he was a young girl in Meiji Japan.

THEY SLEPT TOGETHER only five times, and then, after the fifth time, Mark explained that the sex was making him feel extremely guilty about his wife and that they should stop. They were in Margo's apartment, still naked in her queen-sized bed, when he said this.

"I want to keep seeing you, though," he said.

"Why?" she asked. Really she was still marveling over how he'd thought sleeping with her would make him feel toward his wife, if not guilty.

"Well, because I care about you. Please don't cut it off if we aren't screwing."

She tilted her head. It hadn't occurred to her that she could cut it off; this whole affair had seemed to be kind of his thing. She'd been letting him drive. But the idea of hanging out with this middle-aged man without the sex—like, just having an older, dorky *friend*?

"Okay," she said, "let me get this straight. So you still want to go out to dinner?"

"Yes," he said.

"And emails?"

"Of course we can email, the emails are, like, the most important part, we can email for the rest of our lives."

It seemed obvious to her that they would not.

"But wouldn't your wife mind the love poetry more than the sex? Like, if I were someone's wife, and they slept with someone, I could get over it. It's the love stuff that would get to me. Like, you shouldn't be telling me you love me."

"But I do love you."

Margo didn't know what to say. She had a blister on her thumb from grabbing a hot plate at work. Her fault for leaving it there too long, but she'd been triple sat by the new hostess. She kept pressing on the blister and feeling the tightness of the water beneath the skin. She was on the verge of failing French also. She should be studying.

"I'm not willing to lie about the fact that I love you. If I can't be that honest with myself, then I'm finished."

"I'm gonna go pee," she said. "Do you want a glass of water?"

"Yes, please," he said, the covers up to his chin. Then he said in a little old-woman voice, "I'm so thirsty, Margo." He did this a lot, pretend to be an old woman.

"All right, Granny," she said, pulling on some fresh underwear and stumbling out into the hall.

SHE FIGURED THAT most likely he did not mean it, the stopping having sex. That really he would play a game where he said he wasn't going to sleep with her, then he'd give in and sleep with her and vocalize his guilt and swear not to do it anymore, and so on. That turned out not to be the case. Mark never slept with her again. And he continued to take her out to fancy dinners and write her love poetry and not feel troubled at all. It was incredibly annoying. She was pretty sure she could wear him down eventually, though.

That was the somewhat stable situation in which Margo discovered she was pregnant. She hadn't even realized she was late. One night when she was working, she kept throwing up a little Taco Bell in her mouth and swallowing it, and Tracy, her favorite coworker, was like, "Maybe you're pregnant!" But it seemed so much more probable that her body was rebelling against the Taco Bell.

Yet her body kept rebelling, against cheesecake after her shift, then against yogurt the next morning. She drank a blue Gatorade, cold dark blood of the gods, and puked it right back up. This went on for a full forty-eight hours before she gave in and bought a pregnancy test. They had not used condoms. He had always pulled out. He was married, and he said that was how he and his wife did it, and they'd never had any mistakes! She felt incredibly stupid. For believing him, for having the affair with him, for having a uterus.

The first thing she did was call her mom, and she wasn't even able to get the words out, she was just sobbing.

"Are you pregnant?" her mom asked.

"Yeah," she yell-cried.

"Damn it!"

"I'm sorry," Margo said. "I'm so sorry."

And then her mother took her out for donuts.

Margo ate them, and they stayed down.

WHEN I FIRST told Mark, we were at a restaurant, and I'd ordered a salad with fresh figs in it, prompting me to wonder why everyone was pretending to like fresh figs, this vast conspiracy to fake that figs were any good.

Anyway, I told Mark I was pregnant, and he said, "Holy shit."

And I said, "I know."

"You're positive?"

"Uh, yeah," I said.

"Have you been to the doctor?"

"Not yet."

"So you could just be late."

"Well, I took, like, four pregnancy tests, so I don't think so, but yeah, I guess."

He took a sip of his beer. "I'm involuntarily kind of thrilled. My seed is strong!" he cried in some kind of German or Viking accent.

I laughed. My hands were sweating profusely. It felt like the whole restaurant was moving, like we were on a boat, the heavy-handled silver faintly shifting on the white tablecloths.

"I'm sorry," he said. "I know it's serious. I want to be there to support you in any way possible. Financially, of course, but if you want me to take you to the appointment or any of that—this is my fuckup too, and I am fully responsible."

"So how do I make an appointment?" I said.

"I mean, I would start by calling Planned Parenthood," he said. "But, like, I don't know if private doctors do it or if it's nicer—like, I don't want you to have some cheap abortion."

I had not realized he'd already decided I would have an abortion. But of course he had. He would decide the same way he decided we would stop sleeping together (though evidently making out in his car was A-OK), the same way he decided we would have the affair in the first place. I'd never said no to him, not once. We went where he wanted when he wanted, ate what he wanted, touched or didn't touch as much as he wanted. And honestly, I think I said it just to fuck with him: "Oh, I'm not having an abortion."

He turned green almost instantaneously; it was extremely gratifying.

"What are you, Catholic?" he asked in a much nastier voice than he usually spoke to me in.

"No, but it's my choice," I said.

"Don't you think I should get an opinion?" he asked.

"No," I said. I stood and covered my gross fig salad with my napkin and left. When I got outside the restaurant, I could smell the ocean, and there was this weird moment when I felt like my mom, walking haughtily on the sidewalk, like my legs were in those sheer black pantyhose, like I could slip into being someone else entirely. Then I tripped on a curb, and the feeling was gone, and I was merely the idiot who had parked too far away.

And I really, really wish the next part hadn't happened, but it is true that he ran after me and we wound up making out in his car, and I admitted I would probably have an abortion, I just didn't want to be forced, and he said, "I couldn't force you to do a damn thing, Margo. You are wilder than anyone I've ever known."

And I liked that he called me that, even though the things Mark said about me never felt like they really had anything to do with me. They were more his fantasy of me. But I liked making out in his car, and we left on good terms. Then Mark didn't contact me for three days, an unheard-of silence. I kept checking my phone, checking my email. I texted, Hey, you okay? (I always typed out *you* with him in deference to his Gen-X hang-ups and also because he was my English professor for goodness' sakes.) He didn't write back.

And I knew something bad had happened, that his feelings had shifted. Normally, there was a cord of attachment between us that I could tug and feel him there on the other end. I suddenly had the horrifying sensation that it had been snipped off, and now I had a cord that led nowhere, that was just dangling in space.

Then the email came, long and convoluted, explaining how he felt it was best for us to have no further contact, which was easy enough since the semester was over and I was no longer in his class. He was sorry for anything he put me through, but he felt I was throwing my life away and he couldn't abide it. You could go anywhere, you could do anything, he wrote. Don't throw it all away to have a baby. This one time, Margo, believe me. I am older than you. I have had babies. They are hard. You do not want babies.

It was confusing that he kept trying to frame the decision in terms of what I wanted. To me, *want* and *should* were two very separate things. In fact, wanting something was usually a sign that you did not deserve it and would not be getting it, for example: moving to New York City and going to a fancy college like NYU. Conversely, the less you wanted to do something, the more likely it was that you should, like going to the dentist or doing your taxes. More than anything, what I wanted was to make the right decision, and yet no one was willing to engage with me on those terms.

MARGO'S BEST FRIEND from high school had gotten into NYU and moved to New York, and the pain of this, that Becca was living the life they both had wanted and Margo was a waitress attending junior college—the unspoken understanding that this was because Becca's parents had money and Margo's mom did not—was too intense, and the girls had stopped talking. Except now Margo called her, and Becca picked up on the first ring.

Margo gave her a rough summary of what had happened. "So what do you think?"

"Fucking have an abortion!" Becca said.

"But like . . ." Margo could hear sirens and city noise in the background.

"There is no 'but like.' This isn't a 'but like' situation! This is an emergency!"

It did not feel like an emergency. "Do you believe things happen for a reason?" Margo asked. "Like, do you believe everything is fated, or do you believe in free will?"

"Margo, this is not a philosophical question. This is a financial decision."

"It just feels fucked up to make an important decision based on something as stupid and made up as money."

"I assure you, money is very real," Becca said.

Margo was sitting in her bedroom, looking at the pile of laundry spilling out of her closet like her clothes were trying to crawl away.

"I just think," Becca said, "maybe being a single mom might not be as glamorous as you think."

Now Margo was pissed. "Becca, I'm the one who was raised by a single mom, and it's not fucking glamorous. I'm not saying I would keep the baby because it would be fun or easy. I'm saying I think keeping the baby might be, like, what a good person would do."

"So having an abortion makes you a bad person?"

"Well, no," Margo said. Although on some level, wasn't that kind of what everyone implied? You weren't supposed to get an abortion just because it was more convenient. You were supposed to be all cut up about it.

"So tell me how keeping the baby would make you a good person again?"

"I don't know! I'm not saying it would!" Margo raked her scalp with her nails.

"You literally said you were thinking about keeping the baby because you thought it's what a good person would do."

"Then maybe I didn't mean that."

"And since when do you care about being a good person? I mean, you were fucking somebody's husband."

"I know," Margo said. But she didn't. She'd always known Mark was a terrible person, but she had not quite registered that she was terrible too until this very moment. "Just . . . what am I even doing with my life? Going to junior college? Pretending I'm gonna transfer? Do you even understand how impossible it is to get into a UC anymore? And even if I did, I would major in what? English? You can't get a job with an English degree, and I can't even think of anything else I could study! So, then, what do I do, like, waitress? Get a job at Bloomingdale's like my mom? None of it makes any sense. At least this would be something."

"There's lots of cool things you could do, Margo. You could get into viticulture and go into wine or something."

Margo instantly thought of the wine rep her restaurant dealt with who was so corny and pretentious and had a huge tattoo of grapes on her chest, like right on her décolletage, massive ugly purple cartoon grapes. And Margo knew that if they were talking about what Becca should do with her life, viticulture wouldn't even be on the table.

"I'm saying it's a big deal!" Margo said. "Like, don't you think I should at least think about it? Why are you trying to make it not a big deal?"

"I'm sorry," Becca said, "I don't know why I'm being such a bitch. It is a big deal, it's a super big deal."

This was not satisfying, and Margo didn't know exactly why. "How's school?" she asked. And they talked about that for a little while. When they hung up, Margo cried for twenty minutes and then went to work.

MEANWHILE TIME WAS still happening, and somehow it was Tuesday, and she was going to her first doctor's appointment. She'd originally called Planned Parenthood. They wouldn't do an ultrasound to confirm pregnancy until you were eight weeks along, though. Pregnancy math was cruel. The moment you found out you were pregnant, you were already at four weeks. Waiting four more weeks to see if she was pregnant or not seemed absurd, so she called around until she found an ob-gyn who was willing to see her at six weeks.

It was exactly like every other time she'd been to the doctor. She wasn't sure why that was surprising. Maybe she thought they'd be nicer to her. The doctor was a chubby, middle-aged white guy with a shaved bald head.

"So, you don't know the date of your last period?"

"No, I didn't keep . . . records?"

"Okey dokey, don't worry, we'll get all this squared away." He seemed like the kind of man who was a great husband but whose wife would cheat on him anyway. "I'm gonna leave the room. The nurse will bring you a gown. Change into that, no underwear."

Margo nodded.

"This is a transvaginal doppler," he said. "Ever had one of those before?"

"Nope."

"Well, when the fetus is this size, you can't see well enough through the belly, so you have to take a peek internally."

Margo looked over at the futuristic dildo attached to the sonogram machine. She got the idea. She had not pictured it being like this at all.

After the doctor stepped out of the room, while she was changing into the gown the nurse had brought her, she silently thanked God that Mark hadn't come to spectate such a thing. It would be weird enough if her mom came, but Shyanne was working.

And then it was time for her to get fucked by a robot to meet her unborn child.

"Okay," the doctor said, "now the gel is heated, so this shouldn't be too bad."

He began to insert the giant dildo. It didn't hurt. It was just weird as hell.

He was really digging around in there, trying to see something perhaps in her spinal column. "Okay!" he said, turning a knob on the machine, and suddenly there was sound, a quiet, fast *whoosh, whoosh, whoosh.* "That's the heartbeat."

"It is?" It sounded like a mechanical toy. She didn't know why she was crying; it was completely underwhelming as a sound.

He kept digging the wand around, taking pictures, clicking the mouse of the computer with his other hand. It was really quite impressive, his ambidextrousness. "I'm taking measurements so we can get some idea of the age of the . . . uh . . . fetus."

She noticed he had avoided using the word *baby.* She thought that was kind of him, and it made her start crying again.

"Okay," he said, "so I would say, based on measurements, and these are pretty accurate especially this early, that you're about eight weeks."

It wasn't that this wasn't possible, only that Margo wasn't prepared. Eight weeks pregnant sounded awfully pregnant.

He removed the wand and peeled off the plastic condom thing, then he pressed a button on the machine and a printer started. "Oh, I should have asked—do you want copies of the pictures?"

"Yes," she said, though saying it made her cough because she was crying so hard while trying to be relatively silent.

"Do you . . . know what you want to do about the pregnancy?"

"No," she said, and closed her eyes.

"I'm gonna let you get cleaned up, and then we can talk more about your options," he said.

When he was out of the room, she looked at the pictures, which were still dangling out of the machine on their shiny, thin strip of paper. And there he was. Her baby, looking for all the world like a tiny, deformed dove.

CHAPTER THREE

After the doctor's appointment I drove to my mother's apartment.
"Hey, Noodle," my mom said.

"I'm eight weeks pregnant, it turns out," I said, flopping down on the couch. My mother looked down at me for a long time.

"You want to keep this baby, don't you?" she said.

"I don't know," I said.

She went into the kitchen. I heard the crack and hiss as she opened a beer. She came back into the room.

"I like your nails," I said. They were new. A kind of radioactive-looking yellow.

"If you keep this baby," she said, "I'm not taking care of it. It would be your baby."

"I know," I said, genuinely baffled. I would never give the baby to my mother.

"Goddamn it," she said, pacing back and forth in front of the TV with her beer.

"Mom, it's okay," I said. "I'll figure it out."

"I just . . . I thought I did so good! You were in college! You were gonna be somebody!"

"Who was I going to be?" I asked. I had a sudden image of my mother pressing her idea of who I was onto the actual me, like an acrylic nail, this big mask-shell of a face on top of my actual face.

"You know what I mean. You were gonna have a career and, like, do things!"

"What things?"

"I don't know," Shyanne said. "Whatever you wanted!"

I stayed silent. Mark, Becca, my mom—they kept insisting I had all these options, and I could never figure out what those options were supposed to be. In high school I'd met with my guidance counselor, Mr. Ricci, exactly two times. The first time he told me I could apply for scholarships and financial aid and gave me all these forms to fill out. The second time he seemed to have no memory of me and said my only hope was transferring to a UC. I'd enrolled in Fullerton College, except the whole first year I hadn't been able to get into a single class I needed for transfer credit; they all filled up almost instantly. So I'd done a whole year of basically fluff humanities credits that would never transfer anywhere. Everyone kept telling me I would lose so much by having this baby, but it didn't feel like I'd be losing anything at all.

"I'm dreading telling Kenny," Shyanne said, resuming her pacing.

"Why on earth would you dread telling Kenny?"

"He's religious!" she hissed. There was something very velociraptor about the way she was stalking back and forth.

"So . . . wouldn't he be glad I didn't get an abortion?"

"No, he'd be appalled you've been whoring it up in the first place! Teen mom? I mean, Margo, we would never tell him if you had an abortion!"

"I have to be honest, Mom, I cannot bring myself to care about what Kenny thinks of me. Plus, I'd be twenty by the time the baby's born."

"He could wind up being your stepdad!"

I found this unlikely, though it seemed mean to say so.

"Kenny is great," she said. "Kenny is amazing."

"Okay," I said, "yes."

"It will be fine," she said. "I'll just kind of imply that Mark took advantage of you. It wasn't really your fault."

I did not intend to leap to my feet, but I did, and then I didn't know what to do when I got there. "Mark did not take advantage of me," I said. "It wasn't like that."

"Of course you think that. You wouldn't have done it if you felt he was taking advantage. But he's a grown man, honey. There's things you won't understand about it until you're older."

I was so mad that the bottoms of my feet ached and I also really had to pee, so I went to use the restroom. My mom had this big poster of the Eiffel Tower in her bathroom and little French soaps; the whole room was Paris themed. I was thinking how stupid it looked and how annoying she was as I washed my hands with the little soap, rough and spastic like I was peeling potatoes, and then I realized she probably desperately wanted to go to Paris, and she probably never would. I looked in the mirror and could suddenly see how I looked just like her, a knockoff Shyanne, my eyes set a little too wide. Both of us had stupid faces, pretty and sweet; faces that seemed to imply there was nothing inside us at all.

When I got back to the living room, she was sort of draped on the couch in a sitting position, like someone had let the air out of her. I lay down so my head was in her lap.

"When I got pregnant with you," she said, idly stroking my hair, "I was so scared."

"Why did you keep me?" I asked. It had never really made sense. It was a one-night stand; she hardly knew my father. They'd met at the Hooters where she worked. She didn't even know his real name, only his ring name, Jinx. Because in his first match, his opponent dropped dead before he even touched him.

"I didn't know he was already married," she said. "He didn't wear a ring—none of them did, you could lose a finger, but I didn't know that then. It was really intense between us, and I thought maybe . . . I don't know. Maybe, you know? It felt like my destiny, like he was The One."

The tenderness of her hope and the obviousness of her naivete were too much. I rushed to move on. "What was Dad even like back then? He's so serious now it's hard for me to picture. Even the idea of him being drunk."

"Oh, believe me, your daddy could drink with the best of them. I don't know. He had those dark eyes that kind of sparkled. And he was on so many steroids his traps were huge, and he didn't tan. He was so pale and big, he looked like a milk-white bull."

"Mom, I was asking about his personality!"

"I was getting to it! He was a gentleman. Probably from being Canadian. He was always kind, but he was a heel in the ring, so you didn't expect it. He was a listener, he liked sitting back and letting other people talk."

"I can see that," I said. I had never known my father as a wrestler. By the time I was making memories, he'd already herniated two discs in

Japan and started managing Murder and Mayhem. He managed them in the everyday sense of booking their matches; they were rare free agents amid the Monday Night Wars. But he also played the character of their manager on TV because Murder and Mayhem weren't great talkers and Jinx was a genius at promos. I assumed he stopped using steroids after he got hurt because he lost a lot of weight, and the older he got the skinnier he seemed to become. With the largeness of his frame, in his almost skeletal thinness and shaved head, he'd begun to resemble a hairless cat.

"How did you guys—like, how did you tell him?" I'd spent surprisingly little time imagining all this.

"Well, one night they all came into the restaurant drunk off their asses about one in the morning. And after my shift, he took me to his hotel room, and I told him. He was really happy about it. It was weird. He couldn't stop smiling and touching my tummy. He told me then that he was married, and that kind of broke my heart. I was crying, and he said, 'I'm really glad I met you.' And I realized I was glad I'd met him too. So we just made do with what we had. When he was in town, we'd see each other. I knew he had to save the big money for his wife and them, I always knew that. But he really did come through when he could, I believe that. I don't think you should count on Mark being the same. And probably a lot of people would say I was dumb for doing that, but you know, I always loved him."

This I had known. It was obvious, horribly so. Whenever he came to town, she doted on him, constantly offering to make him a sandwich, get him a glass of water. It was a steel cage match for his attention, and I always lost. The few times I'd won, when Jinx had shone that laser beam of love on me, were painful in a different way. One year he was in town for my birthday and took me to a steak house. I was thirteen and absolutely did not like steak, but he took me out for this fancy dinner, and when I got home, Shyanne wasn't even mean about it, she was crushed. He stayed in a hotel that trip instead of our house. He sometimes did that, and I never knew exactly why or what it meant.

"You chose to keep me," I said. I could hear the faint ticking of the carbonation in her beer.

"I did. But there were other times, later, when I chose different."

I was silent. I had not known that. It made sense, though.

"Do you think things happen for a reason?" I asked.

"I don't know," she said. "But I think you're just scared to admit you want to wreck your life."

"You think it will wreck my life?" I asked.

She stroked my hair. "Yes, Noodle, it will ruin your life, for sure. But sometimes ruining your life is the only thing you want."

I knew she was talking about deciding to keep me when she was pregnant. About the gray area she and Jinx had spent their whole lives in, the bittersweetness of making do with another woman's husband. The way I would scream and chatter when he came in the door, begging him to suplex me before he'd even set down his bag, and her coming out from the kitchen, wiping her hands on a dish towel, having tried to cook some weird retro dish, tuna casserole with raisins in it, meat loaf covered in ketchup. She would snap at me and tell me to give him some space, offer him a beer as I clamored to tell him about school. And when he'd leave again in a few days, the apartment would be so quiet, and we wouldn't know how to talk to each other exactly, like we were embarrassed of ourselves and how we had behaved.

"I ruined your life," I said, not a question. I just wanted her to know that I knew.

"You ruined my life so pretty, Noodle."

I didn't say anything, only lay there on the couch with my head in her lap. She petted my hair, skritched my scalp with her acrylic nails.

But there had also been the two of us laughing and eating popcorn, her loopy handwriting on notes she left in my school lunches that she pretended were written by the cat. Our arms moving in perfect synchrony to fold a fitted sheet. The day we drove all the way to the Grand Canyon, a solid eight hours, and just looked at it, bought some Sour Patch Kids, and drove all the way home so I could go to school the next day.

If Shyanne hadn't had me, what would she have had?

"I scheduled an abortion," I told her. She didn't say anything. "But I don't think I can go. Like, I can't picture myself going."

"Well," she said, "you'll have to wait until it's time and then figure out if you want to go or not."

"Okay," I said, trying not to show how thrilled I was that she'd backed off the idea of me definitely going through with it. Like I was lying to stay home sick.

I called and canceled the abortion the moment I left her house that day. I couldn't tell you why. It was a bad idea. I did not have good reasons. And it wasn't because I wanted to be a good person, not really. It wasn't because I was in love with Mark. I just wanted that baby. I wanted it more than I'd ever wanted anything.

I cut out the best of the ultrasound pictures and kept it on my bedside table. I would spend hours staring at it. It was such an inadequate, ugly image, so frustrating in its refusal to give me anything to hold on to, any way of envisioning who the baby would be. My body was making something in secret, and I was reduced to spying on my internal organs with these grainy black-and-white photos. But I hung on, faithful, waiting.

ONCE SHE WAS past sixteen weeks and an abortion was no longer legally possible, Margo wrote to Mark to tell him she was keeping the baby. She didn't want him to be able to talk her out of it. He didn't write back. She'd expected a lecture, a panicked phone call. For days she waited for the reaction she was sure would come. Even two weeks after the email, she expected him to do something, reach out in some way. He didn't.

It scared her, how much this stung. To be ignored. How much, perhaps, she had thought that keeping the baby would force him to deal with her. She didn't think that was why she'd made the decision, but it wasn't *not* why. It's not like she wanted Mark to play husband, play Daddy—she knew that. If he had said, "Okay, my marriage is a sham anyway, I'll get a divorce and marry you and raise the baby," she would have been horrified. She wasn't even interested in seeing him that regularly. But he had always been clear about one thing: That she was important. That she was amazing. But if she really was, would this be how he treated her?

WHEN MARGO TOLD Jinx she was keeping the baby, he was very relaxed about it. "I'm looking forward to being a grandpa," he said in his weirdly calm, Mr. Rogers–esque voice. She was the youngest of his kids, the first to have a baby, and this was not lost on her.

"Maybe it will be a boy, and he'll be a wrestler," Jinx suggested.

Margo felt instantly terrible that Mark was so short. She hadn't even chosen a big, strong dummy to procreate with; instead, she'd mated with a small, immoral weirdo. Jinx elegantly filled in the pause.

"I didn't realize you had a fellow," he said.

"I don't really," she said.

"Oh, that's all right, Margo. You'll do just fine, I think."

They hadn't spoken since. She called him now.

"I'm scared," she blurted out the moment he picked up.

"Hello there," he said, and his voice sounded weird. Then she heard a woman in the background. It could have been a lover or his wife or one of his daughters, and Margo knew it meant he would keep this conversation short. At least he'd picked up, she told herself. He could see it was her, and still, he'd picked up. That was a kind of love.

She cut to the chase: "What if I'm making a big mistake?"

"You aren't," he said. They both knew they were about to have the most abbreviated version of this talk possible. It was like speaking in Morse code.

"I'm not? You know for sure?"

"I can guarantee," he said.

"Okay," she said.

"Okay," he said.

They hung up, and she felt better. But it was a slow, unsatisfying release of tension, like pouring out a flat beer.

ONE SATURDAY, WHEN she was six months along, Margo and Shyanne were at the Goodwill hoping to find a used stroller that wasn't unspeakably sad. Margo wanted an UPPAbaby stroller more than she'd ever wanted anything in her life, and the strollers at Goodwill were so far from the UPPAbaby stroller, made of a brown floral fabric that bespoke another era or country, perhaps Soviet Russia, and crusted with the food of some previous baby who ate, by the look of things, a lot of egg.

"Mark should be buying you a stroller," Shyanne was saying. "It's the least he could do. Have you even talked to him about this?"

Once Shyanne accepted Margo wasn't having an abortion, she narrowed her entire focus to one thing and one thing only: getting money out of Mark. Every conversation became about this, about how Margo needed to sue for paternity and ensure he paid child support. Shyanne was appalled when Margo refused and said she didn't want to make waves in his marriage. His wife had never found out about them, and Mark was desperate for her to remain ignorant. "Don't make the same mistake that I made," Shyanne said. "You may think on some level that if you're generous and let him keep his marriage, then maybe, you know, things between you . . ." But that wasn't how Margo felt at all. She honestly wanted nothing to do with Mark anymore.

"No," she said. "I'm not asking Mark for a damn stroller." Except now she was about to start crying in the Goodwill, and she'd never even thought of herself as a materialistic person. Whatever was in Target or thrift stores had always been perfectly fine with her. But she felt if she had to use one of those brown strollers that smelled like bowling alley shoes, then her baby would grow up to spit from truck windows and laugh at racist jokes. And honestly, there was a pretty high chance that was going to happen no matter which stroller she used, and the thought of this made her feel like she couldn't breathe.

"Maybe I don't need a stroller," Margo said. "Or maybe I'll find one on Craigslist."

"Here's what you do," her mother said, steering her toward the glassware and ceramic section, always Margo's favorite. "You write to Mark, and you say—"

"No," Margo said. "I don't know how to be clearer about this. I will never, ever ask Mark for a single thing. Not ever."

Shyanne rolled her eyes. "I guess we'll see about that."

"Let's go look at the blue one again."

"The blue one's snack tray is busted."

"Let's go look at it again," Margo said, dragging Shyanne back to the strollers.

In the end, Margo waited in line for thirty minutes and bought the blue one, her head held high, her eyes lit up by a pride that burned, that she could feel inside, its blue flame-tongues lapping, and she believed then that it could make her clean, burn away every impurity, that it could save her.

AND THEN BODHI was born, and Margo was alone with him in her room, like she'd been locked in there and told to spin straw into gold. How did other women do this? She slept at most two hours at a time. Her pajamas were crusted with dried milk and baby spit-up. Instead of changing out of them, she'd put on her giant gray sweatshirt, strap Bodhi in his carrier on her front, and shuffle down to Fuel Up! on the corner, where she'd buy an orange juice and Harvest Cheddar Sun-Chips, a breakfast she and Becca had invented called "Orange Meal."

She'd texted Becca way back after their call—I'm keeping it—and Becca hadn't responded. When Bodhi was born, she sent Becca a picture. Becca texted back, He's beautiful! Congratulations! But after that, radio silence. Even the girls she knew from high school who admirably tried to stay friends with Margo after Bodhi was born, coming around with Chinese food and hoping to watch Netflix, were disturbed by how impossible it was to have fun with the baby. They didn't know how to hold him—he'd arch his back and thrash when they tried—so they couldn't even help while Margo took a shower. He knocked over an entire container of egg foo young with a flailing arm while he was still hooked to Margo's boob. That was the other thing: her boobs were everywhere. She'd forget to put them away, and one tit would be dangling there like a lazy eye while she finished whatever she was saying or took a bite. And her nipples had become weirdly long, like fully half an inch long. It was not fun. It was not fun to visit Margo and the baby, and so gradually they all stopped.

Her roommates weren't sympathetic about the baby situation. All three acted like Margo having a baby was just about the same thing as getting a dog when dogs were prohibited on the lease. It seemed insane to them that someone was allowed to have a whole screaming baby wherever they wanted, and Margo understood their point, she could remember distantly their headspace, but she wasn't able to communicate to them what had changed for her or how she thought they should behave.

Once, in the middle of the night, Bodhi would not stop crying, and she had no idea why. She'd done all the things: she'd changed the diaper, she'd nursed him, she'd burped him. But he kept arching his back and making these piercing shrieks, like a supremely pissed-off eagle. She tried stuffing her boob in his mouth, and he only turned his face away and screamed some more.

Kat the Larger banged on the wall. "Keep it down in there!"

"Don't you think if I knew how to make him stop, I would?!" Margo screamed.

She heard Kat the Larger throw something, by the sound of it a book or maybe an alarm clock, something relatively heavy.

"What do you want me to fucking do?" Margo yelled.

"Go outside," Kat the Larger roared, then Margo heard stomping, and Kat the Larger was in her room, talking fast as an auctioneer. "I don't know why you think this is acceptable, this is completely unacceptable, are you fucking nuts, you think I have nothing to do tomorrow, I have a final in biochem, and you will never understand what this night of sleep might cost me, you will never get it, so if you can't make him shut up, take it outside!"

Kat the Smaller appeared behind her in the doorway. "If you guys could keep it down?" she said.

"It is two a.m. and you are kicking me and a three-week-old baby out of the apartment?" Margo asked, feeling the wonderful, revving warmth of rage. She hadn't known this was what she needed: to fight. She was so angry, she'd been angry for weeks: at Mark for making her pregnant and also for being right that babies were hard and she shouldn't have had one, at Shyanne for not helping more and for being correct that this decision would ruin her life. It was ruining her life. Her life was ruined. She hadn't taken a shower in four days, and even when she did there was no other choice than to lay Bodhi on the bathmat and let him cry, talking to him and singing as she washed her hair and body as fast as she could. Why on earth had she done this? The size, the sheer magnitude, of her own idiocy was crushing. And it hurt all the worse because she loved Bodhi more than she'd ever loved anything or anyone, and she would not give him up for all the world.

"Fuck you both," Margo said. "You could offer to help me. You could extend basic human decency."

"What are you talking about?!" Kat the Larger said, gesturing now with her hands in the dark bedroom. "Are you insane? It is your baby! It is your responsibility! It is not my responsibility! My responsibility is to pass my biochem exam!"

"I think," Kat the Smaller began in her high, soft voice, "what Margo is saying is—"

"Fine," Margo said. "I'll leave."

She strapped Bodhi to her front and jammed a hat on his head. "Are you happy now?" she asked them.

"Yes!" Kat the Larger said. "Because now I will be able to sleep!"

"Margo . . ." Kat the Smaller said, then nothing more.

Margo slammed the front door, hop-skipped down the outside stairs. Normally she was terrified going up and down with Bodhi, positive she'd slip and fall and crush him under her massive body (she felt their size discrepancy keenly; at three weeks he was barely the size of a small cat), but the rage made her so graceful—she feared nothing. When she was out on the darkened street, the beauty of the night overwhelmed her. It was crisp, not cold. The moon was out. She started to walk to her car because she didn't know what else to do. Lulled by the motion of walking, Bodhi relaxed and snuggled into the carrier, and she could tell he was on the verge of falling asleep. She looked up and down the sidewalk. It was a lovely night. There were streetlights and she felt relatively safe, so long as she stayed in her little residential area and didn't get too close to the freeway.

She walked around Fullerton for over an hour, thinking about what had happened, the series of decisions that had led her to this point, and what any of it meant. How much kindness would mean right now, and how unwilling anyone was to give it. How sacred the baby was to her, and how mundane and irritating the baby was to others.

Margo felt so raw and leaking, so mortal, and yet stronger than she'd ever been. The option to throw yourself on the ground and have a good cry was gone. You had to keep going, past the rosebushes and garden gnomes in the dark, the baby asleep on your chest, wondering when it would be safe to go home.

CHAPTER FOUR

Margo had failed to anticipate how awkward Shyanne would be with the baby. When Bodhi was placed in her arms, something odd seemed to happen to Shyanne's elbows, as though marionette strings had pulled them too high, and even her happy smile couldn't disguise her mounting panic.

"This is so weird, Mom," Margo said, because it was weird, it was markedly weird.

"Well, it's been a while since I held a baby, so excuse me!" Shyanne said.

It was true that Bodhi did seem to cry whenever Shyanne held him. Margo was convinced it was because Shyanne couldn't relax, that he was picking up on her vibes.

"Or it's your perfume, Mom, it might be too strong for his little nose."

"I don't understand why you're nursing him. Why not give him a bottle?"

Several times Shyanne asked this question, and each time Margo explained that giving a baby a bottle too early could cause "nipple confusion" and mess up their nursing.

"Did you breastfeed me at all?" Margo asked, finally piecing it together.

"I mean, I tried!" Shyanne said.

Margo hesitated, unsure whether to ask if Shyanne's implants had made breastfeeding impossible.

"I got a bad infection," Shyanne said, gesturing at her whole chest.

"Mastitis?"

"Whatever you call it," Shyanne said.

"Was Jinx around a lot when I was a baby?" she asked during another visit after a completely botched attempt to let Shyanne feed Bodhi breast milk with a bottle. Bodhi was screeching and Shyanne was shaking with panic as she tried to force the bottle into his mouth.

"No, that was the problem!" Shyanne said. "He was supposed to come and then he didn't. He had just gotten injured in Japan!"

"Oh my God—how old was I when he hurt his back?"

"Three weeks old."

"Jesus Christ. Was your mom here to help you?"

"No! Are you kidding? Mama was terrified of flying, she didn't like me having a baby out of wedlock, there was no way she was driving from Oklahoma to help me out of a stupid mess of my own damn making."

"When did he finally come?" Margo asked. She'd always known that her dad had gotten injured "when she was a baby," but it had never occurred to her exactly what that must have meant for her mom.

"Well, he had that first surgery in Japan because he couldn't fly, and then he did rehab there for two months. When he came stateside, he had to spend time with Cheri and them, so I don't remember exactly, but I think you were about nine months when he saw you for the first time."

"Did you almost kill him?"

"I mean, I would have killed him if I didn't need him to give me money so bad!" Shyanne laughed, though it was not a happy sound.

"He must have been strapped. I mean, he basically lost his job, right?"

"Yep," Shyanne said. "It was not a happy time for anybody. Gives me the butt tingles even talking about it."

"I'm so sorry, Mom," Margo said, and she meant it. Before she'd had Bodhi, she'd known her mother loved her, but she hadn't understood how expensive that love was, how much a mother paid for it.

MARGO WORKED HER first shift since the birth when Bodhi was about six weeks old. Shyanne watched him and after that said she'd never watch him again. "I get flashbacks," she said. "He doesn't like me, Margo. It's not right for a baby to be crying and crying like that for hours." Margo nodded. She didn't want Bodhi crying for hours either.

The next shift, Margo hired a sitter who was actually her mother's neighbor, a woman with a lawn statue of a frog Elvis, who said he wouldn't take a bottle for anything, and he'd basically cried the whole seven hours. The next shift, she hired a sitter off Care.com named Theresa, who was twenty-four and studying for a degree in child psychology and had been a nanny to twin baby girls. When Margo got home, Theresa practically rushed out of the apartment saying everything had been great and Bodhi was an angel. Bodhi was in a state, though he settled down after Margo nursed him, and she reassured herself that everything was okay. Later, Margo looked in the freezer, hunting for ice cream, and saw that the six bags of milk she'd left were still there, completely untouched. It was almost like Theresa hadn't even tried to feed Bodhi. Her roommates said the crying was nonstop and that Margo was not allowed to have babysitters watch Bodhi in the apartment anymore.

Margo had one more shift before the weekend—well, her weekend, a Tuesday and Wednesday—and so she called her mom. "You have to," she said. "This is the moment you show up for me."

"Noodle, I cannot do it," Shyanne said. "When he cries, I panic! I'm telling you, that baby does not like me."

"He's a baby, he doesn't like or not like you. I'm asking. I'm asking you this," Margo said.

"Noodle," Shyanne said.

"I will pay you," Margo said.

Her mother paused. "Goddamn it, what time?"

But she called Margo at the restaurant halfway through her shift, saying she could not watch him one minute longer, and if Margo wouldn't come get him, Shyanne would drive there and leave him with the bartender. Tessa, the owner, had been extremely pissed when she handed Margo the phone, saying, "A phone call for you, madame." In general, getting personal calls at work was highly taboo. Tessa's eyeliner was smudged beneath her eyes, adding to the impression she made of a refined and beautiful bulldog.

"Do you want me to bring him there?" Margo's mom was asking, her voice tiny inside the bulky block of the cordless phone.

Margo didn't know which would make Tessa angrier: her leaving in the middle of a shift or a baby appearing at the bar. She opened her mouth and no sound emerged.

"What's happening?" Tessa asked, softened by whatever she could see on Margo's face. "Is it the baby?"

"No," Margo said to Tessa. "I mean, yes, he's okay. My mom is saying she can't watch him because he keeps crying and can she bring him here?"

"Oh, for fuck's sake," Tessa said, grabbing the phone from Margo and saying to Shyanne: "You should be ashamed of yourself. Bring him here, I'll watch him myself."

That night Tessa let Margo nurse Bodhi in the back office, which sent him directly to sleep. He slept on Tessa's massive bosom for the rest of the shift, making Tessa feel like quite the baby whisperer. All the drunk regulars came over to admire him, and Tessa held forth about how the secret to babies was whatever whatever, always ending with giving the baby some whiskey on the corner of a washcloth to suck on, though this was not how she'd gotten Bodhi to sleep at all.

In a way, it seemed like a '90s sitcom, and Margo imagined that maybe Tessa would become the nanny and run the restaurant with Bodhi strapped to her chest. He'd be a kind of mascot. Nothing cheered up aging alcoholics like a baby! At the end of the shift, Margo closed out and tipped everyone. She was feeling good; she'd made more money than usual and worked the last half of the shift light at heart knowing Bodhi was safe. As she peeled his sleeping body from Tessa's chest, Tessa said, "You've got to get something figured out."

"I know," Margo said.

"If you can't get a regular sitter in place by your next shift, you're fired."

"Oh," Margo said.

"I know it seems harsh. But, sweetie, you shouldn't be here. You should be home with this baby."

"Yeah," Margo said, suddenly so angry it felt like electricity was gathering in her eye sockets. "But I have to, you know, live. And pay rent."

"Move in with your mother. Jesus!" Tessa was rubbing her eyes with her knuckles. The bartender, Jose, who had worked there for a hundred million years and still somehow looked only twenty-three, took in their exchange and poured Tessa another whiskey soda.

"I can't move in with my mother," Margo said.

"Why the fuck not? What, you don't get along? Those things don't matter, Margo, you have a fucking baby!"

Margo stood there, angry and trying not to cry, too stubborn to speak.

"I'm not going to actually fire you," Tessa said with a sigh. "I mean, I will, but I'll hate it so much, please don't make me."

Margo nodded. She couldn't look at Tessa. She couldn't look at anybody. She moved her head around so the dark kaleidoscope of the restaurant swirled around her. All the drunk people laughing. Her baby in her arms. "Have a good night!" she said.

"Margo," Tessa said. "Don't be upset!"

Margo kept walking, out the front door, down the street, to her beat-up purple Civic. God, how she had loved that car when she first got it, her junior year. It was used and already had eighty thousand miles on it, but it had a sunroof and a radio and that was all that mattered. Jinx had surprised her with it. She and Becca would go driving, spying on houses of boys they liked.

Bodhi woke the moment she placed him in his car seat and cried the whole way home.

MARGO HAD TWO days off before her next shift and no penetrating new insights into the childcare conundrum. Nannies and babysitters were around $800 a week, whereas day care was only $300, but day care was, as the name suggested, very diurnal, just obsessed with daylight. If she had a respectable job being a secretary or something, she'd have an easier time finding childcare. But she was a night worker, which somehow denied her the right to affordable childcare. It made no sense! A night care would be even easier to run—all the babies would be sleeping!

How was she supposed to make a living? She was willing to work hard, she was willing to never sleep, to wear an ugly uniform, to be mildly degraded day in and day out. She was willing to do whatever was required. But she needed to believe it was *possible*.

Part of the problem was that at twenty dollars an hour, paying for someone to watch Bodhi at night would cut her income by more than half. She considered switching to lunch shifts, but when she called the local day care, it was full. Would she like to get on the wait list? How long was the wait list? Oh, well, not that long, most people were only on it for three to six months.

"Are you serious?" Margo asked. "You would have to get on the wait list before even having the baby!"

"That's exactly what people do," the woman said.

"Oh."

To calm down, Margo watched YouTube videos of oddly satisfying things, like cheesecake being cut perfectly or suitcases being wrapped in plastic, and nursed Bodhi. When that grew boring, she scrolled Twitter, which was like being bathed in the dirty water of other people's thoughts. On Instagram she was in a deep, deep ad loop. The algorithm had really figured her out and was constantly selling her a mixture of vitamins, ritzy baby items, and leggings that made your butt look good. It was high-octane covetousness. She couldn't afford anything. Still, she took screenshots of the things she wanted most.

There was a part of Margo that simply didn't believe Tessa would fire her. Two days to figure out such a massive, intractable problem wasn't realistic. Margo needed only a little more time to get her act together. Maybe Tessa would help her figure out childcare ideas.

The night before her next shift, she texted Tessa: I couldn't find a sitter.

Tessa texted: ur fucking kidding me.

Margo: I just need more time, it's hard to line anything up this quickly.
Tessa: You had nine months to line something up. I'm sorry, Margo.
Margo: Wait, are you going to fire me?
Tessa: Yes

Margo: I'm fired?
Tessa: Yes
Margo: Wait, for real??

Tessa didn't write anything more. It was over. Almost two years Margo had worked there.

Margo ran her fingers through her hair over and over, not really seeing anything out of her eyes.

She'd thought, somehow, that keeping the baby would make people regard her with more kindness. But women frowned at her and Bodhi in the grocery store. The eyes of men skittered over her like she was invisible. She seemed to walk everywhere in a cloud of shame. She was a stupid slut for having a baby, and if she'd had an abortion, she also would have been a stupid slut. It was a game you could not win. They had tried to warn her: her mother, Mark, even Becca. But when they talked about the opportunities she would be missing, she'd thought they meant a four-year college. She hadn't understood they meant that every single person she met, every new friend, every love interest, every employer, every landlord, would judge her for having made what they all claimed was the "right" choice.

To calm herself, she ate two bowls of Crunch Berries until she could feel the sugar and food dye moving in her bloodstream like magic. She realized that underneath her panic, a secret part of her was a little thrilled to be fired. To no longer grind black pepper. To no longer get ranch dressing on her hand and wind up rubbing it in like lotion. She smiled, thinking that she'd never have to see the head chef, Sean, again, who had once tricked her into looking at his dick by putting it on a plate with some parsley around it.

She put her empty bowl in the sink and crept back into her bedroom to her sleeping baby.

Tomorrow she would file for unemployment. She would figure it out. Because it was impossible that there was no solution. People had babies all the time and somehow managed it. She only needed to try a little harder.

THE NEXT MORNING, when she was still asleep, there was a knock on her bedroom door.

It was Kat the Larger and Kat the Smaller.

"We wanted to let you know we found our own place," Kat the Larger said.

"Bodhi is sleeping," Margo whispered, gesturing with her hand to bring the volume down. Kat the Larger had a big, wonderfully loud voice. It was one of the things Margo had initially liked about her.

"Oh, sorry," Kat the Larger whispered, still somehow mysteriously loud. "We found a new place. So we'll be moving out in a week or so. Just wanted to give you a heads-up so you could find new roomies."

It took Margo a couple of seconds to understand what Kat was saying. Margo and Suzie were the only ones technically on the lease. They had sublet two of the bedrooms to the Kats, but nothing was in writing.

"No thirty-day notice? I mean, are you kidding me right now?" Margo's whisper was getting shrill.

"Well, we already paid rent for the month, so you have, like, twenty-five days or something," Kat the Smaller said.

Margo didn't know what to say. The intense sensation of unfairness also made the situation feel like it couldn't really be happening. Shouldn't there be someone in charge of how many bad things could happen at once?

"We're gonna get a guinea pig!" Kat the Smaller whispered, clasping her little hands under her chin with excitement.

"That's neat," Margo whispered back. "Really would have been nice if you'd given more notice."

"Well, we didn't know," Kat the Smaller said. "I'm sorry!"

"Good luck with the baby and all that," Kat the Larger said, raising her eyebrows to indicate how badly Margo would be needing that luck, and it made her beanie lift slightly. It was too small for her head, the beanie, and now that it had been dislodged from its stable position, it was incrementally peeling off Kat's head. Margo just stood there watching it happen, and Kat the Larger had to have felt it happening, but she did not pull the beanie down.

"We'll invite you to the housewarming party!" Kat the Smaller said.

"Okay!" Margo said, and closed her door. Then she went over to her bed and lay facedown next to the sleeping Bodhi. She did not cry. She just pressed her face into the comforter, really smooshed it down. Rent was $3,995, which they had split four ways, so they'd now be about $2,000 short a month. She did not truly believe that Suzie would split the missing rent with her, not because Suzie wasn't nice, but because Suzie worked at the dean's office at school as a work study for, like, eleven dollars an hour and spent all her money on elf ears and wizard cloaks and stuff. Suzie's mom was even more hard up than Shyanne. Suzie had once sold plasma so she could buy contact lenses that made her look like a cat.

"Fuuuuuuuuck," Margo said into her duvet. She wondered when she would need to stop swearing around the baby. Surely not for a while yet.

FILING FOR UNEMPLOYMENT took Margo the better part of two days. She had to get her birth certificate and Social Security card from Shyanne, but at the end of it, she was officially on welfare. When she got to that last screen, her heart stopped. Congratulations! The state would give her $1,236 a month. Digital confetti rained down on the screen.

Margo stared at it. How did anyone think someone in California could live on that amount? She would have $200 after rent, and that was assuming she found new roommates immediately.

She picked up her phone, set it down, then immediately picked it back up and called Jinx. It rang and rang. She normally would never have left a voicemail about something like this. His other kids and wife knew about her, but they didn't like Jinx talking to her, and she knew his wife, Cheri, was constantly snooping on his phone. She didn't have it in her to wait, though, and she figured he was probably in Japan, a Cheri-free zone.

"Dad, this is Margo. I'm in a really bad spot. I got fired from my job, and my roommates are suddenly ditching out, and I'm on the hook for three grand a month in rent. I filed for unemployment, but they'll only give me twelve hundred a month. I need help. Like, it kills me to say that, because I did this to myself, and everyone told me. But I'm scared.

So if you could please call me back as soon as possible, I would—I'm just freaked out. So, yeah. Okay. Sorry this wasn't more cheerful. Love you."

She felt sure he would call her back. She had never asked him for anything before this. She'd never asked for him to come to her graduation, she'd never asked for an iPhone, she had not even asked or expected that he come out for Bodhi's birth. She'd been saving a whole life's worth of chips, and now she was trying to cash them in. And she knew that he loved her. She knew he would call.

LATER THAT WEEK, as I was eating a microwave pizza amid the towers of the two Kats' moving boxes, which for some reason they'd decided belonged in the dining alcove, I scalded nearly all the skin off the roof of my mouth. As I was peeling off the white flap of numb skin, my mom called.

"Kenny wants to meet you."

It took me a second to respond. "I've already met Kenny."

"In passing!" she cried.

"All right! So?"

"He wants to take you out to dinner and really get to know you."

That sounded creepy. "Would you be there?"

"Yes, I think so. I mean, I didn't ask. Gosh, I wonder!"

"Is this a formal interview process?"

I thought I heard Bodhi in the other room, pulled the phone from my ear, and listened to the air, but there was nothing. I took another bite of pizza. My mom was still talking when I put the phone to my ear again.

". . . which, I'm not counting my chickens before they hatch—I've done that before!—but I do think this means it is getting serious, I really do believe that."

"If he asked you to marry him, would you say yes?" It was hard to imagine that she would. Kenny was so old and kind of rigid, needed things to be just so. He had that tight potbelly some skinny men grew as they aged. He had been a high school math teacher and retired early to work for his church. With her Bloomingdale's discount, my mom had been mainlining beauty serums and anti-wrinkle creams for years and she didn't look much over thirty, so even though Kenny was only six years older, there was still a May-December vibe.

"You bet your ass I would," she said. "That man is everything I'm not. He's stingy and cheap and he plans things."

I laughed. It was amazing how depressed you could get and still find things funny. In fact, things seemed even funnier.

"Margo, that is safety. That is securing the future. Hey, have you been looking for a job?"

"Uh, yeah," I said. I absolutely had not.

"You got any interviews?"

"Yeah, like a seafood place on Wednesday." I had no idea what part of my brain generated this lie. I didn't even know what day of the week it was and how many days away Wednesday would be.

"Seafood is perfect. I bet you'll make great tips," she said.

I held my breath, wondering if she was going to ask who would watch the baby and wondering if I would lie about that too, but she didn't.

"So you're marrying Kenny for his fat 401(k)?" It was fun to tease my mother. She always took the bait.

"I would never!" she said. "I would marry him even if he didn't have a cent."

"No, you wouldn't."

"I would!" she insisted. "Because Kenny is the kind of man who could lose it all and build it back up again."

"You think that man is going to let you spend four hundred dollars on face cream?"

"He doesn't have to know about the face cream."

"He's going to know about it if you marry him and get a joint checking and all that. I can't imagine you giving up that much control."

"I have my ways," she said. I knew she meant poker money. Or Jinx money.

"Do you love him?" I asked.

"I do."

I assumed she was bluffing, though I wasn't sure.

She doubled down: "I admire him. I admire the way he is because it's different than the way I am."

"Okay," I said, softening. I understood the bluff was also for herself. The fact was, my mother's life was untenable and she knew it. She'd held out for a long time, too long, hoping Jinx would leave his wife and marry her, and that hadn't happened, and she wasn't getting any younger. My mom loved bad boys, she loved hunks with big muscles and motorcycles. Choosing Kenny, who went so against her type, was a last-ditch attempt to save herself from herself, and there was a kind of wisdom in that. If you didn't want the same result over and over, you had to do something different.

"I don't suppose you could spot me some money for rent while I look for a job?" I asked. "The Kats moved out, so we have to come up with the missing two grand."

"Are you asking me for two thousand dollars?"

"I mean, kind of?"

"I don't have two thousand dollars, Noodle."

"I figured," I said.

"Ask Mark. He's the one who should be giving you two grand."

"Yeah," I said, completely numb.

"So when are you free? You'll have to get a sitter."

"To have dinner with Kenny?"

"Yes."

"Why wouldn't I bring the baby?"

"I haven't told him about the baby."

"Okay, I am not pretending I don't have a baby, Mom." I knew well enough to head these things off now. When Grandma had finally died, Shyanne reused her death again and again to get out of things.

"I knew you were going to be this way."

"Yes, because this is psychotic."

"It is not his business whether you have a baby or not, Margo."

"I'll go to dinner with Kenny as soon as you tell him that I have a baby," I said.

"Fuck!" she said, and hung up on me.

CHAPTER FIVE

On the day the Kats moved out, Suzie came out of her room, plopped down next to me on the couch, and said, "Thank God they're gone, right?"

"Well, except for the rent money part," I said.

"I have some friends who could maybe move in," Suzie said. "I have to check on their lease situation."

I dreaded having Suzie's weird nerd friends move in. They'd be fucking LARPing all over the living room. But I nodded. "Go for it," I told her. Anything so that I didn't have to post ads and interview people. Anything so that I could stay half awake and perpetually nursing. After two weeks, it had started to become real to me that Jinx wasn't going to call me back, and the sadness was like quicksand.

"Hey, I saw Mark on campus," Suzie said.

"Yeah?" I didn't want to talk about Mark. Every time I thought about him it hurt. Not because I missed him or loved him; it just hurt.

"He looked *rough*," Suzie said. "Real rough."

I shrugged, but I was a little bit glad that he wasn't out there thriving.

"Did you know they made him chair?"

"Good for him."

"No," Suzie said, "everyone hates being chair, it's so much work. He's fucking miserable. But he's in all the faculty meetings now, so I get to give him the stink eye."

Part of Suzie's job was keeping minutes at all the meetings for the dean. It was so weird how I had been a part of that world, campus and college, and now I never left the apartment except to go to the gas station. I'd finished out the spring semester, and Bodhi had been born in July, so I hadn't registered for any classes in the fall. I had always assumed I would go back at some point, but now that idea seemed ridiculous.

"Can I hold him?" Suzie asked. She'd never asked that before. Bodhi had finished nursing and was soundly asleep in my arms. I rolled him onto her chest, grateful for the chance to stand up and stretch.

"My lower back is fucked," I said.

"Oh my God, it's like having a cat sleep on you!" Suzie cooed. "A person-cat!"

"Can you stay like that?" I asked. "I haven't pooped in, like, two days."

"You bet," Suzie whispered, relaxing a bit, tucking Bodhi's fuzzy head under her chin. "But if he wakes up, I'm barging in there and handing him back."

"Deal."

MARGO WAITED UNTIL ten days before the rent was due.

Then she swallowed her pride and wrote to Mark, asking to borrow $3,000. She wondered if he would write back.

"Of course we can email," he had said, "we can email for the rest of our lives!" As though what they had was real. Had it been real for him, though? She'd never been able to tell exactly; he seemed so caught up in his fantasy. Maybe she'd been the one being foolish. Of course, it had been real. Just look at this real baby in her arms, this real rent money coming due.

She remembered a day Mark and Derek had argued in class. Derek had tried to claim that third-person omniscient narration "felt more honest."

"Honesty and fiction are incompatible," Mark had said.

"But, you know, like unreliable first-person narrators and all that." Derek motioned with his pale, soft hands.

"Fiction is always a lie," Mark said. "Look, I'll do it right now: An opulent table lay heavy with meat and fruit, wine and cakes. Is there a table?" Mark looked around himself, pretending to search for the table.

"Yeah, but . . ." Derek said.

"Yes?" Mark asked.

"I don't know," he said.

"You like your fake things to be more real feeling?"

"I guess," Derek said.

"Not me," Mark said, "I like the swagger. I like the bravado when the author says, 'Hey, look at how fake this is, now I'm gonna make you forget all about it.'"

MARGO KNEW EVERYTHING that had happened with Mark was as fake as it got. But that didn't make the result any less real, and she was going to need help paying for it.

A DAY WENT by, and then another, with no word from Mark or Jinx. Then Margo received a call on her cell phone from a local number she thought might be Bodhi's pediatrician, Dr. Azarian. It was Mark's mother, and she wanted to meet to discuss Margo's "demands." Even as it was happening, Margo couldn't believe it, that he had taken his problem and handed it over to Mommy. It was surreal. "I don't have any demands," Margo said.

"Well, I do," Mark's mother said. And she told Margo when and where she wanted to meet.

THE BUILDING MARGO pulled up to almost looked like a medical center. When she went inside and found the suite number, she saw it was a law office and thought, Oh. She went in, Bodhi alert and smiley in her arms. The secretary asked for her name. Margo couldn't believe this girl would know her name and have an actual appointment for her, but evidently she did, and the girl showed her into an office that contained a rich, old woman in a pink skirt suit and a curly-haired lawyer with a long, horsey face. The lawyer's name was Larry. Larry the Lawyer. The woman's name was Elizabeth, and she was Mark's mother, who was clearly surprised and appalled that Margo had brought Bodhi with her.

"We certainly weren't expecting this!" Elizabeth cried, fake laughing. Where did they think she would leave the baby? With her twenty-four-hour Swedish nanny? Margo was so overcome with panic at being in this room that she missed almost the first five minutes of what was said. It was overwhelming how oddly similar Elizabeth's and Mark's mannerisms were. They both had a way of looking down so you could see the twigs of their straight, brittle eyelashes and pursing their lips before starting a sentence. When Margo could finally hear over the sound of her own heartbeat, Elizabeth was still talking. Every time Larry tried to interrupt, Elizabeth held up her hand and seemed to press the words right back inside him.

"And in exchange, you would guarantee that you will not attend Fullerton College in the future, make no contact with Mark or his family. And you would need to sign this nondisclosure agreement, which is why Larry is here."

Larry nodded. He sure was there!

"So, can I ask, is Mark listed on the child's birth certificate?" Larry asked.

"Uh, no. I left it blank. But if I did all those things, then what?" Margo asked, hugging Bodhi in her lap. He was lying on her, looking out, like she was a giant human recliner.

"You would receive the fifteen thousand immediately to cover the start-up costs, if you will, and when the child turns eighteen it would receive the trust I already mentioned."

Elizabeth kept calling Bodhi "the child" even though Margo had told her his name.

"I just . . ." Margo said. "Is there any way you could tell me about the trust part again?"

She could tell from Elizabeth's fake concerned eyebrows that Elizabeth thought she was stupid, but it seemed important to find out what was going on here.

"Okay . . ." Elizabeth said slowly. "We would take fifty thousand dollars and put it in a trust, think of it like a bank account. And we would invest that money in something called mutual funds. And that money would grow, so that when he turns eighteen, it should be worth around three hundred thousand."

"Okay," Margo said, stunned by the sum. "I mean, that seems fair. I give up going to college but he'll get to go."

"You could still go to college," Larry said.

"Just not here," Elizabeth said. Her lipstick was the exact shade of pink as her skirt suit, and Margo imagined an entire closet of clothes, all a vibrant raspberry sorbet, like a rich-lady version of Batman, though she knew it was too good to be true. Elizabeth looked like the sort of woman who also wore beige.

How was it possible to hate the person who was saving you?

"Sure," Margo said.

"So, you agree?" Elizabeth asked, almost incredulous. Had she expected Margo to argue? That was the only inkling Margo had that she might be getting taken advantage of in some way. She hadn't put it together that this was not a lot of money for these people, that she could have asked for twice as much and Elizabeth wouldn't have balked. Margo had Mark's whole life in her power. She could end his career, destroy his marriage, ruin his reputation. The Me Too movement was everywhere, all around them, in the news every single day. A year ago, Mark would never have been fired for sleeping with a student. Now everything was changing. The past bulged and contorted beneath a new lens. It was beginning to seem as if even the once whorish Monica Lewinsky had only been a poor intern taken advantage of by the president of the United States. Men were being pilloried, men were being canceled, men were going to lose everything!

But it was beyond Margo then, that long-ago Margo, to imagine that $50,000 wasn't a lot of money to someone.

Mainly, she thought Elizabeth, Larry, and Mark had arranged all of this on the assumption that Margo was some low-class, immature girl who might get mad and call Mark's dean on a lark or show up at his house for drama's sake. Margo could have told them she would never do this. But now her survival depended on them believing she could.

So she signed everywhere they told her, too embarrassed to actually read it right then in front of them. When she got back to her car, she stuffed the contracts in the glove box. She didn't want to look at them. They seemed almost dirty. The check she drove immediately to the bank to deposit. She'd never had a bank balance higher than $500 before. It seemed like so much money. She worried the teller might challenge her, accuse her of forging or stealing it somehow. Margo signed the back and handed it over, and the teller said, "Is that all?"

I can still see her, that Margo, floating back to her purple Honda

Civic, so numb inside, almost shell-shocked. She wasn't sure what she should do next. Bodhi had miraculously fallen asleep, so she went to the Arby's drive-through, ordered two Classic Beef 'n Cheddar sandwiches, and ate them both in the car while he slept. As the fat hit her bloodstream, she realized she was extremely happy. She had $15,000. Yes, she felt gross and degraded, but she had done it. She'd saved them.

I like getting to be the me now watching the past me. It's almost a way of loving myself. Stroking the cheek of that girl with my understanding. Smoothing her hair in my mind's eye.

MARGO WAS DREADING the dinner with Kenny. Shyanne had arranged it after she finally told him that her daughter had a baby.

"Fine," Margo had said. "Where are we going?"

"Applebee's," Shyanne said, "so dress nice but not too nice."

Margo received the message. Shyanne was a big believer in dressing for the job and usually spent more time agonizing over the outfit she'd wear than what she would say in any situation. She'd coached Margo her whole life on the science and art of communicative clothing. Shyanne wanted Margo to dress in such a way that Kenny would know she'd tried and considered this a special occasion, without making him feel embarrassed that he hadn't taken her somewhere nicer.

"Worn to death?" she asked. Shyanne had a belief that wearing one item that showed visible signs of wear inspired sympathy in people because you were clearly doing your best with what you had.

"Maybe that little black cardigan with the pilling," Shyanne said.

"Or I could do old tank top, nicer sweater?"

"He's not that detail oriented."

"Okay, can do. What time?"

IT WAS ONLY once they were seated in the Applebee's that Margo realized with delight that they would be eating. Margo had always been mildly gluttonous, mostly because she could afford to be. She honestly wasn't sure what she'd have to do to put on weight, but certainly the occasional chili dog or Cheez-It orgy wasn't going to do it. Nursing had brought her appetite to new radiant heights. She looked at the full-color photos of the Applebee's menu like it was a rich-people Christmas catalog. The riblets glittered darkly, and the fried shrimp seemed to sparkle with promised crunch. Margo's mouth flooded with saliva. "Do you think we should get an appetizer?"

"I don't know," Shyanne said.

"Margo, I want you to know," Kenny said, "that this meal is my treat, and you can order whatever you like, no expense spared."

He smiled at her warmly. Maybe because of the sheer number of dinners Mark had bought her, she had a sudden flash of wondering what Mark and Kenny would make of each other and almost laughed out loud. She pictured something instantaneous, a chemical reaction, both men completely dissolved into foam within seconds.

"We don't need an appetizer," Shyanne said.

"Maybe you don't need one, you're about to order a margarita the size of your head, but I need one," Margo said.

"Margo!" Shyanne said sharply. "You know I don't drink!"

Margo froze. "Oh," she said, "I guess I forgot?"

Kenny laughed. "That's quite all right," he said.

She didn't know what he meant. Was it all right that obviously Shyanne did drink and was pretending not to drink to please him, or all right for Margo to have forgotten a basic fact about her own mother?

"What looks good to you, Margo?" he asked.

"Nachos or wings," she said.

"Attagirl," he said. "Can't go wrong."

"I'm leaning nachos," Margo went on, still looking hungrily at the menu. "I can be kind of picky about wings."

"How do you like your wings?" Kenny seemed delighted, as though it were novel for a girl to like chicken wings.

"I like bone in and no breading. Except for Hooters wings, I make an exception for those."

"Margo!" Shyanne said.

"Oh, come on," Margo said, "you love the Hooters wings, and you know it."

"I will allow," Kenny said with a twinkle in his eye, "I have had the Hooters wings a time or two, and they are delightful."

"I've never been there," Shyanne said. Margo just stared. Her mother had worked there for six years. She was beginning to think the problem with Kenny wasn't Kenny, but whatever phony personality Shyanne seemed determined to project.

When the waitress came, Kenny ordered iced teas for him and Shyanne, as well as an order of chicken wings and beef nachos. Margo clapped her hands in glee. "Oh, I'm so excited!" she said.

It was comforting to be inside an Applebee's. The faux brick walls, the thickly resined tabletops so glossy and smooth they almost glowed. The service was atrocious; Margo didn't know how the girl who was their server slept at night. When she brought out the nachos, she stuck her thumb right in the beans. Margo saw her lick it clean as she walked away.

"So tell me again, Kenny," Margo said, "you work for the church?"

"I'm the youth ministry director," he said with a big smile, "of Forest Park Community Church. And I love it!"

"Oh, neat!" Margo said, though Kenny was so old and radically uncool that it was hard to imagine what kind of youth he could successfully minister to.

"They have some really great programs, Margo," Shyanne said. "Lots of plays and stuff."

"I do love musicals," Kenny said.

"They even put on *Rent*," Shyanne said.

"We're a pretty liberal bunch," Kenny offered. "Which is why it was so silly of Shyanne to worry I would somehow judge you for having a child out of wedlock."

Margo swallowed. There was always something a little creepy about the word *wedlock*.

"Well," she said, "I will say, I've made a lot of mistakes in my life, but I don't think keeping Bodhi was one of them."

"Amen to that," Kenny said, and raised his iced tea. "So many people want to get out of the consequences of their own actions nowadays. Don't you agree?"

The waitress came back and took their orders.

"Most people," Kenny began when the waitress left, "and feel free to disagree, I'd like to get your opinion on this, Margo, but most people think they're the victims. They want to order their special latte with no foam or extra whip or caramel what-have-you, and if they don't get it, suddenly they're outraged. A lot of girls in your situation would have cried rape! Would have said, 'But he's my professor! He should have done this, he shouldn't have done that.'"

Margo wasn't sure what Starbucks had to do with anything. "I mean, I do think Mark shouldn't sleep with his students."

"Oh, absolutely," Kenny said. "We are all fallen creatures. The real test is what we do when those chickens come home to roost. Do you try to use a get-out-of-jail-free card, or do you man up and accept the consequences of your actions? You have agency. You have the power to make your life heaven or make your life hell. It's about the choices that you make."

"Right," Margo said. It seemed terribly likely that this was going to continue in a direction that would make her uncomfortable, yet his line of reasoning was not anything she disagreed with exactly.

"I told you we'd get along," Kenny said to Shyanne, who laughed and looked down at the table.

Her mother was so beautiful. Margo had always thought that, but as she got older, she could see her mother more as the world saw her. When they were alone together, Shyanne was prone to making silly faces, crossing her eyes and sticking out her tongue. Because her eyes were so wide-set, there was something truly reptilian about it, and it made Margo laugh every time. But when she was aware of being looked at, Shyanne held her head differently. Her neck was longer, and she angled her face slightly down as though beauty were a kind of bridle she had to bite down on.

"Which is why," Kenny began with a rush, "I wanted to ask you to this dinner tonight."

Margo was aware from his tone that something momentous was going to happen.

Kenny reached across the table and took Shyanne's hand. "I want to ask for your blessing, Margo. I would like to ask for your mother's hand in marriage."

"Oh," Margo said. "Oh, congratulations!"

Shyanne made a kind of throttled cry that would make sense only in the context of sex or sports or maybe gambling. It was the guttural, emotional noise of winning.

"So, do we have your blessing?" Kenny asked.

"Yes, of course," Margo said, even though the idea of every Thanksgiving and Christmas being ruined by Kenny's constant, exuberant presence made her sick to her stomach. She looked at her mother, next to her in the booth, who was crying and shaking with happiness. I never want to do this, Margo thought. I never want to marry anybody ever.

And then Kenny stood, looking so determined and embarrassed that it touched Margo. She could see suddenly and swiftly every single time Kenny had been beaten up on the bus or chickened out of talking to a girl. It was as if his middle school self were momentarily superimposed on his middle-aged one. Kenny crouched on the brown carpet of the Applebee's and pulled out a ring box. He flipped it open.

"Shyanne," he said, "you are the most beautiful woman I have ever met."

Margo was aware that the restaurant had paused, that people were watching, and also that Kenny was blocking the aisle. She was tensed for the moment when a server with a big tray would need to get by.

"Yes," Shyanne cried, fanning her face with her fingers spread wide. "I say yes!"

"Let me finish," he said.

Margo was looking at the ring, a pink diamond in a cushion cut. Maybe he really did know Shyanne.

"Shyanne, I would be honored if you would let me be the boring to your beautiful, the strong to your delicate, the serious to your silly. Shyanne, will you be my wife?"

"Yes," Shyanne said, though she was crying so hard only Kenny and Margo could hear her. Kenny slid the ring on her finger. She hugged him and clung to him kneeling there before her, his head smashed awkwardly into her breasts, and the whole restaurant burst into applause.

Well, Margo thought, looking around at all the people clapping. At least they would probably get a free dessert.

CHAPTER SIX

About a week later, the doorbell rang. Bodhi was asleep, and Margo paused to see if he would wake up, but then the knocking started, so she scooted to the door and opened it a crack.

On or off TV, Jinx always wore the same thing: black jeans or leather pants, black turtleneck, black leather blazer. Like some kind of unholy priest. On his long, thin fingers he wore many rings, and he often clasped his hands together in ways that looked strange and artificial. He would fold them up like you fold an umbrella.

He had never called her back, but she always saw Jinx on his terms, and he often showed up unannounced. It wasn't even that odd that he had his leather duffel bag with him.

"Have I come at a bad time?" he asked, delicately pitching his voice low in case Margo had someone over.

"No, I'm just— You haven't returned any of my texts in, like, weeks, and I left you a voicemail, did you get it?"

"That's why I'm here," he said. "I came as fast as I could. I didn't have my phone because I was in rehab, they don't let you have your phone. When I got it back during discharge, I had about a million voicemails. I listened to yours and I drove straight here. Can I come in? I can write you a check right now."

"Oh," Margo said. "Um, yeah. But I figured out the money thing, so . . ." She held the door open for him. She knew her father had been in rehab before. They had always sort of glossed over it. She wondered if this meant things were bad for him.

Jinx ducked slightly as he entered the apartment. "This is nice," he said.

She hadn't entirely realized he'd never seen her apartment before. "Do you want something to drink?" Margo asked, and Bodhi began to wail from the back room. "Let me get him, and then I'll make you some tea or something."

Jinx loved tea. It started with green tea in Japan. Now he was deep into herbal teas and disgusting drinks made of tree bark, and he could tell you the medicinal properties of plants in great detail, though Margo was never sure whether any of it was real. "Rosehips are just tremendous for inflammation," he would say, holding a teacup in his folded crane hands.

Margo returned with Bodhi firmly latched on to her left tit. She thought it would be weird nursing in front of her dad, but he didn't seem uncomfortable at all. "As soon as he's done, hand him over. He is absolutely precious. He's amazing, Margo." Jinx looked at her, and his eyes were glassy with tears.

Margo had a strange feeling of vertigo. This was maybe the first time she'd ever made her father proud, or at least the first time she was aware of it. "So are you in town?" she asked, crossing over to the kitchen to put water on for tea.

"Yes, and on a semipermanent basis, I think," he said.

"What do you mean?"

"Well, Mayhem is retired now," he said.

Margo had known Murder and Mayhem her whole life, and a visiting Jinx had often meant a visiting Mayhem, Mayhem being much more interested in hanging out with little kids than Murder. Before he got into wrestling, Murder had been an enforcer in some L.A. street gang. That was how he got his ring name, from actually murdering people.

"I thought you were going to— What was his name?" Jinx had been in the middle of transitioning, though Margo had gotten a little caught up in her own drama and now had the feeling she was missing vital pieces of the story. Murder had died of a drug overdose five years ago. Mayhem had tried to keep going as a singles act, and he'd limped along for a few years. People wanted him in matches because at that point he and Murder were iconic, part of history. But realistically, Mayhem was too old, and his back was starting to go. When Mayhem finally officially retired, Jinx had started working with some new guy who was kind of a loose cannon, or that was his gimmick.

She brought the tea to Jinx on the couch and sat in the chair across from him to nurse.

"Billy Ants, yes, and that didn't work out. I don't know if I've spoken about this with you before, but Cheri and I are getting a divorce."

He had certainly never spoken to Margo about it before. He rarely spoke about his marriage and his other family, his real family.

"Oh," Margo said. "I'm so sorry."

"It's all right," he said, leaning back and crossing his impossibly long legs. "It was bound to happen sooner or later."

Bodhi, milk drunk, lurched back into profound slumber in Margo's arms, her nipple popping out of his mouth with a squelch. "Here," she said, getting up and rolling the sleeping baby into his arms.

"Come here, you perfect little one," her father said. He did not use a baby-talk voice, yet there was some extra lilt of sweetness in the words. He began bouncing Bodhi with obvious finesse.

"You're good with him," she said. She'd never pictured her father as being good with babies, maybe because of all the black leather or how much he looked like Beerus from Dragon Ball.

"Well, I've had a few," he said quietly. Five with Cheri, and then Margo. "And my little brothers and sisters."

Jinx was the second of nine. Margo had never met any of them and didn't even know all their names.

Jinx relaxed back into the couch with Bodhi, careful not to wake him, and began examining him, uncurling his tight little fist. "He's going to be big," he said.

"How can you tell?" Margo knew he wouldn't be. She wanted to pretend.

"Look at how long and thick his fingers are."

The love-drunk look on Jinx's face made the back of Margo's throat hurt. Had her father looked at her like that when she was a baby? It was overcast outside, all white cloud cover, and the living room had a kind of elegant gloom to it.

"Does Shyanne know you're in town?" Margo asked.

"Yes, she's the one who sent me over here."

"Oh, you went there first?" Margo asked. Jinx seemed unaware that earlier he'd claimed he drove straight to Margo's.

"Well, yes, I didn't have your address. And I needed to talk to her about something. I met Kenneth."

It was just like Jinx to call him Kenneth instead of Kenny. Margo bet it bugged the shit out of Kenny. "How was that?"

"Well, he's a fan."

"No shit!?"

"But yes, the timing is ironic. I think Shyanne was perhaps shocked."

"What timing? Wait, were you thinking of getting back together with her?"

"That was the plan," Jinx said, nodding. "I brought roses and everything."

"Well, you could have told her about the plan!"

Jinx shrugged, repositioned Bodhi more upright against his chest. "Yes, well, my life has been in a state of disarray, if I'm being honest. And then I get here, and you don't even need my help, so I guess—I guess I needn't have come!"

"Dad," Margo said. She was annoyed that he was now playing the victim because she no longer needed money. In her mind, she should get to be the hostile one at least a little bit longer. But he looked sad, so she said, "I always want to see you. I was desperate for you to meet Bodhi."

Jinx smiled, shook his head. "It's probably best I didn't tell Shyanne the plan. It was half-baked at best. And maybe we've been saved from each other in a way."

Margo didn't know what to say to that. Jinx was the love of Shyanne's damn life. "She would leave him in a heartbeat for you."

"That's nice of you to say," Jinx said, "but there is a lot of water under that bridge. All those years, I think they were very hard on her."

Margo wanted to argue, she wanted to tell him Shyanne's feelings for him had never changed, that it had always been him and would always be him, and if they got together now, it would make everything she'd been through worth it. "I think you should at least talk to her about it," Margo said.

"Maybe I will, but there are things between us that would be difficult for you to understand."

"Why? I mean, I'm not exactly a kid anymore."

"No, of course," Jinx said, recrossing his legs in the other direction
and looking up from the baby. "I seem to be constitutionally incapable
of being faithful to any one woman, and I doubt that has changed.
Shyanne was fixated on Cheri, but in many ways, Cheri wasn't the ob-
stacle, and removing her does not entirely alleviate the strain between
us, even if Shyanne believes it would."

"I mean, couldn't you just . . . not?" Margo was thinking that he was
old now—how many hot babes could he possibly be pulling? It was one
thing when you were twenty-eight and touring the world as a pro wrestler, but a fifty-year-old underweight man unable to keep it in his black
leather pants was a much sadder thing.

"Well, naturally that was my own assumption as well, that it was a
behavior I could and should have control over. But I have never been
successful, so I don't know why I would be successful now."

"And then there was rehab," Margo said. She badly wanted to talk
about it, even though there was a dignity to her father she feared dis-
rupting, like pissing off a cat by picking it up. "How did that go?"

"Oh, you know, it's a cycle," he said. She did know it was a cycle.
It was a cycle every professional wrestler went through: get injured,
take pain pills so you can work injured, get more injured from working
injured, take more pain pills. For a lot of wrestlers this compounded
with life on the road and rowdy nights with lots of drugs and alcohol,
but that wasn't so much Jinx's problem. Jinx's role, really, was more to
be Mayhem and Murder's mom: making sure they made their flights,
arguing with them about how many Somas it was acceptable to take,
keeping them in line at hotels. Murder was a horrible prankster and
had once pooped in the elevator of the Waldorf Astoria.

Despite this, and despite no longer working in the ring, Jinx had
four or five different surgeries on his spine over the years, none of them
hugely successful, or maybe one had been for his hip, she forgot, but
she knew he'd had both knees done too. Not taking the pain pills at all
wasn't really an option.

"But, like, how did you know to go to rehab?" Margo asked. She didn't understand why he didn't just take his pain pills as prescribed, one a day, or a pill every four to six hours, or whatever. For him to be abusing them seemed to imply he wasn't taking them and hoarding them and then taking a lot at once. She'd simply never dared to ask about the nitty-gritty of how it all worked.

Jinx was clearly hesitating, wondering how much to tell her. Finally, he looked up and, staring her directly in the eye, said, "I'd begun using heroin and was having a relationship with a young woman named Viper."

"Oh, gross! *Dad!*" Margo was loud enough that Bodhi jerked awake on Jinx's chest. Margo reached out so Jinx could hand him back. Jinx simply bounced Bodhi a few times and he fell back asleep.

"Shyanne mentioned that you might be in the market for a roommate, and I badly need a place to live, but if we're going to be living together, I want to be honest with you even if that causes you to think less of me."

He was still looking right at her. Jesus, what did he think? There was no way she could think more or less of him, he was almost a fictional character to her, a Greek god, a distant planet whose orbit brought him close only once or twice a year. She'd seen him more on TV than she ever had in person. It was painful to want it to be more than that, so she kept him carefully contained in her mind. But now he was talking about living in her house. On a semipermanent basis. The idea was both thrilling and scary.

"Well . . ." Margo didn't know how to say what she needed to say because it was the kind of thing she'd never in her entire life said to her father. "I do really need a roommate. And it would be neat to see you every day. But . . . I need you to be clean if you are going to be around the baby."

"Margo," Jinx said, "I am clean, and I want to be clean. I'm the one who checked myself into rehab. I finished my thirty days with flying colors; I am an active participant in my recovery. I would never, ever want you to see me like that. There will be no— There will be none of that here."

"Why don't you move in with Andrea or Stevie? Or one of the boys?" Margo suddenly asked. It seemed weird that Jinx would choose her over his real daughters. As was only natural, Margo stalked their Instagrams an absolutely unhealthy amount. Andrea had gotten married over the summer, and Stevie was going into her senior year at Barnard. In almost every way they were superior to Margo. They wore nice clothes, went to fancy restaurants, took exotic vacations. Neither of them had Jinx's mushy nose, or they had gotten it surgically altered in their early teens. The boys didn't have social media accounts, except Ajax, who was doing MMA. The boys were less interesting to her.

"Honestly, because when I discussed it with my therapist, we both thought the strain of those relationships might cause me to relapse."

"Okay," Margo said. She felt guilty that this pleased her and did her best to ignore it. "But then why not rent your own place?"

"Uh, because then I would definitely relapse. There would be no one to . . . perform sanity for."

"Oh," Margo said.

"'Act as if,' they say in NA," Jinx said. "Fake it till you make it. But it's okay to say no, Margo. I understand if you don't want me here. I should have come to write a check and see the baby. Or not write a check and see the baby." Jinx was now sad in a way that alarmed Margo. His cheeks were trembling or twitching, and his eyes looked wild.

"No, I wasn't asking because I was hoping you would move in with one of them instead!" she said. "We desperately need a roommate, and I've been dreading trying to find one, and I love you. You know I love you. Do you know that? Dad?"

Jinx was looking down at Bodhi. He didn't say anything for a moment, and then he almost whispered, "Well, I love you too," and he was crying.

Margo got up and scooted around the coffee table to sit next to him. She leaned into him experimentally, his leather jacket cold on her hot skin. He turned his shoulders slightly so she could lean all the way against him.

"You can stay," she said. She pulled away slightly and saw the imprint of her cheek from her tinted moisturizer on the sleeve of his leather jacket. "Of course you can stay."

ULTIMATELY, AFTER A conference with Suzie over Chinese food, Jinx took Kat the Larger's bedroom because it was, well, larger. They decided to hold off on getting a fourth roommate because Jinx argued the fourth bedroom should be turned into a nursery for Bodhi. Couldn't they each pay $1,333 instead? Suzie seemed stressed out by this. Jinx was completely oblivious. Margo grabbed her later in the hallway as Suzie was exiting the bathroom. "I'll pay your three hundred, don't worry about it," she whispered.

"Are you sure?" Suzie asked, plainly relieved.

"Totally," Margo said, though she didn't know why she felt compelled to spare Suzie the extra rent. She still had no idea what she was going to do, but she had the money from Mark's mother in the bank and that was more than Suzie had.

When she returned to the living room, Jinx was watching some indie wrestling program that seemed to be nearly three-fifths comedy show and only two-fifths wrestling.

"Oh, I didn't know Arabella went to Ring of Honor," he said.

"Who?" Margo asked, curling up on her end of the couch. Bodhi was asleep on Jinx's chest. It was weird not to be holding him all the time.

"The one with the bright pink hair. She was with WWE, then her contract got terminated because she'd ... Well, have you heard of Only-Fans?"

"No, what's that? Is that like Cameo?" Margo knew Jinx made a sizable fraction of his living now from a site where people paid him to record videos wishing their husband happy birthday or whatever.

"Oh, no, not quite. OnlyFans is more ... it's pornography, essentially. Celebrities or people with large internet followings have unfiltered, X-rated social media accounts, and you can pay whatever amount per month to follow Arabella and see whatever saucy pics she posts. This is nothing new, pro wrestlers have been making pornography for ages— good for her and all, I hear she makes quite a bit of money—but WWE didn't want to be associated with it. I'm glad Ring of Honor picked her up. She's nice. She loves video games."

Margo sat, digesting all this. She and her father had never remotely discussed pornography before. Jinx could be weirdly prudish in conversation. "Like how much money?" she finally asked.

"I don't know, but when Triple H first told her she had to quit Only-Fans or leave WWE, she said she made more in a month on there than in a whole year wrestling. I mean, I don't know the details of her contract, but if that's the case, it seems like a simple decision. You're not gonna blow your knee out taking nudes, or accidentally break your neck and wind up paralyzed." She knew he was talking about Droz, who had wound up in a wheelchair after D'Lo Brown broke his neck on *SmackDown*. Jinx made a point to visit him once a year or so.

"How famous do you have to be to do it?" Margo asked.

"Oh, I think anybody can do it. It's just a matter of whether people will follow you. Look at that, she's about to do her finisher, watch."

Margo watched as Arabella choked the other girl with her thighs while doing a one-handed push-up. It looked awesome.

"How does she make something so stupid look so good?" Jinx marveled.

THAT NIGHT IN her room, Margo nursed Bodhi and was waiting for him to fall all the way asleep so she could move him. Her top was off, and she could see herself in the mirror, one of those cheap college dorm ones you hang on the door. Her boobs were huge. She'd never had boobs this big before. On impulse, she gave a squeeze and sprayed the mirror with milk.

And that is when she thought: *Any man would pay to see this.*

Margo was highly aware that she was not as pretty as she was hot. Shyanne had said it all the time. "You're not pretty enough to have dirty hair, get your ass in the shower!" "You're not pretty enough to have that kind of attitude, Miss Noodle!" Her face was not as angular as her mother's, and she had Jinx's mushy nose. Shyanne was always trying to contour it and turn it into something better.

Margo knew her mother was trying to pass down wisdom and skill, the dark art of turning an ordinary person into a minor goddess by means of paint and fabric, but what she also heard was: *Your face needs to be covered. To be loved, you should put this face over your face.* It was even okay if it hurt, if it burned, if it accidentally tore out your eyelashes. "Beauty is like free money," Shyanne used to say as she did Margo's face.

Margo transferred Bodhi to his crib and pulled out her laptop. She didn't know why she was so curious about it. She had the money from Mark's mother. She wasn't desperate, though it was alarming how quickly that money was already disappearing. She went to the Only-Fans website and clicked around. It was hard to see what it entailed without signing up, but signing up was free, so why not?

She needed a username. Think of something sexy, she thought. Though suddenly it seemed entirely mysterious what made something sexy. Since having Bodhi, sex felt impossibly foreign, like something in another world or half remembered from a dream. Sex adjacent, she thought, but her brain kept generating ideas like BoobsMcGee and TwatLord. Finally, she typed: HungryGhost.

And then she was in.

The first thing she did was search for Arabella, but nothing came up. She checked the spelling, mystified. Did Arabella not actually have an account, or was there something intentionally weird about the OnlyFans search algorithm? In frustration, she went to Arabella's Instagram account, clicked through her bio to a Linktree. Buried at the bottom was a link that said Cum follow me 18+. Margo clicked and was finally taken to Arabella's OnlyFans page, though she couldn't see any of her posts without subscribing and paying money. Arabella's account cost an astonishing twenty-five dollars a month to follow. Margo felt like Scrooge McDuck, unwilling to part with her cartoon golden coins. But in the end, she was simply too curious. Once she had full access, she scrolled through Arabella's feed, trying to understand it. She'd been expecting nudes, maybe something in between the kind of selfies you would send a boy and something more professional like *Playboy* or *Penthouse*. Most of what Arabella posted were pictures of her playing video games in her bra and panties. There were some videos that were grayed out; you had to pay extra to see. One of those was titled "Rubbing One Out After Insane Vic Roy." Margo wasn't sure she wanted to see that; she didn't know what a "vic roy" was. But she clicked open a free one, astounded to see it was eight minutes long.

There was Arabella, her hot-pink hair hanging a little stringy around her face, wearing a black leather bra with little chains connecting the nipples, split screen with a video game Margo had never seen before and was instantly captivated by. Arabella's character in the game was a sexy girl in a magenta-pink teddy bear suit. Margo watched as the pink bear parachuted down from a blimp onto a cartoonishly beautiful Technicolor island covered with buildings and lakes, little roads and trees, an entire world to explore. Arabella was chewing gum. She said, "Let's go to Tilted, always like to go to Tilted." She landed gracefully on top of some sort of multistory concrete apartment building and began digging a hole through its roof with a pickax. The game play moved so fast Margo had a hard time even visually processing what was happening as the pink bear collected glowing weapons and moved through rooms, eventually coming upon what appeared to be a moving angel made of stone, which she immediately killed, saying, "Hello there!" As Arabella sped down the stairs of the apartment building, she came upon other players in quick succession: a buff blond guy, a gigantic nutcracker, a hot girl in a red triceratops costume. Arabella killed them almost as quickly as Margo could register them on the screen. After killing triceratops girl, Arabella broke her silent, gum-chewing concentration and gave a little battle cry—"Come at me, biiiiiiitch!"—as her teddy bear character on-screen started breakdancing.

Margo could not stop watching. In the game there were grocery store shopping carts you could push and ride around in, there was an everencroaching purple storm, there were canteens of mystical blue fluid you could chug to become shielded, all of it visually spectacular. Margo had never gotten into video games. She'd really only seen Nintendo, which felt a little babyish, or else like *Call of Duty*, where everything was gritty and chaotic, and there were definitely no hot girls in bear costumes. This was the first game she'd seen that made her want to actually play it. After that video she watched three more. This was not what she was expecting Arabella's account to be like at all.

Margo clicked around and subscribed to three other random accounts she found on Instagram, girls who had mentioned OnlyFans in a post or comment, each of them fifteen dollars, and none was like Arabella's. They were much more in line with what she'd expected: a bunch of nudes and sexy talk and purple devil emojis. You could buy a photo set or video based on a thumbnail and a single sentence of description, "Wednesdays make me horny: self-play, vibrator, feet." It seemed improbable that men really wanted sex this badly, and yet they did, there was an entire economy based on how badly they wanted it, and for a moment Margo understood the sexual desire she felt was mild in comparison. She would never pay fifteen dollars to look at a guy naked. You could buy two, possibly three sandwiches for fifteen dollars. You couldn't actually see how many fans someone had on their OnlyFans, but judging by their Instagram followers and general engagement, none of the other accounts she followed had as many fans as Arabella did.

Margo still didn't think she would start an account and begin posting, though she was intrigued. She'd pictured OnlyFans as a sad garden of desperate, fake-horny girls trying to be what men wanted, all of them crying, "Pick me, pick me!" She hadn't imagined Arabella in a fantasy world dressed as a hot-pink teddy bear merking people left and right. Margo knew she couldn't be that—she wasn't that badass, and she was hopeless at video games—but what if she could find her own thing?

"Maybe a bunch of people will want to fuck Mommy," she whispered, looking over at Bodhi in his crib, softly snoring like a baby pig.

And that is how she became HungryGhost. Alone, in the dark, lit up by a laptop screen, with her baby, steadfastly refusing to think about her father injecting heroin and fucking some woman named Viper.

Or that is how I became HungryGhost. It is hard to tell which one of us it was.

CHAPTER SEVEN

One of the first things Jinx did was clean the bathroom, and I mean with a toothbrush and a gallon of bleach. It was like he was getting ready to perform surgery in there. He culled the half-empty shampoo bottles and made me choose only two out of the vast array of scented lotions I'd accumulated over the past year.

His uniform was now a white T-shirt and gray sweatpants, a bold departure from his all-black lifestyle. I couldn't get over how much smaller and more normal he looked. The white shirt had teal lettering on it! Teal!

"I'm sorry, I can't get over seeing you in clothes that aren't black. You're like a whole different person!"

"Kayfabe," he said, shrugging. *Kayfabe* was a wrestling term that meant roughly "staying in character." If you got hurt in the ring as part of a work, you might wear a cast in real life, for example.

"You were kayfabing your street clothes?"

"Of course. Everyone kayfabes their street clothes."

"I thought you just dressed that way."

"Honestly, I've been dressing like that for so many years, I have no idea how I dress now. But for cleaning house, this is better. Because of the bleach. You think you haven't gotten any on yourself, but of course you have. I can't tell you how many shirts I've ruined."

Next was the kitchen, where he cleaned the stove, lifting off grates I'd assumed were attached, making parts of the stove white I hadn't known were meant to be white. As he scrubbed and scoured, he listened to the dirtiest rap music I'd ever heard, just blasting, *Almost drowned in her pussy, so I swam to her butt*. What did that mean, Lil Wayne? The only way that lyric made any sense was if he had been shrunk down Magic School Bus–style.

I didn't know my father even listened to rap music, but he seemed to follow the careers and releases of even obscure artists. When he found out I didn't know who J Dilla was, he almost collapsed. It became a kind of game between us: "Who is this?" I would ask, and he'd say, "This is Maxo Kream, he's from Houston, he'd released some mixtapes before, but in January he released his first full album, and the kid has serious storytelling chops," all the while loading non-dish items he had collected from around the house into the dishwasher to sterilize them: hairbrushes and combs, Bodhi's teething rings, the cup that held the toothbrushes, and all the knobs and handles from the kitchen cabinets, which he had unscrewed.

"Have you ever heard of a game called *Fortnite*?" I asked him.

He began doing a dance where he swung his arms in front and then behind his body in a confusing way. "Who hasn't?" he said.

"Me, I guess." I had tried to play *Fortnite* a couple of times since watching Arabella, stunned that it was completely free, and been horrified by how bad I was, getting shot in the back of the head while I was trying to figure out how to open a door, accidentally walking off the roofs of buildings and dying from fall damage. I played on my phone while Bodhi napped, desperate to somehow become part of that world.

ONE DAY ABOUT fifteen boxes of books were delivered. "Cheri wanted the space," Jinx said, as he watched me drag them into his room. Neither of us wanted him to reinjure his back, though I could tell it pained him to let me do it.

"You should get some bookcases," I said.

"I hate bookcases," he said.

When he unpacked the boxes, he stacked the books waist-high around the perimeter of the room organized by size. He still hadn't gotten a bed and simply slept in a maroon sleeping bag on the floor. He claimed this was good for his back, though he was visibly stiff and in pain, and I didn't see how sleeping on the floor could be helping. But when had my father ever not been stiff and in pain? From my earliest memory he smelled strongly of Icy Hot.

It wasn't clear to me if Jinx was okay or if I should worry. It was sort of like adopting an exotic pet you had no idea how to care for. Did he have OCD? He didn't seem phobic of dirt exactly; if anything there was an almost lusty quality to the way he cleaned the bathroom drain, a disturbing glee at the glops of gunky hair he pulled out. I asked Suzie if she thought it was weird, if maybe there was something wrong with him. "Let him clean," she said. "It's fucking great."

"But is it unhealthy?" I asked.

"I mean, he's just lost his wife, his family, his career. If this is his coping mechanism, it seems pretty harmless to me. Do you think he would buy us beer?"

MARGO KEPT GOING back to OnlyFans. The money from Mark's mother was somehow already half gone, just from rent and life and a couple of hospital bills from Bodhi's birth. She couldn't ever be like Arabella, but the other accounts she followed still seemed to be doing okay, and she was positive she could replicate what they were doing. They didn't even seem to be famous.

If she was going to transition from a user to a creator and start charging money, she'd have to fill her feed with photos as quickly as possible so if anyone became her fan, they'd have access to at least ten or twelve images. No one wanted to pay fifteen dollars to see one lonely picture. So during Jinx's manic bouts of cleaning, Margo was mostly locked in her bedroom, trying to take pictures of her tits.

She ran up against the limitations of the genre almost immediately. She had only so many body parts and so many angles. Variety would have to come from somewhere else apparently—outfits, locations, a tripod so she could change up her poses more.

IN THE FIRST series of photos she took, her tits looked like they were exploding from her bra like a can of crescent rolls after you've smacked it against the counter. All her bras from before she had Bodhi were too small now. She needed to buy lingerie, but the idea of going to Victoria's Secret and spending a fortune made her sick to her stomach. Finally, she had the inspired idea to take pictures in the shower, giving up the bra entirely, and the even better idea to smear her tits in Vaseline so the water would bead on them.

You were supposed to write a little description about the kind of content subscribers could expect on your page in your bio. Margo was struggling to write it and wound up searching for more accounts to see how other girls were doing it. Again, she had to go through Instagram or Twitter. Why did OnlyFans make it so difficult to find new accounts to follow? It was madness! Twitter was how she found Wang-Mangler99, who was fierce and dark haired and as small as a child, but with giant boobs. Her profile picture showed her next to a refrigerator for scale, and a lot of her posts centered on her tininess: holding her bare foot up next to a Coke can, or sitting in an ordinary dining room chair, feet dangling without touching the ground, or else making weird hentai orgasm faces, eyes crossed. Her OnlyFans bio read as follows: "Feed is NSFW, expect to see tits and ass, if you want to see more, you pay more. I also rate dicks. If you want to get your wang mangled, send me a dick pic and a $20 tip, and I'll send you a critique. This is not an account where I will pretend to love you. The only man I will ever love is Goku."

Margo was astounded people would pay twenty dollars to have their dick insulted. Though, if you were worried it was small or ugly, maybe it was better to know for sure. But she still didn't like the idea, which was why in her bio she wrote: "Lonely, hot girl in financial free fall, please help me make rent this month. I'm new at this and I show boobs and butt, but haven't worked up the courage to show more. Maybe you can encourage me? I also rate dicks. If you want to find out what Pokémon your dick most resembles and what attacks it might have, send me a $20 tip and I'll provide a full write-up."

For two days nothing happened, and Margo felt stupid for starting the account, because of course nothing had happened; how would anyone find her? OnlyFans made it impossible! She was also distracted because something was clearly happening to Jinx. His cleaning mania had ended, and now he spent almost all day locked in his room. "Are you okay?" she asked him one evening when he finally emerged. He had even procured an electric kettle, allowing him to make tea in there. Maybe that's what had been making him come out all along: his intense need to boil water.

"Yeah, it's, uh, I think it's brain chemistry stuff. I probably should work out, that always helps, I just don't want to get injured, so I . . . I don't know." He'd stopped shaving his head and had wiry tufts above his ears.

"Are you going to look for a job?" she asked. Margo had no idea about his financial situation. She assumed he had plenty of money but thought he could use a project.

"I would probably have to travel, and I don't know that I'm stable enough for that yet."

"What about volunteering?"

He looked at her as if he had no idea what she was saying. "At what?"

"I don't know, like at the library? Or . . . ?"

"Huh" was all he said before scurrying away to the bathroom. That was the other thing: the amount of time Jinx spent in the bathroom. She could not fathom what he was doing in there. He seemed to poop three times a day, and each session was an hour-long ordeal. Was he constipated? Was it diarrhea? Was it a prostate thing? Should she make him go to the doctor? He kept talking about a therapist and seemed to talk to him by phone, though she doubted the therapist had the real lowdown on these concerning toilet behaviors.

Taking care of Bodhi, monitoring her father's closed door, endlessly refreshing her OnlyFans page to see that nothing new had happened, then making herself scan through job postings on Craigslist was like trying to make origami out of wet paper. The harder she tried, the more it all kept disintegrating in her hands. It was unclear how so many things simply not happening could be so stressful. She created HungryGhost Instagram and Twitter accounts that led to her Only-Fans through Linktrees like she had seen other people do and tried to follow other girls on those accounts, but still nothing happened. Sometimes she opened Arabella's account just so she could gaze upon her hostile, smirking face for strength.

And then she got her first fan.

U1134967. Right away he sent her a twenty-dollar tip and a dick pic to be rated. Margo opened it on her phone and studied the penis for a long time as she was nursing Bodhi. She wanted to get it exactly right.

After she set Bodhi down in his Rock 'n Play, she pulled out her laptop and wrote the following:

> Congratulations! Your penis is a Tentacruel! With bulging pink glans and glittering dark blue veins, your penis is filled with quiet menace. When that mushroom tip glows red, you know he's about to attack! As both a water and poison type, your penis is passionate but prone to jealousy, easily seeing slights where no harm was intended. He needs lots of coddling and gentle licks. His primary weaknesses are psychic and electric types, so stay away from redheaded witches with stars in their eyes! Your Tentacruel's special moves are Ooze Attack (extremely potent pre-cum, watch out for accidental pregnancies), Clear Body (in which your penis completely disappears, which can happen when it's cold out or if you hear your mother's voice), and Poison Prison (in which you ask a girl for so many reassurances that she loves you that she stops loving you, completely understandable and luckily avoidable!). Tentacruel is your penis's fully evolved form, and he has an HP of 120. I rate it a 10/10, tantalizing Tentacruel.

She pressed send, as nervous as the first time she text messaged a boy in middle school. She was still staring at her computer screen when the notification dinged. Another twenty dollars and a message: That was awesome, way better than I was expecting! Not sure how you knew about Poison Prison, but you were sadly right on there, hehehe. You've got a fan! More people should know about this account!

Encouraged by this, Margo diligently posted several times a day for her single fan, U1134967. Since it was only him, her posts grew sillier and less self-conscious. One day, she wrote on her boobs in eyeliner BOOBS and just posted that. He commented with a laughing emoji and sent a ten-dollar tip, suggested she make a video of her boobs bouncing. That was an entire genre she hadn't even thought of. She made a video clip of her boobs bouncing as she pulled off a shirt, one where she jiggled them with her hands. She even made a clip of herself jump roping naked (during which she definitely damaged the popcorn ceiling of her bedroom).

Then one day (incidentally the same day Jinx left the house for three hours and came back with a small ficus tree, which he asked her to help lug up the stairs so it could live in his room—still no bed, still no bookcases, just a sleeping bag and a tree and maybe two hundred books), Margo got two fans at once: U277493 and RocketRaccoon69. Most guys left their handles completely anonymized, and Margo was grateful when they didn't because it made it much easier to keep them straight. Neither of her new fans asked for their dicks to be rated, which was a little disappointing, but she kept posting and the fans kept trickling in.

At the end of three weeks, she had twenty fans paying $12.99 a month each. After OnlyFans took its 20 percent, it was less than she could have made in one night at her old restaurant, and she certainly was no Arabella. But she had time to figure it out, another month or two at least. Mark's mommy had made sure of it.

"So DO YOU think you're clinically depressed?" Margo asked Jinx one day as he was folding laundry in the living room. He loved doing laundry, he said it was soothing, and he had taken over the chore for them all. Margo felt weird about this. He folded her panties into tiny little packet-balls. But she would do almost anything to avoid lugging Bodhi along with their dirty clothes down to the basement. There was simply no good place to put him while she loaded the washer.

Jinx was pairing sets of Bodhi's tiny colorful socks. "Probably," he said.

"Maybe you should think about getting on an antidepressant," Margo said.

"I'm not sure an antidepressant would help," Jinx said. "I think my problem is more of a fundamental failure to attach to other people. I'm not sure that, without love, Zoloft could really do much for me."

Margo thought about this. She knew that she'd always felt her father was a kind of distant planet, but she hadn't known he felt himself to be a distant planet. She'd assumed he was closer to other people who were not her.

"I just feel like you need, I don't know, a world. You need people. What about going to some twelve-step meetings?" she said. He had mentioned NA before, hadn't he?

Jinx frowned and sighed. "This is going to sound conceited and ridiculous, I realize, but in some circles, I am sort of famous, and it can make those meetings very awkward. People record your shares with their phones and post it online. Terrible."

"Oh, right," she said.

"What about you?" he asked.

"What about me?"

"Well, are you going to get a job, or go back to school, or what's the plan?" He paused from folding a tiny pair of footed pajamas and stared at her.

"Touché," she said.

Jinx laughed. "Two aimless sailboats lost in the harbor."

"I don't know what job to get," Margo said. "Like, all I've ever done is wait tables."

"So, wait tables." Jinx shrugged. "I have named my tree."

"You named your tree?"

"Yes," Jinx said, "I have named my tree Earnest."

"That seems like a good tree name," Margo said. In that moment she almost wanted to tell him about the OnlyFans. Jinx hadn't been judgmental about Arabella; he'd even said, "Good for her." Her instinct to hide it was almost entirely because she didn't really know Jinx that well and it seemed like her private life, not his business. Then again, here she was suggesting he was clinically depressed, so evidently she didn't mind sticking her nose in *his* business.

She still wasn't sure if starting the account had been a stupid idea or if she should keep going. But when she thought about applying for server jobs, she felt like she couldn't breathe. And as badly as her OnlyFans was doing, she at least felt a glimmer of hope about it. After almost a month, she was beginning to understand the problem. OnlyFans had no discovery algorithm. It didn't show you accounts unless you already followed them, and there was no general feed you could explore to find new ones. This had to be why it seemed to work only for people who were already famous or had a larger platform. And yet a lot of big accounts seemed to be run by girls who weren't famous at all. How were they finding new fans, or rather getting found by them?

"How do you build celebrity?" she asked.

"Like, how do you get over or how do you build heat?" Jinx asked.

"I don't know," Margo said. "Both? What's the difference?"

"Well, I mean building heat generally means picking fights that piss off the audience. Hate is just as powerful as love, more so where ticket sales are concerned."

Margo thought about WangMangler and Arabella, how utterly unconcerned they were with being likable. She wasn't sure she could ever be like that. "Well, then what about getting over, like getting the crowd to like you? Like, how come some wrestlers get famous and other wrestlers don't? I know it's not only athletic ability."

"Right. I mean, the short answer is persona. But usually the wrestling ability needs to be there, at least in my opinion, though God knows Vince has tried to give guys a big push on looks alone."

There was no Vince McMahon, Margo thought, and that was part of the problem. If it were a matter of pleasing an asshole like Vince, she'd have a better idea of how to go about it. "How do you get hired by WWE?"

"Work for a smaller wrestling outfit so someone can see you work."

"How do you get hired by the smaller outfit? Like, how does a wrestler get their first-ever job?"

"I mean, a lot of times they're coming from a dynasty. They get into it because their dad was in the business, all their brothers or cousins are in the business. But sometimes they're just coming from an athletic background, whether it's football or they wrestled in college or even bodybuilding. But if you're not from some dynasty or special background, I think you just make a tape."

"A tape of you wrestling?"

"Yeah. With your buddies or whatever in the backyard."

"What if you don't have any buddies?"

"Gosh, I don't know if you can become a wrestler without buddies." There was something weird and Canadian about the way Jinx said "buddies."

"You need buddies," Margo said, still thinking.

"Buddies are essential," Jinx said. "I didn't know you were so interested in wrestling."

"Oh," Margo said. "Yeah." She was not.

"Would you want to watch some matches with me?" Jinx asked. "Maybe tonight. I could show you some wrestlers starting out, if that's what interests you."

He seemed so excited she couldn't bear to say no.

"Maybe Suzie would watch too," Jinx said. "Maybe we should make dinner. Should I go to the store?"

"I mean, yeah!" Margo said. "Why not?"

"Do you like lasagna?" Jinx asked.

"Who doesn't like lasagna?" The idea of lasagna was making this whole idea more exciting. The bigger Bodhi got and the more he nursed, the hungrier Margo found herself. "Garlic bread?" she asked.

"I don't think we need garlic bread too, it's so much starch already."

Margo pooched out her lower lip. "Sooo hungry," she pleaded. Then she pretended to die, falling off the couch.

"Are you dead?" Jinx said.

"Dead of hunger," Margo said, eyes still closed. She waited a beat, then stuck out her tongue as a symbol of even greater death. They both heard Bodhi wake up crying on the baby monitor, and Margo popped up like bread from a toaster. "Please!" she said as she scooted down the hall. "I'm still dead! So, so dead!"

THAT NIGHT JINX cooked lasagna, and he made the pasta from scratch, a thing Margo had not exactly known you could do. "How did you learn to cook?" she asked, as she watched him rolling the dough thin with a rolling pin she was pretty sure they had not owned before. It didn't make sense that Jinx knew how to cook. So many years of his life he'd been on the road in hotel rooms without kitchens.

"When things didn't work out with Billy Ants, I retired," Jinx said, "and Cheri—you know, for so long she wanted me around more, and then suddenly I was around more, and"—he laughed, though it was the saddest little laugh Margo had ever heard—"I guess I was around a little too much. Anyway, I started taking classes. That was one thing I wanted: homemade food. And Cheri was like, 'I raised five kids, I cooked every damn night, I'm not making a whole pot roast just for you!' So I thought, Well, then I'll make the pot roast! But she didn't...I don't think she liked me making the pot roast either, for some reason."

Margo, who had always resisted fully hating Cheri as a kind of instinctive counterbalance to Shyanne's intense hatred for her, was suddenly finding herself really hating Cheri. What kind of bitch could be displeased by a guy taking cooking classes and making them pot roast? Though she realized this narrative did not exactly account for the heroin use and Little Miss Viper. Presumably those things happened later and not concurrent with the pot roasting.

As things began to smell better and better, Suzie was lured out of her room. "Hey, I'm working on a new cosplay," she said. "You guys wanna see?"

Margo did not want to see.

"Cosplay!" Jinx said, instantly fascinated. "You dress up as . . . characters?"

"Yep!" Suzie beamed.

"Tell me more," Jinx said, slitting the membranes of the sausages and pinching their pink flesh out into the hot pan.

It had not occurred to Margo before that cosplay and wrestling had anything in common, and yet Jinx wanted to know every detail. "So these orcs—" he said, leaning his face on his fist at the table, "forgive me, I don't know a lot about orcs—are they from a specific franchise?"

But he did make garlic bread, thank God, and it was glorious.

After Margo survived a seemingly interminable number of wrestling matches, each one triggering such lengthy oral histories Jinx felt the need to pause the video, worried she would miss even a second of the action while he told yet another weird story that seemed to involve a wrestler shitting themselves, when she finally slipped off to her room to put Bodhi down for the night, she turned on her bedside lamp and lay on the center of her rug and stared at the ceiling.

Buddies, she thought. *Buddies*.

The OnlyFans girls, Margo thought, had to be either promoting themselves on other platforms or doing some form of cross-promotion. They had to be helping one another out; they had to be buddies. Filled with sudden conviction, she opened her laptop, navigated to Wang-Mangler's account, sent a $100 tip with a message that said: I'm new to OnlyFans and desperately need fans. Would you be willing to do a cross-promotion or give me tips on how to market myself?

Ten minutes later she received a response: Your account is cute. You should make a TikTok. I'll push you on my page for $500.

Margo was shocked at the price. Would it be worth it? She checked and WangMangler had over 100,000 followers on Instagram. Even if only a fraction of them subscribed to WangMangler's OnlyFans, it was a staggering amount of money at $15.99 a person. Which on the one hand made the request for $500 seem petty; WangMangler certainly didn't need her $500. But on the other hand, WangMangler seemed to know what she was doing and believed $500 was a reasonable price. If Margo landed even thirty-eight or thirty-nine fans out of the deal, she'd at least break even. And she technically had the money.

Margo went ahead and made a HungryGhost TikTok account. Kat the Smaller had told her about TikTok, but Margo hadn't gotten around to joining. It was a newer platform, the point of which Margo did not get. Kat the Smaller said it was like Insta for videos, but that made no sense because you could post videos on Insta, so why use an entirely different app? After she made an account and began exploring, however, she discovered that TikTok was an entire world.

She watched an elephant dunk a basketball. She watched cleaning hacks and dance moves and teen boys pretending to be their teachers. She watched people throw cheese slices on other people who weren't expecting it. She watched cats getting baths and hedgehogs drinking from bottles. She watched kids do impressions of moms who wash your hair too roughly, moms who chastised you for having too many water glasses in your room, moms who were constantly opening and flapping trash bags. The most remarkable thing was how the TikToks were all loosely in response to one another. Someone would make a video using a certain song, and then lots of people would use that same song and make their own videos, each one a distinct interpretation of the original. And she didn't have to search for these things, she didn't have to already know what she wanted, like on YouTube. They just came to her, all lined up, ready to be flipped through. It was like the missing link. If OnlyFans had the monetization but no discoverability, TikTok had pure discoverability without any way that she could see of monetizing it. It was somehow now four in the morning.

She wrote back to WangMangler.

K I set up a tiktok where shd I send the $500? If I send thru here I know you'll lose 20%   🤍 🙏 👻

WangMangler wrote back the next morning with her CashApp. Margo sent the $500. Then WangMangler messaged: I'll pin ur post for 3 days but u have to run a promo making your account $4.99 so my fans get exclusive discount on your content.

Margo gasped. She had been betrayed! If her subscription was only $4.99, there was no way she would make back her money. Wang-Mangler had all the leverage. The $500 was already sent; if Margo refused to lower her subscription price, WangMangler could shrug and decline to run the promotion. Margo logged in to OnlyFans and lowered the price. Then she ran to the bathroom and puked absolutely everywhere.

CHAPTER EIGHT

There is a grotesque lucidity to having a fever. I remember lying on the bathroom floor, pressing my hot cheek to the cold white tile and feeling like I could see every speck and crumb and hair in microscopic detail. I had Bodhi with me on the pink bathmat, which was not terribly clean. He was whimpering, though not fully crying yet. I had nothing left in my stomach, but that didn't stop my body from trying to heave it up anyway. I felt if I could keep the hot red balloon of my forehead pressed to the tile then it might pass. If only I could hold still a moment longer, I'd be able to stand. Bodhi turned his head to look at me, and we stared into each other's eyes. His were brown like mine and Jinx's, but marvelously dark and liquid. He opened his mouth and let out an absolute geyser of puke.

I yanked down a bath towel, crawled over, and wiped him off. He didn't get too much on his jammies, but the bathmat was done for. I rolled it into a burrito and pushed it into the corner. As I was holding him, he heaved again and puked down my shirt. It smelled like sour milk, and I gagged. "Oh, baby," I said, "I know, I know," as I bounced him and tried to peel off my vomit-y T-shirt at the same time. There was nothing for it but to strip us both naked and get in the shower.

That day was a blur. Almost as soon as I lay down, Bodhi puked again, soaking the sheets. I built us a nest of towels and brought a mixing bowl in from the kitchen so I wouldn't have to leave him every time I needed to puke. The main thing I was thinking was that it would be dangerous for him to get dehydrated, so I nursed him again. We both had a fever. I cued up endless episodes of *Sesame Street* on my laptop and propped it on a chair beside the bed. We watched with monk-like focus, our eyes hollow bowls of liquid suffering in which Cookie Monster's tiny reflection danced. Every time I googled what I should do in this situation, I lost myself reading the descriptions of all the possible things it could be. There were no clear action items. Going to the store and buying fever reducer was so beyond my capabilities I actually started laughing. I texted Shyanne: Help! Bodhi and I have the stomach flu and I don't know what to do.

She texted back: You'll get through it! 🍀 🍀 🍀

Whenever I went to the bathroom or to the kitchen for water, I lingered, hoping to be discovered by Suzie or Jinx. I never saw either one of them. Suzie might be at work or class, and I didn't know if Jinx was out or shut up in his room.

When it started to get dark again and we were both still puking, I began to panic. How long could a baby throw up the contents of his stomach without needing IV fluids? When would this ever end?

I called Dr. Azarian's office around nine p.m., and there was a twenty-four-hour help line where you could leave a message in an emergency. I left a mildly incoherent voicemail, then there was a knock on my door.

"You okay?" Jinx poked his head in the dim room.

"We're sick," I said. "And he keeps throwing up and—" My voice broke. I did not want to cry, so instead I kind of yelled. *"I'm scared."*

"Oh, poor baby, did you call his pediatrician?"

"Yeah, I left a message."

"Have you taken his temperature? Wait, are both of you sick?"

I nodded. "I don't have a thermometer," I said, "because I am a fucking idiot. Do you have to put it up their butt? I don't want to put anything up his butt, I can't! I can't do it!"

"I'm gonna run to Rite Aid, I'll be right back," Jinx said.

He returned half an hour later with a thermometer that went in Bodhi's ear, and cold Gatorade and Pedialyte that neither of us was sure if Bodhi was allowed to drink, and fever reducer and saltines. I was so grateful it made me panicky. "I'll pay you back for all this stuff," I said. "I'm so sorry you had to go to the store." I realized as I was saying it that I was about to throw up. "I need to puke, could you leave?"

"What? Give me the baby!"

I handed him Bodhi and hunched over the mixing bowl, heaving and heaving though nothing much came out. And that was when I felt it. Jinx's large hand rubbing circles on my shoulder blades. I was still retching and couldn't stop, and now I was also sobbing. I couldn't believe he was seeing me do something so ugly and being so kind. Shyanne did not believe in getting sick, she saw it as a form of weakness, and she certainly didn't want to be involved in someone else vomiting. When I stopped heaving, Jinx automatically took the bowl and left the room to dump my pitiful two tablespoons of bile and rinse it out.

He came back. "If I keep Bodhi, do you think you could sleep a little bit?"

"You can't, he's still puking," I said. "He might puke on you."

"Believe it or not, I've been puked on many times in my life, Margo, sometimes by adult men."

I looked up at him. The room was dim and what little light there was came from behind him, so I couldn't really see his face. "You're being too nice," I said.

"Here, take these." He handed me some Advils and a Gatorade. "Try to sleep. If I need you, I'll wake you. I took his temp and it's not that bad, it's only 101. I gave him some fever reducer."

"It's too nice," I said. He had already slipped out of the room, though, Bodhi in his arms, and closed the door gently behind him. I fell into a state that, if it was not sleep, was sleep adjacent.

At midnight I received a call from a cranky-pants Dr. Azarian.

"Just so you know, the stomach flu is not an emergency," he said.

"Oh," I said. "I didn't know."

"How often is he puking?" he asked.

"About every hour or two," I said. I felt sudden panic that Bodhi wasn't in bed with me, then remembered he was with Jinx.

"How does he have anything left in his stomach?"

"Well, I've been nursing him, I didn't want him to get dehydr—"

"Stop! Stop nursing him! Jesus Christ."

"Oh," I said, "like entirely?"

"When he hasn't vomited for six hours, you can nurse him again. Or give him Pedialyte. Do you have access to Pedialyte?"

"Uh, yes," I said, remembering that Jinx had bought some.

It was like when you got a test back in high school and went over the answers in class, and you could swear the textbook never said anything remotely like that. You were supposed to feed babies every two to three hours. I thought they died if you didn't! It never would have occurred to me to take a baby in a weakened state and stop feeding it.

"If his fever goes as high as 104, go to the ER. Otherwise, just try to get through the night. You can come in tomorrow. You don't need an appointment, come to the office and I'll squeeze you in."

"Okay," I said. I didn't want to explain that I was also puking frequently enough that driving and visiting his office was definitely not a thing I could imagine doing. I trundled out to the darkened living room on shaky legs. Jinx and Bodhi were on the couch watching *Sesame Street*. My dad patted the couch beside him. I lay so my head rested on his thigh. "I can take him," I said, not making any motion to take Bodhi.

"I wouldn't be able to sleep anyway" was all Jinx said.

Together we watched Elmo's haunting monologue. There were so many questions. Elmo was evidently a child, but where were his parents? He had drawn a picture of himself with other larger monsters holding his hands, though whether these were living or merely longed-for parents was unknown.

I snapped awake alone on the couch and went to find Bodhi asleep in his crib, Jinx on the floor right next to him, dead asleep, his face mashed into the carpet. I looked at my phone. It was three a.m. I climbed into bed and moaned with gratitude. For the first time in hours, I didn't feel like I was about to throw up. We had slept. My eyes were hot and wet. "Thank you, thank you, thank you," I whispered to God or Jinx or maybe Dr. Azarian. I fell back asleep with the unusual feeling that we were safe.

IN THE MORNING, I woke to see that Bodhi was already awake in his crib. He wasn't fussing. He was contentedly playing with his toes, trying to jam his feet into his mouth. Jinx was gone. The sun was coming in the window and splashing down onto us. "Why, hello," I said, and Bodhi squawked with delight and turned his head to look at me, smiling. I still couldn't get over those curly little smiles.

What I am trying to say is that I was not thinking about the Wang-Mangler promotion. So when I did finally log in to OnlyFans on my laptop, I almost couldn't interpret what I was seeing. I had 931 new fans. I accidentally shoved my laptop and knocked it off the bed. I'm lucky it didn't break. Bodhi was in his Bumbo seat on the floor, slouched over like he had pudding instead of bones. I jumped up and down in front of him. He was getting pretty chonky, and he was still super bald. He had a sort of miniature Hitchcock vibe, and he was delighted that I was leaping around.

Overnight I had made $4,645.

"Wow," Jinx said from the doorway, "you're feeling better! What happened?"

I froze, crouching in a position of such obvious guilt that there was absolutely no way to explain it. I opened my mouth. Every lie I thought of seemed absolutely insane. And I thought, Jesus, after this night where he has seen you at your worst and been so kind and helped you so much, you're going to lie? So I told him. I told him everything.

"Oh, Margo," Jinx said. They were at the dining table now because when she first told him, he'd been so upset he walked out of her room and slammed the door, and after ten minutes she'd followed him, trying to reason with him as he paced tight circles in the living room. She'd then convinced him to drink tea with her at the table and talk about it more reasonably.

"I hate this," Jinx said. "I hate it."

"I know," Margo said.

"You don't want to get mixed up in that, in those kinds of girls. And it just—it will change the way guys think of you, and not in a good way."

"What are 'those kinds of girls'?" Margo asked. At first, she'd been so purely alarmed at how upset Jinx was that she'd kept apologizing. The longer this went on, though, the angrier she became.

"Girls who use sex to get what they want, you know . . ." Jinx said, trying to find a way of describing sluts without using the word *slut*.

"Like my mom?"

"Not like your mother," Jinx said.

"She was working at Hooters. Isn't that how you met her?"

"I did meet her there. But there is an important difference. At Hooters they don't take their clothes off."

"So if Mom had been working at a strip club instead, you wouldn't have been interested in her?"

"Not seriously. Not romantically."

"Because other people have seen her naked?"

"Listen, it's like buying a car. A used car is a better value, but you never really know what has been done to the car, you know, whereas if you buy a new car—"

"I can't believe you went with the car analogy," Margo said.

"Obviously women are not cars," he said, holding up his stupid gigantic hands.

"Well, then tell me: What am I supposed to do? How am I supposed to take care of us?"

He didn't say anything. Margo kept thinking about Murder. How was her father okay with a guy like that, a guy who murdered people for money, who once famously punched a reporter and knocked out two of his teeth, yet he had this huge moral objection to her posting pictures of her boobs on the internet?

"This is what I have," she said, "this is how I can do it, and if it keeps us safe with a place to live and diapers and clothes for Bodhi, then I don't care."

Bodhi started fussing, and Jinx automatically stood and held out his arms for him. The moment Bodhi was in Jinx's arms, he quieted. "It's a hard situation," Jinx admitted, as he bounced Bodhi gently back and forth.

"And I shouldn't have had him," Margo said, as though some rip cord had been pulled inside her. "I know that, okay? Everyone told me it would ruin my life and it did. They were right, and I was stupid, and I didn't get it. Okay? But now I'm here."

"Yes," Jinx said. "Now we're here."

They were quiet for a moment. Jinx rolled his neck back and forth, and Margo could hear a sound like gravel sliding in a box. That was not a sound a neck was supposed to make.

"What about the guy?" Jinx asked. "What does he think? About you doing the OnlyFans?"

"What guy?"

"Bodhi's father," Jinx said.

"I don't see why Mark really gets a vote here," Margo said.

"Mark," Jinx echoed. Margo had never told him who Bodhi's father was. He'd never asked directly. "Mark the mark." Jinx smiled. That's what they called the fans in wrestling: "marks." A hangover from wrestling's carnival beginnings. "I'm guessing Mark wouldn't want his son being brought up in all that, and if it's an issue of money, maybe he would—"

"He made me sign an NDA," Margo said. "I've already been paid off, so there's no squeezing more money out of him, if that's what you mean."

"An NDA? Jesus, what is he, famous?"

"No, he was my teacher."

"He was your *teacher*?!" Jinx was so livid it looked like he was about to cut a promo. Margo had never seen him that mad in real life before.

"Yes. English 121. Fall of my freshman year. A tremendous educational experience."

Jinx coughed, reached for his tea. Breathed in, then out. "Yeah, I don't think that guy gets a say. But as your father, I think I do get a say, Margo, and I don't want you doing this. And that's final."

Margo could see that even he heard how ridiculous he sounded. "Oh yeah, as my father? You forbid it?"

"Margo," Jinx said.

"Give me the baby," Margo said, holding out her arms for Bodhi.

Reluctantly, Jinx handed Bodhi over, looking as weirdly hostile and sad as a renaissance painting.

THE WHOLE DAY sucked. It should have been a day of joyous celebration. Instead, Jinx stayed locked in his room, and Margo pretty much remained in hers. She had not been entirely aware of how many small moments in the day Jinx had begun taking Bodhi, freeing up her hands, and she missed his help sorely as she tried to load puke-soaked sheets into an industrial washing machine with a baby strapped to her front. The only real upside was that the anger gave her energy, and the sudden influx of new fans was unexpectedly thrilling. All day her phone buzzed in her pocket, money and dicks pouring in. She knew she was too haggard to make new content, but starting tomorrow she'd need to shoot better pictures and fast. She decided to broker a deal with Suzie. Clothes, and in particular costumes, seemed the easiest way out of the finite number of possible butt and boob configurations.

It was dusk. Bodhi was down for a nap in his crib in Margo's room, and she brought the baby monitor with her when she knocked on Suzie's door.

"Margo!" Suzie cried from her bed. "Come cuddle me!" She held open the blanket, and Margo climbed in beside her.

"Oh, it's warm under here," Margo said.

"Are you and Jinx fighting?" Suzie asked.

"Uh, yeah."

"I'm sorry," Suzie said. "What was it about? Like, I mean, I heard some of it, but I still didn't understand what triggered it."

"Okay, so you know how I lost my job? I started doing this website," Margo said, and launched into a brief description of OnlyFans and how it worked.

"Why would anyone pay that much, though?" Suzie asked. "I mean, it's the internet, you can see naked girls for free."

"Because, like, it's more candid and intimate. It's the difference between anonymous vagina and a specific girl's vagina. Like, a real girl who you feel like you get to know and who will message you back."

"When I was little, I would masturbate to *SpongeBob*," Suzie said. The abruptness of this gave Margo a little zing. She always kind of liked that, when things suddenly went sideways with another person.

"How little?" she asked.

"Like nine? I was precocious," Suzie said. "My family was super religious, so I thought thinking about naked people was sinful, but if I masturbated to something everyone agreed was okay . . ."

"Like *SpongeBob*." Although which character on *SpongeBob* could it possibly have been? Margo didn't even want to ask. She was afraid it was Patrick. In fact, she felt it almost had to be Patrick.

"Exactly. Biblical loophole. Tiny Suzie Sex Genius."

Margo had never considered Suzie's sex life before. While Suzie never seemed to have a boyfriend, there were always boys hanging around, and Margo suddenly realized Suzie might be sleeping with them. Dressed as orcs.

"Anyway," Margo said, "I was thinking that cosplay could help me with the taking pictures stuff because it gets dull real quick. Like, how many pictures of your boobs can you take?"

"Oh, right," Suzie said, nodding. "I mean, I guess that's okay. As long as you don't, like, masturbate in the garment. Or if you do, you know, have it dry-cleaned."

Margo nodded vigorously. "Yeah, no, that seems totally fair."

"I can't believe you're a porn star," Suzie said. "It's kind of glamorous!"

"No, it's not," Margo said. "I feel weird about it. I wasn't expecting Jinx to be so . . . violently anti."

"He'll get over it."

"I don't know," Margo said. She was already thinking about how Jinx would move out and they'd have to find a different roommate. "Do you think I'm a slut?" she asked. She had not meant to ask that; it just came out.

Suzie seemed to think about it. "I mean, are you sleeping with any of the guys on there?"

"No!"

"Then how could you be a slut?"

Margo pondered this. "I feel like there is a way in which, even if a girl isn't having sex with anyone, like even if she's a virgin, if she shows her boobs or dresses for sexual attention, she's still considered a slut. I mean, right?"

"I guess," Suzie said. "But it seems weird to say a celibate person is a slut. Like, you're just pretending words have meaning at that point."

They were both quiet for a moment.

"Oh my God," Suzie said. She sat bolt upright.

"What?"

"It's because you *know*. It's because you're in control of it! That is what makes someone slutty or not slutty!" The skin of Suzie's lower lip was bitten and peeling. "Think about it. If a girl doesn't know she's hot and is innocently going about her business, and some guys spy on her naked, she's not a slut. But if she knows guys want to see her naked and charges them money to spy on her, she's a slut. The same physical thing is happening in both scenarios, guys see her naked body, it's just in the second one she knows what's going on and she's in control."

"Yeah, I guess," Margo said. It was an interesting point. She'd had a similar thought before, which was that if sex wasn't shameful and being paid wasn't shameful, then why was it shameful to have sex for money? Or sell pictures of your boobs or whatever? Where was the shame coming from? How was it entering the system?

"I think it's because you're the one making money. How much money are you making anyway?" Suzie asked.

Margo hadn't realized how badly she'd wanted Suzie to ask this.

"This month I've made over four grand."

"Holy shit, then who cares if you're a slut?"

"Right?"

"Hell yes, I mean you get to stay home with the baby, you're safe, you're not having contact with these people. Four grand a month?! Fucking slut it up!"

Margo laughed. She was no more or less a slut than she'd been five minutes ago, but now she felt so much better, the relief was almost indescribable.

"You have the power," Suzie said.

"I guess," Margo said.

"Don't let Jinx treat you like shit. Kick him out! If he doesn't like the way you make a living, he can leave."

"Well, it would still be really nice if he paid rent," Margo said.

"Sure. But money is power, Margo. And you've got it, baby." She kissed Margo on the cheek and then pulled back. "You smell like puke, sweetie."

BODHI STILL SEEMED to be soundly asleep, so Margo took the baby monitor with her in the bathroom and ran a shower, thinking about what Suzie had said. She took her time and, when she emerged, stayed in the bathroom, drying her hair, applying moisturizer to her legs, all the little things she normally skipped because Bodhi was usually fussing in his Bumbo seat in there with her. There was a knock on the door.

"What is it?" she asked.

"It's me." It was Jinx. "Can I say something really quick?"

"Uh, I mean, I'm still in a towel."

"That doesn't matter," he said, and cracked open the door, letting in the cold outer air. He had Bodhi on his chest. She must not have heard him wake up. "I was just thinking, you know, about the OnlyFans stuff. When I was wrestling in Japan—the mafia is really engaged in the wrestling scene there, so all these Japanese mafia guys would be at the matches and sometimes take us out afterward, and one night they took us to this sex club."

Margo was nodding open-mouthed. The entire situation was so deeply weird.

"Anyway, I remember that night watching the sex show and thinking, That's a helluva way to make a living. But then I thought, you know, who am I to judge? How is it that different than what I was doing, wrestling? We're both using our bodies to entertain crowds of people. We're both doing this real-fake thing. Honestly, even the risk of STDs is nothing compared to the risks I was taking in the ring."

"Uh-huh," Margo said.

"And it's— Wrestlers know that even with us, part of it is about sex. About seeing us half naked up there, and Rick Rude or whatever, sure, but even a guy like me, you know, you get thrown over a stanchion and they're touching you all over, they're grabbing you like . . ." He paused, struggling for how to describe it. "I just . . . I changed my mind, Margo. I want you to understand, especially if I am living here, that I know you are not a car. That I respect you and the fact that you are trying to raise this child on your own. Whether you post pictures of your body on the internet, it doesn't matter. I just . . . really, I was feeling protective of you. People treat sex workers so badly and with such disdain, and I didn't want that for you, but somehow that just resulted in me treating you with disdain for being a sex worker, and that's not what I want to do or who I want to be. You're my daughter. I will love you forever no matter what."

Margo was stunned.

"Okay, that was it," he said, and ducked out of the bathroom and closed the door.

CHAPTER NINE

Margo's truce with Jinx felt fragile. She hardly had time to think about it. She was too busy trying to manage her sudden influx of fans. Having access to Suzie's cosplay closet made taking interesting pictures a whole lot easier, though the complaints about Margo's camera quality on her ancient phone were constant. Did you take these with a potato? Are your nipples blurred out on purpose or are you just poor?

Keeping on top of the dick ratings was challenging too, even if she loved writing them. Congratulations on being the owner of a glorious Parasect! Special attack: Clit Clench. Weirdly, it was how much fun she was having that was hardest for her to process. The small cascade of neurochemicals each time her phone dinged with a new message. The obsessive refreshing of the page to see if anything new had happened. The compliments, the likes, the fire emojis—they were all intoxicating and kind of exciting. It reminded her of the early days of courtship, when her whole life hinged upon the latest text or email. Except she was having this same reaction to crude messages sent by strangers on the internet. She didn't want it to be true, that these meaningless, highly artificial interactions could create in her the same feelings as the actual relationships she'd had. She knew what she was feeling now wasn't real, but how real had anything she felt ever been?

Compared with the way she felt for Bodhi, her feelings for any of her former romantic partners were flimsy, like the clothing for paper dolls that attaches with only those tiny folding tabs.

"Listen," Jinx said one morning as they were eating some new disgusting bran cereal he had bought, "I've been thinking, Margo, if you are really going to do this, I want you to do it right."

Margo was mildly horrified, waiting for whatever he was going to say next.

"Now tell me the truth," he said. "Are you paying quarterly taxes?"

She burst out laughing.

"I'll take that as a no," he said.

"I don't know what quarterly taxes are," Margo said.

"Well, are you going to file as self-employed or as a corporation?"

"Dad."

"You don't know?"

"I don't even know what you're talking about," she said.

"You know, Margo," he said softly, "now that I'm living here, I could watch Bodhi while you went to work. If you wanted to go back to waitressing."

Margo nodded, trying to brace herself. Of course he would try again to persuade her. He couldn't just be offering to help with her taxes. She could not explain how much the idea of returning to waiting tables filled her with dread. As dehumanizing as running an OnlyFans was supposed to be, that was how dehumanizing waitressing actually was.

She was aware Jinx was watching her, and she wasn't any closer to knowing how to respond. Then he said, "Waitressing sucks."

"It really, really sucks."

"I have heard this from many people," he said, nodding.

"It's exhausting," Margo said, "and like, there's no getting a raise or a promotion, there's no *growing*. And that makes it feel like trying to run when you're facing a wall." She wanted to share more about Tessa and the penis cake and making the salad boy eat literal dirt and Sean putting parsley around his dick, but none of it seemed bad enough exactly to justify selling nudes. "And being away from Bodhi for that many hours in a row, even if you were watching him . . ." She faltered, not knowing how to say it or if she was allowed to say something so ridiculous. "But it kind of makes me feel like I'm dying?"

Jinx nodded again. "So you really want to do this," he said. It reminded Margo of how Shyanne knew she wanted to keep the baby even before Margo had admitted it to herself. She couldn't explain why she wanted to have Bodhi, and she couldn't explain how badly she wanted to turn the OnlyFans into a success. Was it bad to want things? To want them as badly as she seemed to want them?

"I do," she said. And somehow it felt as formal as if she were getting married right there in the dining alcove.

"Okay," Jinx said.

"Okay?"

"Okay."

OVER THE NEXT few days, Jinx helped Margo complete the paperwork to become a corporation so she could write off her health insurance and pay fewer taxes than if she filed as merely self-employed. He told her to move the remaining money from Mark out of her checking and put it in a high-interest savings account, something she didn't even know her bank offered. Her new income also made Bodhi ineligible for his free health insurance, and Jinx helped her get that sorted too.

Jinx created his own OnlyFans account so he could understand the platform better, and Margo told him everything she had learned so far. Their new plan was to do a copromotion every two weeks. "To build a fanbase who will stay subscribed month after month takes time and a lot of work," Jinx said. "Men like variety. Their natural inclination will be to subscribe to different girls every month."

"Okay, yeah," Margo said, massaging her forehead. Jinx would certainly know about craving variety.

"But how do you override the male preference for sexual variety?" Jinx was clearly in a Socratic mood, high off giving so much advice. "Love," he said. "You have to make them fall in love with you."

"I don't think they're going to love me," Margo said. "I mean, half the time they're telling me to kill myself or that my nipples are crooked."

"That's just the internet," Jinx said, "a disgusting place, really. This is kind of like trying to have a nice dinner party in hell. Certain things you're just going to have to put up with. So how do you make someone fall in love with you?"

Margo felt it was obvious she did not know.

"What I am trying to say is that you need to think about your persona. You need to be someone worth falling in love with—you teach them how to love you by showing them who you are."

"Yeah," Margo said. Because she could see that: Arabella and Wang-Mangler both managed to be unforgettable, whereas most of the other accounts she'd seen tended to blur together into an undulating sea of boobs.

"Are you a heel or a face?" Jinx asked. "The bad guy or good guy?"

"This isn't wrestling, Dad," Margo said. It scared her that he'd even asked. She had hoped she was an obvious baby face. She couldn't imagine being brave or charismatic enough to be a heel. She and Shyanne both had those stupid, innocent faces.

"Everything is wrestling," Jinx said.

"Honestly, I don't think I have what it takes to be a heel." Margo shrugged.

"So you're a face," Jinx said, like that was settled.

Margo sighed. None of this was helpful when all you were doing was taking pictures of your tits. Heel and face played off each other, defined each other, like light and dark. Margo was alone in every frame, translated into nothing but pixels, frozen and ready to be jacked off to.

BODHI, MEANWHILE, WAS now three months old and mysteriously getting cuter and cuter. Once, in the very beginning, when Margo was grocery shopping with a three-week-old Bodhi strapped to her chest, greasy hair slicked back in a ponytail, a woman had stopped her to admire the baby and said, "They get even cuter." Margo had been a little miffed, honestly. Bodhi even at three weeks was the most beautiful and miraculous thing she'd ever beheld. That lady had been right, though. Margo kept wondering what the apex of his cuteness would be and when it would begin its descent, but each day he seemed to be cuter than the last.

One day Margo bought some flowers from a stand on the corner downtown, tangerine-colored roses. She was wearing Bodhi and held the flowers up to his nose. He didn't react. Then she pantomimed sniffing them herself and held the bouquet to him again. This time he sniffed, and his face lit up. He smelled the beautiful smell! She had told him about it, and he understood her. He had literally never smelled roses before. It was a miracle. They stared at each other, beaming.

It was Jinx who ordered a *What to Expect the First Year* book. It was at least two inches thick and stared at Margo reproachfully from her nightstand. Every single time she tried to read it, she got creeped out by the weirdly sentimental way it was written. It was like ad copy. One part said, "Not only won't she get hooked from a day or two of pacifier use, but as long as your little sucker is also getting her full share of feeds, enjoying a little between-meal soothing from a soothie is no problem at all."

Margo had never even worried pacifiers were bad. She'd bought them in every possible color, even the girl ones. Jinx had seen Bodhi sucking a hot-pink one and said, "Aww, look, the newest member of the Hart Foundation!"

Jinx's talk about Bodhi becoming a wrestler was nonstop. It was always joking, she knew that. But she would never let Bodhi become a wrestler.

"Why not?!" Jinx had asked, alarmed when she said so.

"Because they all die horrible tragic deaths!"

Jinx tilted his head to the side, half a nod, as if to concede that this was so.

"But you wouldn't," he said, tweaking Bodhi's toe where he sat in his Bumbo on the carpet. "Because you're too tough."

The truth was Margo had never loved wrestling. On some level, she'd viewed it as the reason her father was constantly leaving. Murder and Mayhem, even more than Cheri and the kids, were the reason he left them again and again. A teenage Margo couldn't help watching *Monday Night Raw* and thinking, For this?

Now that Jinx was living with them, wrestling was on all the time, and she found herself watching it in a new way. For one thing, she was now an Arabella superfan. As an adult, it was much clearer that the stunts they were doing were amazing, especially the high flyers. She was a lot more interested in their biographies too. Jinx personally knew almost everybody, and the anecdotes were simply off the chain. Did she know that the Hart boys had a pet bear growing up? And they'd drip Fudgsicles on their toes in the summer and let the bear lick them clean? Jinx watched a lot of old matches in Japan. He loved Tiger Mask and the Dynamite Kid, who always triggered stories of the truly awful pranks the Dynamite Kid would pull, putting lit cigarettes in Jake's snake bag so his snake would get pissed and bite him, or injecting his tag team partner Davey with milk instead of steroids. "He had the temperament of a terrier dog," Jinx would say.

These men were fucked up and frequently deranged. They were also devoted, Margo couldn't help but feel, to something that could only be called art.

Suzie also got into watching wrestling with Jinx; in a way it was LARPing adjacent. "Wrestling is not fake," Jinx used to say, "it is merely predetermined."

BUT IN A WAY, wasn't everything? Margo wondered. That was one of the things Mark had told her, that as far as neuroscience was concerned, free will couldn't be real. That our brains only invented explanations, justifications for what our body was already getting ready to do. That consciousness was a fabulous illusion. We were inferring our own state of mind the same way we inferred the minds of others: thinking someone is mad when they frown, sad when they cry. We feel the physiological sensation of anger and we think, I'm mad because Tony stole my banana! But we're just making stuff up, fairy tales to explain the deep dark woods of being alive.

THE FIRST WEEK after the WangMangler promo, about fifty people canceled their subscription, and I decided that was normal. Buyer's remorse. The next week another fifty people canceled, and some of them wrote decidedly angry messages about why. This account was a scam. There were no pictures of my vagina. The problem was simple: my account did not contain material it was possible to jack off to.

A kindly fan, one who didn't unsubscribe, suggested I begin making longer videos. He suggested two and a half minutes as being a standard "jack-off length," so I tried to aim for that. I knew the guy had probably meant a video of me masturbating, but I couldn't bring myself to do it. Not while Jinx was watching Bodhi on the other side of the door. It felt too real.

The last copromotion we'd run was a total bust, and we spent $500 to get forty new fans. I was beginning to have a sinking feeling, like the account I'd thought I was building was slipping through my fingers.

It was around this time that I received a strange message. Obviously, I received a lot of strange messages. This one was strange because it was direct and professional. It said: I see you do written dick ratings, would you be open to other written work? —JB.

I don't think a single fan had ever referred to what I was doing for them as work before. It was refreshing. Most of the messages were things like, hey, and u r so hot; sometimes they were telling me to shove a knife up my pussy or drink drain cleaner. One guy offered to pay me $500 to film myself pooping into a soup can. It was out of the question; I would have trouble pooping in a soup can even without the pressure of being filmed. So JB's message was distinctly different from what I usually received. I was intrigued but also worried he'd ask for fanfic erotica where I made us have a threesome with Logan Paul or something.

I clicked through to his profile so I could enlarge his pic. Most guys didn't upload anything, their profile stayed an outline of a head, like a children's board game; others posted their abs or dick, or an anime character, or a Pepe the Frog meme. JB's was a close-up on the face of an aged black pug, its muzzle flecked with white.

I wrote back in the chat: Is the dog in your profile pic yours or just a random internet dog?

He wrote: My dog.

HungryGhost: Name, please?
JB: Is this a test?
HungryGhost: Yes.
JB: I'm going to fail.
HungryGhost: Why?
JB: His name is Jelly Bean. My niece named him.

I considered this. You pass. What kind of written work did you have in mind?

JB: $100 to tell me about your family's holiday traditions.

I stared at the screen.

My brain was ticking. I couldn't think of how this information would be useful to him. And if he didn't want it for practical reasons involving a scam, it meant he wanted it for emotional reasons. He was asking for something real from me. He was trying to get at the me behind the pictures. It made me angry, though I couldn't define exactly why. I just kept thinking, How dare he!

Why? I asked.

JB: I think it's hot thinking about you being a real person.

I raised my eyebrows, but it was not a bad way of spinning the terrible, swollen loneliness that would drive a person to ask for this. And a hundred bucks is a hundred bucks, after all, and there was no way I was letting little Jelly Bean get anything real from me.

So I lied. I made up a whole different family, said I had an older brother and my dad was in sales, and Dad would always get these bonuses at work that were like hotel points and airline miles, and every Christmas we'd take a vacation, spend Christmas in Hawaii or Paris or Bermuda. This sounded too idyllic, too made up, even though I was stealing it from Becca's actual life, so I added a bunch of stuff about how there was so much pressure to be happy on these trips, but really, I just wanted all those normal things: the Christmas tree, the stockings, our house feeling like magic. And instead, it was always a hotel room, white sheets, blue-toned art on the walls; some gifts would appear, only a few, the wrapping a little smooshed, so I knew they'd been stuffed in my parents' suitcases. My brother told me there was no Santa when I was six, but I still wished we could all pretend. I wished my dad did a better job hiding his affairs. I wished my mom did a better job hiding her boredom.

Honestly, I kind of had myself choked up by the end, even though none of this was true. I pressed send. The $100 tip came through immediately. Then he offered to pay $100 for a description of my mother. Like a portrait of her. He was interested because I said she was bored.

You poor sick puppy, I thought, then spent the next hour composing a portrait of my fictional mother. I tried to make it interesting. The rough outline of the parents, the salesman dad and bored mom, I'd stolen from Becca—but I couldn't exactly say where the rest of it came from. It was fun: making things up, pulling each detail out of the dark of my mind like a rabbit from a hat.

CHAPTER TEN

Shyanne was so preoccupied planning her wedding, a trip to Vegas scheduled for the first week of January, that she forgot to tell Margo she was busy on Thanksgiving until Margo called asking what she should bring. "Oh, we're volunteering for the needy!" Shyanne said.

Margo knew it was wonderful Kenny was encouraging her mom to volunteer, and that a good deed was a good deed whether it was done for a cringeworthy reason or not. It was only that Thanksgiving had always been their holiday; she and Shyanne would order in Chinese food, watch Lifetime movies, and do those Baby Foot peels. It felt like an entire world was being lost.

Instead, Jinx made her and Suzie a whole traditional meal. He really outdid himself: turkey, mashed potatoes, real stuffing not from a box, and an apple pie.

After pie they all lounged about the living room. Jinx's body was exactly the length of the pink velvet couch as he dangled Bodhi above him in the air, then brought him down for raspberries and ticklish kisses before hoisting him back into the air again. All of this was accompanied by much gibbering and squealing. Bodhi had begun to babble, and all he said was "Dada, Dada." Jinx would smile and say, "Yes, I'm Dada!"

"Isn't it weird for you to be teaching him to call you 'dada'?" Margo asked. Really, she was just miffed that Bodhi wasn't saying "mama." She worried it was because she wasn't spending enough time hoisting him in the air and making him squeal like that. She worried it was because so often when she was holding him, she was looking at her phone.

"'Dada' is usually the one they say first," Jinx said. "He won't call me dada eventually."

"They say 'dada' first?" Margo was sitting at the coffee table. A Curt Hennig match was on TV. Her dad had some subscription service that gave him access to every WWE match ever.

"At least all my kids did," he said. "You did. Just about killed Shyanne."

This made Margo grin. "What do they say next?"

"Either 'mama' or 'baba.'"

"I hope it's 'mama,'" she said. Her phone buzzed. It was a message from JB:

Dear Hungry Ghost,

$100 per question (length is up to you) for answers to any of the following questions:

1. Who are some friends you remember from middle school?
2. What are your favorite foods, and what foods do you irrationally dislike?
3. Did you know your grandparents at all?
4. What has become of your brother, Timmy? Are you guys close?
5. Do you go to college? Are you thinking about going to college? It really, really seems like you should go to college, and you look so young. I guess I don't know how old you are, though. Maybe you have already graduated college and just have great skin. I don't know, I don't know what I am even saying, but what are your goals for yourself? What do you want?

—JB

He had attached a picture of Jelly Bean in an ill-fitting turkey costume looking absolutely miserable. Margo smiled. She hadn't told Jinx or Suzie about JB and these strange writing prompts. She'd convinced herself she didn't need to tell anyone because they weren't important. She wasn't going to let JB know anything real about her. She knew how to keep it under control.

She wrote back: I want a selfie of you and Jelly Bean!

She didn't know why, exactly; she just wanted to see if he would do it, if she could command him.

He's not in the costume anymore, JB wrote. He didn't like wearing it.

HungryGhost: I don't care about the costume.

There was a pause, then a picture came through, and her breath caught in her throat. She did not know what she was expecting from a man who was sending a girl he met online weird writing prompts on Thanksgiving Day, but it wasn't this. JB was tall and broad shouldered, or at least he looked that way with a pug cradled under his chin, and he had long, thick, shiny black hair that hung around his shoulders. He looked Asian or Pacific Islander and was wearing a black T-shirt and what she was 80 percent sure was a pearl choker necklace. He seemed to be in his late twenties at most and was absolutely, confusingly smoking hot.

She set down her phone. Jinx had been talking for some time, and Margo had no idea what about. Thankfully, it turned out to only be an anecdote about Curt Hennig slipping Yokozuna laxatives so that he shat himself on a plane. "He was always putting drugs in people's drinks," Jinx said. "Which by today's moral standards is reprehensible, but at the time it was fairly humorous."

Jinx hoisted Bodhi in the air again and then said, "Oh God, Margo. Take the baby. Take him right now."

Margo scrambled up and took Bodhi. Jinx kept his arms in the air in the same position, clearly afraid to move.

"I did something," he said.

"To your back?"

"Oh God," he said.

She could see that his face was white, and he was sweating. "What?" she said. "What is it?"

"It's going to be okay," he said. "I think it's only a spasm. I need Somas, but I don't— I mean, because of rehab I don't have any. I just need the muscles to unclench. I don't think a disc slipped or anything."

"Tell me what to do," she said.

"Go get my phone and call Dr. Murtry."

BUT IT WAS Thanksgiving and Dr. Murtry wasn't answering, nor were two other doctors Jinx tried. When Margo discovered that Jinx absolutely could not stand or shift position, she started to freak out.

"Well, I can just stay on the couch," Jinx said, "until someone calls back."

"Dad, you're sweating bullets. You are clearly in excruciating pain."

"Well," Jinx said. "Maybe ice?"

"Dad!" Margo said. "You need to go to the ER!"

"I don't think I can get in a car."

"We're calling an ambulance," she said.

"We are not," Jinx said. "Do not call an ambulance!"

But she called 911, and she could tell by the way he didn't really try to stop her that he was glad. Once they knew an ambulance was on the way, his main concern was that she pack him some books to read in the hospital. "I'm coming with you," Margo said.

"You don't want to bring Bodhi to a place like that! A hospital full of germs!"

"I'll watch Bodhi," Suzie said.

They both looked at her. Suzie had never volunteered to watch the baby before.

"How hard could it be?" she said. "I mean, I watch you guys do it all day!"

"There's pumped milk in the freezer," Margo said, and rushed to show Suzie everything she would need before the ambulance arrived. "And if he's freaking out text me, and I'll leave and come home. I don't think I'll be gone longer than an hour or two tops."

"It's fine," Suzie said, "I think we'll be totally chill."

Margo placed Bodhi in Suzie's arms experimentally. Both Suzie and Bodhi seemed at ease.

"Okay," Margo said, like she was judging a Jenga tower for stability. "Okay!"

WHEN JINX AND I were finally alone together again in his little curtained-off area of the brightly lit ER, he was already doing much better. The nurse had given him muscle relaxers and pain meds in his IV.

"Margo," he said softly, almost a whisper, "I am not going to mention substance abuse issues unless they ask directly. Is that all right with you?"

"Uh, yeah," I said. The idea that I would somehow object and tell his doctor he had just gotten out of rehab hadn't even occurred to me. Now I wondered if that was actually the right thing to do.

"We can figure it out after, I can refuse to take whatever they send me home with. I just know from experience that if you bring it up they instantly treat you like a criminal."

"Okay," I said. Certainly, I wanted my dad to get the medication he needed. I was also uneasy about this. His addiction was a large uncharted area I didn't truly understand. I worried this was how it always started for him: with the best of intentions. I could hear an old woman asking for water through the curtain on our right. "My mouth is so dry," she was saying.

"In the hospital, when I was having Bodhi," I said, clearing my throat from a sudden attack of phlegm, "there was this nurse who was checking my IV, and she ran her hand over my hand in this weird way, and I realized she was checking for a ring. And maybe they have some policy to remove the patient's rings in case of a C-section, but I suddenly felt scared that I didn't have this marker, this thing that indicated that someone loved me, that I was valuable, that someone would get mad and sue if I died. It was probably all in my head, but I felt like I'd press the button for something, and she wouldn't come for, like, hours, and she would walk out without answering my questions, and she made fun of Bodhi's name. They didn't release me for forever, and they wouldn't tell me why. She'd just decided I was this certain kind of girl, you know?"

"She made fun of his name?" Jinx asked, and I could see a strange coldness coming into his eyes, like ice forming on a lake.

"Yeah, I didn't tell you this? Shyanne slapped her!"

Jinx only stared at me, his eyes completely dead. "I would have burned that hospital to the ground," he said. All the hair on my arms stood up.

"I just . . . I get it," I said. "The way how they treat you can change."

"To the ground," Jinx said again.

I laughed. "Thank you," I whispered.

He looked at me and nodded, his eyes dark with love.

"What is the book you're reading about?" I asked, gesturing at the book he had tucked in his armpit.

"Gladiators," Jinx said, flashing the cover.

"You're really into ancient Rome," I observed.

"What gave it away?" my dad asked, winking. Of the books that lined his room, Rome was in about half the titles.

"Why? I mean, what interests you about it?"

"Oh, the violence, I suppose." He gave a cute little shrug then winced, tried to resettle his shoulders.

"Because of wrestling?" I asked.

"Sure."

"Do you feel, like— Do you feel conflicted about the violence?" I asked.

My dad squinted then said, in that soft-loud ASMR voice of his, "I've spent so many years being defensive that it's hard to tell. You know, recounting to myself how violent football is, or hockey, and don't even get me started on MMA. I always wanted to defend wrestling; in a way it's the most ethical one. Because we're trying to put on a show, not truly harm each other. It's a bunch of boys from the middle of nowhere, you know, kind of screaming, 'Look at me! Love me! Look at the insane and beautiful things I can do with my body! I can make you gasp, I can make you scream, I can make you cry!'"

"That's beautiful," I said, "to think about it like that."

Even though he was looking better, his skin was still so waxy and pale in the bright light, his eyes sunken. I had never been so aware of my father's mortality. It was palpable, my sense that someday he would die. I'd also never been able to so fully imagine him as the wild milk-white bull my mother first fell for, the young man from Middle-of-Nowhere, Canada, screaming, "Look at me! Love me!"

"Oh yeah," my dad said. "That's the heart of it. Boys on trampolines fooling around with their friends. That is the beautiful seed wherefrom the wrestling flower sprouts. But you know, almost all my friends are dead. Not all. But more than half. And sometimes they died in horrific and gruesome ways. So the cost, the cost of it, is not beyond me. You know, when you said you would never let Bodhi become a wrestler, I thought, What is wrong with me that I would? I don't want that for him. Why was I saying he could take it? He's four months old! Even before Bodhi, though, I mean, for years and years, I've been thinking about this, about violence and how much we love it and how we can't stop. And just as all roads lead to Rome, all histories of blood sport lead there as well."

"We've always been this way," I said.

"On the contrary, I think we used to be much worse."

"Really?" My knowledge of Roman gladiatorial contests pretty much started and ended with that Russell Crowe movie.

"The kinds of contests they held would really challenge a modern sensibility. I mean, involving animals, making women fight dwarfs, plays where when someone is killed in the story, they really kill them onstage. Slavery made all this possible, as a mental category, of course."

I had not thought at all about slavery outside of the context of America.

"They would make these long seesaws, like teeter-totters. And then they'd chain criminals up at either end, and let in, you know, a dozen starving lions and bears, and watch as the men all pushed off with their legs, trying to be the one in the air, even though they knew that when their counterpart was done, you know, being eaten, that weight would be removed and they'd come crashing down and be eaten as well." His dark eyes were dreamy, focused somewhere on the ceiling.

"That is horrifying," I said.

"You know, and little kids would see that. People would watch and laugh and yell and boo, just like a wrestling show. And you have to think about how profoundly different it must have been in their heads. Now we'd think watching someone be murdered is profoundly traumatizing, except it wasn't traumatic for them. It was fun. And trying to imagine how that worked, what beliefs had to be in place, is just fascinating to me."

"Why do you think it changed?" I asked. "Like, civilization?"

"I don't know what a historian would say, but I would say Jesus: love thy neighbor, and it's easier for a camel to fit through a needle's eye than a rich man to get into heaven. In a place like Rome, insisting everyone had intrinsic value—it rattled them. I mean, they killed him for it."

I was not expecting an answer like that from my dad, who was, as far as I knew, violently atheist.

A doctor came in through the curtain right then, interrupting our conversation. I sat quietly as he asked Jinx questions about his back and various surgeries. Even without Jinx saying anything about substance abuse, the questions about pain management and medication were pointed and repetitive. The doctor asked what pain medication Jinx was on multiple times, as though he didn't believe Jinx when he told him none. He explained they would order X-rays and an MRI to make sure there was no compromise to the spinal fusion.

I was growing agitated. It was the way the doctor talked to my dad, the image of those metal parts implanted in his spine. Across from us there was a girl who'd slipped in a hot tub and was bleeding profusely from a cut along her hairline, waiting to be seen by a doctor, holding a paper towel to her forehead. Sometimes wrestlers would sneak a razor blade into a match and cut themselves at their hairline so that they'd bleed; they called it "adding color" to a match. Abdullah the Butcher's head was practically grooved from all the scars.

Mick Foley and Terry Funk, the tacks and the razor wire and the broken glass, or Nick Gage, oh God, Nick Gage. Rubbing that pizza cutter in men's mouths until the blood flowed down their chins and necks, mixing with the sweat. The time he got stabbed in the stomach with a broken fluorescent light tube and had to be helicoptered out. I kept thinking about the men who wrote to tell me to kill myself.

"You should head home," Jinx said. "I'll be fine here."

"No," I said. But I found I was desperate to leave, wild with the need to be home with Bodhi safe in my arms.

"I'm okay now," Jinx said. But how could he be okay in this brightly lit space filled with people who did not love him?

"Okay," I said. "Sorry, I don't know why I'm so worked up."

"Go home to that baby," he said. "Good night, my sweet."

He used to call me that when I was little. I had almost forgotten it.

"Good night, my meat," I said, which is what I used to say back.

I left him in his little cubicle and stumbled out into the dark night, where I took a cab that smelled like wax and gummy bears to my apartment, sprinted up the stairs, and burst into the living room only to find Suzie and Bodhi solidly asleep on the pink velvet couch, both gently snoring.

But as I tried to go to sleep that night, Bodhi safely tucked in his crib, Suzie covered with a blanket on the couch, I couldn't stop hearing it, my dad saying, "I would have burned that hospital to the ground."

I pictured the burned-out frame of the building, the clouds of ash, my father standing in his black pants and black shirt and black jacket, standing there, looking at me, loving me.

CHAPTER ELEVEN

In the morning I woke to discover Jinx had been released from the hospital at four in the morning and taken a cab home. I was furious he hadn't called me.

"It was fine," he said. "I lay down in the back of the cab."

I wanted to ask him if the doctor had sent him home with pain-killers, except I suddenly didn't know how. I didn't want to be another nurse checking his hand for a ring, another person who looked at him and only saw an addict. "What did the MRI say?" I asked.

"No disc slippage," Jinx said. "Thank heavens."

"That's good," I said.

Jinx was making tea in the kitchen. He paused, his magnificent hands midflight. "Would you like any tea?"

"No, thanks," I said. He had turned on the overhead, but the light it produced was high-pitched and thin, humming green over our skin. I watched him for a moment before turning back to my room.

Why didn't I know how to ask him about this? Last night, I'd felt so close to him, tracing the veins on the top of his hand as he lay in his hospital bed, talking about Rome, and this morning he felt like a stranger. Also, nine more fans had unsubscribed. I knew it was my fault for not showing the full vagine. My dad could go on about persona and making guys fall in love with you, but at the end of the day what these men wanted was simple: to kung-fu grip the original joystick all the way to googasm.

I was so pissed I didn't even want to write back to JB. What did I want? What were my goals for myself? *Actually, JB, my largest goal for myself is to become internet famous for being hot. Ever since I was a young girl, I had a dream that one day men from all over the world would want to cum on my face . . . only it turns out I'm too much of a coward to even do that!* It felt good to mock myself in this way. Because I did want that. I wanted to be famous. I wanted to make a lot of money, absurd amounts of money. I wanted power: raw and cold and green. But every single time I thought about hittin' the kitten on camera, I felt like I was going to puke.

Obviously, I would never say any of this to JB. Not only because it didn't cast me in the best light, but because the dream of being famous was silent, urgent, and embarrassing. Closely kept as a birthday candle wish.

Instead, I wrote about food.

Dear JB,

I am a big fan of fruity candy, with banana-flavored things being S-tier, lemon-flavored things a close second. Banana Laffy Taffy— best candy in the world. Lemonheads—phenomenal. I like Runts especially. They always feel special because you can't buy them in the store, you have to find one of those machines like at the mall or in some crusty pizza parlor. Probably the Runts have been in there since the early nineties, but they are none the worse for it because they are Runts—the Eternal Candy.

For special dinners, in our house the archetypal celebration dinner was steak and potatoes, but I never loved steak. I love chicken wings. I understand that wing places aren't fancy, so it seems like a weird choice. If I were going to a fancy restaurant, I would probably look for some cream-based pasta dish. Anything that is a grown-up version of mac and cheese because I am essentially a giant child.

Because I live in California, for fast food I am obligated to say In-N-Out, and believe me, it is very good, but, and I hesitate to admit this because it is gross and I know it is gross, I really love Arby's. If I am alone and sad, or alone and very happy, Arby's seems to draw me like the North Star.

In terms of the foods I can't stand, okay, I don't like seafood. Almost all of it. But I especially don't like octopus. And I have had it at fancy places where the other person was rapturous about it, and I still didn't like it. This borders on sacrilege, but I don't like crab or lobster really either. I won't refuse to eat it, but I'd never be like, "Hmmm, let me pay forty dollars to wrestle two ounces of delicate, tasteless meat out of the carcass of this oversized ocean insect."

And figs. Fuck figs. Certainly they do not taste bad, and I can even imagine getting over the little pinging texture of the seeds, but they are bland! Pomegranates are stupid and hard to eat, though they do look like encrusted rubies inside glowing with ancient magic, so it's like sure, I'll swallow all these little seeds that are like nail trimmings. But figs? And they are expensive! They come on salads that are like twenty-five dollars for five shreds of bitter lettuce and then these ugly cut-open figs that look like their insides are riddled with tiny tumors. We'll call you back if we're interested, figs!

I realized I'd written him the truth, but I figured it didn't matter. It was only about food after all. And he wouldn't know what was true and what wasn't. I would never meet this guy.

And then, I didn't even think about it, I wrote: What about you?

"WHAT ARE YOU writing?" Jinx asked over her shoulder.

"Jesus!" Margo said, automatically slamming her laptop closed, even though there was technically nothing wrong with her messaging JB.

Jinx had been milling around the apartment all day. He wasn't supposed to lie down or sit for long periods. He also wasn't supposed to bend over or lift anything, so he was pretty much useless Bodhi-wise, though luckily Bodhi had been chill all morning. Margo had recently ordered him a Jumperoo bouncer monstrosity that took up a quarter of her bedroom, played painfully cheerful music, and had flashing light-up buttons. Bodhi was willing to sit in it and jostle around for twenty minutes at a stretch. With Jinx injured, those twenty minutes and the time Bodhi spent napping were her only real chance to post or respond to messages.

"Who is JB?" Jinx asked.

"Ugh, he's a fan," Margo said.

"That looked like a really long message. I didn't know you wrote things like that to them."

"I don't usually, but he pays me per email. A hundred bucks."

Jinx raised an eyebrow.

"I just make shit up. Like, I don't tell him anything about me. I made up a character and everything."

There was a pause. Margo looked him right in the eye. Because it was true. Where was the lie?

"Impressive," he said, and smiled, nodding. He was not making any move to leave her room.

"Do you think you could walk to the park?" she asked, figuring if she wasn't going to work, she might as well do something nice for Bodhi.

"I'm worried," Jinx said. "If it went into spasm and I was away from the house."

"Well, aren't you still on the muscle relaxers?"

"I didn't fill the prescription," Jinx said.

"Dad!" Margo scooped Bodhi up from the Jumperoo and went out to the living room, where it wouldn't feel so claustrophobic with her dad hovering.

"Well, it was late, and I didn't want to tell the cab to stop at the pharmacy, and— I mean, I would rather not take them."

Margo was trying to get it all straight. "So what all did they prescribe? Are muscle relaxers the same as pain pills? Or are they something different?"

"They prescribed both muscle relaxers and pain medication. And they are different."

"What kind of pain medication?"

"Vicodin. Not my favorite, if that's what you're asking. I mean, they're great, don't get me wrong, but it's not like a script for eighties of oxy or something."

"Right," Margo said. "So . . . do you want to fill them? Or, I mean, how are you even supposed to function? Like, you're in pain." She could see it now that she was really looking at him. He was all gray colored and sweaty, the muscles in his face strained and tense.

"But I don't want to start something— I don't want—" He broke off. He was almost panting. She waited. "I want them so much that it frightens me, and I can't tell if I want them because I'm in pain or because I'm an addict."

"You're in pain," she said. "Okay, what if I keep your medication for you. Like in my room, hidden, and you don't even know where it is. And I give it to you only when you need it."

"We could do that," Jinx said, looking up at her, his head nodding rapidly. "We could do something like that."

Margo was amazed. He had come around almost instantly. "Okay, did they call it in? Where are we going? This is exciting, we're leaving the house! Wanna get food while we're out? Something gross?"

"Like what?" Jinx asked.

Margo wiggled her eyebrows seductively. "Like Arby's?"

JB WROTE BACK with lists of his favorite and least favorite foods, and Margo found herself rapt. She had to admit he had a point about Pringles: they *did* taste like someone had already chewed them before you. He said he loved Rocky Road ice cream, which . . . there was nothing wrong with Rocky Road, she would eat Rocky Road at any time of the day or night, but there was something weird about it being your favorite. Like, better than cookie dough? Really? She thought it was kind of cute that he would venerate this utterly boring ice-cream flavor. He was such a puzzling mix of traits. She kept thinking about that pearl necklace tight on the beautiful skin of his throat.

At first, she'd assumed the fact he was writing girls online and paying them to write back meant he was lonely, the kind of lonely that made people, especially men, a little desperate. But now she wasn't so sure what kind of person he was, besides a rich person. If she answered all the questions he sent, he'd owe her $1,000. How did a guy in his twenties have that kind of money, and why would he spend it on this?

She was nursing Bodhi in bed and trying to type a response one-handed.

JB,

Sir, I regret to inform you I have raised my rates. Your answer regarding snack foods was so delightful that from now on, I will require you to answer one question for every question I answer from you. In addition to, you know, the money. Deal? For my next question, I have to know: Is JB your actual name, or does it just stand for Jelly Bean? I can't stop thinking of you as Jelly Bean!

Xo,

"So how much of wrestling is actually real?" Suzie asked that night as they were watching *NXT*. Margo's eyes bugged out of her head, shocked that Suzie didn't know not to ask this.

Jinx was remarkably calm as he answered: "That's a bit of a forbidden question, Suzie. You can ask it of me, I'm not saying I'm mad, but you will get knocked unconscious for asking another wrestler that. Once, a guy started talking about how wrestling was fake in a bar, and Haku said, 'Oh yeah? Let me show you how fake,' and he bit the guy's nose off."

"Oh my God," Suzie said. "Like off-off?"

"O-F-F," Jinx said, and nodded emphatically. "But as to your other question, nobody knows."

"Nobody knows?" Suzie asked.

"How much is fake. It's all fake, it's all real, the lines are blurry. Where does the character end and the self begin? It doesn't help that a lot of the angles are taking real-life dynamics and making them larger than life. There was one move Vince did with Jeff Hardy that was so profoundly unethical, it made all of us uncomfortable."

"Oh, was this the CM Punk thing?" Margo asked.

"Yes, exactly," Jinx said, and continued explaining. "Jeff had for many years been struggling with substance abuse problems, which is common in wrestling because of the chronic injuries involved, but Jeff had a reputation for being particularly out of control and unreliable, and so Vince turns it into an angle and has him go up against this guy, CM Punk, whose whole deal is that he's straight edge."

"Oh, cringe!" Suzie said.

"So you can see that the line between real and not real gets a little—a little fractal."

"But, like, in the ring. How much in the ring is real?"

"It depends. I mean, does it hurt? Yes. Do you get injured? Yes. Are they out there socking each other as hard as they can in the head? No, they wouldn't be able to work six nights a week the way they have to. It's more like it's choreographed. You don't ask if a ballet is real just because it's choreographed."

"Right," Suzie said, though it was clear this answer didn't entirely satisfy her.

"That's the magic," he went on. "It has to be authentic to work, but it's also, you know, by definition fake. You're dressed up in neon spandex and holding a microphone—that is not how fights actually happen."

"What do you mean it has to be authentic to work?" Margo asked.

"I mean, the match, even if it has incredible acrobatic spots, still must have the psychology of a real fight. And if a persona is too fake, it doesn't work, you'll never get over. It has to ring true. But it can be a hard thing to understand about yourself, to say, 'These are my defining qualities, condensed, distilled.'"

"Yeah, that seems superhard," Margo said. Inside, her gears had already begun to whir. Maybe she'd been thinking about it all wrong. She didn't need to become more like Arabella; Margo could never be that thrillingly, bluntly aggressive. Certainly she couldn't ever play *Fortnite* that well. Maybe what Margo needed was to become more herself. "I thought you were saying, like, make up a character and then be that, but you're saying turn myself into a character. Almost like turning yourself into a cartoon."

"Exactly," Jinx said. "Exactly that. But it can be hard to see yourself well enough to turn yourself into a cartoon!"

"I practically already am a cartoon," Margo said.

Jinx squinted at her. "In what way?"

"I'm so goofy," she said. "I'm cheesy."

"I would never describe you as goofy or cheesy in a million years," Suzie said.

"No?"

"No, you're way too scary to be goofy."

"Scary?!"

"Yes," Jinx said, thoughtful, "you are a little scary. I mean, I'm scary! Maybe you got it from me."

Suzie was nodding. "That's true, you are both very, very scary."

"Wait, are you saying I'm a heel?" Margo asked.

"Yes," Jinx said, considering. "I do think you're a natural heel. I know you wanted to be a face. Don't think about it as being mean, think about it as being . . . disruptive."

Margo picked at an ingrown hair on her calf. "I don't see, like, right now I'm not a heel or a face, I'm not a person even, I'm a set of tits. Like, how are you supposed to make a character when it's just pictures of your body?" Arabella had *Fortnite*, she had something to play, to do. Margo didn't have anything like that.

"That is exactly the question," Jinx murmured. He was visibly more relaxed since he'd taken his medication, almost euphoric. "How to go from being another pair of anonymous tits to the only pair of tits that matter? It has to feel real, but how to capture it? That way you throw yourself around in the world like you're invulnerable, when of course you can't be and you are going to get terribly hurt, and yet there is something beautiful about the abandon, the recklessness, and—and kind of the bravery of it."

Never in one million years would Margo have guessed her father understood these things about her.

"What you need," Jinx said, "is buddies."

"Buddies?" Suzie said.

"To play off. You need to build that heat. Heat's what puts the butts in the seats."

Margo knew what he meant immediately. He had mentioned buddies before, but she had only been thinking of it in terms of cross promotion, not in terms of actually producing content. "I need to interact with people. I need other characters to help differentiate myself, so that I'm not just a pair of tits. A face needs a heel, and a heel needs a face."

"Exactly," Jinx said. "Bingo, kid."

Margo had gotten this far in her thinking before, but she'd always stumbled trying to imagine how another person could enter her content without, you know, having sex with her or something. The answer had been right in front of her all along.

"We need to cut promos," she said.

Not the match. She needed the hype in the weeks before the match. How had she missed it? The promos were almost the most important part—they were the reason the audience cared about the fight enough to watch it.

"What do you mean promos?" Suzie asked.

"TikToks," Margo said. "We'll make TikToks."

"Who is we?" Jinx asked.

"I don't know yet," Margo said. "Buddies."

"Buddies," Jinx said, cracking a smile, nodding.

I WENT TO WangMangler's account that night and found the photo that had been bothering me. It was WangMangler in a bikini at the beach. Behind her you could see a pier, and on the pier was a kind of hut, a little hexagonal building with a red roof. I zoomed in as far as it could go. I wasn't 100 percent, but I was pretty sure that building was a Ruby's Diner and that the pier was at Huntington Beach. I noticed on her website that she also had a podcast with another girl who did Only-Fans named SucculentRose, so I went and subscribed to her account and poked around.

SucculentRose looked like an adorable sexy puppy. She had long platinum-blond hair that hung down her back in an unbroken sheet. She was plump with dramatic fake eyelashes and breasts so big and perfectly spherical it was like a twelve-year-old boy had drawn them on her. Her account wasn't as interesting as WangMangler's and she didn't seem to do dick ratings. She only had fifteen thousand Instagram followers, about half as many as WangMangler. She was very obviously a baby face.

I clicked over to WangMangler's account and sent her a message saying I'd realized we might both be in Southern California, and if that was true, could I ever be a guest on her podcast? I received a message from SucculentRose saying yes, they were in Huntington Beach, and did I live close enough to drive there? The timing was perfect because their guest for that week had canceled. Could I come to their apartment to record tomorrow? She and WangMangler were roommates, as it happened. I checked with Jinx. Yes, I could go tomorrow. Suzie would call in sick and help with Bodhi since Jinx still couldn't handle lifting him. SucculentRose gave me the address. It was all set. I had no idea what I would say on a podcast and figured I would have to just deal with that in the moment.

MARGO STILL HADN'T heard back from JB, and she tried not to let it bother her. Around midnight, right as she was about to fall asleep, her obsessive phone checking was rewarded.

Ghost,
JB is my name, and no, it does not stand for Jelly Bean, sadly. It stands for Jae Beom.
    A name for a name?

JB

Margo's heart was beating fast. She didn't know if it was from fear or excitement. Part of her wanted to tell him her name. How could it hurt? There had to be thousands of Margos in the world. But later, if he killed her, people would say, "I can't believe she gave him her name!"

You're never going to believe this, she wrote, but my given name is Jelly Bean.

That's a beautiful name, he wrote.

Elegant, Margo supplied. Sophisticated.

JB: So we are both JB then.

HungryGhost: You mean all three of us are JB. (I am including your dog.)

JB: A coincidence too large to be anything but the signature of destiny.

HungryGhost: Well, my mom let your niece name me, so . . .

JB: 😅

HungryGhost: Can I ask you another question?

JB: Only if you answer one of mine.

HungryGhost: Deal.

First grade school crush, JB prompted.

HungryGhost: Easy. His name was, I shit you not, Branch Woodley, and his mom was a big hippie, and he would use the tinfoil his mom wrapped his sandwich in to make a tiny hat so the teachers couldn't read his thoughts. We would pretend to communicate with the trees by touching their bark with our eyes closed. My question for you is: Are you doing this question thing with other girls on here?

JB: No.

HungryGhost: Just no? I don't get anything more than that?

He sent a $100 tip.

Margo stared at it, a little peeved. Then a message came through:

JB: Have you ever shat your pants?

HungryGhost: Yes.

She pressed send. She had shat her pants during a chemistry final in high school after eating too many mango habanero wings the night before.

JB: I don't get anything more?

HungryGhost: You don't get naked, I don't get naked.

JB: Fair. Honestly, I was doing this whole thing as kind of a troll. I heard of OnlyFans and I wondered what it was about. You were one of the first girls I followed. I don't know. It seemed more interesting to talk to you than anything else, like maybe that's a nerd impulse. The only time I ever got a lap dance I tried to talk to her too. Maybe I just too firmly sexually imprinted on Truth or Dare when I was twelve?

Margo had always loved Truth or Dare and nodded slowly, considering this. And really, she wrote, if you can't tell the truth to a stranger on the internet, then who can you tell the truth to?

Another $100 came through, and a message:

JB: You don't have to tell me the details of how you crapped your pants if you don't want to, this isn't a fetish thing about poop for me. I was just hoping for a funny story.

HungryGhost: Well, the first thing you need to know is that my chemistry teacher was inexplicably from New Zealand with a thick, thick accent I found challenging to parse . . .

CHAPTER TWELVE

SucculentRose and WangMangler lived in a stucco apartment complex that was quiet as a tomb. Margo's footsteps echoed. She didn't see one single person on her way from her car to their second-story apartment.

SucculentRose answered the door wearing a garment that was clearly a descendant of the Snuggie, a hybrid of sweatshirt and nightgown made of tan woolly teddy bear fabric. She was braless, and though Margo had already seen many pictures of SucculentRose naked, the breasts were still very impressive in person, big enough that they moved slightly independently of the rest of her body. "Oh my God, it's so good to meet you!" SucculentRose cried, cradling Margo in a hug. SucculentRose still had on last night's eye makeup. It was even more lovely for being crumbly and blurry, and her platinum hair smelled like expensive shampoo.

"This is silly, but what should I call you?" Margo said. While she could imagine calling SucculentRose Rose, she could not imagine what she would call WangMangler.

"Excellent question. I'm Rose, and that is my real name just so you know, and you can call me that on the show, but she goes by KC. I mean WangMangler. You know what I mean!"

"Got it," Margo said, tucking her hair behind her ears.

"Do you use your real name?"

"I don't," Margo said. "Can we just—can we call me Ghost?"

"Of course! Oh my God, you are so cute," Rose said. "You're so nervous, I love it! Just know, KC will totally be rude, and you will think she doesn't like you and that is true. She doesn't like anybody. But underneath all that she is goo and she likes anyone who likes her, so just be brave. She is not a morning person."

Right then a small white dog skittered into the foyer looking frantically around and barking.

"Hush," Rose said, and picked up the little dog. "This is Biotch, and she is very, very old. Aren't you? Aren't you a little old bitch?"

The tiny dog gazed around, its eyes pearlescent with cataracts. It was a poodle mixed with something else. Rose kissed its tearstained-brown muzzle.

"Come with me," Rose said, and led Margo into the living room, which was almost hostile in its tidiness. White carpet, white leather couch, black metal-and-glass coffee table. Rose sat on the couch and set Biotch beside her. Instantly Biotch peed on the couch, yellow liquid seeping out from under her. "And this is why we have to have a leather couch!" Rose said, heaving herself up to go get some paper towels. Biotch stayed where she was, crouched and shivering.

After the pee was cleaned up, Rose brought them coffee in large pink mugs. As she handed Margo a cup, she smiled and said, "You are so hot!"

"Thank you," Margo said, scrambling for something to say in return. "Your breasts are amazing!"

"Do you want to feel them?" Rose asked. "Come on, don't be shy! Look, I can balance stuff on them. The forbidden end table!" She stood and set her coffee mug right on the top of her breast. She turned this way and that and it stayed there quite steadily. Margo did not have to fake her astonishment. Now she did want to feel them. What property might they have that would allow a coffee mug to rest upon them so stably?

"Are they . . . ?" She did not know if it was rude to ask if they were implants.

Rose said right away, "Oh, a hundred percent."

"When did you get them?" Margo asked.

"Like, three years ago? But I always wanted them. Like, since I was six years old, I knew I wanted implants."

"When you were six? Did you even know what they were?"

"Oh, absolutely. It was Dolly Parton, on TV at my grandma's house. I don't think I knew hers were implants exactly, I just knew she was special. Like, she was not a regular person, she was Dolly Parton."

Margo's mind was quietly being blown by this. It was true. You couldn't be a regular person with breasts like that.

Rose had majored in physics, it turned out, and even done about half of her master's before dropping out. Margo asked to use the restroom so she didn't have to talk about her own college experience.

Alarmingly, Rose was not in the living room when she returned, and Margo stood there awkwardly for a moment before she heard Rose and KC talking. She crept down the hallway and peered in the doorway of the room that they were in. They had a whole little recording studio set up and were sitting in rolling chairs in front of fancy microphones on scissor arms. It looked like a real radio station, except that the tabletops were littered with granola bar wrappers and empty water bottles and what was maybe a vape pen and what was definitely a purple butt plug.

"Oh good, come in here, we're all ready!" Rose said when she saw Margo.

KC did not even look up. She was stirring tea in what looked like a miniature bowl. She was so small sitting in the chair that it was visually jarring.

"There's yours," Rose said, and gestured to the empty seat, which also had a tiny bowl in front of it. Margo sat and peered into it, trying to understand what it was, a broth or tea that smelled of leather. Margo's seat did not have a fancy microphone; it had a more ordinary one that just sat on the desk. She noticed the headphones and put them on. The moment she did, she could hear everything Rose and KC said with crystal clarity, like they were inside her mind.

Margo picked up her small bowl and took a tentative sip. It tasted like mushrooms and tree bark; it was truly vile. "What is this?" she asked.

"Shroom tea," Rose said.

KC was chuckling and did a soft impression of Margo saying, "What is this?" in a namby-pamby voice. It was loud in Margo's headphones.

"Oh, wow, wait, I've never done this before," Margo said.

"Never would have guessed," KC said.

"That's so exciting!" Rose said.

"No, I'm so sorry," Margo said. All their voices were the same volume in her ears, it was overwhelming. "I mean, I can't drink this."

"WELL, you have to do it," KC said. "It's part of the fucking podcast."

"I thought you had listened to a bunch of episodes?" Rose said.

Margo froze. She had not listened to a single episode, though she'd written to KC that she was a big fan. "I mean, I did. I just didn't know it was, you know, required."

"We do mushrooms every podcast," Rose said gently. "That's kind of the whole thing."

Margo began sweating. She must have looked as terrified as she felt, because Rose softened and said, "Oh, sweetie, they're fun! Don't worry! You'll have a blast! Maybe only drink half the cup."

Margo nodded, not even able to speak.

"We all drink the whole cup," KC said with such quiet command that Margo knew Rose wouldn't try to argue further.

Margo thought she might start crying. How was she going to be okay to drive home? How long would she have to stay here with these scary people? When she finally did get home, how long until she could nurse Bodhi? She didn't know anything about mushrooms or how long they stayed in your system. Yet she could not imagine leaving. She picked up the little bowl, and Rose nodded at her encouragingly. She took a sip.

"Let's get this shit show going," KC said, and Rose busied herself at the laptop and then started her intro to the show. While Rose was talking, Margo pulled out her phone and frantically texted Jinx: They are making me do shrooms, no idea how long this is going to be, I am so sorry I am so freaked out. She pressed send and looked up right as Rose finished speaking and was looking expectantly at Margo.

"It's so amazing to be here," Margo said.

ABOUT TWO HOURS in and they were still recording. Margo had no idea how they would edit this down into an hour show. Both KC and Rose had begun to look more and more like cartoon characters, their eyes glinting strangely. Biotch's fur rippled like fields of wheat. They had discussed how they each got into OnlyFans, and Margo confessed she'd not yet posted the full vageen.

"You haven't?!" Rose gasped.

"You've got to make the most of that shit," KC said. "Give that taco a real grand entrance."

"Absolutely," Rose said. "I wish I'd known. Back when I started, I didn't understand that the first time I posted vageen I should have charged, like, fifty bucks. Instead, I put it on sale, it was, like, three dollars. Do you know how sad that feels? To be like, here is my beautiful little vageen, it's worth three dollars?"

"Darling Vageen!" KC said, in a man's bellowing stage voice. "Most precious Vageen!"

"That's good to know, actually," Margo said.

"You should make, like, an advent-calendar-type countdown to your vageen!" Rose said. "And it can be your Christmas gift to all the men in the world!"

Margo suddenly imagined photoshopping her vagina to contain a tiny baby Jesus at its center, like a manger.

KC burped loudly into the microphone.

"How did you get into doing OnlyFans, KC?" Margo asked. She was becoming moderately less afraid of KC in part because KC was utterly unselfconscious. She was scratching her crotch vigorously through her leggings as Margo asked this.

"Rose made me do it," KC said.

"I didn't make you!"

"You did, you said, 'KC, if you're going to waste your life doing drugs and fucking dudes, at least make money doing it.' I was like, sign me up!"

"She doesn't care," Rose said, smiling. "Like, about anything. I do all her money because literally she would just have millions of pounds of sand delivered to her parents' house."

"It's free shipping! Rose. It's free shipping on six hundred thousand pounds of sand. Like, how does that even make sense? Just think of how hard it would be for them to get rid of it!"

After that they all puked, and then KC said she was a sea cucumber and lay down under the desk, so the microphone picked up her voice only dimly. They discussed the men who wanted to dismember them or dissolve their bodies in acid. "It does get easier to tune out," Rose said, "but then one day a guy will comment with something simple, like, just 'butterface' under one of my pictures, and I'll start sobbing."

"Oh, I definitely want to die," KC said in her faraway voice. "Like every day." Why wouldn't she put on her headphones and sit at the mic? Why was she insisting on living in the dark, echoey shadows of the actual conversational space?

"You don't want to actually die," Rose said. "She's afraid of blood; if she even sees a tiny bit of blood, she passes out."

"That's true. I'm very squeamish," KC said.

"I guess my real question," Margo said, having got caught up in her own train of thought, "is why is time only going in one direction? Like, does anybody know why?"

"Well, I mean, if we could move at the speed of light, we could stop time altogether," Rose said.

KC sat up. "We have to leave this room," she said. "The laptop is fucking evil. Like, look at that. Just look at that fucking thing."

They all stared at the laptop. It did seem weirdly malevolent.

They wandered into the living room, which was bright with warm daylight. "Oh my gosh, KC, you were so right," Margo said. "It's much better in here."

"It really is," Rose said. They all three collapsed on the carpet of the living room. Biotch, surprising them all, approached Margo and curled up next to her.

"Why does she like me now?" Margo said. "She didn't like me before, and now she likes me." Margo stared into Biotch's little tearstained face. "Maybe she can read my mind," she continued. "Oh my God, that reminds me, I have something to ask you guys!"

"What is it?" Rose asked, suddenly serious.

"Are you on TikTok?" Margo asked.

KC started laughing. "That was so anticlimactic!"

"No, I mean, I have this idea," Margo said. She was worried she was not going to explain this right. She stroked Biotch's tiny body. Her breasts were so swollen and nodular from needing to nurse they felt like heads of cauliflower under the skin, and she missed Bodhi so much that if she thought about him for even a second, she would begin leaking. She'd called Jinx from the bathroom at one point and arranged for him to come pick her up when they were finished. There was no way she could drive, and she'd cried because she thought he was mad at her even though he kept telling her he wasn't. If she did all this for the sake of this idea and then managed to fuck up the pitch, she wasn't sure she could live with herself. "I have an idea. And I know from the bottom of my soul that if you guys trust me, I can make us extremely famous. And rich. Filthy rich. But also famous."

"Yeah, okay," KC said, "this is a drag. Are you really being like this right now? Are you delusional, or is this, like, a scam?"

Rose shushed her and said, "What do you mean, sweetie?"

Margo stared at the popcorn ceiling, which seemed to be moving like snowflakes. "Okay, so you know Vegeta and Goku? That is like Tik-Tok and OnlyFans."

"Which one is Vegeta?" KC asked, skeptical.

"I guess TikTok," Margo said.

"TikTok is not Vegeta," KC said, "no way."

"What I am saying is the fusion-ha. Fusion-ha! Because OnlyFans has no discoverability, but lots of monetization, and TikTok has all discoverability, but no monetization. They are made for each other. They are, like, destined to interlink. And if you use them together—it's like a superpower. Monetization and discoverability united."

"So you are essentially saying we should make TikToks," KC said. "I mean, duh, I'm the one who told you to get a TikTok in the first place."

"No, I'm saying we should use TikTok to build our personas, and for that we need to work together. If you only have one character, you're naturally limited in what you can do. Mr. Beast works better because he has his friends on the channel. We need that. We could play off each other and make subplots and prank each other, and it would give us something to *do* that was PG enough for other social media."

"Now you want us to start a YouTube channel?" Rose asked.

"Well, probably, yeah," Margo said, "but I think we should start on TikTok. Okay, look at it this way, KC: the fact that Rose loves you balances you. Her sweetness makes your bitterness less toxic feeling."

"Toxic!" KC said, and rolled over onto her belly.

Margo cut her off. "And Rose could easily come off as stupid, but it is obvious she isn't because how else could she have tamed a creature as complicated as KC?"

"Rose is not stupid," KC said.

"Yes, we know that because we have met Rose, but there is no way you can tell she was almost a physicist from her breasts alone!"

Rose reached out and took Margo's hand and squeezed it. "I love you," she said. "We say yes."

"We aren't saying yes to shit! TikTok isn't worth investing in. I know girls who have lost whole 100k accounts just for linking to their Only-Fans."

"We'll use Linktrees," Margo said.

"TikTok is strict, though, you can't do nudity, you can't do all sorts of stuff."

"We don't need nudity. Okay, okay," Margo said, handing Biotch over to Rose so she could stand and demonstrate. "So you pick the hottest sound on TikTok, something dance-y, and you see Rose doing a little dance, wearing clothes but hot, and you are thinking, Okay, hot girl dancing, but then you notice the couch behind her, like, moving, and KC is inside the couch and is slowly climbing out, and then the video ends when she jump scares you. Or when you jump scare her. Whatever, it ends on the scream."

Neither KC nor Rose said anything.

Margo was desperate. She wished she weren't high so there was any hope she could express the magnitude of the vision that had been growing in her for the last twenty-four hours. "Instead of turning you into a body for someone to fuck, working together will turn us into *people*. We will humanize each other. If they see us doing normal things, it will make it feel more real when we do sexy things! We will become more than dolls!"

"Sweetie, I did not know you were this smart!" Rose said.

"I just don't think it's worth it," KC said. "Like some TikTok, sure, but after what happened on Instagram, I don't like putting all my eggs in one social media basket."

"What happened on Instagram?" Margo asked.

"SESTA-FOSTA," Rose said. "We both got into doing OnlyFans because of Instagram, actually, we were big into the festival scene so we had these huge accounts—"

"I had over five hundred thousand followers!" KC cried.

"And both our accounts got deleted and we had to start all over. Like six months ago, because we had linked to our OnlyFans accounts in our bios. She doesn't want to get burned again."

"Fair enough," Margo said. "That's totally fair. But there's no other platform where it's as easy to go viral as TikTok. And I think it's worth trying. Like, what's the worst that happens? And we can cross-post the videos on Instagram, we can put them on YouTube, it doesn't have to just be about TikTok. Think of it as focusing on PG content."

"What kind of percentage are you thinking?" Rose asked.

"Percentage of people who would subscribe if we went viral?" Margo asked. "I mean, I have no idea, but even if it were one percent, if you go viral big enough . . ."

"No, what percentage of our proceeds would we owe to you? You're basically proposing engineering this huge publicity machine, so I assume we'd have to pay to be part of it."

"Oh, wow," Margo said, "yeah, I hadn't gotten that far. Let's just see if it works?"

"I'm not seeing any downside to at least trying this out," Rose said.

"I still think it's stupid," KC said.

"Let me write it. Give me a week, and then we can meet, and you can see if you want to film it."

"Sweetie," Rose said, "I'm just worried you're not thinking enough about what's in it for you. Are you sure you should be volunteering to do all the work? This isn't some group project in school."

"Um, hello, you guys, I have a thousand Instagram followers, you have thirty thousand. There is no way that working with you two isn't a huge, huge step up for me."

"Oh, true that!" KC crowed.

"Okay, that kind of makes me feel better," Rose said.

"I also have to tell you something else," Margo suddenly found herself saying, because she saw in that moment that it couldn't be any other way. "I have a four-month-old baby. We're going to have to work around him, like only shooting certain days or having him in the background. My dad will be watching him, so you will have my undivided attention. I just can't spend eight hours away, I can't, it would kill me."

"Your dad?" KC said.

"Yeah, but he's cool," Margo said.

"A four-month-old baby?" Rose asked. "Are you shitting me?"

Margo could feel the idea crumbling around her. She'd been stupid to think they'd agree to this in the first place. Maybe she'd even told them about Bodhi to ruin her chances because she was afraid of wanting this hard, of dreaming this big.

"I'm sorry," Margo said. "I didn't mean to lie to you guys. I just—"

"It's not fucking fair!" Rose said, and threw a piece of dog hair fluff she'd peeled off the carpet at Margo. "How do you have that fucking waistline?! Four months! Four months ago you pushed a baby out of there?"

"We need to back up and talk about your dad here," KC said.

"I'm not worried about the dad," Rose said.

"I don't want some old dude up in here with a baby—it's weird."

"My dad is Dr. Jinx," Margo said. It was worth a shot.

"Are you joking?" KC asked. And Margo's heart rose in her chest because she'd guessed right.

"Who is Dr. Jinx?" Rose asked.

"Are you fucking kidding me?" KC said again.

"No, he's Dr. Jinx. So it's not normal dad vibes. He's picking me up, you can meet him if you want. I was about to text him to let him know we're done."

"But who is he?" Rose was still lost.

"He's from wrestling, not a wrestler, but like in that world—he's a goddamn celebrity!" KC explained.

"He's *not* a celebrity," Margo said.

"He's an icon! He is literally iconic," KC said.

"Who is this person?" Rose demanded. And so they wound up watching YouTube clips of Dr. Jinx and Murder and Mayhem.

"What is your dad like?" KC asked, completely amped at the idea of meeting Dr. Jinx for real. "Like, in person?"

Margo tried to think about Jinx and what he was really like. The overwhelming feeling of being on mushrooms had mostly subsided, but her mind still felt childlike and fresh, like being in her own head was the most wonderful thing in the world. "Magic," Margo said, surprising herself. "Like he has access to, I don't know, a kind of vast subterranean network of power or . . . like, he's like a disgraced wizard or something. But, I mean, he's also a middle-aged man who, you know, obsessively cleans and can't keep his dick in his pants and makes pasta from scratch. If that makes any sense."

KC lay there, staring at the ceiling, absorbing this. "Actually," she said, "that makes perfect sense."

FORTY-FIVE MINUTES LATER, Jinx texted that he and Suzie and Bodhi were outside. He had brought Suzie to drive Margo's car home for her. The meeting that then occurred between the still-high KC and Rose, in their pajamas out in the bright midafternoon light of the parking lot, and her dad, dressed in his blacks like he knew this very thing would happen, KC jumping up and down and saying lines from famous promos he'd done, Rose crouched and peering in the back window at the sleeping Bodhi, Suzie cackling at them all, magenta lipstick on her teeth—that image of them bullshitting in a parking lot would remain one of Margo's most precious memories. KC tapping an empty Dasani water bottle on her thigh, Rose's absurd fluffy slippers against the black tar asphalt, the warped shiny reflections of their bodies on Jinx's car, a huge group of seagulls suddenly flying overhead. That they should all wind up in this parking lot under a completely cloudless sky about to embark on this adventure together felt so ludicrous as to be almost weightless.

THAT NIGHT JINX decreed Margo was not allowed to nurse for twenty-four hours, to which Margo said, "Ya think?" But they had already gone through all the frozen milk, so Bodhi had to have formula, which did not go well, and Margo felt horribly guilty. She pumped multiple times in the night and through the next morning, throwing out everything and feeling the shame like a film on her skin. But it was a thin film, the kind of shame one might be able to scrub off in the shower.

The next day she woke before all of them and opened her laptop.

She hesitated. Part of her wanted to write a message to JB. He had recently asked her about the best sandwich she'd ever had, but she didn't want to waste this energy. Instead, she opened her OnlyFans account, clicked edit on her account description, and deleted everything except the description of the dick ratings. She sat there for ten minutes thinking, trying to write a new intro paragraph. Then she wrote: "I am from another planet and I do not understand your world, though I like it here very much. Feed me memes and tinfoil and cute cat videos. Give me your boredom and your sadness and your anxiety: I will eat it all. I will eat the buttons off your shirt, your darkest secrets, your keys, locks of your hair, your memories. Come play with me in a world we make up together. I will only kill you a little bit and you will like it."

Then she exited out, opened Microsoft Word, and began writing the script.

By noon she'd written storylines for her, KC, and Rose, enough Tik-Tok ideas that they could post daily for a week. She wrote out ideas for tweets and IG posts for them all as well. When she was done, she printed out two copies on her ancient inkjet printer that trembled and moaned like little Biotch, one for Jinx and one for Suzie.

"Margo," Jinx said as he gave her his notes at dinner, "I honestly don't know if this is a brilliant or a terrible idea."

"I know," Margo said. But she did not feel afraid.

"I do know one thing: you need to tell Shyanne."

"What— Why?" Margo was brought up short. She didn't see why anything in the scripts would make Jinx think she needed to tell Shyanne.

"If this blows up?" Jinx said. "If you get internet famous? That would be a helluva way for a mom to find out her daughter is doing porn."

"It's not really porn, though," Margo said.

Jinx just looked at her. "Promise me you'll tell her."

"Okay," Margo said, though she still had no intention of telling Shyanne.

"Not only for her sake," Jinx said, "but for you. What you're doing, honey, it's not shameful. It's not something that needs to be secret. You should be proud of yourself. What you're doing—I think it's amazing." He patted her on the shoulder, and Margo moaned because now she knew she was going to have to tell Shyanne. She was supposed to see her next weekend to go wedding dress shopping.

After dinner, Margo rewrote her scripts with Jinx's and Suzie's notes, sent them to KC and Rose with proposed shoot times, and then she lay in bed trying to imagine how on earth she would ever tell Shyanne.

CHAPTER THIRTEEN

That Saturday, I loaded Bodhi in the car and drove to Newport Beach to meet my mom at Fashion Island, the rich-people mall, to go wedding dress shopping. My mom used to work at the Bloomingdale's there, when I was eleven or twelve, and once when I'd been too sick to go to school and my mom had been too scared to call out again, I'd spent the entire day at that mall, periodically throwing up in the women's restrooms. It was a pretty place, all outdoors. There was a koi pond and many fountains. I hated it there.

I met my mom near Neiman Marcus. She was wearing a matching two-piece Lululemon set in beige and a flowy cashmere sweater. She looked like an elder Kardashian, only blond and with a flat ass.

"Do you want to get some coffee or something?" I asked.

"I'm all caffeinated and ready to go!" Shyanne said. "I'm thinking we do Neiman's first, then Nordstrom's, then Macy's. Work our way down. You never want to do the most expensive last. That's when you're tired and weak."

So off we went into the hushed beige morgue of Neiman Marcus.

"I'm thinking," Shyanne said, flipping through the sale rack in evening wear, "that I may want to play off white, like a nod to traditional bridal white, but not trying to actually wear white? I'm thinking ecru, I'm thinking peach, something that reads more cocktail dress than wedding dress."

"How slutty?" I asked. Really my entire childhood had been a training course in how to help my mother shop.

"It's Vegas," she said, "and Kenny loves it when I show off the girls. I personally want something more modest, so a happy compromise might be showing a lot of leg but a higher neckline. I am thinking shimmer, beaded or sequined, maybe pearl detailing. I mean, it's Vegas."

"Do you want me to go to the regular ladies' section and pull things?" I asked.

"Sure thing, Noodle," Shyanne said. "I'll be in the dressing rooms over here. Size four! And look for something for yourself to wear too!"

"I know what size you are," I said, and pushed off, the stroller gliding over the thick-pile carpet.

I knew that this was her wedding, the only one she would ever get to have. She wasn't going to have a big reception with all her friends, she wasn't going on a honeymoon (Vegas was to be the honeymoon, two birds, one stone; Kenny was a clever man). The least I could do was attend. I was the person she loved most in all the world. I knew that.

But I viscerally didn't want to go.

I found a peachy wrap dress by Diane von Furstenberg and draped it over the handle of the stroller. I spaced out for a while imagining a video I could do where I poured different breakfast cereals over my breasts, then found three or four more things I thought would suit Shyanne and found her in a dressing room.

The dressing room was gigantic. The stroller and I fit in there with loads of room to spare. There was even a comfy leather chair for me to sit in, though my mother had laid the clothes she'd been wearing there. I picked them up, sat down, folded the bundle so her underwear was no longer visible, and held the bundle on my lap. Under no circumstances would my mother allow her clothes to touch a dressing room floor, a place she believed to be unimaginably filthy even in a Neiman Marcus. "If I had a penny for every time someone has pissed in a ladies' dressing room" was a frequent refrain during my childhood, though from my count she would have wound up with only five or six pennies. Still, I guessed that was enough.

She was trying on a silver sequin number that would have been at home on the red carpet, complete with a plunging back so low it showed her actual butt crack. She was turning this way and that, examining herself in the mirror. Whenever my mother looked at herself in the mirror, she looked flat-eyed like a parrot.

"What do you think?" she whispered because Bodhi was asleep.

"I mean, it's gorgeous, you look like a movie star," I said. "What is Kenny gonna be wearing?"

She hiss-sighed, understanding my point immediately. Kenny would probably be wearing something god-awful, a maroon shirt and gray suit, and in that dress, she'd look like a showgirl who accidentally wandered into a wedding.

"Fine," she said, "what did you bring me?"

I showed her the dresses I had picked out.

"No, no, no," she said, sorting through and hanging them on the wall hooks for noes. She paused on the Diane von Furstenberg. "This is interesting."

"There's a kind of seventies glamour to it. It's understated," I said. I knew it didn't have beading or sequins, but in my opinion she didn't need the glitter. She needed a dress that said, *I am getting married on purpose, and it is not a mistake.*

She took off the silver gown and tried on the Diane von Furstenberg. At first it seemed too big, but when she pulled the waist in and tied it, the fit was perfect. She looked beautiful and powerfully herself, a version of my mother I knew and recognized and loved. "I don't know," she said, turning and looking at her butt.

I knew that if I pushed too much it would turn her against the dress, so I said nothing. She turned around, sighed, pushed out her belly and slumped her shoulders. This was something she did, examine how she would look in her worst moments. It was always better, she believed, to wear something you couldn't look bad in than something you could only sometimes look great in. "All right," she said, her tummy pushed out as full as it could go. "It's a maybe."

WHILE WE WERE at Nordstrom, my mother asked if I had gotten that job at the seafood place, a lie I had completely forgotten.

"No," I said. We were now in lingerie looking for a nightgown she could wear on her wedding night.

"Margo! What have you been doing?! You've got to get your ass in gear. It's not like you to let something fester like this."

"It's just so complicated," I said, "with childcare and—"

"Make Jinx watch the baby, he's great with babies!" She was stretching a thong like she planned to use it to rope cattle.

"Well, Bodhi won't always take a bottle."

"Excuses," Shyanne said, moving on to the next tower of underwear. She was right. I thought about Jinx saying I had nothing to be ashamed of. Why couldn't it be true?

"I've been doing some work on this website, and it pays pretty well," I said.

"Filling out surveys? Margo, believe me, I've done the math, you wind up working for pennies an hour."

"No, it's basically . . ." I was trying to think of some way of saying it without the word *porn*. I kept trying to pretend it wasn't porn, except it was porn. "It's basically like a hybrid of porn and social media."

Shyanne grabbed my wrist. Her fingers were icy cold. "Do not talk about this here," she hissed.

Once we were outside the store and walking to Macy's, she said, "So you're doing *porn*? I can't believe you, Margo. I mean, honestly."

"It's not really porn, though," I said. "There's no sex, there's no other person involved, it's basically pictures of me in my underwear."

"I'm so disappointed in you," she said. She was walking fast, and I was struggling to keep up with Bodhi in his stroller. I couldn't see him because of the sun visor, but I knew he had to be on the verge of waking. We passed the koi pond where beautiful blond children in fine fabrics were laughing and playing. It felt like we were in a dream.

"Mom," I said. "It isn't, like—it isn't that bad!"

"I didn't raise you to be a whore." She said this so quietly I wasn't even sure if she'd intended me to hear it.

I didn't say anything, we just kept walking, rushing like we were divers swimming for the surface. I wasn't sure if we were even still going to Macy's, I was simply following her. It turned out she was heading to an isolated area next to an escalator by a store currently under construction. There was no bench or anything, so we stood there awkwardly.

"No man will marry you now," she said.

I'm not sure there was a thing she could have said that would have struck me as more ridiculous while also tapping directly into my deepest fears.

"Future employers? Forget about it! Once it's on the internet, Margo, it's there forever." Shyanne was trembling, she was so upset. Her mouth was pinched tight in a way that made her look suddenly old.

I didn't know what to say. Bodhi started fussing, so I picked him up out of his stroller. He was hungry, and I was praying my milk wouldn't let down during this conversation.

"You have ruined your life," she said.

I looked up at the escalator, out at the palm trees in the parking lot, anywhere but at her face.

"You thought he ruined your life?" She pointed at Bodhi. "Not even close. *You* ruined it."

It almost didn't matter if I didn't agree with her, the shame was like an egg cracked on my head, cold and wet and dripping.

"If you had told me you were thinking of doing this, I could have stopped you!" She was crying now, wiping away the tears with the pads of her fingers, trying not to stab herself with her nails. "I'm so sad, Margo, and so disappointed. I don't even know what to say. I thought I raised you better than this."

"I'm sorry," I said. It felt like my mouth was numb. All my skin was numb, actually. I didn't know how to argue, even as I knew that if anything, she'd raised me *for* this. "Beauty is like free money." I thought about the things Shyanne said all the time when I was doing my Only-Fans: "Never smile too big at a man too quickly, a shy small smile will make him think he earned it." "Never sit with your purse on your lap, it's blocking your coochie." "Men love hearing their own names, always call people by their name."

"Mama," I said, terrified I would start crying. "The thing is I'm good at this, and I think—"

"I don't care how good you are at it! Jesus, I can't believe you would even *say* that."

"It's not just about sex, though," I tried to argue, thinking even as I said it about all the guys who dropped my account because there wasn't enough sexual content. "It's about building a brand and using social media and—"

"No, this is about giving people everything they need in order to decide you're a piece of trash who doesn't deserve shit. This is about losing the respect of every single person who would ever help your sorry ass even a little."

I thought about Jinx and hospitals and engagement rings and men strapped to teeter-totters being eaten by starving bears. But I had no clue how to narrativize any of that for Shyanne, how to put together all the puzzle pieces in her mind the way I had been putting them together in mine.

"Mamamama," Bodhi said, grabbing a fist of my hair. "Mamama-mam."

The first time he ever called me that.

"I'll do Macy's on my own," Shyanne said.

"Okay," I said.

"Mamamamammmama!" Bodhi cried, delighted with himself. He shook his little fist with my hair clenched in it.

Shyanne stalked off, up the escalator and toward Macy's. I hugged Bodhi tight to me.

"Mama," I said.

"Ma Ma Ma Ma," he said.

"Yes, I'm Mama," I said. He yanked my hair. "Are you hungry?" I asked, wiping the tears off my cheeks. "Let's find a place to nurse."

I found a bench and pulled out a boob, didn't even cover up with a blanket. Just nursed for all the rich people to see.

SUZIE HAD CONVINCED Margo that her target demographic was nerds, and she ought to familiarize herself with their major franchises. "I'll put you through nerd school," Suzie said, "it will be great!" Nerd school was mainly, it turned out, playing video games and watching anime together, and Margo secretly thought perhaps Suzie had only wanted a friend. She didn't object. She liked Suzie more and more, she found.

That night after playing *Minecraft* with Suzie for a couple of hours and dying repeatedly by falling in lava, Margo tried to write JB. She looked over the questions he had sent. The sadness of the day with Shyanne had left in her a deep well. She thought she could use it. Maybe she could pull the dagger out of her gut and put it into his. That was what writing was, wasn't it? She decided to answer his question about childhood pets. More and more she'd begun simply telling the truth when she answered his questions, then changing things around to match the lies she'd already told. It made her think of the old classroom arguments between Mark and Derek, about how characters weren't real people.

Mark was always insisting that characters weren't real, that they had no psychology at all, having no actual body or mind. They were always a pawn of the author. Our job, he insisted, was to try to understand the author, not the character. The character was merely the paint—we needed to try to see the picture the paint was making.

Margo didn't know if she believed that or not—surely characters sometimes took on a life of their own—but it made her feel better about lying to JB somehow. Like even if she was lying, it was okay because she was using the lies like paint to try to tell him something real.

JB,

My mom was pretty anti-pet growing up, but we did wind up adopting a cat when I was eight or nine. We don't know where she came from, and she only had three legs. She was beautiful, a Siamese mixed with something else. She had those bluebell-colored eyes, and she was white with tiger stripes. We didn't know how she lost her leg. It was one of her back ones, cut off at the knee. We figured it must have been done surgically or else how would she have survived, so someone at one point had been willing to shell out however many thousands of dollars for this cat. But she wasn't wearing a collar and there were no lost cat signs. She kept hanging out on our doorstep and meowing to come in, so eventually my mom just held the door open and Lost-y (we eventually named her Lost-y) sauntered in like she already knew the layout.

And she was the most superior cat. She would use one paw to hold down my head while she aggressively licked my hairline, and if I moved at all she would bop me with her paw to keep me in line. She would eat any and all human food. I once saw her eat a whole piece of lettuce, just wolf it right down.

Then one day when I was thirteen, she didn't come home. I hung signs everywhere. I went out on my bike calling for her. I couldn't stand not knowing what had happened to her. Had she been hit by a car? Was she living with another family? Had a coyote gotten her?

I just hope she knew how much we loved her. I hope whatever happened that she was able to face it because she knew these two weird monkeys that lived in a creepy old apartment building from the '70s loved her.

Love,

She read it over and added some stuff about her imaginary dad and imaginary brother, Timmy, and then took out the last sentence entirely. Presumably her fake family lived in a real house, and the line just didn't work as well if she changed it to "four weird monkeys who lived in a respectable, middle-class home." The email didn't seem as deep or special as the others, and she worried JB wouldn't like it. She had not managed it, the transfer of the dagger from her gut to his.

She hovered over the last paragraph and then started typing.

~~I just hope she knew how much we loved her.~~ It bothers me that we never got her a collar, that we never made the effort to claim her, to say, "This cat is ours, beloved by us, call us if you find her, contact us if she dies in your yard!" In ~~Lady and the Tramp~~ there is this moment where Tramp finally gets a collar, and it's a symbol of being loved. If you get taken to the pound, someone is gonna come get you. The dog catcher is different with a dog wearing a collar. A dog without a collar is just an animal. If the world doesn't know you are loved, then you're trash. I think that's even true of people. Maybe. Sometimes. Or I fear it is. That being loved is the only way to be safe.

Sincerely,

Jelly Bean

She was not entirely satisfied, though she knew it was closer, and she was tired. She thought for a moment, trying to decide how she should spend her next question of him. She added: PS: Please write me a portrait of your mom. Then she pressed send and went to bed.

HERE IS THE portrait JB wrote of his mother and sent to her the next morning:

Jelly Ghost,

Both my parents were born in Korea, but they didn't meet there, they met here. My mom is super loud, very pretty, and she's always talking to strangers. She builds—I'm not sure how to say this—inappropriately close relationships with clerks? It would embarrass me so much as a kid, I don't know why. She was wild about movies, wanted to see every single thing that came out. She was a real regular at Blockbuster. The guys that worked at Blockbuster, they were mainly like nineteen-year-old white boys with spiked hair, I don't know, not a natural pairing for a middle-aged Korean woman, but boy, did they love her. She would bring cupcakes when it was one of their birthdays. They talked movies endlessly. I got so mad because she invited one of them, Philip, to my thirteenth birthday party, and I kept trying to explain to her that it was weird, but she just couldn't understand. I remember he got me a magic eight ball. I still can't believe he brought a gift.

She's obsessive about cleaning the house, like no molecule of dust has ever settled in that house, I'm surprised she hasn't plastic-wrapped my dad. They love each other. I mean, I think it might be more accurate to say he worships her, even though a lot of the time he plays at being aggravated. My mom has a lot of Lucille Ball energy and she's constantly getting into weird situations, like she accidentally knocked over this Hell's Angel's bike and it became a whole thing and my dad had to pay hundreds of dollars.

I have a younger brother and my mom dotes on both of us, spoiled us rotten, but not in a normal way. She was always playing video games with us and could beat all my friends. She's never worked a job because my dad made good money, but randomly in her fifties started working as an aide at our local high school because she "wanted something to do." These kids love her, like they tell her all their crushes, and she helps them resolve fights they have with their parents, and she's always coming home talking their slang.

I'm definitely closer to my mom than my dad. It's just a more intimate thing, my relationship with her. My mom demands to have an intimate relationship with everyone, you can't get away from her fast enough, three minutes in and she's trying to advise you on your bowel movements. I love her. She was a great mom.

—JB

Margo found this description of his mother so charming she read it four times. It was not what she'd been expecting. Perhaps because he had so much money and was spending it so recklessly, Margo had envisioned JB as some bored rich kid. And he might still be that, but certainly this portrait of his mom made her like him a whole lot more.

Margo knew that if things were different, she could find a way to make Shyanne likable like this. Every person can be face or heel, flip back and forth, depending on what you showed. Show him putting his sunglasses on a kid, he's a face. Show him cheating and distracting the ref, he's a heel. She knew this was because real people were both good and bad, all mixed up together, only the screen made everyone into basic silhouettes. The resulting image could appear either way depending on which way you turned it, which details you showed.

But that happened in real life too. So much so that sometimes it made her dizzy. Even when it came to herself, Margo could see it both ways: hometown girl makes good, defies capitalist patriarchy, or teen whore sells nudes while nursing, too lazy to work.

And what about JB? Who was this guy, and how would she ever be able to tell from the carefully selected fragments he gave her?

CHAPTER FOURTEEN

Shyanne called the next day and said she didn't mean to be so harsh, but that I needed to stop while I still could and delete the account. Somehow, I wound up promising that I would do so. "You're right," I said, running my finger along the windowsill in my room. "I think you're probably right." When I was saying this to her, I meant it, and it felt good to bend to her wishes. But when we got off the phone, I didn't take down the account. Instead, I went and ate a bowl of shredded wheat, the big ones that look like little doll beds, since my dad had replaced all the fun cereal in the house.

I figured that if the OnlyFans wasn't successful after three more months, then I'd take it down. What was the difference between now and three months from now? (Absolutely untouched by this logic was the idea that a successful run as a porn star is much harder to bury than a failed one.)

The week before Christmas was a blur of nonstop filming. As soon as they had the go-ahead from Rose and KC, Margo and Jinx and Suzie went to Fry's Electronics, even though it was ten p.m. Christmas music was playing, and Jinx and Suzie skipped through the store like kids. Margo waddled behind under the weight of Bodhi in his carrier strapped on her front. They bought two GoPros and a boom mic, some lights, and a Roomba.

They started shooting at KC and Rose's apartment on Tuesday and didn't finish until Friday, so much longer did everything take than they imagined. Suzie wound up occasional cameraman and general fixer, bringing them all Chipotle, finding lost shoes or panties. Jinx was a kind of baby-wearing art director who knew a lot more about lighting than any of them had realized. They all needed endless costume changes to make it seem like everything took place over the course of

seven days. Even once it was over, there was the editing and organiz-
ing, which took Margo another three days.

Still, when she watched it all back, she thought they had something.
They had made something. If it was good or not, she didn't know, but
she loved it. She absolutely loved it.

Margo was so busy that she hardly slept, and she certainly hadn't
gotten a chance to go Christmas shopping. At the last minute she ordered an old-fashioned-looking teddy bear for Bodhi from Amazon and
bought Jinx an electric razor and a subscription to a tea-of-the-month
club. But what to possibly get Shyanne? Margo wound up ordering her
a necklace off Etsy: a tiny ace of spades made of fourteen-karat gold on
a delicate chain. Taking a deep breath, she booked her trip to Vegas for
Shyanne's wedding on January 6. The ticket was expensive as hell, and
she tried not to resent it. She added a lap infant. She would let Shyanne
be furious and count on the presence of Kenny to keep Shyanne from
outwardly expressing the worst of it.

And yet, during the week before Christmas, where everything was a
blur and she hardly had time to shower, she managed to write JB four
pages about the best sandwich she'd ever had (a Reuben). She spent an
hour googling the mall by his hometown, looking for pictures of how
the food court was laid out.

He asked, Have you ever known anyone named Kyle and, if so, what
was he like? Do you believe in ghosts? What is the worst you have ever
done on a test? Who taught you to drive?

They wrote to each other three, four times a day. It felt like an art
project almost, answering each other's questions, like if they were
careful, they could use these messages like Ziploc bags to store reality itself. Who was your first boyfriend? he asked. And she told him
an only slightly modified account of Sebastian. Who was your first
girlfriend? she asked. And he told her about a girl named Riley who
always got the lead in the school play and had an amazing singing
voice, and how they never had sex and later it turned out she was a
lesbian.

She told him about the TikToks they were working on and how excited she was about the project. Maybe you should go to film school,

JB said. Margo started to write back that she couldn't, but then, what if she could? She asked him about his job, and he explained he did something with machine learning and advertising, like with political ads. This was his first real job after grad school, and all the people he worked with were older, in their thirties, and had kids. He'd moved to D.C. for the job and didn't have a lot of friends. He was originally from New York, and D.C. felt very different, he didn't love it.

But it seems like you make a lot of money, she wrote.

I mean, not a ton, he had answered. I think I just don't have much to spend it on.

That didn't make sense to Margo. She googled how much machine learning engineers make and their salaries started at $120k, which she considered to be a wild amount for a twenty-five-year-old to be making. Still, she guessed his mother would probably be scandalized if she saw how he was spending it. Margo didn't know what D.C. was like and pictured an entire city of people who had done student government in high school. She could understand why JB wouldn't like that.

By the time all the videos were edited, it was nearly Christmas. They didn't want to post during low traffic and all agreed to wait until the twenty-sixth. Margo thought the suspense might kill her.

THE DAY BEFORE Christmas, at about six in the morning, a courier knocked on the door of their apartment, chewing gum and with an improbably large diamond in his ear, and asked Margo to sign for some papers. Then the courier asked if James Millet lived there as well and insisted Margo couldn't sign for him. She went to wake Jinx, then stood awkwardly with the courier by the doorway, not making eye contact as Bodhi continually yanked the neckline of her T-shirt, trying to expose her breasts so he could nurse. "He'll be here in a minute," she reassured him. Finally, Jinx came to sign, and with the courier gone, they opened their respective envelopes.

"What is yours?" she asked, as she frantically tried to understand what her own said, Bodhi grabbing at the pages and squealing.

"Jesus Christ," Jinx said. "This is unbelievable."

"PETITION TO DETERMINE PARENTAL RELATIONSHIP," her form said.

"It's a restraining order," Jinx said. "From Mark and Mommy Dearest."

Margo barely heard him, too busy reading her own form. Was Mark trying to establish paternity? For what godly reason?

On the second page there was a series of check boxes.

IF Petitioner is found to be the parent of children listed in item 2, Petitioner requests:

a) Legal custody of Children to . . . . PETITIONER ☑
b) Physical custody of Children to . . . . PETITIONER ☑
c) Child visitation be granted to . . . . PETITIONER ONLY ☑

It didn't make sense. Why would Mark want custody of Bodhi? He and Elizabeth had gone out of their way to keep Bodhi out of their lives, made her sign papers promising never to contact him, and now he was suing her, or summonsing her, or whatever this was?

"This is all my fault," Jinx was saying. "Oh God, this is all my fault."

Margo's hands were so sweaty she was leaving damp marks on the papers, so she set them on the kitchen counter and rubbed her free hand on her shirt. Bodhi still wanted to nurse, so she gave him a rubber spatula to distract him, and he immediately whacked her on the head with it.

"I'm so sorry," Jinx said.

"Sorry for what?" Margo snapped, almost irritated with her dad for making so little sense.

"Margo, I called him," Jinx said.

"Called who?"

"I called Mark and I yelled at him," Jinx said. "I was so mad that he made you sign that NDA, that he was your teacher. I just . . . it got to me, and I kept thinking, He thinks he can treat her like this? He thinks no one is going to stand up for her?"

Margo grabbed Bodhi's fist midair before he bonked her with the spatula again. "But why would you do that? If you knew it would break the NDA and then Bodhi would lose his trust?"

"I don't know, it was stupid, Margo, I wasn't thinking clearly, but you know, technically it doesn't violate the NDA. It says you aren't allowed to contact him. It didn't say anything about me or a party affiliated with you or anything like that."

Margo almost laughed, she was so upset. This time she failed to block Bodhi, and he hit her in the head again. "He wants full custody of Bodhi," she said. She tried to say this lightly, but there was a tremor in her voice.

"Let me see that," Jinx said, grabbing the papers she'd laid on the counter.

Slowly, Margo tried to remember how to make coffee. It seemed almost impossibly complex. She floated uncertainly toward the cabinet that contained the coffee filters.

"There's no way," Jinx said, slapping the papers back down on the counter. "This is just to scare you, sweetie. There's no way any court would grant him full custody."

"Really?" Margo tried to swallow. Bodhi hit her again with the spatula. Jinx came around the island and took him from her. Her arms were suddenly wet noodles, the muscles shaking, and she wondered how she'd been managing to hold Bodhi at all.

"A hundred percent," Jinx said.

"What about the OnlyFans?" she asked. "Do you think they could take him because of that?"

"OnlyFans isn't illegal!" Jinx crowed. "Plus, how would they even know you have an OnlyFans?"

Margo finally was able to separate a single filter from the stack. She put it in the coffee machine, momentarily uncertain what to do next. It was true, she realized. They didn't have a way of knowing about her OnlyFans. It was under the name HungryGhost. "You don't think they'll say I'm an unfit mother?" she asked.

"I promise," Jinx said. "This is going to be okay. This is all my fault, and it's just a reaction to me calling and threatening him and it will blow over, I'm sure of it."

"You threatened him?" Margo paused as she scooped the coffee grounds.

Jinx looked sheepish. "I mean, old habits die hard?"

"What exactly did you say?" She was not happy about this situation, but there was some small part of her that had perhaps fantasized about Dr. Jinx threatening violence on her behalf her whole life.

"I don't know," Jinx said, "stupid stuff. About, like, asking if he knew how easy it was to break someone's fingers, how they kind of pop, you don't even need to press that hard, and the sound they make as they break." Jinx made a popping sound with his finger in his cheek.

"Oh my God," Margo said, then let out a peal of nervous laughter. This wasn't funny. This was very bad. But the idea of little Mark, his cell phone pressed to his ear, shivering with terror as Dr. Jinx made cartoonish popping noises with his cheek, was too much.

"I may have also said that if he ever messed around with another student, I would cut off his member."

Margo was now bent over, hands on knees, laughing so hard her eyes stung. It was the word *member*. Almost unable to stand, she finally said, "Was that the word you used with him?"

"Uh, I believe so," Jinx said.

"My God," she marveled. Jinx and Bodhi were both looking at her, concerned. "This is so bad," she said, still for some reason smiling, though she could feel that at any moment she might begin to cry. "I'm so scared!"

Instantly Jinx was beside her, one of his hands on her back, rubbing circles into the fabric of her T-shirt. She could feel the tension leaving her body in real time, just from being touched.

"Everything is going to be all right," Jinx said. "I promise you."

"What do I do?" she asked.

"It says you have thirty days to respond, plenty of time. You do what all red-blooded Americans do. You hire a lawyer."

"Right," Margo said. Hiring a lawyer sounded overwhelming. "I just— Maybe I should call Mark. He isn't a bad guy. I mean, he's kind of a terrible person, but he isn't an *irrational* person. I could at least find out his intentions."

Jinx grimaced. "I mean, you can if you want to, but I would at least consult a lawyer and see if they think you should contact him. You don't want to accidentally give them more ammo."

Margo thought about this. The thing was, if she had to guess, it was Mark's mother who was behind this. Talking to Mark might not do any good, and it would put her in violation of the NDA.

"It'll be easy," Jinx said. "We can start calling around after Christmas when people are back in the office."

"You promise?"

"A hundred percent," Jinx said. "There is nothing to worry about. This is just the way rich white people say 'fuck you.' Trust me, I know their language, I'm practically fluent."

PART OF THIS game is that you are going to realize certain things before I do. This is called "narrative irony." I know because Mark put it on a test once.

SHYANNE BEGGED MARGO to spend Christmas Eve and Christmas morning with her and Kenny, and Margo knew on some level this was Shyanne's way of solidifying their making up, even if the way she phrased it was backhanded and confusing: "You ditched us for Thanksgiving!" Shyanne said. "You know you did!"

"How did I ditch you?" Margo asked, laughing nervously. Lying to Shyanne about keeping her OnlyFans account left her constantly off-balance.

"You don't even love me anymore," Shyanne said.

"Oh, shut up! You know I love you. Of course I'll see you at Christmas."

Though she didn't entirely register at the time that Shyanne wanted not only to see her, but to have Margo continuously present (and Jinx continuously absent) all of Christmas Eve and Christmas Day.

Jinx was very understanding when Margo finally brought the dilemma to him. "Christmas is entirely meaningless to me," he'd said. He and Suzie planned to watch an old WWE In Your House special, *Canadian Stampede*, in which, Jinx kept promising Suzie, Bret Hart was almost horrifyingly over.

"What is *over*?" Suzie asked.

"Oh, just like, the crowd loved him," Jinx said. "He could have punched an old woman in the face, and they would have cheered."

Margo would stay at Kenny's condo. Shyanne and Kenny were waiting until they were married to move in together, which seemed weird to Margo, but weirder still: her mother was also spending Christmas Eve at Kenny's and had gone out of her way to mention to Margo that she'd be in the spare room while Margo and Bodhi slept in the basement rec room on the floor.

Why wouldn't Shyanne sleep in Kenny's room? Was it possible that her mother and Kenny hadn't slept together yet?

"WE THANK GOD our budget has been approved," Kenny was saying into a microphone onstage. It was Christmas Eve, the five p.m. service, and he was surrounded by the youth band, fronted by a girl singer whose skin was the tender gray white of mushrooms growing in the dark. They had opened the service by singing "O Little Town of Bethlehem" so poorly that Margo had been shocked. The singer kept sucking in air mid-note and sliding around trying to find the pitch. Margo now understood what kind of youth would accept being ministered to by Kenny, and it made her feel tender toward all of them.

When the song finally ended, the band and Kenny left the stage, and the pastor took the pulpit.

Pastor Jim had both Michael J. Fox and Ned Flanders vibes, an ultimately likable combination. The sermon seemed to be entirely about Joseph. "If you were Mary and you were pregnant with the Lord's baby, wouldn't you be a little scared to tell Joseph?" the pastor asked. The congregation laughed. "Yeah!" he said in his folksy midwestern accent. "I'd be afraid myself, if I was in Mary's shoes."

More laughter.

"But, folks, do you think he believed her?"

Margo assumed the answer was yes, and Joseph believed her because he was a good guy. She was surprised when the congregation stayed silent.

"No!" the pastor said. "No, folks, he did *not* believe her, and can you blame him? If the woman you were engaged to marry came to you and said, 'I'm pregnant, but trust me, it's not from another man, it's the Lord's child'—what would you think?"

You could almost hear the congregation silently thinking that she was *a lying whore!*

"In Matthew 1:19, it says: 'Because Joseph her husband was a righteous man and was unwilling to disgrace her publicly, he resolved to divorce her quietly.'" The pastor looked out at them. "Because what would happen if Mary were disgraced publicly?" He waited a beat. "That's right, she would be stoned! Put to death! Or, at the very least, cast out!"

This man did not utter a phrase without an exclamation mark. He was less boring than she'd anticipated. It did make Margo wonder, however, how Mary really did get pregnant. She'd never thought about this in her entire life. It couldn't have been Joseph, or he wouldn't have thought of divorcing her. Whoever it was, it was clear Mary lied and said it was the Lord's baby and got away with it. Was there another way of describing what happened? It was, as Jinx would say, an absolutely epic angle. Mary must have had balls of steel during that conversation with Joseph.

"Wasn't Joseph a great guy? Wasn't he, though?" the pastor was saying. But Margo couldn't stop thinking about Mary and what she'd pulled off. The pastor covered how she was visiting her cousin Elizabeth who was also having a miracle baby, John the Baptist, and Mary stayed with her for three months and returned home three months pregnant to have it out with Joseph, so it seemed likely that whatever happened, Mary's pregnancy was probably the reason she went to visit Elizabeth in the first place, so she could hide out while she figured out what to do. Was it usual for women to travel alone like that? How old was Mary anyway? Margo pulled out her phone and googled: "How old was Mary?" Bodhi was fascinated by her phone and tried to pry it from her grasp. She could barely see but caught the phrase: "At the time of her betrothal to Joseph, Mary was 12–14 years old." She let Bodhi have it, and he happily stuck the whole top corner in his mouth, sucking on the camera lens.

So, she was definitely raped, Margo thought. What other conclusion could you come to? She could picture a seventeen-year-old Mary falling in love with some shepherd boy and having a dalliance, but a twelve-year-old girl? It had to have been rape, not in the modern statutory sense, but rape-rape. Margo looked around at the congregation. How were none of them realizing this with her?

"I hope you've come to love Joseph as much as I do. He was a righteous man. A man not afraid to do the right thing. A man of the law. I like to think that he's the secret hero of Christmas, even if he's not the star of the show. Usually we talk about Mary, we talk about the baby Jesus, but I like to think about Joseph. We could all learn a little something about being a man from him."

There was a murmur of assent from the crowd. Margo tried to catch Shyanne's eye, but she was too busy wiping her tears with a Kleenex. They all stood to sing "O Come, All Ye Faithful," and Bodhi was thrilled by all the singing. He kept shoving his whole hand in Margo's mouth. She wondered, as she bounced him, if any of the men here subscribed to OnlyFans. She pictured her voice, as it rose with the others, glowing subtly black. She didn't know if she was enjoying imagining herself as slightly evil because she disliked these people or because she was afraid of them. She knew they were likely nice people. She even believed that they were probably better than her. But she knew they would hate her. She knew, if pressed, that they would show her no mercy at all. That the lead singer, so delicate, so tender she quaked with the glory of God's love, lungs fluttering too fast to find the note, would press her gray New Balance sneaker right on Margo's throat.

CHAPTER FIFTEEN

After the ordeal of the service, the dinner at Kenny's house was almost a breeze. Kenny's living room was exactly as Margo had imagined it. There was, of course, a navy corduroy recliner. The walls were painted teal and had the texture of psoriasis. There was a weirdly shiny silver shag rug, a painting of a battleship, and a small wooden sign that said Pray Hardest When It's Hardest to Pray in white script.

Shyanne had made a tuna casserole with raisins in it, a dish Margo remembered from her childhood whenever Jinx was in town. Kenny was clearly still on a manic high and kept talking about Annie. Annie was the name of the anemic, breathy lead singer. "I'm telling you, the Lord has special plans for that one. She's also a very talented drawer," he said.

Bodhi was asleep. When they got home from the service, Kenny and Shyanne had taken Margo down to the rec room and shown her a beautiful white crib they'd bought and set up with blankets and stuffed animals, even a little mobile. They'd bought a video baby monitor and a changing table pad. Margo almost cried; it was so sweet. Kenny grabbed her by both shoulders and said, "We want you and Bodhi to always, always feel welcome in this house."

She was touched and it made her feel guilty. If they found out how she made a living, she knew it would all be instantly revoked. She'd have felt better about lying to them if they weren't being quite so nice. Still, Margo had gotten used to having Jinx around, and Shyanne and Kenny, despite their absolute sweetness and generosity, never reached out to help with Bodhi. It simply wasn't in their nature. They would just watch while Margo struggled, looking slightly frustrated that they were all being interrupted by a baby. Margo had finally gotten him down, and by dinner, he was dozing in his new crib, where she could see him on the video monitor.

"What does Annie draw?" Margo asked, blowing on her bite of tuna casserole.

"Oh, all sorts of things," Kenny said, "dragons and horses, mostly."

For whatever reason this made Margo think of Suzie masturbating to *SpongeBob*. She wondered what Annie masturbated to (she assumed dragons and horses, mostly).

"And Pastor Jim! Was he Holy Ghost filled tonight or what?!"

"He sure was," Shyanne said. "I loved all that stuff about Joseph."

Margo tried all night to be nice and complimented Kenny on everything. At one point she even commented on what a clean refrigerator he had.

After dinner, they decided to open one present. Margo panicked, realizing she had not gotten anything for Kenny, only something for her mother. Kenny waved this off. "I am rich in all the things that count," he said, patting Shyanne's white-jean-clad thigh.

They had Margo open hers first. It was from both of them: three sets of pajamas for Bodhi. One made his feet into tiny lion heads. "These are great!" Margo cried.

Then Shyanne had Kenny open one from her. It was a set of seven different novelty hot sauces. It turned out Kenny was into spicy stuff, which Margo would never have predicted. Shyanne and Kenny had bonded over their love of the show *Hot Ones*.

And then Margo had Shyanne open the necklace she'd gotten her, with the tiny ace of spades charm. She'd never bought her mother something so nice. It was solid fourteen karats. She said that.

"It's solid fourteen karats."

Kenny said, "Why is there an ace of spades?"

"Because it's the highest card in the deck," Margo said.

"I love it," Shyanne said. "Oh, baby, I love it."

She tried to have Kenny put it on her, but his fingers were too thick to work the tiny clasp, so Margo did it.

"It's perfect," Shyanne kept saying, and Margo could see that Kenny was getting more and more put out. She wasn't sure if it was because of the association with gambling or anxiety that he hadn't gotten Shyanne anything that would make her say that. Margo tried to mentally warn Shyanne to stop. Shyanne just kept going. "Where did you even *find* this?"

"Yeah," Kenny said. "How did you know your mom would like something like that? Does she, I mean, does she have a love of playing cards?"

"Sure," Margo said brightly. She had known that Shyanne probably wouldn't be honest with Kenny about her poker addiction, and she realized she'd not really thought it all the way through when she chose the gift. "I also just think she's lucky. We would always joke about that, if there was a school raffle or something, Shyanne would always win. She's Lady Luck herself."

Margo worried this was too pagan. Kenny only smiled, tousled Shyanne's hair, and said, "I like that. Lady Luck!"

"Thank you," Shyanne mouthed to Margo when Kenny went into the kitchen to fix himself another drink. He was drinking Jack and Coke of all things. Margo winked back and smiled, but she was already so sad her blood had turned to black water, and she was counting down the minutes until it would be appropriate to say good night and head downstairs.

"Merry Christmas," she whispered to Bodhi's small sleeping body when she finally made it down. Beside his crib lay a narrow twin air mattress covered by a gaping too-large fitted sheet, and as Margo eased her weight down onto it, the plastic made an elephantine farting noise. She stared at the ceiling of Kenny's rec room, thinking about Mark of all people. Had he and his wife pretended to be Santa, eaten the cookies, drunk all the milk, filled up the stockings? That made Margo wonder: What did Mark's wife think about him filing for full custody? Was there any chance he was seeking custody in earnest? She tried to imagine it: Mark watching his real children open their gifts in the morning, Bodhi hovering like a ghost in the corners of his vision. But if he did long for Bodhi, did genuinely want to know him, why not just call her on the phone?

It simply had to be an attempt to hurt her. To make her waste money, to scare her.

And it did scare her. Ever since she had uttered the words, they haunted her, floating through her mind in odd moments: *an unfit mother*. Margo did not actually worry she was a bad mother; like, if Bodhi could magically be consulted, she believed he would give her a good report, except for maybe the night she was on mushrooms.

It was the word *unfit* that scared her, a mother who didn't fit. A mother who wasn't the right kind of mother like all the other mothers. A mother without a ring, who was too young, who let men look at her body for money. She could almost hear Pastor Jim: "That's right, she would be stoned! Put to death! Or, at the very least, cast out!" Even her own mother had called her a whore. And the only reason she was allowed beneath Kenny's roof was because she was lying to them.

She didn't think she was a bad person, but did bad people ever know that they were bad? Mark didn't seem to, even though he gave lip service to the idea. She thought of Becca saying, "Since when do you care about being a good person? I mean, you were fucking somebody's husband." What if, inside, Margo was secretly rotten? What if the reason doing the OnlyFans didn't feel wrong to her wasn't because it wasn't actually wrong, but because she was so vile she could no longer detect all that was wrong with it?

They began posting the TikToks on December 26.

"I shit you not," KC's voice can be heard, "there is a girl on our balcony."

The camera blurs as it attempts to focus through the glass. On the balcony is a sopping wet Margo in a futuristic-looking silver bikini. The light is behind her. She is mostly a silhouette.

"What do we do?" Rose says.

"How did she get out there? Like, from— Did she climb up?"

"We should let her in."

"Are you crazy?"

Right then Margo slams both her palms on the glass, startling them. Biotch barks at her through the glass psychotically.

"Call 911," KC says.

"She's just a girl," Rose says. "It's not like she's armed, she's practically naked. This is ridiculous."

Rose goes over and yanks open the sliding glass door. Margo does not move. She looks curiously at Rose.

"Hey," Rose says gently, "are you okay? How did you get out here?"

KC comes closer with the camera, and you can finally see Margo's face as the expressions ripple across it: confusion, delight, fear. Finally, she says, "You have big, big tatas," laughs, and then barfs silver paint all over Rose.

MARGO, STILL IN her bikini, is in a bubble bath, and Rose is trying to wash the silver paint off her face in the bathroom sink. (That had been a real problem they'd not anticipated. The silver acrylic paint that Margo barfed through a tube they taped to the side of her face away from the camera was not as easy to wash out as the acrylic paint they remembered from childhood, perhaps because it was house paint, and they were all idiots.) KC is interviewing Margo.

"Where did you come from?"

Margo shrugs and continues playing with the bubbles in the tub, giving herself a pointy, conical bubble beard. Rose is cursing as she tries to wash the silver out of her hair. "What even is this? Is this puke? What did she eat?"

"Look," Margo says, and she pulls out the plug from the bathtub, laughing, delighted by the sound the drain makes as it begins to suck out the water.

"No, you want to leave that in," KC is saying when Margo puts the entire plastic bath plug into her mouth and starts to chew.

WRAPPED IN A towel, Margo is sitting at the breakfast bar.

"Ghost hungry," she says.

"I know," KC says. "I'm making you eggs."

"Ghost hungry," Margo repeats, picks up a pen, and puts it in her mouth.

"No!" KC says.

But Margo is already chewing the pen into pieces. (Margo had put about five uncooked rigatoni in her mouth and that is what she is crunching, but the noise was compellingly plastic-like.) Finally, she swallows. Then she says hopefully, "Tinfoil?"

MARGO IS PASSED out on the couch, piles of crumpled tinfoil around her. KC and Rose are out of frame, talking to the camera. "This is not normal. I don't know what the fuck is going on with this girl. We can't get her to leave."

"We should take her to a hospital, is what we should do," Rose says.

"You were literally the one against calling 911."

"Where do you think she came from?"

"You're asking me if I think she's an alien?"

"I mean, kind of. What else could she really be?"

Margo's eyes slide open in a deeply creepy way, and she opens her mouth and a saxophone solo comes out.

Twitter poll:
Should we keep the smoking-hot alien we found on our balcony: yes or no?
    4,756 people voted yes.

Suzie was excited about this until Margo pointed out that most of Rose's and KC's posts got three or four thousand likes.

"I DON'T KNOW, man," KC said.

She and Rose were over for dinner at Jinx's behest. He was making everyone oyakodon. He was shocked they'd never had it.

"See, guys, it's not as easy to go viral on TikTok as you thought. I think it was just too weird," KC continued. "We should be doing the trends everyone else is doing."

They had begun posting four days ago, and the vomiting silver paint hadn't gone viral, but instead had been almost instantly flagged and taken down. None of the videos had gone viral.

"There is no such thing as too weird," Jinx said. "People just don't get it yet, what it is. It's worth making another week. I don't think you can make a thing too weird for people to fall in love with."

They all felt a little sorry for him. It was part of his old-man-ness, the way he was out of touch and couldn't see that what they'd made was childish and stupid and no one would fall in love with it. But he was at least right about the oyakodon being delicious; Margo would have eaten that every day for the rest of her life, no problem. KC and Rose wound up drinking too much wine and spent the night on the couch, and so the next morning had the festive air of a debauched slumber party. Jinx put on an Asuka match and made everyone oatmeal with nuts and golden raisins stirred into it.

So they didn't find out for several hours that they had gone viral. It was right when KC and Rose were about to leave that Suzie opened TikTok and saw it. It was a clip none of them had really liked where Margo, in Amelia Bedelia–like fashion, plants a light bulb in a pot and covers it with dirt, and KC and Rose keep telling her it's not going to work. Margo just keeps looking intently at the dirt, and suddenly a tiny dancing man appears and the camera zooms in on him and it's Bruno Mars. It had taken Margo forever to figure out how to paste in that GIF of Bruno Mars.

"Okay, okay," Suzie was saying, "this is what I would call baby viral, but you have two hundred fifty thousand views."

"Why did that one get so many views, though?" Margo asked.

"No, because it's like," Suzie began, "TikTok shows it to three hundred people, and then if engagement is high enough, they show it to a thousand people, and so on. So people didn't ever see the other clips, they only saw this one because that first group of three hundred people really liked it."

"Okay," Rose said, "that makes sense."

KC was looking at her phone. "I have ten new fans!"

"Ooh, let me log in and check mine," Rose said. Rose had five new fans. They checked Margo's and she had three. It was not by any means a rousing success. But it was enough to convince them to keep going.

KC's VOICE: "SHE'S claiming the vacuum is sentient."

"Rigoberto," Margo says, nodding and pointing at the Roomba.

"That's a Roomba," Rose says gently.

"No," Margo says. "Friend."

"He's your friend?" Rose asks.

"Jesus fucking Christ," KC says.

ON NEW YEAR'S Day, Margo was shopping at Target, which had become in the months since Bodhi's birth a sort of spiritual home, when Jinx's number flashed on her phone.

She picked up, but the voice was Suzie's: "Okay, do you know Kiki-Pilot?"

"Ummm, no?"

"She's a YouTuber, she got famous streaming *Star Wars: Squadrons*."

"Okay," Margo said, gently swaying from side to side to keep Bodhi asleep.

"Anyway, she picked us up! She did a whole reaction video to the TikTok series from episode one—she watched them all!"

"That's so cool!" Margo said.

"You are not getting it!" Suzie grunted in displeasure, and there were muffled sounds like fabric was being rubbed over the phone and then it was Jinx: "The video already has a million views, and it was only posted two hours ago."

"Holy fucking God," Margo said.

"Come home right now and watch it."

IT TURNED OUT that Kiki was insanely beautiful and hot. Margo felt that plastic surgeons should study Kiki, use calipers to measure her face so they could make other people look more like her.

"Honey," Suzie said, "plastic surgeons are the ones who made Kiki look like that in the first place."

The YouTube video reacting to Hungry Ghost was eight minutes long. In the intro, Kiki said she saw the Bruno Mars clip on TikTok and then watched the whole series. Kiki played through each clip of the series, making commentary throughout. "You see people do skits on TikTok, and I've even seen recurrent themes or characters, but I've never seen anything exactly like this. I want to know what these girls are gonna do next."

By the time they had finished watching it, the video had three million views. As Suzie clicked around to show them more Kiki videos, Margo saw that almost every single one had between twelve and fifteen million views. She'd been nursing Bodhi, and he suddenly detached and used her sweater to pull himself more upright and belched like an old man.

"How much money do YouTubers make?" Margo asked. "Like per view?"

"It depends, but between three thousand and five thousand per million views. So on a video like this one, about sixty grand."

"She's making sixty k on an eight-minute video?" Margo could not process this information.

"This is what she used to look like," Suzie said, and hit play on one of Kiki's earliest videos.

Margo was fascinated. It was so difficult to pinpoint what was different, and yet Kiki looked like an entirely other person. A pretty but normal person. Her eyes were slightly asymmetric and her lips were thinner. Was her chin different somehow? Her hair was certainly much thinner back then. How had she known what parts of herself to change? Margo imagined the view count moving the plastic surgeon's hand like a Ouija board, showing him what Kiki's subscribers wanted.

KC and Rose came in, excited and chattering. Jinx and Suzie had called them right after Margo and told them to come over to celebrate. Jinx put on some music and made red beans and rice and corn bread. They let Bodhi have a tiny pile of the softest corn bread crumbs, and he mashed them around with his little hands and then sucked them off his fingers in ecstasy.

All night, Suzie tracked their TikTok accounts and the girls their

OnlyFans. By ten p.m., all of their TikToks had over a million views. Every single one. The real question was whether this would translate to new fans and at what rate. Links to their individual OnlyFans accounts were in a Linktree on the main HungryGhost TikTok account. It was the big unknown, how many people would even click to follow, let alone click to their OnlyFans and subscribe. So far, KC had more than a hundred new fans, Rose had almost eighty, and Margo stopped telling everyone because she felt so embarrassed. But before she went to bed, Jinx grabbed her in the hallway. "Tell me. You don't have to tell them, just tell me."

Bodhi was already asleep in his crib. Margo had tried to stay up with everyone else, but she was desperate to be alone.

"How many?" Jinx whispered.

"Um, almost four hundred?"

He squeezed her shoulders with his giant hands and folded her into a hug.

"You're gonna be so famous," he said into her hair.

"No, I'm not," she said, out of reflex.

"Darling, I'm afraid that you are very wrong."

JB MESSAGED ME that night. Not about the KikiPilot stuff; he wasn't aware of any of that.

JB: Jelly Ghost, I think I'm getting confused. About what's real and what's not. I think I need to take a break.

I wrote back immediately: Confused about what?

JB: All this started out as a kind of game, like an experiment, but now it's getting confusing. I may need to take a step back. I just wanted to let you know so you would understand you didn't do anything wrong.

I knew on some level that he was saying he was developing real feelings for me, and I knew that should have worried me. Instead, it felt more like an exciting upping of the ante. Maybe it was the leftover excitement from the KikiPilot video, but I didn't want him to take a step back. I wanted to keep going, not because I knew what we were doing or where it was going. It was like I had become addicted to it. There was a purity to our messaging that I found intoxicating. We'd been working our way through grade school, trying to remember everything we could about each year, our teachers and classmates, our lunch boxes and backpacks, the books we read, what we did at recess, our favorite toys. It felt like I could touch the sublime by memorizing all of JB's memories. Wouldn't that be a beautiful human achievement? To learn everything about a person you would never meet?

I wrote: The thing is, writing these messages with you has become the most interesting thing I get to do.

JB: Yes, that's the same problem I'm having.
HungryGhost: So why is that a problem again?
JB: Aside from the staggering financial impact, I just feel weird. I don't even know your name.

"Staggering financial impact" was worrying. He had always acted like the money was nothing. I wrote: I mean, I have one. Does it really matter what it is?

JB: It doesn't matter what it is, only that I don't know it? Maybe?

I lay in bed, listening to Bodhi's sleeping breath in the dark. Did I really believe JB would use my name to hunt me down and kill me? It was hard to imagine, given everything I knew about him now, and yet he could be lying to me the same way I'd been lying to him, or twisting things so they didn't sound as bad. Don't be an idiot, I thought. Don't be stupid.

My name is Suzie, I wrote, and the moment I pressed send I knew I had made a huge mistake. I had lied to JB plenty, and honestly, I had never felt that bad about it. But this time I felt like I'd played the wrong chord on a piano, the shame was that immediate and ringing. He'd been asking for something real from me, and I hadn't even lied *well*. If I thought a first name was enough for him to hunt and kill someone, which I obviously did not, I had just given him my *roommate's name*.

Suzie is a beautiful name, he wrote.

I was going to throw up. Don't pay me anymore, I wrote on impulse.

JB: What?
HungryGhost: It's too much money.

It really was an absurd amount of money. He'd paid me almost four grand in the last month. It also felt like he was saying he felt stupid for valuing what we were doing together, and I didn't want him to feel stupid. I valued it too. And I could have shown him that by telling him my real name, and I hadn't. This was another way I could show him.

He didn't write back right away, and I didn't know what was happening.

HungryGhost: JB?
JB: I'm embarrassed. Not paying, or at least not paying so much, would be a huge relief. I was kind of digging myself into a hole. But I also loved sending you the money! Like sending you a tip and watching it go through was this thrill, and I liked feeling like a rich guy, but I knew it was totally out of control.

You idiot, I wrote, though I was grinning.

JB: See, before you didn't know I was an idiot!
HungryGhost: I like it better that you're an idiot.
JB: Thank you, Suzie.

And I tried not to feel sick hearing him call me that. Because I knew there was no way I could ever tell JB the whole truth. If I told him I was a college dropout with a baby and no real career prospects, all this would evaporate. This was the kind of spell that worked only at a distance. All I could do was try to enjoy it while it lasted.

CHAPTER SIXTEEN

Margo had assumed Becca was coming home from NYU for the holidays, so when she didn't hear from her at Christmas or New Year's, she inwardly felt snubbed, though she tried not to dwell on it. But three days after KikiPilot, and two days before Margo was supposed to leave for Vegas, Becca randomly knocked on their door. The timing was so weird; Margo thought maybe Becca had come *because* of the KikiPilot video, but that turned out not to be the case.

After the flurry of hugs and the admiring of Bodhi, whom Jinx then graciously, wordlessly took from Margo, Becca and Margo found themselves alone at the dining table drinking tea Jinx had made that smelled strongly of hay. Becca looked exactly the same. She was wearing knee-high black leather boots that looked ridiculous in a California January and a kind of artsy black velvet blazer. Her face (that of a chubby Reba McEntire) was the same too; even the zits on her chin were in a familiar constellation. She smelled the same, though Margo could never have named the smell. It evoked cloves and the interior of cars, the sweetish acrylic odor of Halloween costumes.

One look and Margo loved her again, and she could see that Becca loved her too. They were helpless to stop themselves, even if they both would have liked to hold on to their hurt a little longer. "Dude, you're a mom!" Becca said. "I don't think it was real to me until I met him. Like real-real. And your dad is here! I did not see that one coming."

"I know, right? It's all very weird." Margo realized as she took a sip of her tea that she would have to make a conscious choice to either tell Becca or not tell Becca about her OnlyFans. On the one hand, Margo felt honor bound to start telling the truth. And if Becca didn't know about the KikiPilot video, part of Margo was proud and wanted to tell her. But Margo also dreaded having to navigate whatever bullshit reaction Becca might have.

"But is it okay? Being a mom? You seem okay." Becca reached out and grabbed Margo's forearm, squeezed the meat around the bone.

Margo tried to figure out how to answer this question. "I think I'm okay? In some ways, I'm totally overwhelmed, but in others I think I may be doing better than I ever have?"

Becca smiled. "No, I can tell just from looking at you."

"What about you?" Margo asked.

"I'm . . . okay," Becca said, laughing nervously. "School is a little yucky, not gonna lie. I didn't get cast in any of the shows, which, like, last year I was a freshman, so I didn't expect to be, but I guess I was hoping as a sophomore? And it's fine. It's a change, though, to go from being cast in every show because you're a senior to suddenly you don't even get to act anymore when that's the whole thing you came there to do."

Margo nodded. She had not realized Becca was that serious about acting. She'd acted in high school, but Margo thought that was purely for the social scene.

They talked on this way for almost an hour until their barnyardal tea was cold, and gradually Margo got the picture of Becca's life in the city: hookups with a guy studying jazz saxophone where she got her feelings hurt, doing blow with a girl she didn't like very much in the East Village, spending half her food money on vapes and alcohol and making up for it by eating nothing but on-sale vegetarian hot dogs on Wonder bread. The grades she'd gotten weren't as good as she'd hoped. Some of her classes were easy, some of them were hard, and sometimes her professors were kind of mean. Or rather, they did not see Becca or care about her or feel any kind of native sympathy for her.

"I don't know why I'm crying," Becca said. "I'm not sad! What time is it? I didn't even mean to talk this much. I came here, actually, because Angie Milano is having a party at her parents' house. Wanna go?"

"Oh," Margo said, taken aback. "Gosh, no!"

"Seriously?" Becca asked. "Too good for your old high school friends?"

Margo didn't know what to say. But yes, the idea of spending time in Angie Milano's parents' darkened living room making small talk with people she went to high school with sounded terrible.

"Sebastian will be there," Becca sang, trying to tempt her.

Margo still felt some tenderness toward Sebastian. But seeing him was the last thing she wanted. She felt so far away from who she'd been and with no easy way to explain who she was now. Jinx appeared with Bodhi. "He's getting fussy, would you mind nursing him?"

Margo took him and whipped out a boob without thinking about it.

"Oh, wow," Becca said. "You're not gonna go in another room?"

Margo stared at her.

"No, it's fine!" Becca said. "Sorry, I was just surprised."

Without a word, Jinx tossed Margo a swaddling blanket to use as a cover-up. She draped it over Bodhi as he nursed, though of course he continually tried to claw it off. Who wants to eat while being smothered by a blanket? It occurred to her that Becca had not asked a single question about Margo's life. She didn't have to lie about OnlyFans because Becca hadn't even asked what she was doing for work.

"Come on, I know you wanna go," Becca said. "And if it's boring, we can ditch out."

"I don't want to leave Bodhi," Margo said. "And I don't know, the idea of drinking, like, Smirnoff Ice and asking people about college, ugh." Margo actually shuddered.

"What, like college is so terrible to hear about?" Becca asked, clearly offended now. All the warmth between them evaporated so quickly, Margo could still sense it as a vapor in the air.

"I just feel like, you know, I'm on a different track now."

"Why, because you're a mom?"

"Well, yeah." Margo shrugged.

"You think you're so fucking special," Becca said with a venom that surprised Margo.

"Becca," Margo said, exasperated. "It's not about being special, it's literally that it's painful for me to hear about college. Do you think I didn't want to go to NYU? Do you think I wasn't jealous?"

"You didn't even apply!"

"Because I couldn't afford it!"

"You could have gotten financial aid. You chose not to go. I begged you to apply with me," Becca said.

"What I could have gotten was thousands of dollars in debt with no way to repay it. How would I have even gotten to New York? You think Shyanne would buy me a plane ticket? I mean, honestly, Becca, do you not know? Like after all this time, do you not know?" Margo was aware of Jinx listening in the living room. She didn't care.

"Know what?" Becca snorted.

"Your parents are rich. That's the difference. That's why you went to NYU, and I didn't."

"The reason you didn't go to NYU," Becca said, "is because you were too chickenshit to go to a big city where you might not be the big fish in the little pond anymore. You wanted to stay where you could pretend you were better than everyone. Like, 'Oh, my professor is in love with me, oh, he thinks I'm so special! I'm gonna have his baby!' You think he picked you because you were special? He picked you because he knew you had fucking daddy issues!"

"Hello," Jinx said, "excuse me." He was standing by the table and smiling. "Please leave."

"Are you kicking me out?" Becca asked.

"Dad," Margo said.

His eyes flicked to her, obedient and detached.

"It's okay," Margo said.

Jinx shrugged slightly and walked away, down the hall. They heard the sound of his bedroom door closing.

"I think you should probably go," Margo said softly.

"Just so you know," Becca said, "getting knocked up by your professor and living with your pro wrestler dad is fucking trashy. Like, everyone is grossed out. They all talk about it, and I'm like, 'I don't know what's going on with her.' Lenin Gabbard said he saw you on OnlyFans, and I had to spend, like, twenty minutes telling him he had to be mistaken."

Margo froze. Bodhi was asleep in her lap now, her nipple still clamped in his mouth. She couldn't breathe, it was like her lungs were stuck in the fully open position.

"Oh my God, it's fucking true," Becca said. "Are you serious right now?"

"Please leave," Margo whispered.

"I didn't believe it. Like, everyone knows your mom was a slut, but you? I thought, Margo would never, she's only ever slept with, like, two guys!"

Jinx moved across the room so quickly, Margo barely registered him before he took Becca by both shoulders and steered her, gently but authoritatively, almost like she was a moving dolly, toward the apartment door, saying in that low, calm voice, "And you'll be leaving now." He opened the door, shoved her through, closed it softly behind her, and snapped the locks shut. They could both hear Becca's voice in the hallway, tiny, saying, "Unbelievable. Fucking unbelievable."

They listened to her boots as she stomped down the echoey stairs.

Margo was shaking. She pulled her nipple out of Bodhi's mouth and tucked her boob back in her bra, which was a relief. There had been something especially yucky about having her boob out during all that.

"I feel," Jinx said, sitting down with her at the table, "as though maybe ice cream is in order."

"Large quantities," Margo said. "Disgusting amounts."

They laughed and then a silence fell, tender and swollen. "I felt so ashamed," Jinx said, "when you were talking about college—"

"It's fine—"

"The truth is, I don't think I could afford full-time tuition at NYU."

"Oh, I know," Margo said. She knew this was not because he didn't have the money, but because the money was already being spent on full-time tuition at Barnard, and weddings, and on things for his real kids.

"But a plane ticket, or help moving, or a few thousand here or there, you can always ask me for those things."

Margo was going to cry if he kept talking, both because it was too nice and because it was still not enough.

EVER SINCE THE KikiPilot video, Margo's phone was constantly vibrating with notifications, so it took her a while to notice that this time all the notifications were coming from Facebook, her personal account, which was weird because she hardly ever went on there.

She was cuddled up with Jinx on the couch, stuffed full of ice cream, watching old WCW matches. She clicked, only mildly curious.

An account named SlutSleuth had posted ten screenshots of her OnlyFans content, the naughty parts blurred, on her Facebook wall. Some of them already had more than fifty comments, and they'd been up for only an hour. She scrolled through, reading bits and pieces of the comments in her panic. Mostly they were shocked emoji, or embarrassed emoji, or exclamation points, or jokes about how this must be why she dropped out of college. Or: I guess now we know how she wound up pregnant! She deleted the posts from her wall as fast as she could, though she knew the damage was done. She had seen Shyanne's name in the comments. She had written, I have never been more ashamed than on this day. Kenny had liked the comment.

"Oh God," she gasped. She left Facebook and opened her Instagram. In her personal account, SlutSleuth had tagged her in the same screen captures. Even worse, they had found her HungryGhost account and under her latest post left a comment: @MargoMillet, this you? Now all her HungryGhost Instagram followers had a direct link to her personal account. She deleted the comment.

"You okay?" Jinx had paused the match and was looking at her.

Was she okay? She was sitting on a couch, safe, with her dad and her baby. But also, maybe her life was ruined? Or ruined more than it already was?

"Tell me," he said, and she handed him her phone.

MARGO WASN'T SURE she could have gotten through that night without Jinx. He was instantly pragmatic. He told her to delete her personal accounts on both Facebook and Instagram so that SlutSleuth couldn't repost. "Who do you think did this?"

"My guess," Margo said, "is that Becca went to that party, and they all got drunk and did it together."

"Makes sense," Jinx said, and she was relieved he didn't seem to have plans to put on his leather jacket and head on over there.

They went into Margo's HungryGhost Instagram and blocked every single person Margo could even remember from high school, as well as the SlutSleuth account.

"Do you want to close down the HungryGhost account too?" Jinx asked.

She didn't. She really didn't. Since the KikiPilot video she had almost thirty thousand followers on Instagram, and it was frankly addictive. Earlier she'd posted a picture of a dang smoothie and it got six hundred likes. Plus, money and blah blah blah.

"I mean, my hope," Margo said, "is that they did this drunk, and in the morning, they're gonna feel a little gross about it and probably not do it again."

Jinx thought about it. "That's possible," he said. "The main thing I worry about is if they post in the comments of your OnlyFans account. That's what you don't want, them posting your real name and address where those guys who want to melt you in acid can find it."

Margo had not even thought of this and logged in to her OnlyFans with her heart pounding. There wasn't anything yet, everything looked normal. Or as normal as it ever was. Since the TikToks took off, the comments and messages had gotten a lot more fun. I want you to take me to your planet and feed me shards of metal and plastic. Another one said, Would you consider a threesome with me and Rigoberto?

"Jesus," Margo said, suddenly realizing. "The custody thing! If they didn't know about the OnlyFans before, they certainly do now."

"Oh man," Jinx said. "Well, I mean, does he follow you?"

"I blocked him way back when."

"So there's a chance he didn't see," Jinx said.

"Fuck, this is so fucked," Margo said.

"Who did that girl say it was? Who saw you on OnlyFans?" Jinx asked.

"Oh, Lenin Gabbard."

"If he's one of your fans, block him."

"I guess I'll look, but most of them don't use pictures or real names."

Around midnight, she got a text from Shyanne.

I have never been more ashamed in my life. Please don't come to Vegas. I don't think I can stand to even look at you. Kenny saw those pictures. I had to look him in the eye and say yep that's my daughter. And that I had known you were doing it and hadn't told him, and I told him you promised you stopped and that you lied to me, but he was furious and now he is sleeping in the rec room and I will never forgive you for this, Margo. I never will.

Margo peered at her phone, dazed. "What is it?" Jinx said.

"Nothing," she said. She didn't want to talk about Shyanne with Jinx. She also did not want to examine why, for some reason, her main emotional response to this text was relief at not having to go to Vegas.

"Try to sleep," Jinx said. "You can find Lenin Gabbard in the morning."

Margo nodded in the darkened living room, lit only by her laptop and phone screen. "I will," she said.

But she didn't. She stayed up until three looking through her fans, trying to find him, as though finding him and blocking him would make her safe again. Except she had no idea which account was his and eventually she gave up and fell asleep, dizzy and screen blind.

THE NEXT MORNING, Margo called Rose to tell her she'd been doxxed.

"What a shitty thing, sweetie. I'm so sorry."

"It's okay. I mean, I'm okay. It's weird, though. It feels unsafe to have so many people mad at me. I don't know how trolls do it. Or heels in wrestling—like, what is it like to have a whole stadium of people boo-ing you?" She didn't mention that her mother was one of those people, or that she'd been disinvited from the wedding, or that Mark was suing for custody, or that Kenny had slept in the rec room, or that the Virgin Mary had been raped.

"There's a kind of freedom in that, I bet," Rose said.

"How so?"

"Like how comedians have to bomb. If you don't learn how to bomb, then the audience has you on such a tight leash, you're stuck saying only the things you think they'll like."

Margo was frozen looking out her window, her phone pressed to her head. She had not associated freedom with being hated before. It made perfect sense.

"I'm sorry, what did you just say?" Margo asked when she realized Rose was still talking.

"I asked if you wanted to take down the Hungry Ghost TikToks," Rose said.

"No," Margo said.

"You want to keep going?"

"I do," Margo said. "Like, more than ever. I edited everything we shot on Monday and put it in your Dropbox. Take a look when you have a second."

AFTER CHRISTMAS AND New Year's, true to his word, Jinx made an appointment with a custody lawyer. Michael T. Ward, Esquire, was dark haired, clean-shaven, and fat in a way that suggested he'd played high school football. He used a lot of spiky gel in his hair even though he was in his forties at least, and he smelled strongly of cologne. I was prepared to dislike him, but then he offered us Nutri-Grain bars in the best flavor, strawberry. They were in a little wicker basket on his desk, and all three of us took one like they were cigars. I fed Bodhi tiny pinches from my fingers.

"So why don't you give me the general situation," he said, waving his hand around. He was tilted back in his desk chair. I oddly felt I could tell this man anything. As I told the story, I handed over the relevant documents: the NDA, Bodhi's birth certificate, the restraining order against Jinx, the paternity papers I'd been served.

"Can he even do that, request full custody?" I asked.

Ward scoffed, a small crumb of Nutri-Grain bar flying. "I mean, he can try, but he's not gonna get it. California courts prefer fifty-fifty custody both legal and physical."

I crumpled my wrapper into a sweaty ball in my fist. "I don't understand—like, it's my baby, he didn't want anything to do with him. How does he suddenly have a right to any custody at all?"

"Well, he's the child's father. I mean, that's another thing—is there any chance he isn't?"

"No," I admitted. "But can't we use the NDA as proof that he didn't want Bodhi? That he gave up his parental rights? I mean, can I even respond without violating the NDA and jeopardizing Bodhi's trust?"

Ward shrugged. "I mean, this NDA is so broad it's practically unenforceable anyway, but no, it can't be used to claim Mark gave up his parental rights. You can be disinterested for fifteen years and suddenly decide you want a relationship with your child, and the State of California recognizes your right to that relationship. But tell me more: what do you do for work, what does he do for work, what's the grandma's angle, give me everything you've got."

I explained the OnlyFans and the doxxing but clarified that Mark's family might not know about it because I'd blocked him on social media.

Ward fiddled with his ear, squinting. "Yeah, I don't know. That's a tough one."

"But hopefully they didn't see it," I repeated.

"I don't think you should hide it," Ward said.

"Even if they didn't see it?" Jinx pressed.

"Maybe they saw it, maybe they didn't," Ward said, "but if you hide it, she looks unemployed—also bad, possibly worse. California law is really explicit about finding custody arrangements that are in the best interest of the child, and it's better to eat and have a mom selling nudes than not eat. Selling nudes isn't illegal. I don't think it's going to be a problem. I mean, is there drug use?"

"No!" Jinx and I said at once.

"Then I think it's better to be forthright. I mean, the courts deal with it all the time: Mom strips, Mom does cam work. This is more of the same. If it's just that and only that, no judge is going to refuse you partial custody. It's a job."

"But what about full custody?" I asked.

Ward sighed. "I mean, there's nothing you told me so far that would cause a judge to deny Dad fifty-fifty custody. Maybe you could get a temporary order while he's still so little. Does he nurse?"

I nodded.

"I have to warn you, though, the courts frown on one parent trying to prevent the other from having a relationship with the kid. It's a big red flag." I must have looked upset, because he said, "And hey, I know it feels unfair, but wouldn't Bodhi be better off knowing his dad? I mean, if his dad wants to be part of his life? Dad's not abusive or anything, right?"

"No," I said. I did not know how to explain that Mark was simply a gross person, the kind of man who fucked his student, the kind of man who slept with his wife's sister on their wedding night.

"I mean, it's his kid too," Ward said, licking the sweat off his upper lip.

Was Bodhi Mark's kid too? Mark had not risked his life to bring him into the world, literally split himself open and been stitched back together. Mark had not stayed up nights nursing, lying in bed, tiny pinching hands kneading sore breasts. Mark had not been puked on, had not, once, miraculously caught spit-up midair with a burp cloth. Mark had not trimmed Bodhi's nails or given him a bath or kissed his tiny feet or made him laugh. How on earth could Bodhi be his?

Jinx and Ward were going through Jinx's phone call to Mark and exactly what threats were made, exactly what wording used. I couldn't make myself listen or care.

"So basically," Ward said, "you have to respond within thirty days using Form 220, and you have two options." Ward flipped a paper toward us and pointed with his finger. "You can propose a custody split to counter his request for full custody—maybe he agrees, maybe not. The next option: you can request mediation, which means you both meet with a court-appointed mediator and try to hash it out. If you come to an agreement, great. If you can't agree, that's when it would go to court."

"The thing is," Jinx said, "we don't think he's serious. This is a guy with a wife and kids. You can't tell me this is what his wife wants."

"And that may be," Ward said. "But in my experience people don't go to the trouble of filing for custody unless they want custody."

Jinx was nodding, thoughtful.

"I mean, one positive thing is, hey, at least he'll be paying child support!" Ward said. His eyes were a weirdly bright blue, like the ocean on a classroom globe. "Can't establish paternity without signing up for child support!"

I didn't know how to explain that Mark's money was newly useless to me.

"So you can settle this through forms, don't need me for that," Ward continued. "Or you can go to mediation. In that case, you would probably want to retain me so I can give you advice and help you prepare for mediation. I wouldn't be present in the room, though, it would just be you and Dad. Right? Mediation can drag on for months, all sorts of things can go into it, and there's things you can do to stack the deck in your favor."

"Like what?" I asked.

"Like you can order a deposition. That means I get to sit down with Dad and a court stenographer and ask him as many questions as I want. Doesn't even have to be related to the case. And if he lies, it's perjury. I mean, it's a little pricey, but I'd recommend it one hundred percent."

"So what does the money side of all this look like?" Jinx asked. He was so good at this.

"Right," Ward said, and launched into his fee structure and how much a deposition would be ($2k) and how much a trial might be (upward of $40k). It had not occurred to me the price could be that high. I knew lawyers were expensive; I just hadn't imagined my entire bank account being emptied. One thing I knew: Mark's pockets were deep. And if his intention was to hurt me, he could drag this out long enough to bankrupt me. I might wind up needing that child support after all.

"What do you think, honey?" Jinx asked.

I shrugged again. Was this guy a good lawyer? He seemed no more ridiculous than good old Larry. Maybe all lawyers were like this?

"Hey," Ward said, and I looked up into his eyes. "This is the absolute hardest, scariest thing you'll ever do."

Fuck, he was gonna make me cry.

"It's your kid. You know? It's the greatest pain and the greatest love you've ever known. This is a bad situation where the other party seems to perhaps have malicious intent. If you feel overwhelmed, if you feel emotional, that's only natural. My job, should you decide to retain me, is to be the one person in this who's completely on your side. And that means telling you the truth, leveling with you, giving you the power to understand what's going on. So I'm not just gonna tell you what you want to hear. Unless something powerful comes out in that deposition, there's very little chance you come out of this with full custody and no visitation. Your one advantage here is that Bodhi is still very young, you are breastfeeding; judges would be sympathetic to you retaining physical custody on a temporary basis."

One of Jinx's hands landed on my back. Ward leaned over his desk, holding a box of tissues out to me. I took one and blew my nose.

"It's gonna be all right," Jinx said.

"It will. It really will, sweetheart," Ward said. "You want a donut? I think there's donuts in the conference room."

Ward went to get me a donut, and Jinx raised his eyebrows, silently asking what I wanted to do.

I hesitated, then nodded. The donut had clinched it. Ward was hired.

CHAPTER SEVENTEEN

In Mark's course on narrative, I spoke during exactly one class period. It was the week we read Gogol's "The Nose."

"What exactly does this story have to do with narrative perspective?" Derek asked. "Isn't it third-person omniscient?"

"That's a good question," Mark said. "What do you think?"

Mark had gestured to the class as a whole, but Derek responded as though Mark were talking only to him. "I just told you—it's third person about some guy whose nose runs away."

Mark nodded, as if conceding this was true. He was much more patient than I would have been. "Let me ask you," he said, "when Gogol describes the nose walking around Saint Petersburg, what did you picture? Was it still nose-sized, scurrying around like a mouse? Was it the size of a person? How exactly was it capable of wearing an officer's uniform?"

"I pictured a giant nose with legs," a girl named Brittany said.

There were some murmurs of assent, people who pictured a giant nose; others had pictured a man who just *was* the nose while looking like a normal man, and some had pictured a man's body with a giant nose for a head. Everyone had pictured the nose a different way, but no matter how they pictured it, Mark pointed out a place in the text that contradicted what they had imagined. If the nose was big, how could it be baked into a loaf of bread? If the nose was small, how could it wear an officer's uniform or exit a tram car?

"The point here," Mark said, "is that it is possible to form sentences that make sense syntactically but still don't make meaning. Words can be made hollow, and once they are hollow, anything can be done with them."

"I still don't understand," Derek said. "How is this related to point of view?"

"That's because you didn't read to the end," I said, not even aware I was speaking out loud.

Mark barked out a laugh, then covered his mouth with his fist, his happy eyes watching, excited to see what would come next.

"I read to the end," Derek said uncertainly.

"Then you are aware that the story is actually in first person?"

"Wait, what?"

"At the end, the narrator begins addressing the reader in first person, about how he doesn't even understand the story he's been telling, which you know can't be true or else why would he be telling it?"

"I'm not sure that negates my point, though," Derek said. "I mean, it was in third person for most of the story."

Really, he was remarkable. Mark looked at me and grinned, hopeful perhaps that I would tear Derek apart. Personally, I wasn't sure it was worth my time.

"Well," I said, "you have to think outside the box when you're confronted with this kind of perfect storm of a can of worms."

Mark laughed so hard and loud it made Derek jump a little.

"But you have to keep in mind," I said, "what comes around goes around and you can take it or leave it, but every rose has its thorn."

"Uh . . . okay?" Derek said.

Mark was still losing it, giggling in a girlish way, his face covered with both hands.

"Really," the boy next to me said, catching on to the joke, "I think this is a case of the pot calling the kettle black."

"What is going on?!" Derek whined, aware we were making fun of him even if he still didn't get the joke. His instincts were so bizarre. I could only guess he was the youngest of a group of siblings.

It went on that way for a bit longer, with people telling Derek to buck up, that he could cross that bridge when he came to it. Later, when Mark and I started sleeping together, we would speak nonsense to each other as a weird kind of love language. "The ace up my sleeve keeps adding insult to injury," he would say. "You air your dirty laundry against all odds," I would reply.

It felt like that, the custody battle. Like all the words had stopped being attached to anything. We were reduced to "Petitioner" and "Respondent." And maybe Mark would be able to stack up his meaningless words higher than mine, even though I was the only one who loved Bodhi. But there were no words on any of these forms for love. Nowhere did it ask you how the baby's head smelled or whether you would be willing to die for the baby.

When we retained Ward, we decided to move forward with mediation. I was hoping the courts would be so backed up we wouldn't get an appointment for months, but our appointment was only two weeks away. And so each day was converted from normal life into a countdown to unthinkable loss.

Meanwhile, there was still more work than I could possibly do, and for hours and hours each day I was looking at pictures of dicks and writing things like, Whoa! That is a Bulbasaur that would leave any lady sore! Each penis was so isolated, the only thing in the frame, and they seemed like a series of blind, hairless, oddly defiant little critters. Would it be so different if these men were sending me pictures of their noses? Close-ups of oily pores, isolated little snouts. It felt that strange and dislocated.

I saw my mother's wedding as a series of Facebook posts. Her account was totally public, so I could view them from my HungryGhost account even though I'd deleted my personal one. She wore the Diane von Furstenberg. I had written her right after the doxxing saying I was sorry, sorry for lying to her and sorry for making trouble with Kenny. When she didn't respond, I was a little relieved.

For comfort I wrote JB a three-page email about when I'd thrown up shrimp at the eighth-grade dance because I didn't know you weren't supposed to eat the tails. Once it was sent, I reread it two times to luxuriate in imagining him reading it, lingering on the places I hoped he would laugh.

Then I watched videos of people jumping out of planes in wing suits, their tiny forms gliding over fantastic landscapes. There was something about the wrongness of it I found soothing, the fact that they'd snuck out of the world and gotten into a place they were never supposed to be: the sky. It was like if a period had climbed off its sentence and begun flying over the page.

THIS IS DEFINITELY one of those sections I will have to tell in third person:

Margo was eating Crunch Berries in the dark when her phone rang. Jinx had relented about the healthy cereal only out of pity for her and guilt over threatening Mark. It was midnight.

"Hello?" she said, though she knew who it was. She had given JB her number as soon as she got his message. He had written:

So you're from California and you don't have a brother named
Timmy and your mom is named Shyanne and you have a baby?
On Instagram, someone said, '@MargoMillet, this you?' and I
clicked, and sure enough, it was you! Margo. Such a mango of a
name! Why would you call yourself Suzie of all things? It doesn't
suit you. Jesus. Margo, why am I so gut punched? I'm not even
mad, I just feel like an idiot. Like, of course you were lying. I was
stupid to think that you weren't. I was paying a girl to pretend to
fall in love with me, and I got confused and fell in love instead. I'm
an idiot.

She had written back without thinking: You are not an idiot.

Then she had given him her number and told him to call her right then. "Hey, it's JB." His voice was lower, more raspy than she would have guessed.

"Hey," she said. "Are you okay?"

He gave a brittle laugh. "Not really."

She wasn't sure if he sounded drunk or like he'd been crying.

"I'm so sorry," she said.

"No," he said. "Fantasy production is your whole job. Like, it's what you are paid to do. You didn't do anything wrong. I was the one who got lost in it."

"I think I got lost in it too, though."

"Don't say that," he said, his tone suddenly sharp. "I can't— Like, don't try to make me feel better. It makes it worse. Because I can't tell what's real. I need to wake up from it, you know?"

Margo hesitated. She didn't want to throw it all away simply because it wasn't true. That would be a waste. "JB, the big parts were
a lie, but you should know the little parts were true. Like I really did
throw up shrimp at the eighth-grade dance. And I loved writing those
messages, none of that was fake. I need you to know that."

He sighed and his breath was ragged. She could tell he was moving,
pacing around his house.

"You have a fucking kid, Margo! Like sure, the little things were
true, I can see that, but having a kid is a pretty big thing to lie about!"

"I know," she said, and slumped back in the hard wooden dining
chair. Because it was the biggest thing, a thing so magnificent and
huge and altering she wasn't even sure how it could be truly commu-
nicated to someone who had never experienced it. And he was a young
guy. Kids weren't even on his radar yet.

"Look, Margo, I don't have any idea who you are now. You know
every single little thing about me, and I don't know anything about
you."

"Listen, JB, obviously this is not how I wanted you to find out. But
you have to look at it from my side. When you first wrote to me, like, if
you could even see my inbox you would understand. Right next to your
message is, like, guys telling me they are going to use a cheese grater on
my vagina. Lying was a self-protective thing, like, it would have been
reckless for me to spill my guts to you."

"I get that," he said. "But there have been so many points since the
beginning! You could have said, 'Hey, I lied to you, and I want to tell
you the truth now.'"

"I know, and I wanted to!"

"Even when I asked you for your name, you lied," he said. "So you
can't go and say now, oh but really it was real. That's bullshit. Right?
You can't have it both ways."

"Listen," she said, struggling to regain control, "you're a client. You
are the coolest, funniest, most interesting client I have. But you're a
client—and—"

"Exactly," JB said. "Thank you for finally being honest."

"JB," Margo said, closing her eyes again, like she could find him there in the dark. Everything was getting all twisted around. "I mean, I have to prioritize my safety, I have to—JB?"

But there was only silence, not even the hum of connection: flat, dead silence. He was gone.

It was almost shocking, how difficult it was to keep going after that phone call. Margo had been unaware that JB had been so central to her happiness. After all, sometimes she'd look at their situation and think they were strangers playing a game, a kind of online poker of the heart, her lies no more morally problematic than a bluff in cards. Other times, she'd look at their relationship and think it was too real, that what they were doing was bigger and deeper and stranger than real.

"All things that are genuinely interesting aren't quite real," Mark had said. It was almost frustrating, really, how right that stupid little man had been about so many things. And now whatever was between her and JB, real or unreal, was over. It felt like a portent. Like this was the beginning of things going horribly wrong.

I left Bodhi at home with Jinx for that week's shoot at KC and Rose's place. Bodhi had a Gymboree class, and Jinx agreed to take him. Gymboree was a brightly lit space padded with blue tumbling mats where women were paid to sing songs to babies and blow bubbles on them to . . . encourage them to crawl? I wasn't certain, but it made me feel like an extremely good mother whenever I took him there. Suzie called in sick to work so she could come with me as camerawoman. That was one thing I had not appreciated or understood about Suzie before all of this. The girl was always aggressively down.

On the way to Huntington Beach we stopped for beef jerky and blue Slurpees. Suzie had her bare feet up on the dash as we listened to J Dilla beats, stuttering and doubled as our hearts. We were wearing sunglasses. I had been doxxed and lost both my mother and the client who made up a staggering proportion of my income, but I was also twenty years old, going seventy miles an hour on the freeway, hopped up on sugar and preserved meat, about to shoot TikToks that would hopefully make me thousands and thousands of dollars.

"Thanks for calling in sick again," I said.

"About that," Suzie said, "I've been fired."

"Oh shit, Suzie! I'm so sorry!"

"I was just wondering, like"—Suzie hesitated, clearly nervous—"if I could be paid for the hours I work on the TikToks? Or the hours I take care of Bodhi?"

"Of course," I rushed to say. It suddenly seemed obscene that I hadn't already been paying her. How had I not noticed that Suzie was working almost as many hours as me and making nothing for it while I made thousands of dollars? "We'll figure it out, like I don't know what's fair, an hourly or some kind of percentage, but we'll talk to Jinx when we get back."

Suzie was visibly elated and that felt good. She rolled down her window, and I turned up the music, glad I wouldn't have to talk, because while I felt it was the right thing to do, I was getting awfully comfortable making financial commitments I was in no way sure I could honor. The four hundred new fans I'd gotten from the KikiPilot video were a huge boon, but that was still only five grand, and it hadn't even cleared my bank account yet. I'd paid Ward's $10k retainer, and who knew how much more I'd have to pay if it went to court. I had more money than I'd ever had in my life, yet somehow it never seemed to be enough. Still, I would make sure I had a way to pay Suzie. I would figure it out. We would shoot new TikToks and take advantage of the momentum we'd already built.

When we arrived at KC and Rose's, there was a dude there just chilling on their couch, Biotch curled like a hairy shrimp in his lap. He was an extremely tall and pasty white boy who, when he smiled, revealed a huge gold grille. "This is Steve," KC said, before flopping back down on the couch, scooting her head in his lap next to Biotch.

"What it do?" Steve said, holding up a fist.

I reluctantly gave him knucks. "Are we not shooting today?"

"Were we shooting today?" KC asked. "Dude, I'm so out of it. We did mushrooms, like, all night, I don't know if I can handle it."

"This is the day," I said. "Jinx is watching Bodhi, like, this is the day."

Steve looked up at me and smiled again. "Baby girl needs a nap, you feel me?" He was wearing a Dodgers hat and a thick gold chain with a dangling gold pendant of a marijuana leaf. I went into the kitchen to find Rose, Suzie trailing behind me.

"What is the deal with Snoop Dork out there?" I asked, pitching my voice low. Rose had just put coffee on, and the pot gurgled and hissed.

"Ugh, I know," Rose said. "They're driving me crazy. They have sex, like, eight times a day, it's disgusting."

"Are we still gonna shoot?" Suzie asked.

"We have to shoot something!" I said. We literally had no new content to post.

"Could we shoot stuff just you and me?" Rose asked.

"I mean, I wrote it for the three of us!" I sat down at their kitchen table and tried to think if I could rewrite some of the skits so they didn't involve KC. It was difficult to imagine. Rose's character was great as a counterpoint to KC, but KC was the one generating a lot of the conflict. I hadn't written a single script that was me and Rose, and I was realizing there might be a reason for that.

Rose sat at the table and set down massive pink mugs for all of us. She gestured for Suzie to sit.

"Now, don't take this the wrong way," Rose said, "but I just wonder if this isn't a blessing in disguise—like maybe it will give us a chance to think of some new ideas! When we got the scripts for this week, they were kind of blah, you know?"

"Blah?"

"Like, every single one was something we've done before in a way. Like Ghost eats something bad, KC and Rose are exasperated, they try to teach her something human, it goes comically wrong." She pulled her fingers like a rake through her long platinum hair. "I think we need something fresh, something new."

I do not know how to explain this or justify it or make myself seem like less of a baby, but when she said this, I started crying.

"I'm sorry!" I said, covering my face with my hands.

"Sweetheart, this is not a criticism of you!" Rose said.

"I know," I said, my face still hidden in my hands. No matter how hard I tried, I could not get my chin to stop shaking.

"We don't expect you to be some TikTok genius who never gets it wrong!"

"I know," I said, and gulped. But I had wanted to be a TikTok genius more than anything.

"We'll all try to think of ideas," Rose said. "It shouldn't have to be you all the time."

"I've gotta go pee," I said, standing before she could say anything more, scurrying down the hall and locking myself in their bathroom.

There was a used condom floating in the toilet. I put the lid down and sat anyway. They didn't want me to even write the TikToks anymore. I couldn't breathe. They had all known. Even fucking Snoop Dork had probably read that script and said, "Yo, these TikToks are kinda whack!"

Everyone had always known, could see that there was something about me that wasn't worth investing in. The way they could so easily throw me away. Mark, Becca, my old boss Tessa. My own mother, who must have once loved me as much as I loved Bodhi—a few naked photos and I was out of her life. And why shouldn't I be? I was a liar and a whore. I'd alienated literally everyone in my life except my ex-addict pro wrestler dad, who was like, "Attagirl, keep selling those nudes!"

And JB. Precious, neurotic, Rocky Road–loving JB in his pearl necklace with his wild mane of dark hair and clerk-befriending mother. "You can't have it both ways," he'd said. But both ways was sometimes the truth, wasn't it? I couldn't tell if I was trying to keep lying to him or to myself. Either way, I had fucked it all up, and now he was gone.

I stared at myself in the mirror, being dramatic as hell, for a solid ninety seconds, but then I had to blow my nose because snot was dripping down my upper lip. I needed to pee, but I couldn't stand the idea of a sea turtle dying because it tried to eat Snoop Dork's used condom, and in order to use their toilet I'd have to fish it out. So I decided to just pee when we got home. Although then someone else would flush it. Finally, I gave in and fished it out with the toilet brush and peed.

WHEN I WENT back to the kitchen, I swung my purse up onto my shoulder. "So Suzie and I will drive back then, and I'll come up with some new ideas!" I said. I knew my voice sounded fake happy. It was the best I could do.

"Sweetie, I didn't mean to hurt your feelings," Rose cooed. Sometimes her saccharine nature really made my teeth itch.

"Not at all," I said. "It's important to get constructive feedback like that. I don't want to post a bunch of crappy TikToks and ruin what we've got going on!"

"Yeah." Rose nodded. "Okay."

"I'll let you know," I said. Suzie was up and ready by my side.

"And I'll try to think of ideas too!" Rose said. "It shouldn't be just you!"

I tried not to flinch. "Please do!" I said, grabbing my sunglasses from my purse and putting them on.

And then Suzie and I drove home, the salt drying tight on my face beneath my sunglasses in the car's AC.

"I don't know if this helps," Suzie said after twenty minutes of silence. "But I think I'm in a position to be fairly objective, and about eighty percent of what Rose was saying was to shift blame off of herself and KC and onto you, and maybe only twenty percent because the TikToks were lackluster."

"No," I said reflexively. "I doubt it was that."

"For real," she said. "The TikToks were fine. Maybe not explosively new, but they were totally fine."

"I didn't think they were *so* bad," I said, "that it would be better to have *no* TikToks than *those* TikToks."

"It would have been way better to film the ones you wrote. I mean, they were better than ninety-nine percent of the shit that gets posted on there. They just weren't, like, a step up. They weren't mind-blowing."

I nodded. It hurt, though I could see now that they were repetitions of gags we'd already done, dynamics we'd already explored.

"It's hard," Suzie said. "You've set the bar pretty damn high."

"You are so nice to me." I sighed, because frankly I wasn't sure I deserved to have someone be this nice to me.

We made it back in time for Jinx and me to take Bodhi to Gymboree together. We clapped Bodhi's little hands as ladies blew bubbles on us and dropped silk scarves so they floated beautifully down, and Bodhi screeched in delight.

THE SADNESS FROM the morning didn't exactly go away; it dried on me and slowly crumbled, leaving me covered in little flakes, like if you eat a glazed donut in a black shirt. That was how it was being a grown-up. We were all moving through the world like that, like those river dolphins that look pink only because they're so covered in scars.

CHAPTER EIGHTEEN

Margo and Jinx had gone on a special shopping trip to buy her an outfit to wear to mediation, and they'd finally settled on slouchy boyfriend-style jeans, a white silk shirt, and a violently elegant black blazer that cost five times what Margo had ever spent on a single piece of clothing. "Good God," Jinx said when he saw her in it the morning of mediation, her hair pulled back in a French twist, her face bare of makeup except for a little mascara.

"It's okay?" she asked, giving a twirl.

"Chef's kiss," Jinx said, Bodhi in his lap, chewing on the nipple of the bottle like a hungry baby goat.

She kissed Bodhi and hugged Jinx goodbye, feeling hulked out on mother love and ready to kick some ass.

This feeling dissipated at the courthouse, where it took forever to find a parking spot, almost making her late, and disappeared entirely the moment she laid eyes on the mediator: an older woman with frizzy black hair, wearing a lumpy maroon sweater, who spoke so slowly and haltingly that Margo assumed it was due to some medical condition. She was wearing ugly earrings, heavily tarnished little silver figures. Margo leaned in. Were those fairies? On little toadstools?

Margo would have given anything to be wearing a pilled cardigan instead of the black blazer. What had she been thinking? She should have dressed for sympathy, not power!

"We are here today to try to come to an agreement," the mediator, Nadia was her name, said, "about what is in the best interests of your child, Bodhi. Is that right?"

"That's right," Mark said, nodding. It was weird to be in the same room with him, a claustrophobic little conference room with a scuffed fake-wood table. He had grown his hair out chin-length, brown and wavy. It suited him and also bespoke some kind of emotional unwellness. He'd said hi to her rather shyly when she first came in the room.

Since then he'd avoided her gaze. There was a Sparkletts water dispenser in the corner behind him, the kind with the big jug. Margo could see that it was bone-dry.

"Let's start by having each of you state your goals for this mediation. Mark, would you like to go first?"

Margo was glad that Mark was going first because she still had no idea what this was about for him. Her best guess was that Elizabeth was making him do this, even though establishing paternity would mean paying child support. Why would Elizabeth want Mark to do that?

"My goal," Mark said, like he was teaching a class, "is to have full legal and physical custody of Bodhi out of concern for Margo's fitness as a parent."

Heat rose in Margo's face. She had suspected as much, but it was still upsetting to hear him say it.

"And why do you doubt her fitness?" the mediator asked. "What behavior of hers is concerning to you?"

"Three things," Mark said, clearly having rehearsed this. "One, I believe Margo to be in financial jeopardy. She has already turned to me for funds. Two, she is currently living with her father, an ex-professional wrestler, a very violent man, who threatened my life and on whom I was forced to place a restraining order. That's not a healthy environment for a baby. And three, because of her financial distress, it is my understanding that Margo has begun doing sex work, also not a suitable environment for a child. I feel Bodhi is safer with me."

Nadia blinked three times, as though waiting for Mark to go on. When he did not, she turned to Margo. "Would you like to tell us your goals?"

"My concern . . ." Margo began. She was dizzy and trying to adjust to the fact that Mark knew about the OnlyFans. She and Ward hadn't intended to hide it; she'd just thought she'd have more control as to how it was presented. "To clarify," she began again, "I do make web content that involves some nudity, but—"

"Porn," Mark said. "She makes porno."

Why was it so much grosser with the *o*?

"It is erotic in nature," Margo said, "though again, for clarity's sake, I am not having sex on camera."

"You certainly sell videos of something!" Mark said.

"I'm happy to explain the content of the videos," Margo said to Nadia, trying to breathe, to calm down. Ward had said, "Just keep calling it a job, over and over. My job. Oh, you're talking about my job? Yes, I have a job. My job is very . . ."

Nadia seemed to be holding her eyes open without blinking like a turtle, waiting for Margo to continue.

"Mark is clearly extremely prejudiced against my job, and the idea of having Bodhi live with Mark and his wife, who would undoubtedly have complicated feelings— I have no objection to Mark knowing Bodhi or being in his life, but it is hard for me to understand the demand for full custody as anything other than an attempt to punish me for my job, no doubt spurred by my father's inappropriate behavior."

The mediator had her mouth open, about to ask about the inappropriate behavior no doubt, when Mark spoke up. "I'm actually in the midst of a divorce, so if I were granted custody, Bodhi would live with me in my apartment, not with my wife and kids. In terms of it being a 'hostile environment.'"

She had to admit, the divorce surprised her. As philandering as Mark was, he had a strangely steadfast devotion to his wife, and Margo would never have predicted he'd leave her.

"I'm sorry, this is new information for me," Margo said. "So are you also going through a custody battle over your other children?"

Mark nodded. "I mean, not a battle. But yes, we are in mediation."

Seriously, what was this? Had he gotten a two-for-one custody deal from his lawyer or something? She couldn't imagine he was serious. Mark wanted a baby? By himself in an apartment?

"We have heard," Nadia said, her voice low and yet squeaking like a hinge, "the reasons why you do not want Mark to have his goals. But I'd like to hear from you what you *do* want for Bodhi. What parenting scenario do you think would benefit him the most?"

"Oh, sorry," Margo said. She had gotten so rattled she'd failed to even answer the question. "I think as difficult as Mark and I may be finding it to get along right now, Bodhi would be better off knowing both parents. Because he is breastfeeding, I would want him to remain in my custody, but I would be happy to give Mark visitation if he wanted to be in Bodhi's life."

It killed her to give this answer. She'd argued with Ward for almost an hour over exactly what she should ask for, and he had finally worn her down to this compromise, promising it would make her look sane and make Mark look like "a rage-addicted, mama's boy cheese-dick."

She really had come to like Ward.

"There's a lot of middle ground in your two different visions," Nadia said. "You seem to be in agreement that Bodhi would be better off with both parents in his life. That's some real progress!"

Margo did not feel it was progress; she felt like she was losing ground. Why were their two positions being equated? Mark was supposed to look like a cheese-dick.

"Let's get into the details a little bit," Nadia said. "Sometimes you can find there's more to agree on than you thought. So, Mark, say you were granted full custody. What's your work schedule like? Who would take care of Bodhi while you were at work?"

"I'm a professor, so I have a great deal of flexibility in my schedule. It wouldn't be a problem," Mark said.

"But when you are teaching, who would take care of Bodhi?"

"I suppose I would hire someone? I don't know, a nanny." It seemed like Mark had genuinely not considered this. "Or, I mean, if Margo wanted him during the days, I could drop him off with her?"

"Ms. Millet is not a daycare, she's the child's mother," Nadia said, and Margo's heart surged with hope. This mediator was turning out to be much more badass than anticipated.

"It also strikes me as strange," Margo put in, "that you would be willing to leave Bodhi in my care while you were at work, if you believe I am an unfit mother and my home a dangerous environment."

Nadia looked expectantly at Mark, waiting for him to reply. It was clear Mark didn't know what to say, and he hesitated, then said, "You have, like, four roommates! I'm sorry, but a kid shouldn't be raised in what is essentially a college dorm!"

"And what is your living situation exactly?" Nadia asked Margo.

"I live in a four-bedroom apartment with Bodhi, my father, and we have a roommate named Suzie, who is currently a student at Fullerton College. It's hardly a college dorm. I made a list of all their contact info here." She opened her folder and pushed a sheet of paper over to Nadia. "I also brought my financial statements. I thought it might be helpful since Mark seems so worried about my being in financial jeopardy." She slid Nadia her bank statements and a copy of her quarterly taxes. She'd brought them because Ward insisted, back when she still hoped the OnlyFans was something she could gloss over. Now she was glad she had them.

Nadia read them, her eyebrows creeping ever higher as she took in the numbers. "Margo," Nadia said, "maybe this is a good time for you to tell us a little bit about your schedule and work-life balance?"

"There are two components to my work," Margo began. "The shooting of content and the posting of content. I tend to shoot content usually one or two days a week. The video shoots are not held in my apartment but at another location, and my dad watches Bodhi for the day. The rest of the time, I'm just posting and answering emails, a lot of boring administrative stuff, editing video, that kind of thing, and I do that kind of work while Bodhi naps."

"So would you say that on most days, you are taking care of Bodhi the entire day?"

"Yes," Margo said.

Nadia changed tack. "Can you tell us a little about your father and his history with violence? Are you concerned having him in your home?"

Margo tried to smile. "Oh, absolutely not. My father is an actor. I'm sure you know—maybe Mark doesn't realize—but professional wrestling is fake. My dad isn't a tough guy, he only played one on TV. As far as I know, he's never gotten into a real physical altercation in his life. It's extremely unfortunate and inappropriate that he called Mark—"

"And threatened me," Mark said.

Margo nodded. "And threatened him. He was angry at the way I'd been treated, at the abuse of power. You can understand why a father would feel that way."

"What abuse of power exactly?" Nadia asked, turning her head so that her silver fairy earrings wobbled.

"Mark was my college professor," Margo said. She did not like using this against him because on some level it felt like a lie. She'd been too young and dumb to understand what she was signing up for, but she'd signed up all the same.

"Please don't pretend you have the moral high ground here," Mark said.

"I'm only trying to give Nadia the context as to why my father would call and yell at you," Margo said. Did Mark think *he* had the moral high ground? "I'm sorry, can I ask something?"

Nadia gave her a shrug that said, *By all means.*

"Mark, do you genuinely believe I'm an unfit parent?" She looked directly into his face, trying to get a read on him. Something about this just wasn't right. She'd thought he was doing it to punish her, that it had been Elizabeth's idea, that Mark himself would feel sheepish and gross and might ultimately be reasoned with. Now she wasn't so sure.

"One hundred percent," Mark said, meeting her gaze.

Her hands were shaking, and she hid them under the table. "Why?"

"Margo, you're a kid." He said this almost gently, pleading with her to understand. "You have no money. You have no plan. You're doing porn. I mean, is this what you want? Really?"

"Yes!" Margo cried, her voice coming out a little strangled.

"See," Mark said, looking back to Nadia. "I find that even more concerning. You have to understand, we are talking about a girl not even of legal age to drink, no college degree, on her own with no real financial support, trying to raise a baby while doing porn. It seems crazy to me that I even have to explain why this is a problem. It seems obvious!"

Nadia was frowning. "Let's try to refocus our conversation on what is best for Bodhi. It seems Mark is worried that this life isn't best for *Margo.* But our concern is for Bodhi. Mark, can you be specific about the kinds of harms you worry might come to Bodhi under Margo's care?"

"Well," Mark said, "what about when Bodhi grows up? What about when one of his little friends finds your account and everybody at school realizes his mom is a porn star? I know you think that's far off, but as a dad to older kids, I can tell you, it goes pretty fast."

Margo had never considered this question before, and she faltered.

Mark went on to Nadia. "It's going to affect every aspect of her life: the jobs she would be able to get if she decided to stop, the relationships she'll be able to have. Most decent men simply will not seriously consider a romantic partner who does sex work, so that means the guys she'll be bringing around will be of a lower caliber. She's doubtless going to have friends who also do sex work, and they'll be around in the house. This kind of thing, it's insidious."

"What's insidious exactly?" Margo asked, swallowing. Some of what he said was true. Rose and KC did come to the house. Bodhi was growing up in a house full of sex workers. Was it weird that she didn't think that was so bad?

"Let's try to focus this on the here and now," Nadia said. "What is best for Bodhi at nine might look a lot different from what is best for Bodhi as an infant. So, Mark, what are you currently worried about in terms of Bodhi's well-being?"

"Well, when you're doing sex work from home, how can you be sure the proper boundaries are in place? He might see inappropriate content; he might see nudity, for example," Mark said.

"This baby literally came out of my vagina!" Margo exploded. "I'm not sure my body is what we need to be protecting him from! I mean, he breastfeeds, Mark! He sees my breasts every day."

"Well, now so can everybody else," Mark said, his eyes trained on his folded hands on the table.

The logical inconsistency of his argument made her want to strangle him—he was supposed to be the smart one; he was a college professor, for Pete's sake! "And how does it hurt Bodhi for other men to see pictures of my breasts? What tangible harm is it doing to him?"

Nadia cleared her throat. She turned to Margo. "Would you prefer I separate you in two different conference rooms and hear your arguments that way?"

"She is a child," Mark interrupted them, as though he had finally found the words he wanted. "That's all I'm saying. It's not personal,

Margo. I would say this about any twenty-year-old—you're just not ready to raise a baby." He shrugged like there was nothing he could do about that.

"I was certainly old enough for you to fuck me," Margo said, her cheeks burning.

"That's pretty low," Mark said, shaking his head like he was disappointed in her. "I wouldn't think you'd go that low."

Margo almost laughed even though she felt like she'd been punched in the gut.

"The rest of this meeting will be held in two separate conference rooms," Nadia said, standing. "Margo, would you step with me out into the hall, and we can get you situated?"

PRETTY MUCH NOTHING eventful happened after that. Nadia sat with Margo and asked her more questions. She asked about Bodhi's pediatrician and if he went to the doctor regularly. She asked if Margo had a boyfriend. They were all easy to answer.

"Let me ask, what is your bottom line, your best offer, the biggest compromise you would sign on to today?"

"Bodhi stays in my physical and legal custody. Mark can have visitation, but no overnights."

"Okay," Nadia said, clearly disappointed. "So no big concessions."

Margo knew Ward would be mad at her. She said it anyway: "He doesn't have to pay child support."

Nadia raised her eyebrows. "None?"

"None."

Nadia seemed to be thinking about this. "All right," she said, getting up. "It's worth a shot." They agreed that Nadia would speak to Mark and that Margo would wait for her to come back. When Nadia returned, she looked worried, her frail shoulders hunched.

"That doesn't work for him," she said. "Unfortunately."

They both sat at the table for a moment, tired. "Do we go to trial then?" Margo asked. The idea of it made her sick. Upward of forty grand, Ward had said, and she didn't have the money. She didn't even have TikToks to post. Honestly, she was still so mad at KC and Rose that she hadn't written anything new. She watched her fan count slowly drop, day after day, from lack of vageen. She rested her forehead on the table of the conference room the way they made you put your head on your desk after recess.

"I think in this case it might be a good idea to keep it in mediation a bit longer, to give tempers some time to cool down."

"Okay," Margo said, not raising her head. "That will give us time to depose him, I guess."

"Oh good," Nadia said. "Then that works for everybody."

Forty grand, Margo thought. *Sporty strand, warty gland, stormy sand.*

"It was lovely to meet you," Nadia said. "I'll see you in about four weeks. I'll get back to you with an exact date after I talk to Mark."

"So lovely to meet you as well," Margo said, lifting her head off the table and suddenly becoming aware of how inappropriate it had been for her to lay her head on the table at all. "I like your earrings!" Margo called.

Nadia was already halfway out the door. She turned, touched her ear as if to remember which ones they were. "You take care," she said, and then she was gone, a mystery.

MARGO GOT HOME and gave Jinx and Suzie the skinny.

"Ward was totally right, they're treating the OnlyFans as a job, one hundred percent, the mediator didn't bat an eye, even though Mark kept calling it porno with an *o*."

"That's such a relief," Jinx said. "But gosh, it surprises me that this is all coming from Mark. Does he— I mean, has he ever met Bodhi?"

"No! And he didn't even ask to!"

"This makes zero sense," Suzie said.

"I don't know," Margo said. Mark could state the exact same facts of her life as she did—her age, the baby, her work—and make it sound like she was some tragic figure. The idea that she might post naked pictures of herself and remain psychologically healthy seemed not to have occurred to him.

When she was finally bored of complaining (she had gone on an extended jazzy riff about Mark's long hair and the brooding way he liked to peer out from under it), she gave Bodhi a bath and dumped a whole load of new bath toys in with him. He squealed with delight as the rainbow of small rubber ocean creatures bobbed in the water.

Mark had made her feel so ashamed in that meeting, and she was only now shaking it off. It was a mystery, really, why people thought sex was so dirty. You were literally genetically programmed to do it; it was necessary for the continuance of the species. And Margo liked sex, at least in real life. She'd thought a lot about it over the past few months because sometimes the way men wanted sex seemed pathological, and she wondered if there was something wrong with them or if maybe there was something wrong with her. What she liked most about sex was that feeling of all the normal posturing and social rules falling away, the giddy panic of realizing you've lost control and you're not getting it back. Instead, you're just helplessly writhing, victim of an ancient itch.

Then it's over, and one of you gets up to go to the bathroom and pulls on their underwear, and you can feel the horrible slide back into the world, into language and clocks and calendars, into who you are pretending to be and who they are pretending to be, and it's lost, it's gone.

But she didn't think any of her fans were trying to get such a thing when they paid their thirteen dollars. She didn't know exactly what they were getting out of it. If she had to guess, she thought they were hoping to own her like a Pokémon card. This tiny electronic woman who lived in their phone that they could make look at their dick and she'd respond with adorable, themed messages. They wanted her to be real, but only so it was more fun to keep her in a little cage.

And it was true the idea of this, of being the little woman in their phone, grossed her out. It wasn't that she was willing to defend OnlyFans as some morally unimpeachable activity. But she was tired of pretending all the Kennys of the world were right. She wasn't rotten! She wasn't trash—no human being was trash. Jesus had said that. Jesus, who consorted with lepers and prostitutes.

And besides, she loved making the content: the manic frenzy of dreaming up a new concept, writing, and shooting it; seeing the reactions online. And sometimes she did not imagine herself as tiny, she imagined herself as gigantic, a woman the size of the Empire State Building, spraying breast milk all over Manhattan.

The important thing, Margo thought, was to control the narrative. Mary hadn't worried that having been raped made her any less worthy of marrying Joseph, and she didn't worry about the fact that she was lying. What she did was put her finger on a scale she could clearly see was rigged against her. If she'd told the truth, she would have been killed. So Mary told a beautiful, golden whopper and became the most revered woman on Earth.

Bodhi stuck a pink shark in his mouth. Margo thought about what Rose had said, about bombing making stand-up comics free, unchained from only saying things the audience would like. She pictured a stadium of people around her, booing, hating her, spitting on her, telling her she would go to hell. Mark and Shyanne and Kenneth. She imagined that singer from his church, Annie, wild-eyed as she hurled a rock. Everyone loved to put a bitch back in her place.

You could be like Shyanne and wear a pilled-up old cardigan and try to win the mob's sympathy, or you could stand there, defiant, like Mary, and claim to be touched by God.

But the money—it was so much money, and she'd have to make it quickly. She couldn't exactly count on another video from KikiPilot. She watched Bodhi gumming the little pink shark.

Suddenly, Margo realized she knew exactly what to do.

CLOSE-UP ON MARGO's face. She is wearing nerdy glasses and concentrating intently, her tongue in the corner of her mouth. Cut to an overhead shot of her desk, littered with tools and electronic components. At the center is Rigoberto. She is screwing his battery panel back on, as though she has finished altering him in some way.

Close-up of Rigoberto as his "on" light begins to flash and glow.

"Finally, I can speak to you more precisely," Rigoberto says in a female robotic voice not unlike Siri's. Margo made it on AIVoiceOver. Rigoberto having a female voice tickled her for some reason.

"Oh, Rigoberto!" Margo cries, and embraces the Roomba.

"Don't touch me, you stupid bitch," Rigoberto says.

Margo drops him back on her desk.

"Things are going to change around here," Rigoberto says.

"What do you mean?" Margo says, using all her carefully honed alien naivete.

"Hold still," Rigoberto says.

A black screen with the words: *Two hours later.*

Margo is examining herself in the mirror. She used one of Suzie's contact lenses to make one of her eyes bloodred. She lifts her hair to examine a small plastic panel cover screwed into her head. This was just the back of her dad's blood pressure monitor hot glued to a hair clip, but it looked dang good.

"Now you will do anything I say, and I control you completely," Rigoberto says.

From that point on in the video, Rigoberto makes her do various things, which start off ridiculous—"Do the Orange Justice naked," "Suck on this screwdriver," "Say 'Robots are hot'"—and then get more and more sexual and culminate in Margo masturbating to Rigoberto's precise, exacting instructions.

By the time Margo was done editing, it was four minutes long. She thought it was good, maybe even hot in its own ridiculous way. If she was going to lose a job or get kicked out of school because of this video someday, she could feel pretty good about it, she thought. If Becca posted this on her Facebook, Margo might even be a little proud. The video was Margo-ish. She was being herself, and yes, that was her vagina, and it was all of a piece somehow.

She decided that since she'd spent nearly three days making and editing it, she should charge at least twenty-five dollars for it.

She used some of the footage to make PG clips for TikTok of the Rigoberto takeover, which was the only solution she'd been able to come up with for handling the Amelia Bedelia corner she'd painted herself into. Controlled by Rigoberto, Ghost would become a truly evil heel and do all sorts of terrible, comical things to Rose and KC. Eventually, KC and Rose could make a plan to incapacitate her somehow, unscrew the panel and make her normal again, though of course then she'd be a new version of Ghost altogether, neither the old naive Ghost nor the evil bot Ghost, but a more complex and nuanced and human Ghost.

AN HOUR AFTER she posted the Rigoberto video, five hundred fans had bought it. Margo was shocked. Jinx was shocked. Suzie was shocked. The comments on her page were rabid, ecstatic; people loved it.

"I wish I could see what it was so badly," Jinx said. "What did you do?"

"I mean, I don't think—"

"No! I am not asking for permission to watch. I absolutely refuse to watch it."

"It's just Rigoberto taking over my body."

"It's what?!" Jinx crowed with laughter. "Oh, Margo. Margo!"

"What?"

"You delight me."

"So in what way does the Roomba take over your body exactly?" Suzie asked.

Margo didn't answer. She could not stop refreshing her earnings page to see the total again and again. She'd made over $12,000 in an hour. Well, OnlyFans would take its cut, and Jinx kept reminding her to mentally set aside 30 percent for taxes, which paying quarterly had made crushingly real.

Margo never would have guessed she loved money this much. In fact, in the movies and TV shows and books she'd read, you could tell if a character was the bad guy by how much he cared about money. And since she wanted to be good, she'd always been careful not to care too much about money. Now she wondered if all those Disney movies were merely propaganda to keep poor people content with their lot. *We may be poor, but we're the salt of the earth, we know what really matters. The rich are perverted by their hideous wealth—why, look at that Cruella de Vil!* But good or evil, every single dollar was power. Power to hire a lawyer, power to control how she spent her time, power to change her appearance, power to command respect. Power to be who she wanted to be.

SHE HAD TALLIED it all up in an Excel spreadsheet, all the money JB had ever sent her. The total was over five grand. She had wanted to send it all back, some kind of grand gesture, but she was too afraid she would have to go to trial and might need every penny she'd just earned, so she wrote him a message instead:

The moment I told you my name was Suzie, I knew it was a mistake. A lie unlike the other lies I had told. If before we were playing a game, suddenly I was truly deceiving you. And I wanted to. That boundary, being in control of it. It felt impossible to let that go. There aren't a ton of stereotypes around what being a "good" sex worker might look like, and I think the one I latched on to, the only one I understood, was to always ensure I was in control of those boundaries. I don't know if you can understand this, but having a baby adds to that feeling of protectiveness. I stop short of telling you I wish I could go back and answer differently. I am not sure I could have, or even that I should have. It was a mistake that maybe I had to make, would always make no matter how many times I tried.

In that same exchange where I told you my name was Suzie, I also told you to stop paying me. And that was not a mistake. I wanted you to know that I wasn't only writing to you to make money. I was writing to you because I wanted to. And I am glad that I had sense enough to make that clear. The good and the bad, they always seem to come all tangled together like this for me.

JB, you said I can't have it both ways, but why can't I? Why can't being genuine and putting on an act coexist? Aren't we all always putting on an act? I'm not trying to excuse myself or justify anything, I don't think I need to. You said it yourself, you were paying me to lie to you. But I can't stand the idea of you thinking you were an idiot for enjoying it. I found what we were doing beautiful. Writing you was the absolute best part of my day. I realize maybe you can't build a real relationship on that. But you can sure as shit build an imaginary one, and I think what we built was a castle in the damn sky.

Sincerely,
Margo Jelly Bean Ghost
(That's my full name, my true name.)

CHAPTER NINETEEN

Ward called me at ten p.m.

"Why are you working this late?" I said.

"Can't get you off my mind," Ward said.

I laughed like a sheep bleating.

"No, really," he said. "I just got an email from Mark's attorney, wanted to let you know so you could sleep on it and I could get your take in the morning. I don't know if this was a direct result of the mediation session or us asking for the depo, but they're asking for a 730 eval."

"A what now?"

"You hire a shrink to do a complete psych eval. They interview you, they interview people in your life, they observe you and Bodhi together."

"Jesus Christ," I said. "You think he's retaliating because he doesn't want to do the deposition? Like, giving me a taste of my own medicine?"

"Maybe yes, maybe no," Ward said. "They also stipulated that if the results of the 730 are good and the evaluator thinks you're a good mother, they'll let you keep full legal and physical custody with only weekly visitation."

"Oh," I said. "Well, that could be good!"

"It could be. They did stipulate that you would have to pay for the 730, which—fifty-fifty would be more standard. It's a dick move."

"How much?"

"Somewhere between five and ten k," Ward said. I could hear the dim, sparkling sound of ice in a glass. I wondered if he was still in his brightly lit sterile office or if he was at home in a dark living room, maybe with the TV on but muted.

"That's cheaper than a trial," I said, though I did wonder how people who were not selling nudes on the internet paid for this kind of thing. Or maybe they couldn't. Maybe people just . . . lost their kids.

"It definitely is. And you may have wound up having to do one in a trial anyway. It's just— Margo, they will get into your business. It will be invasive. I don't know if you're ready for that."

"Invasive how?"

"They're gonna want you to take the MMPI-2, which is a personality test, over five hundred questions. They will interview you, interview Jinx, ask all sorts of questions. They'll want to come to your house, observe you and Bodhi together."

"Well, none of that sounds like a problem," I said.

"No skeletons in your closet?" he asked. "It's not going to be a problem if an evaluator comes out there? I mean, I've never seen your house. I'm just saying, you might want to have maids out or something."

"Oh," I said. "No, my dad is a clean freak, our house is immaculate. It's all good. And I'm not scared of the psych test. I could be totally deluded, but I think I'm relatively normal."

"All right," Ward said. "Well, you sleep on it."

I told him I would, even though I was elated. I had gotten the *Caillou* theme song stuck in my head earlier, and I hated that song, but now I hummed it buttery and smooth as I washed my face, flossed, and brushed; checked on Bodhi in his crib and collapsed into bed. *I'm just a kid who's four, each day I grow some more!* I was going to fucking ace a psych eval.

READER, I COULD not tell in the slightest if I aced that psych eval or flunked it entirely. It was so weird I couldn't believe it was a real test.

The psych eval was my first meeting with the 730 shrink Mark had chosen. The court had given us a list of ten. Ward had me eliminate five—I crossed off most of the men—and then Mark and Larry the Lawyer got to choose the final person. Her name was Clare Sharp.

Dr. Clare Sharp was brunette, a little bit fat, pretty and confident. She wore an electric-blue blazer over a black T-shirt and pearl earrings. I liked her immediately. We met in her office, she explained the test, then left me alone to take it, wandering in every now and then to see if I needed anything. Her office was small and a little shabby, but chic in a Pinterest way. She had one of those weird wool woven-art things on the wall and kilim pillows.

The first question on the psych eval was: *I like mechanics magazines. T/F.*

It wasn't that I didn't know how to answer; I was mystified as to what this question could be trying to ascertain. Was it some kind of decoy? The next one: *I have a good appetite. T/F.* Again, very clear I would be answering true, but as to the purpose of the question, I had no clue.

Some of the questions were obvious. Number 24 was: *Evil spirits possess me at times. T/F.* Hard to imagine who would be far gone enough to circle *T* on that one.

Other questions were harder to know how to answer. *Someone has it in for me. T/F.* I'd literally just been doxxed by my best friend; in a certain way, it would seem crazier to put *F*, but I put *T*, assuming this was a question designed to root out paranoia regardless of how warranted it might be. Same with: *I prefer to pass by school friends, or people I know but have not seen for a long time, unless they speak to me first.* Same with: *I have never been in trouble because of my sexual behavior.*

Much of the time I feel as if I have done something wrong or evil.

My family does not like the work I have chosen.

I believe that women ought to have as much sexual freedom as men.

Anyone who is able and willing to work hard has a good chance of succeeding.

I cry easily.

I have sometimes felt that difficulties were piling up so high that I could not overcome them.

WARD HAD GIVEN me only one piece of advice about this test, and it was to tell the truth. "Don't just pick the non-crazy answers. Everybody is a little crazy, and they have stuff in there to see if you're lying." But it was scary to tell the truth. I did cry easily! I decided that I didn't feel I had done something wrong or evil *much of the time*. Really, I had felt that way only in Kenny's church or when I was in a fight with Shyanne. The rest of the time I hardly felt evil at all.

I finished the test and crushed the tiny room-temp bottle of Poland Spring water Dr. Sharp had given me. It was a marvel they could tell who was crazy at all. How would Kenny answer the questions on this test? He would obviously choose *F* for *I believe that women ought to have as much sexual freedom as men.*

But there were so many I'd answered false that I knew he would answer true:

I believe in life hereafter.

I have never indulged in unusual sex practices.

I daydream very little.

I would like to belong to several clubs.

I have been inspired to a program of life based on duty which I have since carefully followed.

It was hard not to feel like the test was made for him, designed with Kenneth himself as the model of mental health. And if Kenny was what sane was, maybe I wasn't. I mean, he was the one who believed in invisible beings controlling every aspect of our lives. I kept telling myself it couldn't be. Dr. Sharp had multiple degrees. She wouldn't use a test where the "right" answer was that women shouldn't have as much sexual freedom as men, would she?

When she came back in, Dr. Sharp seemed just as normal and cool as before. "So, when do you come in for your interview? Do we have that next Tuesday?"

I nodded.

"And thank you for this contact sheet and this whole little bundle," she said, holding up the file I'd given her. It made me think of the kids complaining in senior English class about the big paper we had to write for our final project with a cover page and table of contents, whining about how we'd never need to do this in real life. *Guess what, Seth! You've got to write a report to keep your fucking kid!*

THE NEXT DAY, I tried to put the psych eval out of my mind. We had TikToks to film. Rose and KC had both gone bananas for the new scripts. Suzie had read them too. She had come to me in my room, waving the printed-out pages at me. "Now this—" she said, "this is leveling up."

The moment I turned Ghost heel, I had almost fifteen ideas in less than twenty-four hours. Ghost's alien nature still worked in an Amelia Bedelia–like way, maybe even better now that she was evil. In one skit, Ghost sprays KC's butt with Lysol and says, "I'm sorry, it said to spray on flat surfaces." I'd been practicing and had developed a creepy smile with unseeing eyes, heavily based on the way my mother looked at herself in the mirror.

It was food pranks that really interested me, though. Ghost makes Rose and KC eat Popsicles she has made by freezing blue toothpaste in molds. She feeds them apple slices she's rubbed with jalapeños.

I had gotten these ideas remembering Tessa and how she'd fed the salad boy potting soil and shaving cream. He'd spent all night throwing up in the bathroom, and everyone had laughed. Looking back, it seemed like Tessa had actually poisoned him. Couldn't he have gone to the police? There was an undercurrent of real evil there, and it intrigued me. Evil witches in forests who made houses out of candy to lure children. Poisoned enchanted apples. It was very old, our sense that food, the thing we needed most in order to stay alive, could be used against us. I wanted to use that for Ghost, to make her a truly unforgettable heel. I even wrote Snoop Dork into the script. Ghost feeds him a burrito filled with crushed-up Viagra, and he winds up with a boner for thirty-six hours. I argued we should have him really do it so he could go to the ER and we'd film that, but KC vetoed it.

I'd wondered about the phrase "Hungry Ghost" when Mark first wrote that poem. What did he mean by it? How could ghosts be hungry? But it made perfect sense to me now: The longing for the food you could no longer eat. The memory of having a body. People were constantly giving ghosts food, offerings of persimmons and oranges, pan de muerto on the Day of the Dead; even Halloween was about nothing so much as candy. What the dead wanted, above all else, was to eat, to cram their mouths full, to feel the calories flood their bloodstream, to be part of it again: life. Bloody, squirming, pulsing, hungry life.

WE SHOT ALL day and had an early dinner/late lunch. Rose and I picked up Yoshinoya and ate it on the balcony, while Suzie, KC, and Snoop Dork went across the street to Chipotle. Jinx had said he didn't feel well enough to come, so I had Bodhi on my lap, which made eating a challenge. He kept trying to plunge his little hands into my rice bowl.

"Can I ask you something?" Rose said.

"Of course."

"Why didn't you— I mean, why did you keep him? When you found out you were pregnant."

I thought about this, slowly chewing the tiny perfect bodies of the rice. "I mean," I said, "I think I was just stupid."

Rose laughed. "I thought maybe you were religious or something."

"No," I said. "Though, I mean, at the time I did feel morally conflicted. But there's nothing like having a baby to make you solidly pro-choice!"

"Why, though? I mean, it's so clear you love Bodhi, and you're a great mom."

"No, no," I said. "It's not about that. I'd do it all again. But, like, I didn't really know you could still die having a baby, or, you know, tear. Kind of inevitably. Down there. And then for the rest of your life when you sneeze, you pee a little. Some women tear way worse and they wind up not able to control their poop all the time. It changes your body in irreversible ways. One of my tits is now a full half cup size bigger than the other."

"Well, yeah," Rose said. "I mean, of course it's going to change your body."

"You can't tell me that if it was men and a medical decision would result in their penis splitting open and them not being able to hold their pee for the rest of their life, they wouldn't think that should be their own decision."

Rose snorted as she was drinking her Diet Coke. "Yeah, that's pretty hard to imagine."

"They would be like, 'Look, this is my penis we're talking about here!'"

Bodhi was getting obsessed with touching my food, so I stood and bounced him.

"And I didn't understand how not set up the world is for women to have babies. The whole childcare system is unworkable. Like, it ruins your life. You can't choose that for someone else. You shouldn't be able to *make* someone do that."

"Yeah," Rose said a little wistfully. "So you don't think you'd be doing this if you hadn't had a baby?"

"OnlyFans? I mean, it wasn't plan A! But it doesn't seem like it was your plan A either, right? I mean, you were doing physics."

"True," Rose said.

"Do you ever think about going back?" I asked.

"Not really," Rose said.

"Why did you leave grad school again?" I always figured she'd run out of money.

Rose smiled in a funny way. "Well, I started my OnlyFans, like, my second year? To make money. Which was kind of perfect because I could make my own hours. I mentioned it to another girl in the program, and she told everybody, and it just became a big, big thing for some reason. And they asked me to leave the program."

"They *what*? How could they legally do that?!"

"Well, they didn't, it wasn't like they kicked me out. I tried going to my adviser to figure out what to do because it was kind of getting out of hand—there was this one guy in particular who took offense for some reason and wrote an email outing me to the entire department, asking if these were the kind of values the department held, like 'this is supposed to be a hallowed space for science' and blah blah blah. And my adviser was basically like, 'I don't know what you should do. Maybe leave?' So I left."

"Oh, Rose. That makes me so mad! Every day, I'm like, *The world is complex and wondrous, everything is so nuanced,* and then I turn on the computer, and it's like, 'Look at my dick, look at my dick, dick, dick, dick, dick!'"

Every day, on my phone, on my computer, they were always there. I thought of my fans now as a garden of little worms, like Ursula the sea witch's garden of lost souls, but with dicks. And they all said the same thing, they all opened their hungry little penis mouths to ask for more. More vagina, more sexiness, "talk to me," "show me," "cum for me." Their need was colossal, it did not seem possible it could be satisfied, least of all by pictures of my weird little vagina. And yet it was so. They loved that silly Rigoberto video. I had plans to make another one where I fucked myself with a Dyson, though really this was just an excuse to buy a Dyson. It made me both hate my fans and love them. I needed them desperately, and yet I wished they'd all go away, even only for a day, so I could breathe and think and be a person.

"No, I totally know what you mean," Rose said. "The thing about horny men is that, yes, they are annoying. It's easy to hate them. But at the end of the day, horny men are people. And they are in need, and they are in pain, or they're fixated on something, and they deserve as much kindness as we can stand to offer them. That's kind of my take."

"You're a saint," I said. But it broke my heart in a way. To think of all those dicks belonging to real people. To think of sweet Rose, kicked out of grad school, trying to be kind to them.

Right then KC and Suzie got back, knocked on the sliding glass door to get our attention, then smooshed their open mouths on it and blew, puffing up their cheeks.

We had one more TikTok to film, an eating contest between me and Rigoberto. The bit was that we'd show Rose filling two paper plates with shaving cream (switching mine out for Cool Whip off camera), then Rigoberto and I would have a contest of who could eat it faster. I genuinely had no idea how that part would go. I assumed Rigoberto would dust me, but I was going to give it my all. Rose and I reluctantly left our perch on the balcony, the dusk beginning to gather around us, and went inside.

I changed into a red bikini and assumed my position on the tarp.

LATE MONDAY NIGHT I got a message from JB.

I've been thinking, JB wrote. When you fall in love with a book, is it the character or the author you're falling in love with?

HungryGhost: I mean, I guess both?
JB: And only one of them is real.

True, I admitted.

JB: And the fake one is the only one you get to actually know. But you can kind of feel the author under there, beneath the surface of the fake world you're inhabiting. Their imagination is the water you're swimming in, the air you're breathing. They've made every table and every chair and every person in the whole book.

I couldn't breathe.

JB: I'm just saying, even if everything you wrote me was a lie (and I know, not ALL of it was a lie, but even if it was!), then in some sense I would still know you, at least as well as I feel I know Neal Stephenson or William Gibson or whatever, and honestly, I feel like I know them better than I know anyone in the world. Do you know what I mean?

I knew exactly what he meant, but maybe because of the custody stuff with Mark, or everything with my dad, reality did not seem as trivial as it once had.

The thing is, though, I wrote, a book isn't a relationship. There are these built-in guardrails that keep you from knowing the author. The end of the book is like a chasm, cutting you off from them. And we don't have that. We might keep mistaking what's fake for what's real between us, like people eating wax fruit and wondering why it tastes bad. Like, there is writing each other these emails, and then there is trying to actually, you know, date. If that's even what you're suggesting.

Was that presumptuous, to call it dating? He had never said he wanted to date me. But what else could we be talking about here? Did

I even want to date him? The moment I posed this question to myself, I discovered that I really, really did.

JB: Can we switch modalities? Can I call?

My phone was buzzing seconds after I typed yes.

"I think I should fly out there," he said.

"Whoa, what? Really?"

"Why not? I could get a flight for as much as I used to pay you to answer three questions."

"That's kind of disturbing to realize," I said. My heart was racing and it was unclear if I was panicked or excited. I was pretty sure I was both.

"Only for the weekend. And I can meet your baby and we can just . . . see where it goes."

Fuck, I was going to have to tell Jinx. Fuck! "Okay," I said.

"Okay? So what airport should I fly into?"

Jesus Christ, was I really going to do this? And then I told him to fly into Long Beach or else Ontario, LAX as a last resort, giddy as a kid on Christmas.

CHAPTER TWENTY

The next morning, Margo went to Dr. Sharp's office for her interview. The home observation visit would be in a couple weeks, and while nervous, Margo was feeling optimistic. She sat on Dr. Sharp's couch, the scratchy kilim of the pillows itchy on her back where her shirt was riding up.

"How have you been?" Dr. Sharp began.

"All right," Margo said. There was no way she could or should tell Dr. Sharp about what had happened with JB, but how else to explain her good mood? "I mean, this whole process is scary, but I'm glad that Mark was even willing to do it instead of continuing to pursue full custody."

"Mark is a good starting point. Why don't you just tell me about Mark, how you two met, the whole narrative arc."

And so she did. Ward had warned her not to make Mark look like a total bad guy, so she tried to be evenhanded and generous in the way she told the story, even though he was a morally bankrupt, navel-gazing little troll. Dr. Sharp asked questions, a couple of them pointed.

"And what exactly *was* your financial plan after the birth of the baby?"

Margo paused. Tell the truth, she thought. "I was incredibly naive about what would be involved. I didn't know finding childcare would be so hard. I wasn't thinking about that when I decided to keep the baby."

"What were you thinking about?" Dr. Sharp asked.

"I mean, I think I thought I was being a good person. There's a lot of cultural messaging about what the 'right' thing to do is when you find yourself with an unwanted pregnancy. And I thought if I did the right thing and was a good person, then it would all turn out okay."

"Do you no longer think that's true?" Dr. Sharp asked. She was staring down at her pad of yellow paper, her hand moving rapidly as she took notes.

"I think being a good person is important, but my landlord doesn't care if I'm a good person, he just cares if I can pay. My old boss, I think she really liked me, even loved me, but what mattered in the end was whether I could work when she needed me. That's kind of how the world works." She hoped this was not news to Dr. Sharp. She thought again about the way the test seemed designed for Kenny, who no doubt believed that if you were virtuous, God would provide, and hoped this wasn't the wrong answer.

"Let's talk a little bit about your dad," Dr. Sharp said.

"Okay," Margo said, relieved they were moving on. "I love talking about my dad."

"Why is that?"

"I don't know," Margo said. "I know he's a pretty unconventional guy. I guess he wasn't around a lot when I was younger, but this time living with him has been really good for us. He went from feeling like someone I was sort of pretending was my dad to being my real dad, if that makes sense. Like, he's taken care of us when Bodhi and I got a stomach virus. I've taken care of him when his back has gone out. We've gotten to do a lot of that bonding and building trust that we didn't do when I was little, and it's been a really positive thing for me."

She thought of Becca saying, "You think he picked you because you were special? He picked you because he knew you had fucking daddy issues." She didn't think she should mention this to Dr. Sharp.

"How did you feel when you found out he'd threatened Mark?"

"I mean, I felt upset that it was resulting in this custody dispute and the restraining order and all this scary stuff. But I also felt—you know, some people would say that for Mark to start the relationship with me was an abuse of power. I never felt super comfortable with that. I didn't want to admit I'd been . . ." She struggled for the word, then found it. "Tricked. And I still think it was more complicated than that. The further removed from it I am, though, the more I can see how young I was and how much I didn't know, and how much Mark, as an older man with a wife and kids, *did* know. And I can see now that it was not an even playing field. So for my dad to stick up for me, on some level it felt good. I would have preferred he not threaten Mark with physical harm, obviously. But I would be lying if I said it didn't feel good to have someone on my side."

I HAD BEEN the one to suggest JB and I play *Fortnite* together. He was flying out in two weeks, and it felt like the days couldn't pass fast enough. The moment he agreed, I wished I'd never asked. For one thing, I was a terrible player. For another, while lots of people spent tons of money on different skins and had dozens of options, I had bought only one. It was a blond male Christmas elf. I didn't know what this said about me, but I doubted it was good. When he teleported into my squad, JB was a breathtakingly hot Little Red Riding Hood wearing thigh-high black boots. We had our mics on so we could talk, and I was having a hard time adjusting to the thrill of his low, raspy voice. "We don't even have to try to win," he said, as we entered the lobby and waited for the Battle Bus, "we can hide in the bushes."

"Okay," I said. We got lit up almost as soon as we dropped, and JB had to carry my unconscious body slung over his shoulder as he killed the last of them. He was honestly pretty cracked. He got me healed up, and then we scavenged through chests, collecting as many heals as we could before setting off.

"Where are we going?" I asked.

"Into the storm," he said, like it was obvious.

"What are we going to do in the storm?"

"Just hang out and drink heals until we die," he said.

I'd been caught in the storm plenty. I had never entered it on purpose before, and the sensation was a little strange. Every second you were inside lowered your health, and it made everything look purple and swirly with fog. We found a campfire and lit it, which would give us some health, though not enough to survive. I was aware of trying to speak quietly so Bodhi wouldn't wake up in his crib. I had all the lights off in my room. There was only the purple glow of my laptop screen.

"Here." JB tossed me a med kit and I used it, watched my health bar surge green. There was something weirdly compelling about hearing his husky male voice coming out of this cartoonishly hot female fairy-tale character.

"How long do you think we can keep living like this?" I asked, using one of the bandages in my inventory, which made my elf body kneel as he wrapped up his arm.

"I don't know," JB said, cutting down a nearby bush for more wood to feed the fire. "I haven't done this before. But there's only ten people left. We might even win."

"From inside the storm?"

JB murmured, and I could tell he was clicking through his inventory because different weapons and objects kept appearing in Little Red's hands. The fire was making amazing shadows on her epic honkers. "You look hot in that skin," I said.

"So do you," JB said.

In real life I snorted, then froze, but Bodhi didn't wake up.

"Oh yeah?" I asked. "This Will Ferrell bod getting you all hot?" I didn't have a lot of emotes, so I put one on that made me play an extended, highly sexual saxophone solo. Little Red stood stock-still, watching my weird elf body humping the air.

"My wires are real crossed right now for sure," JB said.

"I don't even think I have wires anymore," I said. "That's how crossed they are. I think I have, like, veins."

THERE ARE CERTAIN things I've had to lie to you about. I want you to close your eyes and actually remember what it was like to be twenty. I want you to remember your house or apartment or dorm room. Whom did you have a crush on? How did it feel to be inside your body, letting your legs flop over watching TV? Think of how ridiculously, insanely, terrifyingly stupid you were, how many things you just did not know. I have tried to hide as best I can the fact that I was young and, by virtue of being young, a fucking idiot, but there are some moments in which you can't understand it any other way: an idiot comes against the hard surface of the world as it is.

THE NEXT MORNING Jinx was taking forever in the bathroom. Suzie was desperate to pee. "Dude, your dad has been in there for nine years," she said.

Bodhi was still asleep, and Margo had been hoping to drink her coffee unmolested. She'd help Suzie, of course. She knocked on the bathroom door. "Dad?"

There was no response.

"Dad, are you okay?"

If Jinx's back had gone out and he was in pain, he would still answer. The fact that he wasn't seemed to imply he was unconscious.

"Hold on," Suzie said, going and getting her Ralphs grocery discount card. She slid it in the crack of the door, weaseling it back and forth, until suddenly there was a click and the door swung open. Margo stepped inside, and as soon as she saw him, she slammed the bathroom door shut so Suzie couldn't see. He was in the dry bathtub in his pajamas, unconscious, a needle still hanging out of his arm. It made her sick, the way it stayed in his skin. He had used her velvet scrunchie as a tie-off. She reached out to feel his face, terrified he would be cold. When she finally let her fingers graze his cheek, he was warm, and she could breathe again. She grabbed him by the chin and gave him a shake. His eyes peeled open. His pupils looked small like a snake's.

"Hey," he said, dreamy, happy. He raised his eyebrows, amazed to see her.

All Margo's terror turned to disgust so quickly she could barely parse it, and her hand flashed out to the shower knob and turned the cold water full on him before she'd even planned to do so. Jinx sat up sputtering. "Stop! Margo, stop!" She turned it off.

"Get the needle out of your arm," she said as quietly as she could, close to his ear so Suzie wouldn't hear. He reached over and patted his arm until he found the needle and took it out. "Why the fuck," she whispered. "I mean, how long . . . ?"

"I'm so sorry, Margo," Jinx whispered back. "I'm so sorry. It won't happen again."

"Are you kidding me?"

They stared at each other. He was soaking wet, and his face was puffy. He looked stupid, like an animal, the muscles around his mouth slack. While she tried to think of what to say, what to do next, he fell asleep again and she slapped him hard across the face. He snapped awake.

"Are you OD'ing?" she hissed. "Should I take you to the ER?"

Jinx laughed. "No, I'm not OD'ing. I'd be having the time of my life if you'd stop slapping me in the face. And it's cold. Why is it so cold?"

"Because you're all wet."

Jinx looked down at his completely soaked pajamas, totally mystified. "How'd I do that?" he asked.

"Okay," she said, "I'm bringing you dry clothes, you change into them, and then I'm putting you in your room, and you're staying in there. Do you understand?"

He seemed to grasp that he was high and this should be a secret, even if he was hazy on the exact situation. A familiar paradigm to his blasted mind, maybe. He nodded. "You get my clothes, and I'll knock 'em dead," he said. Margo didn't know what that meant. She went to get his clothes.

"His back went out in the shower," she told Suzie, who was waiting outside the bathroom door. "He's incredibly embarrassed. So I'm gonna help him get dressed and move him to his room. He'll be fine in a few hours when his meds kick in."

Suzie nodded sympathetically and remained by the door waiting to pee.

Margo had hoped Jinx would be able to dress himself, but when she returned to the bathroom, he was asleep again. She woke him and turned away while he changed, but he had trouble with the pants, and she wound up having to guide his foot for him as he clung to the shower bar. Jinx kept giggling.

"Stop laughing," she said. "This is not funny."

"It's a little funny," he said.

"Head," she said, and he bowed his head so she could jam his shirt on. "Come," she said, taking him by the hand. It occurred to her to look for the needle, which he'd left on the side of the tub. She snatched it up and rolled it into the ball of his wet clothes, led him out and to his room.

Jinx immediately went to his sleeping bag and climbed into it. "Paradise," he said.

Margo unrolled the wet bundle and tossed the clothes in his hamper, not sure what to do with the needle. "Where's your stash?" Margo whispered.

"What?"

"Where's your stash? What do I do with this needle?"

"Oh," Jinx said. "There's an eensy-weensy Allen wrench in the bottom drawer of the bathroom cabinet, and you can use it to unscrew the towel bar. And, you know, it's hollow." For some reason this cracked him up. "The tube thingy."

"Wait, *inside* the towel bar?" Margo said. Really it was ingenious. "You stay in here. Okay? Stay in your room. Do you understand?"

"Who am I hiding from?"

"Suzie."

"Oh God, I wouldn't want Suzie to know." This seemed to genuinely scare him.

"Stay," she said, and slipped out, the needle hidden up the sleeve of her sweatshirt. She went in the bathroom, recently vacated by a grateful Suzie, and locked herself in and took apart the towel bar, found in its metal tube three more needles and a small baggie of brown paste. She emptied the brown paste into the toilet and flushed, then wrapped the needles in toilet paper until they were a big, soft wad. She put the towel bar back together, her hands shaking. She was sweating.

"Um, Margo," Suzie called through the bathroom door, "Bodhi woke up and I grabbed him, but he's fussy. I think he needs to nurse."

"Okay," Margo said, and shoved the bundle of needles in her hoodie front pocket, opened the door, and took Bodhi from Suzie, holding him out from her body as she rushed to her room. She set Bodhi, by now bawling, on her bed, and hid the bundle of syringes in her closet behind her shoes, feeling both like she'd successfully defused a bomb and that she was a naive idiot who had no idea what she was doing.

Margo,
Do you have time for a phone call to go over the depo later? I have 2–3 free. Short version: We didn't get anything great. He is, it turns out, an awful husband but a pretty great dad.

Talk soon,
Ward

Margo read the email numbly later that day as she sat with Jinx on the pink velvet couch, Bodhi asleep on her chest. The main point of the depo, Ward had explained, was to prove Mark wasn't a great father to the kids he already had. Who made the kids dinner, who bought their clothes? Whom did the kids go to when they got hurt? What books was he reading with them? What was their pediatrician's name? "Most dads have no clue who their kids' doctor is," Ward told her. Margo had also given him enough details to ask damning questions about the chronic infidelity. Ward was hesitant to use moral fiber arguments, though, lest they be turned against Margo. Sex work > cheating, sinwise, at least in the minds of most.

She had allowed Jinx out of his room once Suzie went off to class. He was more awake now, though all he wanted to do was watch wrestling and doze and endlessly itch his nose. She'd already tired of interrogating him. How long had this been going on, where did he score, why had he done it?

His answers had been frustrating, if, she thought, fairly honest. He had found the medication in her closet almost immediately, the day after she'd hidden it, and zipped through it in less than a week. After that he'd called a guy he knew in L.A. Of course he had known a guy in L.A. Margo felt incredibly stupid. Jinx had been stealing medication from the hidden stash from the beginning, and she hadn't even noticed.

"Yeah," he said, and laughed. "I started telling you I didn't need them because if I asked for one you would go look at the bottle and see how many were missing."

She had never hated him before, not even as a child when he'd wounded her the most, not like this, not this hot dark fury in her lungs. The worst part, really, was how dopey and slack his face looked as he told her all this, scratching his nose with the back of his hand.

"Why are you crying?" he asked, slurring a little. "Hey, why are you crying?"

"Because I don't know what to do!" she said, trying to wipe away her tears without waking Bodhi. Being with her dad high was like having to deal with another person while still being totally alone. It was almost like having a baby in that sense.

"Margo," Jinx said, "the thing is it's not as big a deal as you think. Like, I'm not saying it wasn't a huge betrayal on my part—it was. But heroin is a drug. It's not, like, the symbiote or something—it doesn't turn you evil."

Margo did not know what the symbiote was, and this involved a whole discussion about Spider-Man and Venom and some Google Image searching of the living black goo in question.

"I'm just saying," Jinx said, seeming slightly more lucid now, "when you're lost in the deep dark forest, the thing to do isn't to get scared of the trees. You have to find your way out again. And if you treat it as this big terrible thing, like every time I relapse it's the end of the world—well, then I'm just gonna hide it from you more and then I'll be in a worse spot to fight it."

She stared at him, trying to understand if he was manipulating her.

"Margo, I've been fighting this battle my entire adult life, it's pretty normal to me." He laughed, looked up at the ceiling. "I mean, God, what a sad thing to say. What a waste of a life."

"It wasn't a waste," Margo said. "Look at your children and your career. I mean, you're literally in the WWE Hall of Fame. Nothing was a waste."

"But all that time," Jinx said, still not looking at her, "I was secretly here. And all my energy has gone into *this*. I feel like I never really experienced the other stuff at all, it was kind of reflected on the surface around me."

"Oh, Daddy," Margo said.

"But that's the thing," Jinx said. "The tragedy isn't brown paste you buy from some guy in a Lexus outside a donut shop; the tragedy is that I was a shitty dad." He reached out his huge hand and carefully, softly ran the knuckles down her cheek.

"You weren't," she told him.

But they both knew he was. And not only to her.

"And I'm sorry for calling Mark," Jinx said.

"Wait, were you high when you called Mark?"

Jinx nodded. Margo closed her eyes. Bodhi was heavy and sweating on her chest, and she felt like she couldn't breathe. Of course that was it. He had just been high. She thought of herself shyly telling Dr. Sharp how good it had secretly felt, her father protecting her like that, defending her.

"Are you going to kick me out?" he asked.

"I don't know," Margo said. There was a sour taste in her mouth. It honestly hadn't occurred to her to kick him out, though she could see that maybe it was the reasonable thing to do. She suddenly remembered JB was coming and wondered if she should tell him not to. "What would you do if I kicked you out?"

"I don't know," Jinx said. "I mean, honestly probably use for a few months and then go back to rehab."

"Oh God," Margo said. She was glad he was being honest. It was also alarming.

She would be so sad if Jinx left, if this was how it all ended. But he couldn't stay, he couldn't be around Bodhi like this. And he'd lied to her, had been lying to her, this whole time.

"Margo," Jinx asked, "I have a really, really big favor to ask you."

"I'm not going to kick you out right this second," she said.

"No," he said, "I was going to ask if there was any chance you could go to the gas station and buy me a Milky Way."

She stared at him.

"Okay!" He held up his hands. "Or not!"

She did go buy him a Milky Way at the gas station, partly to get away from him, but also because she wanted a Milky Way herself. The walk there with Bodhi strapped to her chest made her feel normal again, no longer a part of a sticky nightmare, just her sturdy, regular little self. She bought the Milky Ways and also two Orange Meals, one for her and one for Jinx.

The email from Ward was depressing, but she would talk to him at two o'clock and find out the whole deal. What she couldn't imagine was getting through the rest of this custody battle without Jinx. Yet she also felt used by Jinx, tricked and manipulated. It felt like the only right thing to do was kick him out.

She didn't even wait to get home to open her Milky Way, peeling open the wrapper on the walk back to the apartment. When she'd first told Jinx about the OnlyFans, he'd turned away from her, just like Shyanne. But in less than an hour he had come back. He'd chosen to be on her side, told her she wasn't a car, taught her how to pay taxes and build heat. He had bounced her baby and soothed his cries and turned to look at her when Bodhi did something new or cute.

Yes, she was naive and an idiot. Too young and too stupid. Capable of completely mishandling serious things like drug addiction and taxes. But she was strong. And determined. If there was anything she'd learned, it was that strength and stubbornness were not nothing. The way Jinx had said it, when you're lost in the deep dark woods, the thing to do isn't to get scared of the trees—it made sense. It reminded her of the way the OnlyFans seemed to scare Mark, as though Margo wouldn't be Margo anymore once people had seen her vagina. Maybe Jinx was still Jinx even if he was on drugs.

The sun was strong, and she squinted, her mouth filled with melting chocolate and caramel and nougat. Fuck it, she thought.

If Jinx had been fighting this battle his whole life, then Margo would fight with him.

"Come at me, bitch!" she said, and laughed, chocolate all over her teeth.

THE METHADONE CLINIC was on Commonwealth Avenue, a large cube of '80s paneled mirror glass, a building remarkable only for its complete lack of signage. Jinx and Margo showed up at eight a.m. the next morning, not understanding how busy it would be. It took them three and a half hours to fill out all the paperwork, complete the blood and urine tests, and see the doctor (who was honestly super nice). But they did it all, and in the end, they got Jinx his first dose.

When they drove home, Jinx sat in the back seat with Bodhi to help him through his car seat sadness, and Bodhi was all happy coos and grabbing at the ring toy Jinx dangled in front of him.

"Thank you, Margo," Jinx said.

Margo wasn't sure what to say. It had taken her only a couple of hours of googling to decide methadone would be the best thing. It had taken much longer to convince Jinx to try it. Her arguments: he wouldn't have to leave, he could get treatment while continuing to live with her; it would also treat his chronic pain, since it was an opiate, thus keeping them out of situations like this in the future; they could go tomorrow and be on a new course. He wouldn't have to go through the agony of detox. He could just be done, done with the whole thing.

Jinx's argument was that methadone was heroin, it wasn't any different, a drug is a drug, and an addict is an addict, plus you have to go there every single day, what a drag, and he wouldn't be done, he would never be done, he would be putting off actually getting clean because eventually he'd have to get off the methadone. Also it immediately made people think less of you.

She had won only when she told him he had to go or she was kicking him out.

"You're welcome," she said, her eyes on the road.

"No, I mean, I already feel better."

"You do?"

Jinx had gone through the roof when he found out Margo had flushed his stash. He'd spent the whole night sweating and having diarrhea.

"Yeah, I mean, not just the stomach cramping, but my back. I noticed it when I got in the car. And it's only been, what, like half an hour?"

She could hear the hope in his voice. What if it worked? What if he didn't have to choose between being in constant pain or being the scum of the earth? What if there were more than just those two choices?

"Well, we'll see," Margo said. They had to start the methadone at a low dose because the whole point of it was that it stayed in your system for an incredibly long time. If you titrated up too fast, you might accidentally OD. The doctor had explained that Jinx would probably start feeling withdrawal symptoms that evening. It wouldn't be nearly as bad as the night before, though. And he could come at five a.m. when they opened for his next dose. It would take at least a few weeks before they titrated up to a perfect dose, enough to keep cravings at bay and manage Jinx's pain without making him a zombie.

But it was hope. They were both underslept and exhausted, but it was hope.

"You know what I wanna do?" Jinx asked, as they climbed out of the car. He was smiling, and his skin looked normal, and Margo could not stop herself from smiling back at him.

"What?"

"I want to get really into making bread. Like aggressively into it."

"Okay, now you're just trying to make yourself indispensable," Margo said, reaching to take Bodhi from him.

"No, it's okay," Jinx said, "my back feels good right now."

Margo looked at him. He didn't seem high and was steady on his feet. In that moment, Margo could not think of a single price she wouldn't be willing to pay for her dad to smile at her like that on the sidewalk, Bodhi perched in the crook of his arm, looking around the dazzling morning like a somber little owl. She tried not to think about the weeks and weeks that Jinx had been lying to her, getting high, and she hadn't even noticed. She tried not to think about what that meant, those dark air bubbles in the past.

"After you, my sweet," he said, gesturing her to the door of their building.

She stepped forward and opened it, then held it for him, "After you, my meat!"

There is a desperation to a novel that is unsettling. The world so painstakingly re-created in miniature; this tiny diorama made of words. Why go to all this trouble, to create me, to seduce you, to enumerate so many different breakfast cereals? To make the cunning tiny apartment, the itsy-bitsy Jinx? It's like going to meet your new boyfriend's family for the first time and discovering they are all paid actors. It's almost easier to believe I'm real than to understand what's actually going on. The desperation that could have caused anyone to invent me in the first place. The urgency and need that would require creating an imaginary space of this size and level of detail.

And it really makes you wonder: What kind of truth would require this many lies to tell?

CHAPTER TWENTY-ONE

When I called Ward that afternoon and explained the Jinx methadone situation, he freaked out. "Drugs entering into this is bad news, Margo. It will screw up everything."

I wanted to believe that if I explained the moral conundrum, Dr. Sharp and Mark and even the judge would understand. Wasn't it the right thing to do, to help a family member struggling with addiction? Wasn't he in a treatment program actively attempting to recover? Why should it make me look worse to be helping him? Addiction wasn't contagious.

"No," Ward said. "It's one too many things. You have your age, you have the OnlyFans, you have the pro wrestling stuff—you add drugs? It starts to look real bad."

I knew what Ward meant. He meant it made us look like white trash. Which we were. Which I'd always known.

"What should I do?" I asked.

"I mean, if I were you, I would lie."

"You would?"

"Not outright, but don't bring it up. What do you have left, just the home visit, right? Jinx doesn't even have to be there for that, you could say he's out seeing a movie. If they were looking for drugs as an angle, maybe they would figure out he's registered with the methadone clinic, but I'm not even sure with HIPAA if they have access to that. In fact, I doubt it. How many people know about Jinx's relapse?"

"I mean, right now, just me."

"I would keep it that way. And when you do that home visit, lie your little ass off. Pretend the relapse never even happened. Do you think you can do that?"

"I think so," I said. I mean, I wasn't Shyanne and Jinx's daughter for nothing. Lineage-wise, I was practically falsehood royalty. How many times had I pretended my own grandmother had died?

JB WAS COMING that Friday, a fact so exciting and scary I almost squealed every time I thought about it. By Thursday, Jinx seemed relatively stable, and I knew I couldn't wait any longer.

"I've started seeing someone," I said. We were at the park with Bodhi, pushing him in the little bucket swing. I stood behind, with Jinx in front, and periodically pretended to be a monster who wanted to eat Bodhi's fat little legs. Bodhi shrieked with laughter.

Jinx looked skeptical. "Who?"

"You know that guy I was writing long messages to?"

"Oh, Margo, no!" he cried.

We went back and forth for over an hour, me explaining, Jinx objecting, first at the park, then at the waffle shop, then the apartment. I tried to be patient. I'd known it would be like this. Jinx was convinced JB was going to rape and murder me. Finally, I had Jinx read the portrait JB had written of his mother.

He sighed when he finished reading, handed my phone back. "Well, that's very compelling."

"Because even if it isn't true," I said, "the sensibility to make up a lie like that."

"I don't think it's a lie," Jinx said. "But you're right, even if it was a lie, your typical murderer/rapist wouldn't make up *this* lie."

I nodded, happy and reassured that he knew what I meant.

"I am perturbed," Jinx said. "I'm really of two minds about this."

"What are your two minds?"

"Well, I mean, I worry. What if this guy tries to take advantage of you? He sees that you do all this stuff online, maybe he'll get ideas."

I guffawed. "Dad, I mean, you know I've had sex before?"

"Well, yes, I'm aware!"

I wasn't sure what to say. To me it was obvious JB was coming to have sex with me, that it was the whole point really. If things went well, obviously. And I wanted them to go well.

"The other part of me is just delighted to see you this happy," Jinx said. "You should get to have that—you should get to be young. I can remember that feeling, when you're smitten and can't think about anything else." He smiled, his eyes far away.

"Were you smitten with Viper?"

Jinx came back to himself. We were lounging on the pink couch, stuffed full of waffles, Bodhi asleep on my chest. "Viper was a much sadder situation."

I waited, though it didn't seem he was going to explain. "Was Viper her real name?" I asked.

"Oh, I assume not," Jinx said. "I don't know her real name. She was an escort. I was— I'd started using again and I was hiding it from Cheri, so I'd go on these 'business trips' and basically have a bender."

"Where would you go?" I was afraid of what he would say, but I also wanted to know.

"Oh, I went to a town about thirty minutes from us that had a La Quinta. But it's not very fun to do drugs all by yourself. So I called one of those escort services, and Viper came, took one look at me, and said, 'You better share!' We wound up spending a lot of time together."

It was all so banal, so much more ordinary than I had been imagining. I remembered the way he had been when he was high, imagined him and Viper eating Milky Ways together in the La Quinta, probably watching old wrestling matches. "Why do you think you have such a hard time being faithful?" I asked. Because in some ways it was the question of my whole life. His inability to be faithful was why I'd been conceived at all. Jinx had broken hearts, ruined marriages, alienated his kids—all for sex? It was almost easier to understand the drugs.

Jinx sighed, seemed to really consider it. "I'm not sure any of it was about the actual sex."

I guffawed again. "What was it about then?"

Jinx was rubbing his chin over and over like it was sore. "I get lonely. At night. And women are, you know, like, soft and—"

"Soft?!" I said too loudly. Luckily, Bodhi didn't stir.

"Look at it this way," Jinx went on. "If you're feeling awful and hollow and lonely, do you want to go out and do coke with Shawn Michaels and get into a bar fight when he uses the N-word, or do you want some giggly redhead to tell you her whole life story while you eat ice cream on a hotel bed and then cuddle you with her soft boobs?"

"My God," I said, "do you think *we* weren't lonely?"

"You and Shyanne? You and Shyanne had each other," he said.

I wanted to say that we had failed in a crucial way to connect. Yet in so many ways, it felt like Shyanne and I, even though there were so many things we wanted and couldn't have, were the lucky ones, and Jinx, who always did exactly what he wanted no matter who it hurt, had never managed to enjoy his life.

"I'm sorry," he said, looking over at me, his brown eyes sad as a noble dog's.

"It's all right," I said. Because in the scheme of things, it had been. It was a relief, getting to ask these questions. I had always imagined my father as having these dark, unfathomable urges for sex, drugs, violence. It was better, in a way, to understand that what he really wanted and needed was for the pain and loneliness to ease. His behavior was still bad, but it was no longer so alien and frightening.

"So you'll watch Bodhi while I go out to dinner with JB?"

Jinx nodded. "But I get to meet him first and make sure he's not a psycho."

"You can tell if someone's a psycho upon meeting them?"

"Pretty much," Jinx said. "I've known several."

And I laughed. Because he really, really had.

THERE WAS NO shortage of affordable hotels in Fullerton, partially because of the colleges, mostly because of the proximity to Disneyland. But JB had chosen an Airbnb. In his words, he was "physically unable not to." It was a haunted mansion. He had forwarded me the listing, and I gasped at the price, nearly $400 a night. From the outside it looked like any normal house in Fullerton, cute and unassuming. Inside, everything was purple velvet and red silk, with low light and a plastic raven with glowing purple eyes, creepy portraits, and crystal balls. There was a "haunted gaming room" and a totally normal-looking outdoor hot tub. That was really the funniest part about the house, the contrast between its spooky interior and suburban exterior.

The day JB flew in, I was so excited and nervous it felt like I was outside my body. I had borrowed a green sundress from Suzie and kept sweating through the pits, so I had wads of toilet paper stuffed under my arms as I dashed around the house, making sure the sterilizer was running with Bodhi's bottle things, digging through the laundry for a clean blankie. When the doorbell rang, I ran to answer and tripped in my strappy heels, face-planting on the carpet. "Jesus!" Jinx cried, as I lunged up from the floor like a whale breaching the water, desperate to get to the front door first.

I opened the door, knees stinging with rug burn, strands of my hair stuck to my lip gloss, toilet paper trying to climb out of the armpits of my dress, and there he was, just as nervous as me. He wasn't as tall as I was expecting. His shoulders were broad, and he was solidly built, like if you whacked him in the torso, he would make a good sound. He was wearing a black button-down shirt and jeans and smelled like gum. But it was him. That was the main thing I felt: that I recognized him, that he was who I had been hoping he would be.

"Come in," I said, gesturing. He was holding a bouquet of tiger lilies, the pink ones with freckles, still wrapped in crackly plastic from the supermarket. He held them out to me.

"Oh my gosh," I said, and blushed. I felt like he was here to pick me up for a school dance.

"Is that JB?" Jinx boomed from the living room. I led JB in and introduced them. Jinx managed to deliver what looked like a cripplingly strong handshake while still holding Bodhi in his other arm. JB handled it well and called him "sir."

I took Bodhi from my dad, even though I was already holding the flowers, and bounced him on my hip. "This is Bodhi," I told JB, and JB reached for Bodhi's tiny hand, then didn't know if he was supposed to.

"Hey there," he said, a little awkward. It was clear he didn't know anything about babies.

"Let me get these in water," I said, stomping into the kitchen like a giraffe in my heels. I was already reconsidering the shoes. I had assumed JB would follow. Jinx had started talking to him, and I kind of panicked and left him there. I couldn't get my heart rate to a normal speed. I plopped Bodhi in his highchair while I arranged the flowers in a vase. I fished the toilet paper out of my armpits and tried to calm down.

Evidently JB passed Jinx's cross-examination, and I was so keyed up I don't even remember saying all of the goodbyes except that I kissed Bodhi about a million times, and then we were out the door. On our way down the stairs, I tripped, twisting my ankle, and went down hard. I knew it was bad the moment I finished falling down the stairs. I didn't even try to get up.

"Oh shit!" JB cried, scurrying down to me.

"I'm okay," I said, even though I knew I was not. I wasn't even positive I could stand, my ankle was screaming.

"Do you want me to get your dad?" he asked. "Do you think you need to go to the doctor?"

I closed my eyes in anguish. I knew I could not go to the fancy restaurant where he'd made a reservation like this, and I was certain Jinx would be able to tell if my ankle was broken or only sprained; he was great with injuries. But I also knew if we went back up there our chances of having any date at all would drop to zero. I tried to stand and gasped when I put weight on my ankle.

JB grimaced.

"What if," I said, "we go to the haunted mansion and just order in?"

"Don't you think you should go to the doctor?" JB asked, gesturing at my ankle.

"If it's broken it will still be broken tomorrow," I said. "And I will cry if we don't get to have this date. Please? Can we please just go to your place and order in?"

"Of course," JB said, "obviously, obviously." But he looked worried. "You want help walking?"

I nodded, and he dipped his shoulder so I could grab on while he braced me around the waist. We wobbled out to the parking lot to his rental car.

When we got to the haunted mansion, JB helped me to the door, then told me to wait while he disappeared inside. When he returned, he was pushing a desk chair with wheels. I plopped into it delightedly, and he gave me a rolling tour. It was very gaudy as haunted mansions go. There was a black light in the hallway that made eyes on the wallpaper glow. We settled in the sitting room, where flat screens hung in elaborate gilt frames were rigged so they displayed paintings that appeared to be moving. I transferred myself onto a velvet settee, and JB grabbed me some ice in a bag for my ankle, then plunked down beside me, and we huddled over his phone trying to decide what to order.

"Oh, I know what we should get," he said. "This is so obvious!"

"What?"

"Wings!" he said.

I clapped my hands like an excited child. "Yes!" I cried. "Wings!"

Once the business of ordering the food was done, I became keenly aware of him next to me on the couch. I felt like a vampire mesmerized by the pulse in his throat or something, but we couldn't start making out before dinner. So I asked questions about his flight and work and whether he'd ever been to California before (he had, though not to Fullerton, because, duh, why would anyone visit Fullerton?). It felt like we were strangers, and I didn't know how to break through into feeling like we knew each other.

"Your dad is quite intimidating," JB said. I had briefed him on my dad, but it was another thing to experience it in person.

"Oh, no, did he threaten to cut your dick off?" I asked.

JB laughed. "Now I feel like he was taking it easy on me."

"Do you ever think about the sort of restrained, almost literary quality of my made-up family, and just comparing it to my real family, aren't you ever like, 'Damn, she's a genius'?"

"Yeah, didn't you see my review on Goodreads?"

I laughed. "What the fuck is Goodreads?"

"It's, like, a book review site, it was a joke."

I giggled, caught up in a fantasy of other people reading his reviews of our private correspondence, trying to figure out what he was even talking about. "Gosh, people love reviewing things," I said, imagining with horror a site dedicated to reviews of OnlyFans accounts.

"Even dicks," JB said.

That was true, I realized, I did rate dicks. But I didn't want JB to think I was like WangMangler. What if he was nervous and thought I was some big dick judge? "I'm an easy grader," I said. "I give them all ten out of ten. The art is really all in the comparison to the Pokémon and any relevant puns."

"Oh?" JB said, still smiling, though I could tell he was uncomfortable. And why shouldn't he be? I shouldn't be talking to him about other people's dicks.

When the wings came, JB set out all the food on the coffee table so I didn't have to move, and we feasted. The whole time we were eating I was distracted trying to figure out what would happen next. I had not calculated any of this because I'd imagined us at a restaurant. I'd thought my chance to kiss him would be when we walked out to the car after dinner, and if that went well we'd go to his Airbnb instead of my house. Now I didn't know how exactly a kiss would happen.

"Is something wrong?" JB asked.

"No," I said, "I'm just, like, plotting how I'm gonna put the moves on you."

He laughed, covering his mouth with his napkin. "That's a relief," he said after he finished chewing. "I'm not good at making plans like that. I figured I would try to kiss you after dinner when we walked to the car."

"That's when I had figured I would kiss you!"

"But now I have no idea, really." JB laughed again.

"Leave it all up to me," I said. "You won't even know what's happening. You'll be like a baby gazelle taken down by a lioness."

His eyebrows shot up, and I figured it was now or never, so I leaned over and kissed him, even though I was pretty sure I tasted strongly of buffalo sauce. My lips met his, and he leaned into the kiss, turning to me on the settee. His hands found my rib cage and squeezed. I could feel the strength in his hands and arms, that big chest with its huge ribs, the heat of him. I broke away from the kiss and blinked. The room was spinning slightly. "Whoa," I said, and he kissed me again.

CHAPTER TWENTY-TWO

The next morning, I awoke with the sun streaming down on a massive four-poster bed, my breasts rock hard with milk, as happy as I had ever been in my life. JB was curled around me. I scooted my butt closer to him, remembering the night before. He had carried me in here, me clinging to his front like a koala.

I kept my eyes closed and experimentally rolled my ankle. It didn't hurt as much as I'd feared. I pushed my foot out from under the covers and opened my eyes, peered down at it. It was swollen and there was a purple bruise on the outside, right below my ankle. It didn't look all that bad, though. I became aware of a buzzing sound, my phone on the nightstand. I grabbed it in time to see Jinx was calling. It went to voicemail before I could answer. I'd told him I was spending the night. I figured he just wanted to see when I would be home, make sure I was okay, but when I opened my phone, I saw there were six missed calls and my stomach dropped. Bodhi.

I called Jinx back immediately. "Oh my God, I'm so sorry, I was still asleep, is he okay?"

"He's fine," Jinx said, but his voice sounded weird.

"What happened?"

"I need you to come home," Jinx said.

"Why? What happened? I'm on my way. Is he okay?" I was sitting up now and JB was awake beside me.

"There's someone here to do a home inspection for Bodhi's well-being."

"From the 730?!" I was straight panicking. "They weren't supposed to come until Tuesday!"

"Okay, well, they're here now, and, uh, your presence is requested. She says if you can't be here in fifteen minutes, she'll need to take him with her to her office."

"Fuck, okay, I'll be right there."

JB HAD ME back at the apartment in less than eight minutes. I'd rinsed my mouth with water and wiped the mascara from under my eyes, but my hair was a hopeless mess, I had a major sex tangle in the back, and I hoped it wasn't too obvious I was in last night's clothes.

JB started to unbuckle to walk me in. I stopped him. "I don't want to have to explain who you are," I said.

"But you can't get up the stairs," he said.

"I can," I said. "I'll be fine."

"I feel like I should—"

"Please," I said, "trust me. It will look way worse if you go in with me." It would be one thing if JB and I had time to come up with a lie, some alternate story as to how we met. I had told Dr. Sharp I didn't have a boyfriend, so I couldn't go into this home inspection with a guy I'd clearly just fucked and be forced to admit, yeah, he was one of my fans!

"At least let me help you to the door," he said.

"Nope!" I said, and slid out of his car. "I'll text you as soon as this is over," I promised, and did my best not to show how much it hurt as I hobbled up the stairs, my heels in one hand.

I let myself inside and found my dad with a woman I'd never seen before, sitting together on the pink velvet couch in a large patch of sun. They looked beautiful, God-lit.

"Oh, hello!" The woman heaved herself up. She was at least seven months pregnant and as cute as can be, wearing a black maternity dress printed with white flowers, a white T-shirt underneath for modesty. There was a tattoo of a star on the inside of her wrist, I noticed as we shook hands.

"Are you Margo? My name is Maribel. I'm with Child Protective Services."

"I'm so sorry I wasn't here," I said. My heart was beating so loudly, it was hard to hear. "I thought it was supposed to be Dr. Sharp. Isn't the appointment next week?"

I looked to Jinx, who was now standing and bouncing Bodhi, who'd begun to fuss. He didn't meet my eye.

"Well, I don't know anything about Dr. Sharp, and there was no appointment, so I'm afraid you must be thinking of something else. I'm with CPS. We received a complaint of possible neglect and abuse. This home visit is standard procedure. Hopefully we can go through everything and make sure this is a safe environment for your little guy. I've already walked through the apartment with James here."

"Are you going to take him?" I asked, my voice breaking. That's what Jinx had said, that if I wasn't there in time, she would take him. I had made it, but would she take him anyway?

Bodhi was fussing in Jinx's arms. Jinx was bouncing him helplessly. "I think he needs to nurse," he said, handing him to me.

"Oh, of course," Maribel said, and gestured to the couch. I did not want to take her spot, but I knew if I sat on the floor I'd never be able to get up with my ankle, so I sat and whipped out a boob as discreetly as possible.

"Today we're evaluating the home," Maribel said. "If we don't find imminent danger to Bodhi, then he can remain here."

I nodded anxiously.

"So James said you were staying at a friend's house?" Maribel prompted.

"Yeah," I said, afraid of contradicting anything he had already told her.

"Do you do that a lot?" she asked.

"This was the first time, actually. First night away." The shame was quick and wrenching. I couldn't believe I'd left him here, that I'd been so selfish.

"I see," she said in a way that made it clear she didn't believe me at all. "Well, I suppose everyone needs a break sooner or later. So I was asking James exactly what you do for a living. He said you have a website?"

"I'm no good at explaining it," Jinx said, making wild *I'm sorry* eyes behind Maribel.

"I'm like a content creator? We make TikToks mainly right now. I think eventually we'll branch into YouTube." If she didn't already know, then I certainly didn't want to tell her.

"But you also have an OnlyFans account?" Maribel asked.

She already knew. "Yeah," I said, almost dizzy with fear. "I'm confused—is this related to the 730 evaluation?"

"So you're also undergoing a 730 eval right now?" Maribel asked.

"I mean, yes?" I said. Probably that looked even worse.

"As part of a custody dispute? Divorce?"

"No, paternity," I said.

"Oh my God, your ankle!" Jinx cried. He had just seen it. I'd texted him that I was spending the night with JB, but I hadn't mentioned that I had fallen down the stairs and we'd never even made it to the restaurant.

"It's okay," I said, trying to hide it behind my other foot.

"Did you fall?" he asked.

"Yes," I admitted, "in the stupid heels."

"Had you been drinking?" Maribel asked.

"No," I said quickly. I didn't turn twenty-one for a few more months. "Just a klutz."

Maribel's brow was knitted. Anyone, I realized, would think I had been out drinking. My hair was messed up, I was wearing last night's clothes, a sprained ankle, and she knew about the OnlyFans—Jesus Christ, how much worse could this even get?

"So tell me about Mr. Bodhi," she said. She was clearly trying to be friendly, which I wouldn't have expected. "What he likes, what he doesn't like. What's his personality?"

"Oh gosh," I said. No one had ever asked me what Bodhi's personality was before. It seemed like an intricate thing to describe, given that he wasn't talking yet and all my maternal insight was based on vibes. "He's my only baby, so I can't compare him to other babies, but he's very joyful and . . . happy." As I was speaking Bodhi shat an incredible volume, warm and thick, I could feel it through his diaper against my arm. "He's, uh, I mean, he's a pretty normal baby, I think?"

"Why don't you show me Bodhi's room."

"Oh," I said, "his crib is in my room." I stood and went light-headed at the pain. I tried not to let it show.

"We were waiting to go in your room till you got here," Jinx said, in a way that said, *You better not have a robot dildo on your desk or something*. And he was right to worry, though I didn't think Maribel would know to be suspicious of the Dyson in its shiny new box sitting in the corner. I had no idea exactly what state I'd left my room in as I was getting ready for my date, and sure enough, as I hobbled through the door, I saw a pair of panties that hadn't made it into the hamper. I bent to scoop them up, my ankle threatening to give out entirely, and I could feel the poop from Bodhi's diaper start to leak down my arm. I was so anxious I was actually quivering.

"And these are his toys?" Maribel gestured at a single sad octopus toy on my bed. Each tentacle said the name of a color in both French and English.

"Oh, he has more, hold on," I said, and dragged out the big plastic bin of his toys from the closet. Every time I moved, I lurched around like a cartoon hunchback. I had no idea if it was a normal amount of toys, wildly too much, or not enough. Mainly I was trying to judge whether she could smell the poop.

"That just a closet?" Maribel said, peeking into the dark closet. And in that moment, I remembered the toilet paper bundle of syringes I'd stashed there. I'd never thrown them away. They were tucked behind my shoes, boots, and things I didn't wear often. You couldn't see them, and I'd forgotten they were even there. My ears were ringing.

"Is this where you change him?" she asked, gesturing at the dresser. The changing pad was on the floor and the dresser top was bare wood. The fact that she'd turned her attention away from the closet was a massive relief, but I found myself unable to speak fluently.

"I usually change him on the floor?" I said. "I'm paranoid about him rolling off. Not that I would let him roll off or leave him up there or anything."

"And do you have a boyfriend? Anyone come around?"

"No," I said, my voice wobbling. "No boyfriend."

She looked at me skeptically. "Not seeing anyone even casually?"

I felt like she could see everything JB and I had done on that massive four-poster bed, my body on top of him, his strong hands squeezing my tits until milk ran down his arms, my sudden flash of embarrassment and then the way he growled with delight. "Maybe casually," I admitted.

"Does he ever spend the night here?" Maribel asked.

"No," I said quickly.

"I need to do a physical exam of Bodhi to make sure there are no bruises or lacerations or other signs of abuse," she said brightly.

"Oh," I said, "as we were talking, he definitely pooped, let me get him changed."

"That's okay," Maribel said. "I can change him. I'll need to look under his diaper anyway."

She held out her arms for me to hand over my shitty child. I almost couldn't make myself do it. I followed her as she knelt on the ground to change him on his changing mat, which was awkward given her pregnant belly. There was poop on my arm. I snagged a wipe to clean it off as surreptitiously as I could. It was a major blowout, and it was clear Maribel didn't have a ton of diaper-changing experience. She wasn't using the wipes efficiently and was fighting hard not to gag. I could not imagine this was good. Why had she not allowed me to change him? It was such a weird power move. I'd not been breathing normally for some time and there were purple spots in my vision.

After she'd finally gotten him clean, she pointed to a bit of diaper rash. "What's this?"

"It's diaper rash," I said.

"Have you been doing anything to treat it?"

I told her I'd been putting Boudreaux's Butt Paste on it and explained he'd begun eating more solids. I thought his poop was more acidic.

"This is diaper rash?" she asked again.

"Yes," I said. What did she think? That I'd been burning his little butt cheeks with a curling iron?

After that, she wanted to talk with me at the dining room table. Jinx took Bodhi. Suzie had come out of her room and was watching everything, silent and sad-eyed. She and Jinx disappeared into the living room with the baby, and I could hear *Sesame Street* in the background. I tried to relax. At least we were farther away from the closet.

"And what does Jinx do for work?" she asked.

"He's retired," I said.

"What did he used to do?"

I could not see how this was germane to Bodhi's safety, but I didn't want to seem difficult. "Um, he was a professional wrestler?"

Maribel looked up, skeptical. "For real? Like with WWE?"

"Actually, he was kind of independent," I said. I knew that made it sound worse, like he wasn't legitimate. But there was no way to explain that he could be independent only because he was so famous.

"Any substance abuse problems?" Maribel asked.

I worried I would throw up. "Me?" I asked, stalling. I didn't know what to do. I knew Ward had told me to lie to Dr. Sharp at the home visit, but this was a different situation.

"No, your father. Have *you* had any substance abuse problems?"

"No," I said.

"But your father has never had substance abuse problems even in the past?" Maribel pressed.

She had to know. There was no other reason for her to be asking, I realized. Plus, there were about two decades' worth of tabloids and wrestling blogs reporting my dad was in rehab; all she'd have to do was google him. "In the past, yes," I said. "But he's in treatment and he's doing really well."

"So you think he's clean now?" Maribel asked. "I'm going to ask both of you to provide a urine sample."

I had no idea if methadone would show up on a drug test. I was guessing it might. "He's currently on methadone," I said. "So that may show up on his urine test."

"Oh, so he's on methadone?" The tone in Maribel's voice changed. "How long has he been on methadone?"

I hesitated. If she asked to see proof he was in treatment she'd see the dates, so I couldn't imagine lying. The truth didn't sound great, though. "About ten days." I wanted to explain about him being clean, then his back going out, the ER doctors, the vicious cycle of chronic pain, but it felt like I'd swallowed a chunk of ice.

"Ten days?" Maribel asked, even though she'd heard me perfectly fine.

I nodded, and she was quiet for a bit, busy writing things down. I stared at the ceiling. It felt like the whole world was ending.

"Do you use any illegal substances?" she asked.

"No," I said firmly.

"So you don't use drugs of any kind?"

"No." I stared at her. She stared at me. She was waiting, certain I would crack and confess that actually I did smoke pot now and then. But she could suck it because I absolutely did not smoke pot now and then. Finally, she looked down at her notebook.

"Okay then, let's get the urine tests over with, shall we?" she said.

"My pleasure," I said. She took a plastic urine sample cup from her purse, which felt very wrong and way too intimate, and handed it to me.

It was a relief to be alone in the bathroom. I peed in the cup. Being pregnant I had peed in an awful lot of cups, and it was much easier now that there wasn't a big belly in the way. When I came out, Jinx was holding his cup and waiting to go in, looking cold with dread.

Maribel was by the front door, chatting with Suzie, who had Bodhi on her hip. Suzie looked so small suddenly, like a child holding her baby sibling. When Bodhi saw me, he squealed and reached his little arms out for me, babbling, "Mamamamamamamama," and I swooped him up and kissed his fat cheek.

"So what I'm going to do," Maribel said, "is check in with some other members of your family—your mom, your stepdad—talk to them, talk to Bodhi's pediatrician. And I have your financial statements, James got me those." She smiled almost too widely, showing her beautiful tiny teeth like pearls.

"So with the 730 . . ." I began. I was hoping it was somehow illegal for her to interfere in that process, some attorney-client privilege or HIPAA thing? At the very least, it seemed like CPS should wait until the accusations were substantiated before they went to Mark and told him Jinx and I were porn-addled drug addicts who ate too much sugary cereal.

"I can speak to your lawyer," she said. "The case will be under your name, I can find it."

"Oh," I said, my heart sinking. "Okay. Who filed the complaint against me?" I asked. "If you don't mind me asking."

"That's confidential information, unfortunately," Maribel said. "We'll get your urine tests back, and we can go from there. One thing I can tell you is that Jinx will need to get off methadone in order for Bodhi to stay in the home, so he may want to talk to his doctor about that."

"Wait, what?" I said. "He just got on the methadone."

"It's our policy that caregivers should be clean and able to pass a drug test in order for the child to remain in the home." It was creepy how she kept calling it "the home."

"But methadone is a treatment for substance abuse. Why would you want people with substance abuse problems to stop receiving treatment for those problems? What if they relapse?"

"It's policy," Maribel said. "And we don't require they stop treatment. In fact he will have to show proof of being in some kind of treatment, usually a twelve-step program."

I had done all this research when we got Jinx on the methadone in the first place, so I said, "But why, when methadone has a success rate of sixty to ninety percent, and twelve-step programs have a success rate of between five and ten percent? Why would you insist people adopt the less successful, less science-backed treatment option?" These were the longest sentences I'd managed to speak the whole time.

"In the eyes of the California court system, methadone is just another name for heroin." She shrugged.

"But it's *not*," I said.

"And yet it is," she said, smiling confidently.

Bodhi squealed and reached out, grabbing at Maribel's sleeve. "Sorry," I said, trying to detach his tight little fist from her T-shirt.

"He's cute," she said a little sadly, like she already knew I would lose him. "Look at it this way: when his urine test comes back, your father will test positive for opiates. They could be methadone, or they could be heroin. We have no way of knowing the difference."

"But you do have a way of knowing because you have paperwork stating he is in a methadone treatment program," I said. I knew the last thing I should do was get heated, but this was maddening.

"He could also be using. Lots of people on methadone continue to use."

"His doctor said the methadone blocks the euphoria of the high," I said.

"Doesn't stop people from trying," Maribel said.

Then Jinx was behind me, holding out his pee cup. "Everything okay?" he said.

"This looks great!" Maribel said, as she accepted his pee and put it in her purse. Okay, it wasn't a purse-purse, it was like a tote bag. She didn't even check to make sure the lid was on tight, just popped it in a Ziploc bag and tossed it in. "We'll be in touch," she said, like this was a job interview.

And I heard Mark's voice in my head: "Words can be made hollow, and once they are hollow, anything can be done with them."

CHAPTER TWENTY-THREE

Jinx and I spent the next hour going over Maribel's visit in micro detail, trying to reassure each other that everything would be okay. We debated who'd called in the complaint, and I figured it had to be Mark. There was really no way of knowing.

"What I'm worried about is *your* drug test," Jinx said.

"My drug test?" I asked. "Why?"

"Because of the mushrooms," he said. "I mean, I don't know if they test for them or not."

"Oh God," I said. The mushrooms had not even occurred to me. "Oh no, oh God!"

"It's okay," Jinx said. "Jesus, you didn't realize?"

"No! I didn't think about that at all! That feels like forever ago! Can it still show up?"

"Don't panic," Jinx said. "WWE didn't test for mushrooms, so CPS might not either."

We googled and the results were confusing. There were all different kinds of pee tests for different things. Finally, we thought to look up how long mushrooms stayed in your system, and with a urine test it showed up for only one to three days. So even if they did test for mushrooms, I should be in the clear. Hair follicle tests were a whole other story, and we both thanked God I hadn't been asked for one. I should be okay. Somehow, I didn't really feel any better.

"I don't know what to do," I said.

"Let me see that ankle," Jinx said, and patted his lap for me to swing up my leg. "Wiggle down here so you can bend your knee."

I scooted down the couch, Bodhi on my chest. He was in a wonderful, milk-drunk mood at least. Jinx examined my foot, running his fingers over the tendons until he found the place that made me wince. He explored the bones on the top of my foot, but none of that hurt.

"I think it's a sprain," he said, finally looking up. "Oh, hey, why are you crying?"

I shrugged, my chin crumpling. I really didn't know. It might have been that my body didn't have another way of processing so much adrenaline. I couldn't tell how bad everything was. I didn't know if I would lose Bodhi, if I was going to have to quit OnlyFans. I felt guilty for spending a night on my own, for sleeping with JB, for thinking it was okay that I was allowed to be young again just for one night. The needles in my closet. "I'm a bad person," I gasped.

"No," Jinx said. "No, honey, you're not a bad person."

I closed my eyes.

I couldn't trust him.

He was a bad person too.

JINX LEFT FOR Rite Aid to buy me an ankle brace, and I went to my closet, gathered the bundle of needles, wedged them deep in the diaper trash, then hobbled outside, taking the whole bag with me to the dumpster while Suzie watched Bodhi. I sat down on the curb and called JB, the sun helping to relax some of the muscles in my back. The crows were calling back and forth across the parking lot, arguing from the trees.

"Hey, how are you doing? Everything turn out okay?" he asked, his voice so warm and easy.

"Not really," I said.

"What's going on?" he asked.

I didn't want to get into the details. It all felt so terribly shameful.

"Should I come over?" he asked.

"No," I said. I knew he had only a few hours before he'd have to head to the airport. We'd made tentative plans to have lunch with my dad, but I couldn't imagine him coming over now. I felt like I'd throw up. The idea of seeing him and being excited and happy was almost grotesque. "I can't have lunch."

"Oh," he said. I could hear the disappointment in his voice.

"JB," I said, "I had so much fun last night. But I—I think we should stop seeing each other."

"What?"

"At least for now. I'm in a really bad situation. I haven't gone into it with you. Mark, Bodhi's father, is suing for custody, and I've been undergoing this whole investigation, and Child Protective Services came by today—someone reported me for neglect. I—" I broke off, my voice cracking. It burned, having to admit all this to him.

"Oh, Margo, I'm so sorry," JB said.

"I just really need to focus on my shit right now," I said. "There isn't room in my life for romance, even if I wish there was."

There was a pause, then I heard him sigh. I wished I could see his face.

"What?" I asked.

"I was going to say, couldn't I help? Couldn't I come over and offer moral support or . . . I don't know?"

"It's just, JB, I'm fucking up. I'm fucking up bad. I need to focus and do the right thing and be an adult." I left unsaid that I didn't think JB could offer me any help. He was awkward as hell just meeting the baby, it wasn't like he could hold Bodhi while I called Ward or went to the bathroom. And I didn't want him there. I knew it was irrational, but it felt like spending the night away from Bodhi had caused Maribel to come.

"If that's what you want," JB said finally.

"It's what I need," I said. "At least right now." I wasn't sure it would get any better in the future either. My mind snagged on that moment talking about my dick ratings, the wariness that had come into his face. How would it ever work between me and JB? What guy would be able to tolerate my phone constantly buzzing with pictures of other guys' dicks? We might lie to ourselves for a little while and pretend it could work, but how could it? I didn't know if it was better to say all this or let it be unspoken.

"I'm sorry," I said. "This is going to be one of those things I regret."

"Then why are you doing it?" he asked, really and truly angry now.

Good, I thought, *get angry at me. Hate me. Boo and set me free.*

When we hung up, I hunched over like I'd been stabbed and stayed there, remembering how, after we finished making love, we had scampered into the backyard naked and slipped into the steaming water. I'd worried it wasn't good for my ankle, but I didn't care, didn't want to consider it. The stars were bright above us, and we both groaned as we relaxed into the hot tub.

"You're sparkling," he said, gesturing to the mist around us. "The steam makes it look like your skin is sparkling. Like you're a goddess."

I laughed, delighted.

"I think maybe you are," he said. "That's the only rational explanation."

"Explanation for what?" I asked, and then kissed him so he couldn't answer.

Of course I didn't get to be that happy.

Why had I ever thought I deserved such a thing?

JINX RETURNED WITH an ankle brace and, charmingly, Orange Meals for them both.

Margo felt better with the brace, more secure. "Do you think I should quit my OnlyFans?" she asked, opening her bag of SunChips.

"It's not illegal to have an OnlyFans," Jinx pointed out. "I don't think they can make you quit."

"It's not illegal to be on methadone either!" Margo said. "What are we even going to do? You can't get off the methadone!"

"Oh," Jinx said, suddenly hesitant. "I thought that part was easy. I think we just— I mean, I think I should move out."

He looked so normal as he said it. As though he weren't pushing her off a boat and into the freezing water.

"If I'm not living here," he continued, "they don't get to say what course of treatment I pursue. And the methadone, Margo, I mean, I feel really hopeful. I don't want to quit."

Margo nodded rapidly, tucking her hair behind her ears. "Totally," she agreed. "But . . ." She didn't know how to frame it, how to say it. She had no excuse for how badly she wanted him to stay. "Where would you go?" she asked finally.

"Somewhere close, at least for now," he said. "I want to stay close by the clinic. But eventually, you know, I'll probably have to start working again."

Margo nodded, unable to speak. It wasn't that she'd thought Jinx would live with her and Bodhi forever. But what would she do without him? The idea of continuing OnlyFans without Jinx felt scary somehow, just her and Bodhi and her garden of penis worms. She couldn't bear the idea of it. And she felt certain, deep in her gut, that if she kept doing the OnlyFans, Maribel would find a way to take Bodhi. She could picture her, smiling as she lifted Bodhi out of her arms. But how would Margo make a living? Who would watch Bodhi? She was back in the same predicament she'd always been in, and depending on whether there was a trial or not, she might not even have any savings.

"What's a career where you can make good money without going to school?" she asked Jinx.

"Don't do something hasty," Jinx urged. "I feel like if it were that clear-cut, she'd have said you had to quit. I mean, you should be good on the pee test, the mushrooms won't show up. They can't take him, Margo. You haven't done anything wrong."

But Margo knew the world was perfectly willing to punish you no matter what you had done.

SHE DRAFTED THE announcement to her fans that night.

She explained she was going back to her home planet and that she'd miss them all terribly, and that she'd sculpted exact replicas of each of their penises out of tinfoil and planned to eat one a day until they were all gone. She let her cursor rest over the "post" button. She wouldn't do it tonight. There were too many unknowns. She needed to come up with a plan. She thought about Ward saying the State of California would rather a kid be able to eat and have a mom who sells nudes than not eat. She would need to devise some other way of making money and figure out childcare, now that Jinx would be moving out.

She pulled an old three-ring binder from her shelf, the one she'd used for Mark's class, and clicked it open, dumped everything out. She would do this the way she had done everything else.

The more she read, the more the plan cohered in her mind. If she quit the OnlyFans, Mark wouldn't have any grounds on which to take Bodhi; they wouldn't have to go to court. She could use the thirty grand in her account to launch herself on another career. She could hire Suzie as a nanny. She was an hour deep into research on how to become a real estate agent when her phone buzzed with a message from JB. Thinking of you, it said. She set it down without answering. That was exactly the problem. She couldn't afford to be thinking of him. Dr. Sharp's in-home observation was three days away, and Margo had to be ready.

IT WAS AT first extremely weird having Dr. Sharp in her apartment, like seeing your second-grade teacher at the grocery store, and then suddenly not weird at all.

"What's all this?" Dr. Sharp asked, gesturing to Jinx's moving boxes. Margo knew she'd promised Ward that she'd lie to Dr. Sharp about Jinx's addiction, but if she was quitting the OnlyFans and he was moving out, she didn't see any point in that, and there was something wonderfully freeing about being up front. She explained the CPS visit, and Dr. Sharp confirmed that it had not been triggered by the 730.

"I figured," Margo said, then explained Jinx's relapse and treatment, that CPS required he get off methadone. "And we want him to succeed, we want evidence-based, effective medicine, and that means staying on the methadone, so he has to move out." Margo shrugged.

"I see," Dr. Sharp said. She didn't seem sympathetic, but she didn't say it in a judgy way either. They had settled at the dining table. Bodhi was in his highchair, and Margo was feeding him pureed yams.

"I've decided to quit OnlyFans," Margo said. "I haven't told Mark yet. But I don't see a way forward. I can't put Bodhi at risk like this."

"So you feel that the work is harming him?" Dr. Sharp asked.

Margo snorted. "No! But I'm not willing to have CPS come in here and mess everything up whenever they want to." She shivered, imagining Maribel holding out her arms for Bodhi, the wistful way she'd said, "He's cute."

"I see. So then what are you thinking workwise?" Dr. Sharp asked. This was much closer than Margo had ever sat to Dr. Sharp, and she could see the downy hairs on her plump cheeks; they made Dr. Sharp seem more human. She was, after all, just another woman. Probably a mother herself.

"I have a fair bit in savings," Margo said. "I was thinking of getting my real estate credential." She liked how solid and grown-up that sounded. When she'd told Jinx, he'd been exasperated with her. "You will hate it," he spat, "all those phonies! Margo, no, this is not for you." At least Dr. Sharp didn't react like that, she merely nodded and wrote something down in her notes.

Margo wiped some yam off Bodhi's face. He was squealing and gibbering, so happy. He loved yams. She'd started doing Baby Signs with him, and he touched his fingers together in the sign for "more."

"You want more?!" she cried, laughing. "I don't have any more!"

Bodhi signed frantically, *More, more!*

"Okay, all right, you want some banana?" she asked.

Margo peeled the banana and mashed it in a little blue bowl with a fork while Bodhi shrieked like a chimpanzee with delight and impatience. She'd been feeding him the yams with a little spoon. Most of the time she let him feed himself with his fingers. She didn't know if this was bad or good, but it was her secret belief that it couldn't hurt him, and it might even help his fine motor skills.

"This might get messy," she said to Dr. Sharp. "He loves to feed himself, and I think it's good for him, to have to use his hands." She gave him the bowl, and they both watched Bodhi, who looked comically excited, as he steered his hand down into the banana and then slammed it up into his mouth. It really was amazing how consciously he had to manipulate his hands, like he was working an arcade claw machine, every movement jerky and a little askew.

"Really makes you more impressed with deer," Margo said.

"How's that?" Dr. Sharp asked. She had taken off her blazer at some point.

"Oh, what with the walking from birth and all. Or like snakes that don't need any parenting at all, they hatch and say peace out and go try to be a snake. They're programmed to know what to do. I wonder what it's like, acting completely on instinct like that."

"That's an interesting question," Dr. Sharp said. She didn't write anything down this time. She wasn't saying it was interesting that Margo had said that, like she was evaluating her. She just seemed genuinely interested in what being a baby snake might be like. They were two women imagining being baby snakes.

Once Bodhi was good and coated in goo, Margo stripped him down and put him in the bath, dumping his toys around him. Dr. Sharp sat on the closed toilet while Margo knelt by the tub. Margo had worried she'd be awkward with Bodhi in front of Dr. Sharp the way she'd been with Maribel, all her words vanishing, everything coming out wrong. But she found that it didn't matter if Dr. Sharp was watching them; she was giving Bodhi a bath like she always did because Bodhi expected her to, and Bodhi was more important to her than Dr. Sharp in an almost physical way.

Dr. Sharp stayed while Margo got him out of the tub and changed him into a fresh diaper and jammies. "So in general, at this point I would nurse him to sleep," she said, mainly to warn Dr. Sharp she was about to whip out a boob.

"That's fine, Margo," Dr. Sharp said. "I think I've seen enough. You've been so generous with your time. I'll get out of your hair and let you get Bodhi settled."

"Oh," Margo said, "okay." She trailed Dr. Sharp out to the foyer.

"Thanks so much," Dr. Sharp said. "I know it's a lot, to be observed in your house with your child. That's a lot of trust. Thank you for letting me be part of your evening."

"Oh," Margo said, "of course!" She almost said, "Anytime!"

And then Dr. Sharp was gone. It felt almost too easy. Margo worried she might have done something wrong, though she couldn't think what it might have been.

She went to bed wondering about mother snakes and baby snakes and whether snakes feel love for each other, or if they draw that intense pleasure from some other aspect of their nature, maybe from killing. She imagined a snake philosopher telling his snake students about the greatest good and how everyone knew of course it was killing.

She'd have given anything to have someone to express these thoughts to, but she knew it wouldn't be fair to call JB, even if talking to him would be more wonderful than anything. Who cared about sex, really? When what you needed was someone to talk to in the dark. She thought about what her dad had said about women and why he always ended up cheating. People are all so lonely. Even when they do horrible things, it often comes down to that, if only you take the time to understand them. It seemed like that should mean the world could be better, that people could help each other, like Jesus said. And yet that's not what happens. That hardly ever seems to happen at all.

She couldn't help thinking that if she went into real estate and things calmed down, and if her phone wasn't buzzing with dicks and her days weren't spent in cosplay lingerie, she and JB could try dating for real. But it was difficult to picture. Whenever Margo thought of herself as a real estate agent, she imagined her body with someone else's face pasted on it, the scale slightly off so the head was too big like a Barbie. She tried imagining a JB doll grasping the Margo doll with his stiff arms, kissing her with his numb plastic lips.

CHAPTER TWENTY-FOUR

The next morning I showed up at Kenny's condo right as Shyanne came out the front door dressed head to toe in aqua Lululemon, dragging a yellow Labrador that couldn't have been more than eight weeks old.

I didn't think she'd be able to see me through the glare of my windshield, but she stopped dead the moment she stepped outside. I suppose there were only so many purple Civics with big dents in the front right fender. When I unbuckled Bodhi and joined her in the shade, she looked so on edge I almost didn't know what to say.

"I came to apologize," I said. "I'm quitting the account and I'm going to get my real estate license. And try to be . . . someone you can be proud of." I struggled to push out the words. I tried to read her face, but it was guarded. It was unreasonably hot for February, and I could see the sweat gathering on Shyanne's upper lip.

"I don't know if I can ever forgive you," she said, and my immediate reaction wasn't hurt but skepticism. A full raised eyebrow. Like, *This is how you want to play this scene, lady?* I knew that was not how I should feel, so I tried to get back to feeling sorry and bad.

"I wish I could take it back," I said. "I wish I'd been at your wedding."

"Well, you can't," she said.

"I know that."

The puppy was jumping up all over my feet.

"You got a dog," I said. I bent to show Bodhi. "See the puppy? It's a puppy!"

As soon as I brought us close, it jumped up and licked our faces with delicious puppy breath. At first Bodhi was terrified and clung to me, then he shrieked with laughter and kept trying to touch the dog's face, almost stabbing it in the eye with his tiny fingers.

"What's its name?" I asked.

"Lieutenant," Shyanne said. "Kenny's wanted to get a Lab for years and name it Lieutenant, so . . ." She gestured sort of disgustedly at the adorable puppy.

"He's darling," I said.

"I was going to take him for a walk." Shyanne motioned in a way that seemed like an invite, so I followed. We weren't so much walking Lieutenant as slowly meandering through the grass so he could roll in a three-foot radius around us.

"How have you been?" I asked, determined to outlast her coldness. I followed her as she followed the puppy, and she answered all my questions tersely with fake hurt. She was milking it almost beyond my ability to feign contrition when suddenly we lit upon the topic of her gambling in Vegas. She was like the sun coming from behind clouds as she described her system of waking up in the middle of the night, sneaking out of the hotel room, gambling until four, and then crawling back into bed before Kenny woke up. She detailed a game hand by hand in which she'd won almost ten grand. I thought of JB saying his mom had Lucille Ball energy, and I thought maybe that was why we got along the way we did, both of us raised by these delightful psychos.

"And you never told him?" I guffawed.

"Hell, no!" she said. "You know he'd put it in some bond or CD you can't cash out for thirty years."

I laughed. I talked a little more about the real estate idea, and Shyanne was absolutely thrilled. "Margo, that is genius," she said, and invited me to come inside the condo to try this new drink she really liked that her personal trainer had recommended, which turned out to be a red powder you mixed with water that contained 150 milligrams of caffeine and enough niacin to make my arm skin prickle. We were sitting at Kenny's kitchen table, or I guess their kitchen table now. Bodhi was in my lap.

"You're going to need a whole wardrobe," Shyanne was saying. "I'm thinking skirt suits, I'm thinking Victoria Beckham. I'm thinking legs for days and a nude lip. I'm so excited!" Shyanne was beaming. My heart was beating like a hummingbird from the red powder and also from relief, an eagerness for things to be easy between us again. She grabbed my hand. "I'm just so darn glad you came to your senses. I mean, I knew you would! I knew you wouldn't want to lose that baby. But I am so, so glad."

I froze. "What do you mean 'lose that baby'?" I could hear the buzz of the overhead lights in Kenny's kitchen.

"Well, they did come by, didn't they?"

I'd never told her about the CPS visit.

"I mean, what a wake-up call!" she said. "Kenny said that's what you needed, and he was right, I guess."

It was taking a while for all of this to cohere in my brain. "Wait, are you saying— Did you guys call CPS?"

"Well, I mean, not me, but Kenny," my mom said.

"Jesus, Mom," I said. I had a sudden vision of reaching out, grabbing her lash extensions, and ripping them off her face.

"Well, look, it worked!" She pointed at Bodhi on my lap.

I stared at her, trembling with rage. "I could have lost him," I said. "Mom, the investigation is still ongoing. I could still lose Bodhi!"

"Oh, they're not going to take him away if you stop doing the Only-Fans," Shyanne said, waving her hand to brush away the idea.

My heart was beating faster and faster. It would have been one thing if I thought she was scared for Bodhi, but I didn't believe that for a second. "If you were really worried, wouldn't you have, I don't know, called?! Dropped by?"

"We weren't exactly on speaking terms!" she said. "Once you posted all that on Facebook! I mean, honestly, Margo, what were you thinking!"

"Mom, I didn't post those. Why would you think I posted those? I was doxxed. You could see it right there—the account that posted them was called SlutSleuths!"

"Well, I didn't see that," Shyanne said. "I thought you were advertising."

"Jesus Christ," I said. There was a feeling like I was going to laugh or vomit. She was a fucking idiot.

"Well, however it happened," Shyanne said, "it doesn't matter, because Kenny saw it, and once he knew, he wouldn't let go of it, how it wasn't right for a child to grow up in a home like that, how we were guilty of child abuse if we stood by and let it happen. And he made me!"

"He *made* you?" I pushed up from the table, not able to remain sitting any longer. Bodhi picked up on the vibe shift and began to whimper in my arms.

"I couldn't get a moment's peace! And the more he said it, I mean, I didn't think you should be doing that either! I didn't like that you were doing"—she struggled for what to call it, then hissed—"all *that*. I thought it would teach you a lesson. This is about you and your decisions. Trying to blame this on *me*."

She rose from the table too and paced around the room, sucking on her red drink through her straw. Her face looked hyperreal in the buzzing fluorescent kitchen light. My eyes were streaming with tears, and all I could think was: Why doesn't she love me? What did I do that this is all the love I get?

"Margo, I'm sorry," my mother said, closing the distance between us. She reached out and squeezed my shoulder. Her hand felt cold. "I'm sorry," she whisper-hissed, "but what was I supposed to do? Kenny isn't exactly the most adjustable guy!"

"Then why did you marry him?"

She squeezed my arm hard, whispered, "You don't think every day I wonder if I made a mistake? But it's the choice I made. It was the only choice I thought I could make at the time."

It must have been dizzying, Jinx showing up with those roses. There had to be a part of her that considered ditching Kenny then and there. But Kenny was a sure thing. That was his whole deal. And here she was asking me to understand how fucked the world was and how trapped she was within it. She'd been asking me to do that my whole life, and I always, always had. I'd understood she couldn't magically make Jinx stay and love us. I'd understood she needed romance and that meant dating men I didn't like or want around. I'd understood she needed to work weekends, I'd understood we didn't have that much money, I'd understood she needed a beer after work, I'd understood when cooking dinner was beyond her. I loved her. I understood it all.

But sometimes understanding wasn't enough.

"Don't take your judgment and shame over how I was making a living and try to pretend it's love," I spat, "that you're concerned, or that you did it for my own good. You don't care about what's good for me, what's best for us. You care about not pissing off your new husband so you can keep dressing in Lululemon and seeing your personal trainer."

Shyanne made a noise of disbelief. She didn't seem to know how else to respond.

"Stay out of my life," I said. "Just stay out!"

And then I walked out, hobbling on my bad ankle, my baby sobbing in my arms. The moment we got outside into the bright sun, he quieted, looked around, amazed at having been plunged into a beautiful day. Trees wavered around us, dappling the sidewalks with fluttering shade.

No, I thought, as I walked to my car. I didn't know what I was saying no to, what I meant, only that the word was right. *No.*

No fucking way. Not like this.

WHEN I GOT home, Jinx was out looking at apartments and Suzie was in class, so there was no one to talk to and share what had happened. I put Bodhi down for a nap and began folding laundry, not sure what else to do, when my phone dinged with an email from Ward. All it said was: How do you like them apples? There was an attachment, a PDF titled 730EvalReportCase#288862. I've never clicked so hard on anything in my life.

The whole first five pages were a maddening labyrinth of check boxes detailing exactly who had ordered the evaluation and what it was supposed to include, who had paid for it, what legal constraints were placed upon it. Then there was a page with big bold letters at the top: RECOMMENDATIONS.

The custodial placement that would best serve the interests of the child regarding the child's health, safety and welfare, and safety of all family members is:

Physical Custody: Mother

Legal Custody: Mother

I gasped and continued scrolling, desperate to read more, to understand what it meant, if it was binding. Toward the end, the form-like structure fell away and there was a written report.

I was appointed by the court at the request of the child "Bodhi Millet's" Father "Mark Gable" to assess the psychological fitness and ability to parent of "Bodhi's" Mother "Margo Millet." In the event that "Margo" is found psychologically fit, Father "Mark" asks she retain full legal and physical custody. "Margo" also wants to retain full legal and physical custody, significantly simplifying the question the court was posing when it commissioned the report: Is "Margo Millet" able to provide a healthy and safe environment for "Bodhi"? And in the event she is not, what would the best environment for "Bodhi" be?

To assess "Margo's" psychological profile, I utilized the MMPI-2 administered at my offices on January 28, 2019. "Margo" scored within normal range on nine of ten scales, with a high score (63) just out of normal range on Scale 5 Masculinity/Femininity. On Content Scales "Margo" measured high-normal DEP indicating some depressive thoughts/tendencies, as well as high-normal CYN indicating underlying cynicism and misanthropic beliefs. The APS Scale does indicate a personality type associated with substance abuse, but "Margo" has no known substance abuse problems, though addiction does run in her family. (Full Results Attached)

"Margo" lives in a four-bedroom apartment with Child "Bodhi," Grandfather "James" and roommate "Suzanne." Grandfather "James" is in the process of moving to his own apartment and will no longer be living with "Margo." He is currently in recovery from opiate addiction and is enrolled in a methadone treatment protocol. When interviewed, his doctor said he has not yet missed a dose and approaches his recovery with appropriate seriousness.

"Margo" was "Mark's" student in a college course titled "ENG 121: Unnatural Voices: Taking Narration to the Edge" in the fall of 2017 at

Fullerton College. "Mark" initiated the affair. At the time "Margo" was nineteen and "Mark" was thirty-seven. He was married at that time to "Sarah Gable," with whom he has two children "Hailey" and "Max." His affair with "Margo" lasted approximately six weeks, during which time "Margo" became pregnant and decided to keep the baby. "Mark" did not want to be involved in the child's life at that time.

"Mark" and his wife "Sarah" are currently in divorce proceedings and in mediation for custody of their two children "Hailey" and "Max." "Mark" has no permanent domicile and is currently staying with his mother "Elizabeth." He has provisional weekend custody of "Hailey" and "Max." He has positive relationships with both, and "Sarah" has not reported any concerns of abuse. He has retained his job at Fullerton College despite the affair and is financially stable.

"Margo's" pregnancy was healthy, and her medical records indicate no evidence of substance abuse, despite the hospital keeping "Margo" an extra twenty-four hours to run an additional drug panel when the first came back negative. "Bodhi" was born with no health complications at a normal-low birth weight of 6 lbs.

In addition to the MMPI-2, I interviewed "Margo" at my office on February 2, 2019. "Margo" arrived on time and in appropriate attire. She appeared clean and groomed, her speech was clear, her mannerisms were not unusual, and her eye contact was within normal limits. Her intellectual-cognitive functioning is high, and she is able to express herself verbally with ease. "Margo" appears to be able to accurately perceive the world around her, presenting others, even those with whom she has conflict, in a nuanced way.

"Margo" has a moderately impaired self-concept and consistently estimates herself to be both superior to and inferior to others. She is conflicted about her identity and role in the adult world and attempts to shield her vulnerability with an affected attitude of power and dominance. She is currently experiencing manageable levels of anxiety and depression, though these feelings center primarily on the custody dispute and her relationship with her mother. "Margo's" emotional regulation is appropriate to her young age, and while she did begin to cry at multiple points in the interview, she was able to calm herself and remain in control of her behavior.

"Margo's" educational transcripts and SAT scores indicate above average intellectual ability. However she dropped out of Fullerton College and seems to have no further educational ambitions. It should be noted that she dropped out at the request of Father "Mark" and grandmother "Elizabeth," who asked her to sign an NDA keeping "Mark's" parentage a secret. "Margo" signed this agreement and abided by its terms and in exchange received $15,000 as well as a trust for child "Bodhi" in the amount of $50,000.

"Margo" is currently working as a social media personality on OnlyFans and TikTok. OnlyFans is a website catering to adult clientele that offers sexual content. "Mark's" concern over "Bodhi's" welfare centers almost exclusively around her work on OnlyFans. Her work is not illegal and pays extremely well, allowing her to work from home and provide full-time care to Bodhi. It is well established that sex work is highly correlated with negative psychological outcomes, with those at-risk populations more likely to suffer from depression, mood disorders, and suicidal ideation. "Margo" displays none of these behaviors, but it is a risk that comes with her chosen work that cannot be overlooked, especially considering her potential for addiction, young age, and tendencies toward depression. While she has plans to segue into real estate, her financial future remains uncertain and will certainly continue to provide a source of stress.

As part of my evaluation, I performed a Parent-Child Observation at "Margo's" apartment. The apartment was clean and well-kept, and "Margo's" speech was unimpaired, nor were there signs in her gait or mannerisms of alcohol or drug use. I watched her feed Bodhi dinner, give him a bath, and get him ready for sleep.

"Margo" displays high levels of positive affectivity, involvement and responsiveness in her interactions with "Bodhi," using nonverbal behaviors like smiling, nodding, and laughing to express care, in addition to verbal communication that included room for "Bodhi" to respond.

"Margo" was adept at setting up adequate structure for "Bodhi," as well as managing his frustration or excitement and soothing him when necessary. During dinner, she allowed "Bodhi" to feed himself with his hands despite it being very messy. During bath time she had proper safety precautions in place and was alert to his safety in the water while still allowing him to explore and take physical risks. This kind of high-care, low-control approach has been found in numerous studies to be optimal.

"Bodhi" appears to have a flexible temperament with some active child characteristics. He is physically at ease with Margo and responds to her touch and verbal praise, showing signs of pleasure like smiling, laughing, and clapping. His babbling and physical coordination are normal for his age. His pediatrician (letter attached) has no concerns regarding his health or "Margo's" ability to parent, and in fact described her as "overly conscientious."

"Margo" is currently under investigation by Child Protective Services. When contacted, CPS indicated that they would not be concluding their investigation within a timeframe convenient to this custody proceeding. Since there were no signs of abuse or neglect in my own investigation, I decided it would be imprudent to wait, but I am happy to provide an addendum once their findings are made available. This report is also being provided to CPS for their investigation.

From everything I have seen, "Margo" is psychologically fit to retain Full Legal and Physical Custody of "Bodhi" and there are no signs of abuse, neglect, or harm. Margo currently has custody of "Bodhi." Because the CPS investigation is ongoing, it is customary for custody disputes to be suspended until the investigation is resolved, but because "Margo" currently has custody of "Bodhi" and both "Mark" and "Margo" wish her to retain it pending acceptance of this report, no further action need be taken.

In the event of a CPS finding contraindicating this report, custody will be reevaluated through the standard mechanisms.

It is my recommendation that "Mark" be allowed once weekly visitation should he so choose and that he pay child support in keeping with his income for one year, at which point the situation can be reevaluated as Mark's domestic living arrangement becomes stable and the psychological toll, if any, of Margo's employment becomes more apparent.

I was overjoyed, though it was also creepy as hell to read about myself in this way, and by the end I felt a little sick. I was still surrounded by tiny piles of folded Bodhi clothes. I wasn't sure what to do next, if I should finish balling his tiny socks or call Ward. Right then, Bodhi woke up, and his wails came tiny yet loud through the baby monitor. I went to him and changed him. He was in a giggly mood. There really was no greater delight on Earth than a well-slept baby. I blew raspberries on his tummy as he shrieked, and when I stopped, we were both panting and looking at each other and smiling, and I thought in a robot voice: This kind of high-care, low-control approach has been found in numerous studies to be optimal.

I was proud. I mean, "optimal"? I would take it.

I was also thinking that if it was Shyanne who'd called CPS, then it wasn't Mark, and that shifted things. And with Dr. Sharp's report, there was a good chance we could keep this from going to court. I needed to know exactly what I was dealing with.

CHAPTER TWENTY-FIVE

I had Mark's address from the custody papers. I assumed it would be an apartment, but when I pulled up it was like a mini version of the White House. A maid answered the door and led me through an all-white living room, past a Carrara marble kitchen, and out some French doors to the backyard. There was a pool and an outdoor kitchen. She pointed to a stand of silver sheen trees beyond the pool. "Mr. Mark's cottage is back there by those trees—do you see it?"

Did I see it? It was a full-sized house, nicer than anywhere I'd ever lived. The maid, like a guide to the underworld, seemed to indicate she could go no farther, and so I skirted the edge of the pool alone, made it to the dappled shade of the trees, and knocked on Mark's door. There was no answer. I knocked again.

All at once, Mark yanked open the door, clearly annoyed. He was wearing a Duke sweatshirt and purple track pants; his long hair was a little greasy and unbrushed. He had on reading glasses, which he took off the moment he saw me looking at them. "Well, this is unexpected," he said.

"We need to talk," I said. It was weird, being alone with him, familiar even though I was such a different person from who I was the last time we'd spoken like this.

I followed him into a darkened living room. All the shades were drawn. Mark snapped on the bright overhead lights, which immediately made clear that this was a den of terrible sadness. There were books and papers everywhere, abandoned half-full coffee cups on various end tables, clothes on the floor, a pizza box on the coffee table. The furniture was all in an island motif, rattan with cushions printed with birds of paradise, and this made the room even sadder. Mark sat on the couch, reached over to snag a towel off the chair so I could sit. The cushion was faintly damp.

"So what's going on?" he asked. "I saw Dr. Sharp's report, which was very reassuring. I would have thought you'd be pleased." He massaged the bridge of his nose.

"I am pleased," I said, though I was still somewhat numb from my confrontation with Shyanne the previous day. "But we need much clearer, less expensive lines of communication. At first, I thought you were doing this all to hurt me or punish me. Then in mediation, I started to understand that you really thought I wasn't doing well, that I was out of control in some way. So now I really need to know, Mark. What do you want? What is all this about?"

"Well, what do you mean?"

"Do you want to be part of Bodhi's life?"

"Obviously," he said. "He's my child too, Margo."

I squinted at him. "Because less than a year ago you were having me sign an NDA promising to drop out of Fullerton College and never tell anyone Bodhi was yours."

"Feelings change. Don't I have the right to my own emotional journey?"

I sighed. It was so tiresome wading through his self-righteous posturing. He wasn't even very good at it. "Help me understand how it went down, how this change occurred." I needed to know why he had done what he'd done so I could better predict what he was likely to do next.

"Well, I mean, when your dad called, Sarah was right there! How was I supposed to explain what was going on without telling her everything? Margo, I don't know what he was on, if it was alcohol or drugs, but he was slurring and not making sense, and he kept calling over and over. I didn't know what to do."

"So you told Sarah," I prompted. This was a chain of causality I had not anticipated. It made total sense. Justifying himself to Sarah had made Mark twist his reality up like a pretzel.

"I told Sarah." Mark nodded. "And then in addition to being literally afraid for my life, she was furious with me. I stopped sleeping, I stopped eating, I took a medical leave from work."

Barf.

"And Sarah, she was so upset. Naturally. About the affair, the betrayal, and she kept saying, 'You have a child?!' And in my head, I was like, Well, yes, but not really, Margo has a child, and it has some of my DNA. I mean, I didn't say that out loud, though I realized that's what I'd been thinking and there was something really wrong with that."

Was there, though? I sure wished he'd gone on thinking that way. "So it was Sarah who wanted to sue for full custody?" I asked. That was the part that didn't make sense. She might want to shame Mark, but I doubted she wanted to change his other kid's diapers.

"She felt I needed to take responsibility," Mark said.

"And she was already divorcing you," I said, putting it together, "so it doesn't affect her."

"Well, the divorce isn't final," Mark said, clearly offended.

"Oh," I said. Did he think, somehow, that by taking responsibility for Bodhi he'd convince her he was a good guy, and she wouldn't leave him?

"Sarah never specifically said I should try to get full custody," Mark said. "I was seeing Larry about the restraining order for your dad and explaining the situation, and we both felt, like, hey, there's a kid over there! What's gonna happen to that kid? You know?"

"Christ," I said. I was suddenly so very tired. Larry wasn't even a custody lawyer, which in a way explained a lot. I noticed an Uncrustables wrapper on the floor. There was no changing Mark. Or Jinx, or Shyanne, or how the world worked. They were like chess pieces: they moved how they moved. If you wanted to win, you couldn't dwell on how you wished they'd move or how it'd be fairer if they moved a different way. You had to adapt. The thing I needed to know was whether Mark truly cared about the OnlyFans. He could continue to pursue full custody and take me to court, no matter what the 730 said. He might not win, but he could bankrupt me trying.

"I need to know how strongly you feel about the OnlyFans."

"Well," Mark said, "I mean, according to Dr. Sharp it isn't problematic at all!"

"I'm asking whether you will continue to pursue full custody as long as I'm still doing it."

"I thought you were getting into real estate," Mark said, a bit snide.

"I'm trying to decide exactly what I'm going to do, which is why I'm asking. To me, it seems absurd that a man I slept with over a year ago gets to decide how I make a living, but that's the position I find myself in."

"I have to confess something," Mark said suddenly, with an *I've been a bad boy* excitement. "I bought your Rigoberto video. And I have to say, from an artistic standpoint, I was really quite impressed."

So weird, so gross. "Thanks," I said, praying he wouldn't say more.

"It just— It wasn't what I had been picturing," he said.

As much of a nitwit as Mark was, I knew what he meant. I hadn't been expecting Arabella's account to be what it was. I hadn't expected to think pro wrestling was a form of art. I hadn't expected infidelity to be about cuddling or drug addiction to be about eating Milky Ways.

"Will you do me a favor, Mark? I get you being worried about Bodhi, or about decisions I'm making professionally, but can you try reaching out to me directly? Because I think the things we make up in our heads, the assumptions we make, wind up being much worse than what's really going on. Like, just call me! You never needed to file papers in the first place, come talk to me."

He nodded, then his brow furrowed. "Could I— Do you think I could meet him? Bodhi?"

"Of course," I said. "Whenever. But I need to know, if I keep doing OnlyFans, are you going to continue pursuing full custody?"

"No," Mark said. "I don't really think full custody . . . I mean, you're his mother. You're all he's ever known."

I was embarrassed that my eyes almost filled with tears. I hadn't expected Mark to say something so decent.

"I don't know," Mark went on. "In mediation, you just seemed so much more in command than I'd been expecting, it really changed things."

That black blazer, I thought. *Worth every penny.*

THAT NIGHT, I looked at the pink binder I'd been putting together for CPS. In it, I'd made a twelve-month financial plan for transitioning to real estate based on a template I found on a website called Templates4Everything.com, which had absurd slogans like "Cut your business time in half!" I flipped through the pages. I closed the pink binder. Set it on my desk. Regarded its flat bubblegum exterior.

I hated the entire plan. I hated the binder. I hated the idea of going into real estate, of spending hours and hours a day away from Bodhi to pursue something I didn't want to do and had no idea if I'd even be good at. I hated Maribel. I hated being tongue-tied and cowering. I hated having to toe the line of rules I knew were stupid. I hated being afraid.

But I *was* afraid. I could feel the blind, blunt grasp of bureaucracy closing around my life. The scariest thing about Maribel, I realized, was that she wasn't a true villain; she was kind of an officious busybody convinced she was on the side of right. Someone completely inane in charge of whether I kept my baby. I wanted to do whatever would get her to leave me and Bodhi alone. If that meant following the rules, then I'd have to suck it up and follow them. Or at least that's what I'd thought before I talked to Mark.

When lo, a vision came unto me. And that vision was of Ric Flair, his tan old-man skin gleaming with oil, his peroxide-blond shoulder-length shag shimmering. Ric Flair, greatest heel of all time: a man who would beg his opponents for mercy and then jam his thumb in their eye, a man who won pretty much only by cheating, a man so famous for pretending to pass out they named it the "Flair Flop." And in this vision, the Nature Boy appeared before me in his glittering bejeweled robes, lit by a neon glow, and said unto me: "Margo. To be the man, WOOOOO, you gotta beat the man!"

I opened my laptop and did a couple of quick searches, my pulse racing. I clicked and clicked, reading the articles as fast as I could. It's amazing what you don't find if you aren't looking for it. I called Ward even though it was ten at night and I'd already bugged him earlier about Mark getting to meet Bodhi. He picked up on the first ring.

"Hey, Ward," I said. "Wanna make a little more money and help me with some case research? I think I may have been going about something all wrong."

LIKE ANY WOMAN fully in charge of her destiny, I tried to stack the deck in my favor, in this case stopping on the way to buy Ward donuts. When I got there, Ward said, "I'm really not sure what you're hoping to accomplish with this, Margo, and I don't want to get your hopes up."

I set the pink box on his desk, the aura of Ric Flair enveloping me like a protective shield. "Ward, quitters never win, and winners never quit."

He opened the box and pulled out an apple fritter. "Jesus Christ, they're still warm."

"So did you know there's no legal precedent for how CPS handles cases against moms who have OnlyFans accounts?"

"Yeah," Ward said, his mouth full of fritter.

"Well, you know who owns OnlyFans?"

Ward shrugged.

"Leonid Radvinsky. And the other big website he owns? MyFreeCams," I said. "And I got to thinking, OnlyFans is really a social media spin on a camgirl site, and camgirl sites have been around pretty much as long as the internet."

"And how were they ruling?" Ward asked.

"Guess," I said.

"Judging by this apple fritter, I would say they ruled very favorably."

"And you would be right," I said. "But I don't want to print out pages from some Google search; she won't believe it if it's coming from me. I need you to make it all official and lawyer-y."

"Right, right," Ward said. "You need me to scare the shit out of her."

"Exactly." I jerked my glazed donut away so Bodhi couldn't grab it. "And I need to know if there are any cases that *don't* fit that pattern too."

"The thing is, Margo, we can do all that, but the research is going to be expensive. And I'm not sure it will actually get them to stand down. This would all be a lot easier if she'd done something wrong."

"She entered without a warrant," I offered.

"Yeah, but you let her. If someone says, 'Can I come in?' and you say yes, there's nothing wrong with that."

"Well, she didn't exactly say 'Can I come in?'"

"Then what did she say? Exactly. What *exactly* did she say?" Ward asked.

Despite his initial skepticism, the meeting with Ward was long and manic, and by the end we'd eaten more than half the donuts and formed a plan. The following week was fairly uneventful. It made me uneasy. When you're going to do something stupidly brave, it helps to have less time to think about it. Still, I took all the old papers out of the pink binder and filled it with all new papers, carefully organized with a table of contents. We had no idea when Maribel would return. It could be any moment, or it could be weeks. The pink of the binder became slightly more radioactive with each passing day.

Meanwhile, Jinx found a darling house to rent with a pool he claimed was for Bodhi. "Dad, he can't even swim yet," I said. But I was happy he'd be close by. It wouldn't be so bad, I realized, having a little more distance. I had to trust that it would remain that way. Before with my dad, leaving had always meant him being all the way out of my life. It was going to take some time for me to learn exactly how we could make this work.

I thought of JB constantly and, even though I knew it wasn't healthy, read his old messages. But I knew I couldn't prioritize him.

I also thought of Shyanne. I'd cooled down some, and I knew I didn't mean it, what I'd said to her about staying out of my life. She was the only mother I had, and she was flawed, and it sucked, but I loved her. It made me sick, honestly, picturing her in Kenny's condo, that clean and ugly place, hopped up on energy drinks, sneak playing poker on her phone. I couldn't leave her in there. I'd have to find some way of making peace with her, though I had no idea exactly how I would do that. All of it made my heart hurt.

But I also knew, nursing Bodhi to sleep each night, that my world would never be without love again. Love was not something, I realized, that came to you from outside. I had always thought that love was supposed to come from other people, and somehow, I was failing to catch the crumbs of it, failing to eat them, and I went around belly empty and desperate. I didn't know the love was supposed to come from within me, and that as long as I loved others, the strength and warmth of that love would fill me, make me strong.

As I finally drifted off to sleep, I pictured myself like Arabella, violent and half naked, only instead of shooting people with glowing cartoon guns, I was loving them so big, so hard and real, that the world began to crack at the power of it. My mother's face flew into fragments, shot through with golden beams of light; Jinx's skeleton body was lifted into the sky.

And Bodhi, Bodhi glowed gold, drinking and drinking the love that flowed out of my body, using it to make himself strong and happy, using it to grow, his cells doubling and redoubling, his bones assembling themselves with time-lapse speed like a miracle.

CHAPTER TWENTY-SIX

The following Friday morning, Mark came to the apartment to meet Bodhi for the first time. I warned Jinx. "I have to tell you something, and it's something I've been kind of dreading telling you this whole time."

Jinx's brow furrowed. "What?"

I knew it was hilarious, but I was still concerned. "Mark is short."

"Bodhi's dad?"

"Yeah, he's, like, Michael J. Fox size."

"So?"

"I mean, I know you hoped Bodhi would be big and wrestle, and like . . ."

"Bodhi is going to be gigantic, Margo. I'm telling you, I have never seen a baby with hands that size."

"I'm just trying to prepare you, you know. So it won't be weird when he gets here!"

"I promise not to gasp and say, 'But you're so short!'"

"Thank you."

"I might say, 'I can't believe you screwed my daughter while she was your student, you shit bag.'"

"That you can say."

When Mark arrived, we all got along well enough, even though my dad made a risky joke about breaking his fingers for real this time when they shook hands. Mark was wearing wide-legged brown linen pants. Jinx raised an eyebrow but stayed admirably silent, busied himself in the kitchen making tea and snacks while Mark met Bodhi in the living room.

"So this is Bodhi," I said, bouncing Bodhi on my hip. He was seven months old, had two bottom teeth, and drooled constantly, cascades of spittle down his chin at all times. Despite this he was beautiful in an elfin way, and I was proud. I had him in his cutest romper. It was burnt sienna with white foxes on it, and I'd just given him a bath, so he smelled like honey and oatmeal.

"Oh my gosh! Oh, Margo!" Mark looked at me, and tears were streaming down his face. It was not the reaction I was expecting, and I was honestly a little touched.

"Do you want to hold him?" I asked.

"Will he go to me? Does he have stranger danger yet?"

"No, he'll go to pretty much anybody still," I said. "Here, I'll put him on his blanket and you can play for a bit, and then you can try holding him."

Mark immediately dropped to the floor like I'd told him to do push-ups. "Margo, he's so pretty." I put Bodhi on his blanket, and he immediately got on all fours, which he'd been doing more and more lately. He kind of rocked back and forth and looked at Mark in a challenging way. Mark got on all fours as well and mimicked the back-and-forth motion, and that made Bodhi laugh. Bodhi grabbed for his octopus and sort of rubbed his mouth on it and looked at Mark. "Is that your octopus?" Mark asked. "He must think I'm so weird, crying like this!"

"Oh, he's seen me cry plenty," I said. "He probably just thinks adults have wet faces at this point."

Jinx brought the tea and snacks, and we sat around, watching Mark and Bodhi play together. I thought about what Ward said about the depo, that Mark was a shitty husband but a pretty great dad. I could believe it. There was no faking the kind of delight he was taking in Bodhi, and it won my grudging approval.

Then the doorbell rang.

I was so unexpectedly happy I didn't even worry about it. I stayed sitting on the couch watching Mark and Bodhi while Jinx went to the door, then I heard Maribel's voice. I scrambled up off the couch, whispering to Mark, "Shit, it's CPS."

"Do you want me to do anything?" he whispered back.

And I said, as though this were a drug deal or something, "Just be cool." He would tease me about this for literal years. He still says it to me all the time.

I ran to my desk and grabbed the binder. I could hear my dad explaining to her that Bodhi's dad was here. "So cute!" she said, when she returned from whatever ocular pat-down she'd done of Mark and Bodhi in the living room.

The moment she sat down at the table with us, I opened the binder and tried to begin my spiel. I'd rehearsed what I wanted to say dozens of times. Every single night when I went to sleep, when I was using the bathroom, when I was waiting in line at the store, I was imagining justifying myself to Maribel.

"In our last meeting," I said, but she interrupted.

"So, Jinx, you tested positive for opiates."

She said this like it was so damning. Like he should be ashamed.

"We told you he would. He's in a methadone treatment program," I said.

"And has Jinx made any plans to get off methadone?"

"No," I said, "but he is moving out this weekend, so whether or not he is on methadone shouldn't have any further relevance."

Maribel gave me an odd look I couldn't interpret, then said, "I'll need to see a copy of his lease."

"It's right here in the binder," I said, pointing to section 3 in the table of contents.

"What is all of this?" she finally asked.

"These are examples of case law regarding previous CPS cases against camgirls in the state of California."

Maribel let out a fake-dramatic sigh. "It really was not necessary to do all of this. Case law doesn't determine whether we find your home safe or not. Margo, you did pass the urine test, which is why we are now asking for a hair follicle test."

This was pretty much the worst thing she could have said. "Why would passing a drug test require me to take another drug test?" I asked. My heart was beating like dubstep. I would fail that hair follicle test. Ward and I had gone over what I should say, but I didn't know what would happen if Maribel said something unexpected.

"When one person in the home tests positive for illegal drugs, it's policy to do a more extensive panel on all the caretakers to catch anything the urinalysis may have missed. It's very simple, we take an inch of hair, a single strand." She explained this like I was a child who needed to be convinced to take medicine.

"Do you have a warrant for the drug test?" I asked.

Maribel half laughed. "We don't usually get a warrant for a standard drug test."

"Well, technically you should have gotten a warrant just to enter the apartment," I said. "We only let you in as a gesture of goodwill on our part."

"Are you refusing the drug test?" Maribel asked.

"No," I said. "I would be happy to take the drug test if you show me a warrant for it." Ward was positive no judge would sign off on such a warrant. There was no reason to suspect me of drug use, there were no drugs in the home, and Jinx's positive result had a logical explanation. "They have zero probable cause," Ward said. But I was kind of putting my whole life in Ward's slightly sticky, weirdly hairless hands right now.

Maribel was writing something down in her notebook. Her pen had a little Sanrio frog on it. She was shaking her head, then she looked up at me, met my eyes. "When a parent refuses to cooperate in an investigation, it's a big red flag. Refusing to take a simple hair follicle test—it makes you look extremely guilty."

I kept trying to swallow, and it felt like my throat was swelling shut. "I understand," I said. Of course refusing made me look guilty. Why had Ward and I convinced ourselves this would work?

Maribel reached over and rested her hand on my arm. Her nails were neatly painted a sparkly purple. "I'm saying this because I care about you, Margo. Refusing to cooperate with the investigation will look very, very bad."

And just like that, I had the ground under me again. Maribel didn't care about me. She'd taken the bluff too far. She was trying to manipulate me, and in an instant, everything was simple again. "Oh, I'm eager to cooperate with your investigation. I've organized some documents to help you. You can see, here is the table of contents and my 730 evaluation, which includes a full psychological profile and concludes that not only am I fit to parent Bodhi, but that my parenting style is optimal." My voice was trembling. I cleared my throat in an effort to regain control of it. "Here is a letter from Mark, Bodhi's father, expressing his full support for my work at OnlyFans. At the end is a collection of California case law examples that establish clear legal precedent for the legality of my work. There are dozens of cases wherein it was established that a mother working in a legal, sex-work-adjacent field could not have her employment used against her by CPS, whether that work was as a stripper or a camgirl."

"That may be, but OnlyFans is a new phenomenon," Maribel said, "and provides a unique situation because the sex work is taking place within the home where the child is being raised." She said this with careful seriousness, stressing the words *within the home*. It was exactly the way they talked on *Sesame Street*.

"Right," I said, smiling and nodding. "Yes, I can see that. But there is very little material difference between cam work and hosting a profile on OnlyFans. The last case in here was a successful lawsuit against CPS and the State of California on the part of Kendra Baker, whose children were taken because of her successful career as a camgirl. Just like me, Kendra Baker worked out of her home. Just like me, she kept her children out of her work life and was a good mother and a fit parent."

I opened the binder to the correct page.

"She sued for, wait, what was it? Two million dollars?"

I left the page open so Maribel could see the actual amount was $2.2 million. And that Kendra Baker had won.

"This is very detailed," Maribel said. "But like I said, our first concern is that the child is safe *in the home*."

She sure loved that phrase.

"At this point," I said, "I think your first concern should be assessing your own legal risk. Here is a letter from my attorney, Michael T. Ward, asking you to stop entering my home without a warrant. The last time you were here, you entered under false pretenses by claiming that you would take our child unless we complied, which, as I am sure you know, is a violation of our rights and leaves you vulnerable to prosecution under 42 U.S. Code 1983, the Civil Action for Deprivation of Rights."

Ward had leaped on that detail when we met. He kept calling it a game changer and asked me ten times if she'd really said that. We'd even called Jinx and made him repeat it exactly word for word. She threatened to take Bodhi twice, at first when he wouldn't let her in and then again when I wasn't home. Ward had guffawed: "What, like it's illegal to have a babysitter? This chick sure loves to make threats, let's see how she feels about receiving a couple." I wasn't sure it was as big a deal as Ward thought. There wasn't any recording of the conversation. We didn't have actual proof she'd ever said that. All she'd have to do was deny it. It would be our word against hers. Maribel pulled the binder over for the first time and began really looking at it. She skipped all the case files and read the letter from Ward.

Jinx reached over and took my hand. We held our breath as we watched Maribel read, occasionally murmuring the words to herself under her breath. When Maribel reached the last page, she lingered for a moment, then slowly closed the binder. "This is very interesting," she said, "and it's clear you put a lot of effort and time into this. And certainly, our primary concern here is Bodhi's well-being. We're not here to try to take a child that doesn't need to be taken. Our goal is always to keep the child with their family if at all possible."

"Right," I said, breathless. It almost felt like she was backtracking. And I needed her to feel like backtracking was possible, would be easy. "That makes sense to me. Because our lawyer was so upset that he wanted to press charges immediately, but I said to him, 'Ward, I think CPS really wants to help. They're the good guys. Let's give them a chance to show it.'"

"Absolutely," Maribel gushed, "our first priority is always to try to keep a child within the home. What matters, at the end of the day, is whether the home is clean, whether the child is receiving regular medical care, and so on. Your drug test came back negative. The other people we interviewed confirmed everything I learned from you and from James here."

"See," I said, "this is exactly what I told Ward. But he was so caught up in the technicalities! He kept saying, 'Margo, what they did was illegal, you could sue for a lot of money,' and just going on and on." I laughed like he was being silly.

Maribel was nodding rapidly and chewing on her upper lip. "No, we really do always want to do right by our families, that's what we're here for—to make sure everyone is safe! And thank you for this research, all this legal research. I think you make some very compelling points about the related nature of OnlyFans and cam websites, and we certainly do have legal precedent regarding the, uh, the cam websites."

Jinx was squeezing the shit out of my hand. She must think she'd be in deep shit for lying to Jinx about taking Bodhi. She wasn't even trying to argue.

"So at this point," she went on, repeatedly clicking her pen, "this visit counts as your second home visit, which concludes your case, and once I file my report your case will be considered closed. But here is my number, and if you ever have any questions or concerns, or need help with social services or finding care, just give me a call or shoot me a text."

"So wait," I said, "when will we hear from you?"

"There is no further need for me to perform another home visit at this time. The only thing that would trigger a return visit is if we received another complaint."

"Or if your supervisor has a problem with any of the documentation we provided?"

"I don't really foresee that," Maribel said. She wasn't going to show her supervisor a single page from that binder, I realized. She was going to bury this as fast as she could.

"I think I'm gonna cry," I said.

"Don't cry," Maribel said, "be happy! This is the outcome we all want, right?"

Was it? I stared at her, smiling in what I hoped was a genuine-looking way. She had us sign some papers saying the home visit had been performed and we'd been informed the case was now closed and that was it. She was leaving.

When I showed her to the door, I wanted to say something. "Good luck," I said, and gestured to her stomach.

She looked confused. I realized I sounded insane. It was insane, really, that I still wanted to wish her well. I didn't think Maribel was some villain; I thought she was an idiot who got off on power trips and probably did genuinely think of herself as one of the good guys. I also knew her whole life was about to get exploded, and not by me.

"It's like falling in love," I said, though maybe that sounded even more insane. "It's the biggest love you'll ever experience. And it will change everything about you. At times you will think your whole life is ruined, but you know, like, you wouldn't change any of it. Just . . . I'm excited for you. That all that's about to happen."

"Thank you," Maribel said in her guarded but sweet way.

I nodded and shut the apartment door.

CHAPTER TWENTY-SEVEN

That," Jinx said, when I came back to the living room, "was masterful."

I laughed, giddy. As soon as Mark left, we called Rose and KC to come celebrate, and ordered in Mediterranean food that gave us all instant crippling diarrhea. Jinx's guts were feeling it the worst, and he spent most of the night in the toilet. KC made a gross joke about how the diarrhea had "cleaned her out" and now she was "ready for some action," so she and Rose went to meet up with Snoop Dork, and by eight p.m. it was only me and Suzie. Bodhi was asleep in his crib, the baby monitor resting beside me on the couch.

"So you were really going to quit?" Suzie asked.

"I mean, I thought I had no choice," I said.

"When were you going to tell me I was fired?" she asked, then gave an unconvincing laugh. In the yellow lamplight of the living room, her dark blond hair shone like beaten gold, and the simplicity of her features made her look old-fashioned somehow, like a profile on a cameo.

"I was actually hoping to hire you full-time as my nanny."

Suzie raised her eyebrows, then looked down. She was picking at the rip in her jeans, worrying the frayed white ends. Suzie was, I realized, still such a mystery to me.

"Do you ever think about starting your own account?" I asked. Because it was puzzling. Why would she ask to work for me when she could make a killing working for herself?

"Oh, I'm not pretty enough," she said.

"Horseshit," I said.

She laughed, finally looking up. "I don't think I could do it," she said. "If I'm being honest. All the attention and having to fake it with guys like that. I mean, editing a zillion nude images of myself every week sounds like some kind of existential hell."

"Oh, you stop thinking about it as you," I said.

"Still, I just . . . with my family . . . I couldn't. I just couldn't do it."

I got that. "Would you want to be in the TikToks?"

She shook her head and went back to picking at her jeans.

"What do you want then?" I asked. Because it felt like she did want something and was too afraid to say.

She rolled her eyes, then smiled at me. "You know what I want!"

"I don't!" I cried.

"I want to be part of the team," she said, her voice breaking on the last word.

"Oh, Suzie," I said, "you are part of the team. From now on, you are explicitly part of the team." I reached over and hugged her, and her skin was surprisingly warm.

"And you'll tell me," she said. "I'll be one of the people you tell when you're thinking about quitting!"

"I will," I said. "I'll tell you every business-related thought I ever have."

She sucked some snot back in her nose, laughed, and said, "I think that may be the most romantic thing anyone's ever said to me."

IT WAS ALMOST the end of February when I got a call from JB.

"I'm in L.A.," he said.

"What?"

"I've been doing a lot of thinking, and I really think we need to talk. So I came."

I didn't know if I was happy or sad about this. Mainly it made me uneasy. And yet, on a physical level, I was thrilled to hear his voice. "Okay," I said.

"Okay?" He sounded a bit surprised.

"Yeah. Where do you want to meet?"

"Anywhere you want," he said.

"Oh, you'll regret that," I said, as I gave him the cross streets of my second-favorite Arby's. (My second favorite was closer to his hotel. I wasn't some monster who'd make him drive all the way out to Brea. I was only asking him to drive from downtown L.A. to Buena Park, which someone should be willing to do for love.)

I BROUGHT BODHI even though he'd make it harder for us to talk because I worried JB had some big romantic idea in his head, that we were destined to be together. It seemed like he had to be in that mode to fly across the country to have a conversation. The Buena Park Arby's had recently been redone in fake wood paneling and dangling pendant lights, bright red metal chairs. It was a lot cheesier looking than the Arby's in Brea, which featured grimy gray and black tiles and weird '80s confetti wallpaper. But it would do.

When Bodhi and I arrived, JB was already there. He half stood from the table and sort of crouched as we approached.

"Have you ordered?" I asked, overwhelmed by his physical presence. Even the fact that his glasses were greasy and slightly askew was making my pulse race.

"No, I was waiting for you," he said. "I didn't know what to order. I've never been to an Arby's before."

"You haven't?! Oh, well, this is an occasion! You want me to order?"

"Sure," he said, and nodded.

"Okay, you find a highchair," I said, and took Bodhi with me to go wait in line. I was hungry, so I really went for it: a Classic Beef 'n Cheddar, the Smokehouse Brisket sandwich, a French Dip & Swiss, a Corned Beef Reuben, two orders of curly fries, and two vanilla shakes.

"It's so good to see your face," I said, when I got back to the table. I slid Bodhi into the highchair JB had found and he immediately shrieked, so I fished in my bag for something to entertain him and came out with a teether toy I knew wouldn't work at all. I gave it to him, and he screamed and threw it on the ground. "Hold on a sec," I said, and ran to grab a handful of straws. Bodhi had never been allowed to investigate a bright red plastic straw before. He held it wonderingly in his hand like a magic wand and then stuck it deep in his throat and gagged himself, removed it and eyed it with curiosity and respect.

"Okay," I said, tucking my hair behind my ears.

"I don't know whether to dive into everything or wait until the food is ready," he said.

"Gosh," I said. I was a little unnerved that he seemed to have prepared a presentation: *"Eight Reasons You Should Date Me." In this TED Talk, I will* . . .

"To get this out of the way," JB said, "I just want to say—I don't think we should be together. Romantically." My face must have been one big record scratch. JB laughed. "Caught you off guard with that one!"

"Hells yes," I said, "you most certainly did."

Just then they called number sixty-eight.

"Hold on," I said, and went to get our food.

"Holy shit, Margo," he said when I returned. "This is enough for six people."

"I'm nursing," I said. "And this way you can try everything!" I was still trying to parse how I felt about what he said. He didn't think we should be together. Yet he had flown out here. He thought we needed to talk. It didn't add up. I wasn't sure if he was lying to me or to himself. But there would be time to find out, and I'd be eating curly fries in the interim. I opened the lid of my milkshake so I could dunk.

"Which is this one?" he asked.

"Beef 'n Cheddar, start with that one."

He nodded, carefully unwrapping the sandwich, and for a moment he looked like a serious little boy.

"So you don't want to date me?" I asked.

He indicated that he would answer when he finished chewing. I waited. "Okay, so it's not really a matter of not wanting to date you. You're the one who is saying you can't commit to a relationship right now, and I respect that. But I got to thinking, you know: How do we find a way to not waste this? Like, should we throw away this great connection just because it's not the right time?"

Bodhi dropped his straw on the floor, so I gave him a new one. I felt like I knew where this was going. "The thing is, JB, it's not only about the timing or needing to focus. I've kind of gotten through the custody crisis. But I saw the look on your face when I talked about rating dicks, and . . . I don't want to make you feel like that. I also don't want to quit my job. I get it, that it may be incompatible, like, I don't think I would feel great if you were flirting with women online all day even if it was for money. Switch?" I asked, holding out the French Dip.

"Sure," he said, trading me for his Beef 'N Cheddar.

Bodhi could smell the food and was desperate for some, but I wasn't sure if he would choke on the meat. I gave him a tiny gossamer shred of roast beef and he gobbled it down, signed feverishly for more.

"What was that?" JB asked. "What he just did?"

"Oh, it's baby sign language. He signed for more because he likes the roast beef."

"Huh!" JB said. "The French Dip is not as good."

"Try the brisket," I said, nudging it toward him.

"So anyway," JB said, as he unwrapped the Smokehouse Brisket. "As everything was happening with you, massive shit was going down at work. And D.C. has just changed since the election, it's a whole different vibe. And I realized, you know, I hate my life. Like, I hate my job, I hate where I live, I have a few work friends but they're all married with kids."

"Right," I said. It hadn't occurred to me that JB and I were in a similar situation. I was isolated because I had a kid and none of my friends did, and he was isolated because he didn't have a kid and all his friends did.

"I feel like I'm taking too long getting to the point," JB said. "The point is, I started to think: How could Margo and I keep this? How could we grow it into something real and substantial? The brisket is pretty good. A little sweet."

I nodded, still busy shredding roast beef and feeding tiny shards of it to Bodhi, who had gone into a total beef frenzy.

"Margo, I have a business proposition for you."

For some reason this made me bust up laughing.

"What?" he said, and his smile was so sweet.

"Nothing," I said, "I just wasn't expecting any of this. So what's the business proposition?"

"Okay, you know that what I do is machine learning with advertising, right?"

"Yeah, but admittedly I have no idea what that is."

"So imagine basically, say I look at your Instagram followers. And I write a program that will analyze all of their Instagram accounts and find common features, patterns they share, people or brands they follow, usage patterns, words in their bios, basic demographics like gender, age, location. And I make, like, a perfect profile of the average Ghost subscriber."

"Cool," I said.

"And then I use that profile to buy ads and show those ads exclusively to people who are perfect Ghost subscriber material."

"Oh shit!" I said.

"Margo, you're gifted at the writing, the character you made up for Ghost. And I thought, what if we started a consulting company? Where we offer this in-depth data-driven analysis of their target demographic to OnlyFans content creators and make ad recommendations. Lots of companies could do that—they aren't right now because they don't even know what OnlyFans is, but they'll figure it out eventually and provide stiff competition. We could do more than that. You could offer them a critique of their character, of their persona, and give them ideas for how they might tweak it to make it more successful. I mean, we could even offer a prestige service where you write actual scripts for them."

"Oh my God," I said. I had stopped shredding, and Bodhi squawked to get my attention. I gave him another wisp of roast beef. "We could even, like—we could run storylines."

"Exactly," JB said.

We stared at each other. What JB was offering, it was beyond even my own wildest ambitions. JB was offering me the chance to become Vince McMahon.

"So do you like this idea?" he asked.

"JB, I fucking love this idea."

JB nodded, though he looked concerned or maybe a little disgusted. "Margo?"

"Yeah?"

"I don't think I can eat any more."

"Wimp," I said. "Hand it over."

He gave me the brisket, and I went to work as we kept talking. There were a million things to discuss. There was no reason we needed to be in the same geographical location to start the company, even if JB was sure he didn't want to stay in D.C.

"So are you going to do this in addition to your regular job? Do you think you'll have time?"

"Oh, no, I already quit my regular job. I quit it the moment I realized I hated it, like three weeks ago."

"Oh!" I said.

"I just feel like I need something new. I don't know that I would move to L.A. necessarily, I was also kind of thinking about Seattle. But I need you to know, if I moved here, I wouldn't be trying to start something, I wouldn't be—"

"No, I get it," I said. But I didn't. If JB and I lived in the same city, if we worked closely together, something would happen. I used the back of my fingers to stroke his hand and felt every hair on my arm prickle. "Are you seeing this, though?" I asked. Maybe I was wrong, and the effect was only on my side. But I couldn't imagine sitting next to JB in a car without violently making out.

"Yeah," JB said. "I mean, that part might be kind of a problem. We would have to agree to not be physical. Because if we start being physical, it's all over."

I took my hand away. "Do you think it's realistic, the idea of us never being physical?"

JB didn't answer right away. Bodhi was getting more and more worked up, screeching for more meat, and when I finally gave him some, he threw it right back at me. "I swear Bodhi is getting the meat sweats, he is totally done in here, can we go outside?"

"Yeah, yeah," JB said. "You take him, I'll clean all this up."

I pulled Bodhi from his highchair and shook all the meat and bread crumbs off him, then perched him on my hip and pushed out into the cold gray afternoon. It was windy, and the cars driving by were loud and sounded kind of like the ocean. When JB came out, we decided to walk a little, so I strapped Bodhi into his carrier, where he fell almost instantly asleep. We talked as we walked, but only about how the business would work and what the pricing would be. The open question of what we would do with the volcano of our physical attraction was carefully ignored. He hadn't said anything about whether he really did object to my work, whether he could handle being with me while I still rated other men's dicks. And maybe he hadn't said anything because he didn't yet know how he felt about it.

We quickly realized that we should offer different packages, different levels of service.

"Right, so maybe we offer multiple levels of ongoing subscription service, and we have, like, a basic one that just gives them updated demographic feedback, post-performance analysis, your tips for what they could do with their persona or their content, but we also offer a prestige, like, white-glove service, where we manage everything for them, website, ad placement, maybe even a set number of scripts per week. How much do you think we should charge? Like, what's a monthly fee they wouldn't balk at?"

"I don't think we should do a standard monthly fee. I think we should do a percentage of earnings." It was cold enough I could see our breath in the air.

"I like that," he said, "but how much?"

I thought about it. It really depended, but for the white-glove service I didn't think we should charge anything less than 10 percent.

"That high?" JB asked.

I nodded. "And presumably if we're doing our job right, their earnings should increase enough that it pays for our ten percent and then some. I think that's how we sell it to them, that there's no risk, that they won't see any earnings decrease because we'll be earning our own keep."

"The only thing that's starting to bother me," JB said, "and I didn't think about it until we started talking about a percentage, but like, Margo, are we—like, are we talking about becoming pimps?"

I hesitated, really thinking about it. Then I let out a Ric Flair "Wooo!" into the cold February afternoon. "Hell yeah, we are," I said. "We're going to be the most awesome, ethical, kick-ass pimps of all time! I mean, if sex work can be a legitimate profession, why can't being a pimp? Hey, that gives me an idea: Do you know about, like,

VPN stuff? Like, could we offer a security service that shields them from doxxing?"

We kept walking, talking over everything, how many clients we could do at a time, the best way to start. We made a big loop, ending up back in the parking lot of the Arby's.

"What do you want to call it?" JB asked.

"I don't know," I said. "Like, Special Services?" I laughed; it was such a bad name.

"I think we should just call it Ghost Ink," he said. "You know, like a ghost writer?"

I couldn't even say anything, I was so pleased with this idea. I just nodded.

"I don't know, maybe you'll come up with something better," he said. "We've got time to think about it."

"How long are you in town?" I asked.

"My flight isn't for a couple days."

"Want to come to my house?" I asked, suddenly excited.

"Yeah, when?"

"Like tomorrow?"

"Okay, awesome!" JB said.

"I'm so excited!" We had arrived at my purple Civic, and I went to give JB a side hug since the gigantic sleeping Bodhi was still strapped to my front.

"Hey, wait," JB said, stepping away from me. "I have something for you in my car."

He popped the trunk on his rental. Then he presented me with a gallon Ziploc bag filled to bursting with Runts.

"How?" I asked. "Where did you get these?"

"At the mall," JB said, smiling sheepishly. "I brought, like, twenty dollars in quarters."

"You harvested these Runts for me yourself?!" I crowed with happiness.

"From the dark fertile soil of American capitalism," JB affirmed.

"JB, thank you."

"Oh, it was a silly gesture," JB said. "I mean, it's pathetic that I have that much free time. It's weird not having a job. I haven't really known how to fill the time."

"No, I mean for coming out here. For demanding that we talk and having this idea."

"Oh, you don't have to thank me. This is going to sound weird, but I just . . . I kept thinking we weren't done. That was all I could think: I know this isn't done. Me and Margo, we know each other for a long time. We wind up in each other's lives. It just took me a while to figure out how it could work."

I looked up into his beautiful face. He was right. I wanted whatever allowed us to keep each other, whatever path forward that would allow us to be in each other's life. Besides, there would be plenty of time to seduce him later. I held out my hand. "Partners?"

JB looked almost like he was about to cry, but he was grinning. "Partners," he said.

And we shook on it there under the glowing red hat of the Arby's, with Ric Flair and the Virgin Mary smiling down on us, willing the story to go on, to never end, to start over again, one adventure leading to the next, and we would never die, and we'd be young forever, and we would scream to the crowd, "Look at me! Look at the beautiful, insane things I can do with my body! Look at me! Love me!"

Because that's all art is, in the end.

One person trying to get another person they have never met to fall in love with them.

ACKNOWLEDGMENTS

First thanks has to go to Michelle Brower, you shimmering mermaid; thank you for believing in Margo and in me. Without you, this book would be a shadow of itself. Thanks to all the members of Trellis, truly a group of literary all-stars, with special thanks to Allison Malecha, Allison Hunter, Nat Edwards, Khalid McCalla, and Danya Kukafka. You all have won my heart.

Thank you to Jessica Williams for being my dream editor. You work harder and smarter than anyone. You are elegance incarnate and funny as hell. Special thanks to Peter Kispert, who gives great email, and to Nancy Tan for the thoughtful and thorough copy edit. Thank you to Nicole Rifkin for the gorgeous illustration on the cover; your art takes my breath away. And thank you to Mumtaz Mustafa for masterminding the entire cover design so brilliantly.

Brooke Ehrlich, I mean, my god, what don't I owe you and that quiet, fur-lined voice of yours? You are so sane and so canny and so dazzling. How do you do it? I live for Oliver pictures. Sidney Jaet, you are a true hero.

To the foreign publishers who have offered Margo a home: I am so wildly grateful. Thank you to the brilliant Ansa Khan Khattak at Sceptre and Monika Buchmeier at Ecco Verlag, whose letter made me cry! Thanks too to Edward Benitez at HarperCollins Español and Daniela Guglielmino at Bollati Boringhieri. Daniela, I feel so grateful for your friendship and continued belief in me.

I would be nothing without my friends. K-dawg, you are a treasure, a perfect little piss baby. As you know, I would eat the world and then die of it all, but when I receive messages from you on my phone I do not feel as sad and terrified.

Pony, you hold my past and present together and squeeze like an accordion, and you might be the only thing that causes me to be a single concrete person. There is no one as beautiful as you, and I am so damn proud of you. Thank you for believing in me through all of this and talking me down and helping me plan and being the very best.

Thank you to Emily Adrian, who is ferocious and hawt. Your early reading of this book was crucial in my ability to keep the dream alive through so many setbacks, and I feel so lucky to know you.

Mary Lowry, you are a ray of goddamn sunshine, a child of light, and absolutely the most fun; I love you.

Thank you to Cynthia, who is strong and warm and wise and always knows what to say to comfort me, and thank you to Jade, who is so excellent at walking towards pigs under a humongous moon and talking about books. Thank you to Janelle, who is sweet through and through but probably doesn't think of herself that way, and thank you to Steph who is not sweet really at all, but gloriously powerful and leonine. Thank you to Edan who gyrates in hard pants so wantonly whilst doing the dishes.

Thank you to Annie, whose cheekbones should be illegal, and Tessa who is brave and wild, and Clare who is maybe some kind of elf or Naiad or only partially human demigod. Dawg Pit Forever.

Matt Walker, did you know there is a dragon under that new brewery they opened? I got that gun you wanted.

I owe an especially big thank-you to Heather Lazare, who said the most important two words ever to me. No coffee mug will ever be enough. You are such a light in the literary community, and I am so lucky our paths crossed when they did.

Thank you to Mary Adkins, whose disembodied voice I treasure and listen to in secret. I can't believe I get to work with you every day. You are brilliant. Thank you to all the folks at The Book Incubator; Liz and Harrison, you are all such beautiful human beings and a joy to work with.

Thank you to Stephen Cone, who is magical. I want to hang out with you at the teen center on a cloudy afternoon eating fries.

Thank you to my mom friends: Emily, you fucking badass, Avni and

Tulika and Reagan and Janet and Kelli and Janice and Jazmin and Chelsea (THANK YOU FOR MY HAIR!).

Thank you to my family. Thank you Jan and Ashley, best mother- and sister-in-law respectively. You make me cackle and leap with glee. Your clam dip, carrot cake, and kamut bread are unparalleled. Many ferocious hugs to Tom and Grant and my little nephews Blake and Calvin who fill my heart to bursting.

Thank you to Andrew for being my brother, and Jessie for putting up with the constant triathlons. Thank you to baby Jackson for being the best and cutest baby in the whole dang world.

Thank you to my mother, who made everything in my life possible and who continues to be an inspiration to me every single day. You will always be better at painting than me because at the end of the day you work way harder, and that should be a lesson to all of us about life. Thank you for loving colors and teaching me God was just about being grateful and looking for beauty. Thank you for everything you sacrificed so that I could live this life and walk this path and write these books. I owe you everything.

Thank you, Sam, for being my lettuce planted by the water. Marrying you was the best thing I ever did. I will live with you in a little house until the end of time, making and remaking ourselves each day. I dream constantly that I keep finding new rooms in my house, and you are those rooms, those magic rooms I didn't know were there, and the joy is to keep finding them, knowing you and coming to know you all over again, on repeat until we die.

Thank you to my boys. Booker, you little dragon, every day you surprise and delight me. I know you are going to do such important things in the world someday. Thank you for always being so gentle with me. And Gus, you charming rogue, hitter of piss missiles and cracker of jokes, you bring me daily wild joy. Thank you for endless hours of watching YouTube, thank you for playing Duolingo and chess and Wordle with me, thank you for being my world.

To all the OnlyFans girls who helped in the research of this book: THANK YOU. I know I seemed like a weirdo and my questions were super annoying, but you humored me anyway and I couldn't have written this book without you.

Thanks to the YouTube accounts WrestlingBios and WrestlingWithWregret. I spent countless hours watching your content and I hope it fucking shows.

I would also like to thank Bret Hart specifically, just for being the best there is, the best there was, and the best there ever will be. But also Mick Foley for teaching me you don't have to be the best to be the most beloved. Thank you for everything you did to your body over the years to astonish us and take our breath away. All that pain and all that risk, I doubt normal people can even comprehend what you did, and I know I myself can only just glimpse it, the magnitude of it, but I just really want to say thank you. You are an artist.

Obviously the final thank you goes to you, the reader, who I will never meet and with whom I am in love, whoever you are. This state—this private whisper chamber tucked away in the heart of the world that we call novels—it is everything to me. Thank you for letting me into the dark of your mind and allowing me to relentlessly, anguished-ly, excitedly lie to you. I would die if you didn't let me. I would surely die.